MEDICAL

Pulse-racing passion

Tempted By The Outback Vet
Becky Wicks

An Irish Vet In Kentucky
Susan Carlisle

MILLS & BOON

TEMPTED BY THE OUTBACK VET
© 2024 by Becky Wicks
Philippine Copyright 2024
Australian Copyright 2024
New Zealand Copyright 2024

First Published 2024
First Australian Paperback Edition 2024
ISBN 978 1 038 92165 9

AN IRISH VET IN KENTUCKY
© 2024 by Susan Carlisle
Philippine Copyright 2024
Australian Copyright 2024
New Zealand Copyright 2024

First Published 2024
First Australian Paperback Edition 2024
ISBN 978 1 038 92165 9

MIX
Paper | Supporting
responsible forestry
FSC® C001695

Published by
Harlequin Mills & Boon
An imprint of Harlequin Enterprises (Australia) Pty Limited
(ABN 47 001 180 918), a subsidiary of HarperCollins
Publishers Australia Pty Limited
(ABN 36 009 913 517)
Level 19, 201 Elizabeth Street
SYDNEY NSW 2000 AUSTRALIA

Cover art used by arrangement with Harlequin Books S.A.. All rights reserved.

Printed and bound in Australia by McPherson's Printing Group

Tempted By The Outback Vet

Becky Wicks

MILLS & BOON

Born in the UK, **Becky Wicks** has suffered interminable wanderlust from an early age. She's lived and worked all over the world, from London to Dubai, Sydney, Bali, New York City and Amsterdam. She's written for the likes of *GQ*, *Hello!*, *Fabulous* and *Time Out*, and has written a host of YA romance, plus three travel memoirs—*Burqalicious*, *Balilicious* and *Latinalicious* (HarperCollins, Australia). Now she blends travel with romance for Harlequin and loves every minute! Find her on X @bex_wicks and subscribe at beckywicks.com.

Visit the Author Profile page
at millsandboon.com.au for more titles.

Dear Reader,

Get your sunblock ready, and prep your taste buds for coffee and Vegemite—we're off to sunny Australia, where the snakes and spiders aren't the only things concerning our veterinary heroes! I had such fun with this one, bringing our wounded horse whisperer and his outback love interest to life. I hope you can soak up some sunshine through these pages.

Becky Wicks

xxx

DEDICATION

Dedicated to Paul and Campbell, two handsome
excuses to visit Australia for real.

CHAPTER ONE

SAGE STEPPED CLOSER to the paddock gate cautiously, the scraps bucket held tight in her hands. Storm was all action and nervous energy, rearing up and bucking violently at the sight of her.

'Steady, boy!' She flinched as the horse's hooves slammed to the sandy ground, his eyes wild with distress. This was the third week in a row that Storm had been inconsolable, refusing to let anyone near him. Ellie shuffled just behind her, twirling a strand of her sun-bleached blonde hair around one finger, as her young veterinary assistant often did when she was thinking.

'I just don't know what to do, Ells.' Sage's voice came out strained. 'I mean, look at him. I can't even get close enough to examine him! If anything he's getting worse. The mayor is going to want answers soon and, right now, I don't have any. Zero.'

Sage's heart ached. Feeling helpless never had sat well with her, especially where animals were involved—it brought back too many bad memories—and Abigail's husband, Amber Creek's beloved Mayor Jarrah Warragul, had brought Storm to her, convinced she could apply her years of veterinary expertise to help convert the wild animal into the doting pet his eleven-year-old wanted. Lucie, Sage's favourite of her best friend's three crazy kids, was beyond excited for rides through the outback on her very first horse, and at this rate Sage was going to have to let the whole family down, hard.

Ellie gave her shoulder a gentle squeeze, still quite understandably hesitant to step her petite frame much closer. 'Did you think any more about what the mayor said, about that vet we saw on TV last month? The one who calmed that uncontrollable racehorse?'

Sage nodded slowly as the image of the equine vet's face flashed back into her brain, throwing her off track for a moment. Rugged, handsome, built like a soldier in a sunhat…the kind of man who lived a life outdoors and could wrestle a croc with one arm. The mayor had suggested she call him; in fact, when she hadn't taken his advice, he had told her just today that he would go ahead and arrange things, which she hadn't told Ellie yet. It was more than humiliating, knowing she hadn't been good enough for the job.

'Ethan Matthews. Yes,' she said on a sigh. 'He used some kind of pressure-point massage to relax that horse.' She frowned as his features grew clearer in her mind's eye. The equine vet was bordering on being the sexiest man alive and not just because of the way his muscles rippled beneath his shirt like a sculpted masterpiece. He radiated the kind of magnetism that could stir something primal in a corpse, even through the TV screen. There should have been nothing more attractive to her than a guy who'd devoted his entire life to caring for animals, the same as she had, but this was her territory. She'd never had anyone else come in and take over before.

'Yes, him,' Ellie said with a dreamy sigh. 'I kind of wanted to *be* that horse.'

Ellie giggled into her hair and Sage rolled her eyes. The two of them had watched the vet in action intently for about ten minutes before realising they were both admiring a lot more than his horsemanship.

'He's supposed to be the best you can get when it comes to problematic horses. And Storm is definitely problematic. Look at poor Karma!' Ellie pointed out.

Sage looked at her newest gelding, Karma, who snorted obstinately from the corner of the paddock. He was doing better after his surgery, but she had her suspicions the healing horse just didn't want to provoke Storm in the same space.

Sage finally told Ellie that Ethan was flying in

tomorrow, and Ellie pretended she wasn't excited about it, even though her eyes practically bugged out of her head. Ethan lived in Queensland, and he was known for some pretty weird holistic practices, which felt more infuriating the more Sage thought about it. She'd been used to handling things her own way for the best part of six long years, and now they were just supposed to let some TV celebrity come in and take over?

'Maybe some of his methods might actually work?' Ellie suggested cautiously, eyeing Sage's fierce scowl.

Sage crossed to Karma, careful not to spook the wide-eyed Storm, who watched her every move suspiciously. 'Don't mind us, buddy,' Ellie told him, keeping close behind her.

She didn't have a choice about Ethan's so-called methods, she thought gloomily. Jarrah wanted him here, and, besides, the horse was too dangerous and unpredictable to have around his growing family. Abigail was five months pregnant with their fourth child and what if this unruly beast got a little too wild, a little too close to her? It didn't bear thinking about! Everyone here adored the mayor and his family, Sage most of all. She would be eternally grateful for the soft cushion they'd given her to land on six years ago when she'd driven into town, looking for work. Abigail knew everything about her past, too: the bushfire that had rendered her an orphaned child at ten years old, the fact that she might have prevented it if she hadn't been such a silly, disobedient kid, and that weird, sudden break-up with Bryce too, just weeks before she'd rocked up here.

Abigail had unbottled Sage years ago, along with the wine they had taken to sharing most Friday nights, and Sage was incredibly thankful that she'd been able to talk to someone about it all. It wasn't as though she went around telling just anyone *why* she'd grown up in the care of a foster family in Perth. Just the thought of all the animals that must have died that night when the fire had spread and killed her family, and Juni too—the best dog who'd ever lived—devastated her.

Keep on moving, keep busy, be a good vet, be good to your community, help the animals.

That was her strategy for life. It seemed to be working most of the time, except for when she saw a dog in distress. That always brought all the trauma rushing back, along with the overwhelming guilt.

Sage squinted against the sun. Why exactly was the thought of Ethan Matthews coming here unsettling her like this? He might well be an arrogant showbiz equine expert, but so what?

Maybe it was something about the look on his face when the camera had panned in, she thought. As if he was carrying some kind of close-held secret he only ever shared with his horses. Something that reminded her of herself.

* * *

The morning sun warmed her tense shoulders as Sage stood with her arms folded over the fence, chewing her lip distractedly under the wide-brimmed hat. She called out to Storm, who ignored her. He'd been restless all night again, snorting and pacing as if an invisible phantom were on his tail. It had taken even longer than usual to coerce him between the stall and the paddock with a broom handle.

The rumble of a truck caught her ears. Turning around, she felt her breath catch as the door of the red pickup swung open and then she was watching Ethan Matthews jump to the dusty ground. All six-foot-something of him.

The sunlight streamed across his broad shoulders, forcing her gaze to the contours of his biceps and the dark, almost jet-black thickness of his hair. He wore it scraped back into a rough, manly ponytail at the nape of his neck and he moved with a quiet confidence that made Sage's pulse quicken. She took him all in as he strode towards her in jeans. A forest-green T-shirt moulded to his sculpted torso, muscular thighs visible through every stretch of denim.

Holy hell...

'Dr Dawson?' He was in front of her, extending a big hand, fixing her with the most piercing blue eyes she'd ever seen. They were striking, rimmed

with a deep green, and were more bewitching
the longer she looked at them. She was suddenly
aware they were roaming her face inquisitively,
turning her cheeks into beetroots. 'Great to finally meet you.'

Finally? She bit back a grimace. So, he'd been
anticipating showing up here for a while, then.
Knowing the mayor as she did, he'd have waited
at least two weeks out of the three before making
the call. It wasn't as if he didn't trust her. He'd
probably just realised she clearly didn't have the
right experience for this task.

Sage adjusted her hat, willing her heart to calm
down. She wanted to stay annoyed, but Ethan
Matthews was so good-looking it was almost
too much to take in—how were they not constantly doing close-ups of his eyes on TV? He
was brooding from a distance, but this close the
effect was devastating. Maybe they were afraid
of hypnotising the nation. At any rate, nope. Such
charm and charisma would *not* work on her.

'Dr Matthews, thanks for coming on such short
notice,' she said after a rather awkward silence.

His grip was strong. That green shirt was doing
strange things to her insides too; he either hit the
gym every single day for an hour or so, or he'd
honed his physique purely from wrestling way-
ward horses. Either way, he was likely all style
over substance; he probably had a huge ego too,

having everyone telling him how great he was all the time. Why was she feeling considerably hotter than she had been five minutes ago?

'Ethan, please,' he said, catching her eyes and holding them in a way that made her feel as though she'd forgotten to put on clothes this morning. This was nothing like when she'd first seen Bryce with his shaggy hair and oversized backpack, she thought, agitated all over again.

Wait…why was she comparing Ethan to Bryce?

'Ethan. I appreciate you being here. It's a long way from Queensland,' she said, forcing herself to be polite.

'I go where I'm needed,' he replied with a trace of a smirk. 'I'm sure I can help the mayor get this horse into shape in no time.'

'Well, good luck with that,' she said, more snippily than she intended. Oh, to be that confident and self-assured! 'Three weeks in and I've barely been able to meet his eyes. The only way I can get him to move anywhere is by waving the broom at him. I feel like an evil witch.'

At that, Ethan stifled a laugh, which annoyingly, rather pleased her to hear. Then his eyes trailed the whole length of her body from her boots right up to her face. Sage had never felt so exposed in her life. Even more than before, she certainly did not want this cocky man all up in her business for longer than he had to be. But still, the way he was looking at her made her swallow hard…

'I'll take you to Storm,' she said, flustered.

CHAPTER TWO

IN THE PADDOCK, Sage watched Ethan's eyes lock onto Storm with sharp focus. Keeping his movements slow and steady, he followed her to the stall of their troubled animal patient, ignoring the creature's indignant snorts and holding up both his hands. Sage stood at his side, casting secret glances his way, taking in the decisive slope of his nose, the sharp angle of his cheekbones. What would it feel like to have those big man hands on her own skin? His forearms were so thick with muscle, she half expected to see him pick up Storm with one arm...

'I'm going in,' he said.

'What?'

She watched aghast as Ethan flicked the latch on the stall door, causing the horse to stop in his tracks and stare straight at him.

'What are you doing?' Panic coiled in her belly as her hand went out to his arm. It was hard as a rock and she withdrew it almost instantly, embarrassed. But he didn't even have the broomstick to move him with, or to use as defence.

'I wouldn't go in there. I just told you, he hasn't let anyone close…' she started. Was this really the right approach, so soon? But Ethan didn't appear to be listening to her. He took one step into the stall and Sage held her breath, waiting for the horse to bolt, or, worse, lunge for them both.

'Easy, boy,' he said, almost under his breath. The horse eyed him warily from the corner. Ethan started lowering himself at a snail's pace to his haunches, murmuring gentle words of reassurance. Storm was still looking at him suspiciously down the length of his long nose, and Sage's heart was banging like a drum. What was he doing? Surely, this tactic would not end well! Still, whatever he was doing, her eyes couldn't help but trace the rugged lines of his biceps, their well-defined curves hinting at the raw strength of this man before her.

'I reckon we should start with some quiet talking,' he said. 'He's scared, and we need to be the ones to show him his fear isn't necessary.'

Sage almost snorted despite herself. 'Quiet talking?' She had already tried that, as well as begging the horse fervently with her dignity firmly squashed beneath her own muddy boots, all to no avail.

Ethan nodded, eyes still fixed on Storm. 'Horses

understand everything about our tone and intentions. We have to speak to his spirit first.'

OK...maybe this was a mistake.

'This isn't some Hollywood movie, Ethan. It's not that simple,' she heard herself say, agitated by both his words and the way he was looking at her, as if he was drawing her out of herself and everything that up to ten minutes ago had been quite comfortable, thank you very much.

Ethan gave a short laugh. 'Trust me, he's waiting for someone to understand him.'

Sage just looked at him. What was she supposed to do with this? She hadn't actually heard much of what Ethan had said to that horse on TV; the focus had been on his actions, his strong, confident energy. He had all the right qualifications, a background in veterinary care that stretched back more than a decade; he'd even been on an episode of *Vets in the Wild*, where he'd tamed a stallion that had already stomped a man down and left him fighting for his life in hospital, but this was just...well—not quite what she'd expected. This was supposed to have been her issue to handle, her problem to solve, yet she was more confused now than she'd been before.

She bit her tongue as he held out a hand slowly, cautiously. Surely it was only a matter of seconds before he regretted this too; Storm was wilder than she could handle with her experience alone and, she'd assumed, Ethan's too, despite being the star of the nation. To her shock, though, the horse took a tentative step towards him.

'He's listening to you, he's responding,' she said in awe, covering her mouth with her hand. OK, so maybe he wasn't just all mouth and muscles as she'd assumed. She'd gone as far as assuming the camera had lied, or they'd at least done some clever editing. But here he was. In the flesh. Succeeding where she'd failed. So infuriating.

Ethan continued to murmur soft words of encouragement from his lowered position on the ground and soon the horse was sniffing warily at his outstretched hand. Sage watched, afraid to move for what felt like at least an hour but was probably only three minutes.

'So, are you a wizard or something?' she asked him eventually, feeling silly instantly.

Ethan finally tore his gaze away long enough to chuckle at her under his breath. No sooner had he flashed her a half-smile, however, than Storm was scrambling backwards and rearing up on his hind legs, spooked by something all over again.

'Move!' Ethan's reflexes were as fast as the horse's. He rose to full standing and before she had a chance to react he was throwing himself between her and the snorting, wild-eyed animal. Sage gasped for breath as Ethan yanked her against him, holding out his other hand to Storm as they backed away slowly through the stall door.

'Steady,' he implored quietly. Did he mean her, or the horse?

Her whole body tensed with shock as he shielded her from the threat of Storm's powerful hooves and she didn't know whether to be impressed by his quick reaction or annoyed with her own slow one as he latched the door behind them. Storm hoofed at the floor repeatedly, kicking up the dirt. Sage's back was still pressed hard against Ethan's chest, his flexed arm like a giant safety belt across her abdomen. For a moment she couldn't even move. Then, embarrassed and maybe more than a little undermined by this man who was still a stranger on her turf, she uncoiled herself.

'I told you, he hasn't let anyone close, so *why* did you do that?'

Ethan fixed his blue gaze onto hers. 'And I told you, Dr Dawson, he's waiting for someone to understand him. He'll only know that we do if we back off now.'

His tone was gruff and assertive and somehow managed to both irritate her and turn her on at the same time. She smoothed down her overalls and was about to tell him that maybe this hadn't been the mayor's best idea when he cut her off by extending a hand, straight at her face. She blinked as he swiped something from the rim of her hat, and a wisp of straw floated to the ground.

'This will take a while. But I'll take the case,'

he said. 'No broom necessary.' Then he tilted his head at her in a brief, courteous bow before turning and leaving the stable. Sage followed him out into the sunlight, squinting, heart still racing. Ethan didn't bother opening the gate to the paddock. He simply scaled the five metal bars with one jump like a two-legged show pony in jeans. Then he swung it wide open just for her to walk through after him.

Sage bit down on the inside of her cheek. How dare he just stroll in and make everything look so easy? OK, so this man had made more progress with Storm in a matter of minutes than she'd made in three whole weeks, but the magic show had to end at some point. Storm was unpredictable at best. He could take many weeks, even months of training. Ethan's confidence would likely wear off just as hers had, but she still might be stuck with him for ages until that happened!

Why was she suddenly wondering how close he'd be sleeping to her? Of course, he'd stay at Yukka Guest House, just like everyone else!

Leading Ethan into the clinic, Sage was acutely aware of his tall, muscular frame behind her. She glanced back at him as he looked around, taking in the examination rooms and medical equipment, the poster of the horse with the kookaburra on its head that hung over the reception desk, and the row of slightly dusty cactus plants in the window. He exuded an aura of quiet intensity that charged the room.

'Nice place. How long have you been here, Dr Dawson?' He ran a finger over one of the cacti as if daring it to prick him.

'Call me Sage. And it's coming up for six years now,' she told him, just as Ellie appeared from the back with an owner and her rabbit, its leg freshly bandaged from its brush with a snare. She introduced them and watched Ellie and the rabbit's female twenty-something owner flush. Both women actually fluttered their eyelashes! Ethan fielded questions from them with brief replies, while casting his gaze first to her, then back to them, causing her to roll her eyes, as well as smooth her frizzy hair from her face so many times it went static.

Ruffled, she called Yukka Guest House in Amber Creek to ask about a room, warning her eyeballs to stop roving over his face from across the reception. But she couldn't help it; he was probably one of the most striking men she'd ever laid eyes on. Not that a TV star with an ego the size of the moon would look twice at someone like her, covered in dust and straw on the outside…a bit of a mess on the inside most days, too.

She tutted to herself. That wasn't entirely fair; she wasn't ugly. And she wasn't always covered in dust and straw either. It was just that she was…well…what man would want to deal with all her baggage? The orphaned child, fostered by a wealthy miner, given all the privileges and advantages she could've dreamed of: a caring new family who weren't her own, but who loved her anyway, an education at one of Australia's most prestigious veterinary institutions, money, freedom…yet who still couldn't date a guy without the same profound sense of hopelessness swallowing her senses, reducing her to an undatable weirdo, incapable of forging an emotional connection. She hadn't slept with more than three people since that doomed relationship with Bryce, six whole years ago. She probably had cobwebs. Not that those three men hadn't all tried to pursue her afterwards; she just had a habit of keeping her heart locked up where it couldn't be broken any more. They all got tired of her emotionally stunted self eventually.

'I've booked you my regular room at Yukka Guest House for tonight,' she told him when they were alone again, as an image of him lounging in bed forced her eyes back away from him. 'After that you can decide if you want to stay there or move…'

He quirked an eyebrow. 'Your regular room?'

'The room I reserve for locums and visitors,' she corrected herself. Could he read her mind or something? He laughed softly. The sound of it made her skin prickle and she cleared her throat.

'That was pretty remarkable, back there,' she

said before she could stop herself. 'I've never seen anyone calm any horse so quickly. Even if it didn't last.'

Ethan gave a modest shrug. 'Just takes patience. And reading their body language.'

The way he said 'body language' while looking at her...

Oh, my.

Sage started quickly tidying up some scattered papers on the front desk. In her hurry, a sheet fell to the floor and it floated in the draught against his leather boot. He bent to retrieve it just as she did, and their hands brushed over the piece of paper. Sage sucked in a sharp breath. On reflection, it was so loud she could've sworn Ellie heard it in the exam room. It must have spoken volumes about the way he was tangling up her insides already in this confined space, but if Ethan noticed, he said nothing.

'So, Mr Famous,' she said bluntly, shoving the papers back onto a pile on the desk and finally retrieving Storm's file. 'I've seen you on TV. How long have you had this gift with horses?'

'Gift?' He smirked, placing the file under his arm as he made a thing of eyeing her exam certificates, framed in a row on the wall. Bachelor of Veterinary Science, Member of the Australian Veterinary Association, and also a specialised postgraduate qualification highlighting her advanced training in veterinary surgical procedures.

'You seem to have some kind of qualification that I don't,' she said pointedly. 'I don't even think you can study for what you can do. Therefore it's a gift, isn't it?' Sage hoped the comment didn't inflate his ego any further. But she'd said it now. His eyes met hers, and her pulse quickened. He was so intense. She'd just caught his bergamot-like scent too: citrus and wildflowers and horses and man. The smell stirred something in her, made her heart start to beat even faster. Maybe she was just a little starstruck, she reasoned, because of the whole TV thing. How irritating.

Ethan rubbed his neck self-consciously. 'I wouldn't call it a gift. Just skills I've picked up over the years. Helps that I'm as stubborn as most horses,' he said wryly.

Sage sensed his humility was genuine and felt a momentary stab of guilt at her prickliness. 'Still, your techniques are quite different from how we practise around here,' she followed.

'I hope that won't be a problem.'

For a moment, she glimpsed a flicker of rebellion in his eyes and she fought the instinctive desire to tell him there was a way of doing things around here—*her* way. Her way hadn't worked so far, had it? Not with Storm. And the *mayor* wanted him here.

'We open at seven a.m.,' she said instead, motioning for the door. She walked him across the dusty forecourt to his vehicle, simultaneously flustered and intrigued. 'I understand you'll want more time with Storm tomorrow…'

'And the other horses,' he said, opening the car door and leaning on it, eyeing her over his crossed arms. 'I need to see how he interacts with the others. I'll be here early, if that's OK.'

She fished around in the giant pocket of her overalls, then handed him a key. 'Sure, that's the key to the back. You'll find the coffee machine there. If it doesn't start, just give it a firm kick.'

'I'll be sure to do that.'

'Any problems, I live just over there.' She pointed to her humble cabin beyond the tree line, where she'd been shacked up since arriving. It was modest to say the least, but it had become somewhat of a home while she tended the small native plant garden around it and kept the wildlife from moving in. Better than paying rent in town.

'You live here too?' he asked, seemingly surprised.

'Yeah, I'm still trying to figure out the irrigation system so we can grow more than cacti but…'

'Can I see?'

She watched as Ethan closed the car door again and made for her cabin. Following him, she prayed she hadn't left any undies out to dry. Thankfully she hadn't, but he seemed curious about her rock garden, and the compost pile she'd constructed to recycle organic waste. Before she knew it, they were discussing the plans for the drip irrigation system, which would eventually deliver water directly to the base of plants, minimising evaporation. He told her he lived on a homestead with his dad that included an equine centre for troubled horses and prime grazing that she knew they only had in Queensland. His late mother had been adamant they turn it into the most climate-conscious place they could for the whole community to enjoy, before she died.

'I'm so sorry you lost your mother,' she told him as the awkwardness snaked around her like a living thing. How could her own mum's smiling face not come back to her, the second he shared that information? Ethan simply nodded at the ground, ending the conversation by making for his ute again.

Suddenly Sage was wondering if he had a wife, or a girlfriend, waiting at this homestead, and found herself looking at his left hand. No ring. That didn't mean anything though, really. And why should she care? Still, they stood there at the vehicle for just a second too long for it to be comfortable. And as his ute rumbled away, she felt the strangest sensation that her entire world had just shifted completely on its axis.

CHAPTER THREE

ETHAN SCANNED THE horizon over his coffee mug. The landscape beyond the borders of the clinic seemed endless, hugged by jagged dunes and rugged, red-earthed wilderness. It was beautiful around here, even at six-thirty a.m., and remote. It wasn't as if he didn't know remote, though.

He and his dad lived this way themselves for the most part in Queensland, just them and the horses and dogs, away from the noise and traffic and…memories, but this was something else. The nearest town, Amber Creek, was four miles away. Babs, the funny and kind woman at the guest house, hadn't been able to stop staring at him when he'd first arrived; was he that much of a celebrity here? The thought was grating.

He could tell Sage wasn't particularly keen to have him here either. He would get her on board, show her it wasn't all camera magic and celebrity draw that kept people calling him where other vets failed, but still he probably shouldn't have agreed to all the TV stuff in the first place. It was just that they'd offered him a lot of money. And with everything he and Dad had wanted to do with the land to honour Mum's dream, their plans for the self-sufficiency workshops, the rainwater-harvesting system and solar panels she'd started implementing before the cancer stole her mobility and mind—well, they'd needed a significant injection of funds. But there was still so much to do. And the mayor of Amber Creek had offered him a significant amount of money to treat Storm. Almost as much as the network.

Clutching his coffee, he rested a boot on the gate of the paddock and sipped the scorching black brew. Dr Dawson… Sage, had been right. He'd had to kick the machine pretty hard to get a decent cup of coffee out of it. He'd also relocated a redback spider more than once over the last few days. Little guy had made a home for himself, nestled amongst the filters.

'I'm almost done, Ethan!' The stable hand, Billy, had shown up ten minutes after him. The lanky kid, dressed in denim shorts and a baseball hat, was mucking out the stalls now, neatly avoiding Storm. Ethan raised his cup at him, ready to address the situation when the kid was out of the way. The horse was snorting again, not as angrily as he had done on day one, but Storm's sweat-soaked coat was reflecting the morning sunlight in a way that concerned him. This was one unsettled animal. The problem was, he didn't know why yet.

He was just placing his chipped mug back by the kickable coffee machine in the back room, wondering yet again why there was a giant NO NAKED FLAMES IN THE KITCHEN PLEASE! sign on the wall, when a shadow appeared behind him in the doorway.

'Morning, Ethan.'

The light cast a warm golden glow over Sage's wavy chestnut hair, loose again today, falling around her shoulders from the same wide-brimmed hat. For a moment he just stood there, and she stood opposite, smiling from one corner of her pretty mouth, seemingly taking in his clean checked shirt and jeans, and the brown leather boots he'd stormed across a thousand paddocks in.

'I like the boots,' Sage quipped.

'Thanks. They were a gift,' he said. Sage nodded from the doorway as if waiting for him to tell a story. Of course, he wouldn't. Carrie had bought him these boots eight years ago, right after they declared themselves an item. If only he'd known back then that the footwear would last longer than their relationship; that she'd wind up with his best friend while he was blinded to it all by grief, reeling from losing Mum.

Sage blinked, offering a slightly nervous laugh before skirting around him. 'I just need a…'

'Right, a coffee.' He moved quickly, but not before catching the scent of her: freshly showered, maybe a splash of fragrance, something floral. She went about putting a new mug under the ancient contraption and hit the button under 'flat white'. Then she pulled her phone out, scanned it unseeingly and slid it straight back into her pocket while his eyes fixated on her movements.

So, here it was again. The same unsettling attraction to her that he hadn't known exactly what to do with on day one. It had probably made things a little awkward, all the little silences between their exchanges. Sage Dawson kind of reminded him of Carrie. And that wasn't exactly a good thing. They were the same slight build, the same height, five-foot-five-ish, with eyes that unpicked you. There was something about her intelligence and determination that had caught him off guard and put him in his place, and she never seemed starstruck like the woman at the guest house. Having her remind him of Carrie wasn't ideal. His ex-fiancé was probably just waking up to another Brisbane sunrise in the fancy penthouse apartment she and Cam had bought after their wedding: traitors, both of them.

'So, how's Storm this morning? Did you get a chance to examine him yet?' Sage was still staring at the empty coffee cup, and the silent machine.

'I was waiting for Billy to finish mucking out. We don't want to startle him.'

'Oh, so Billy showed up.' Sage frowned and raised a knee at the machine. He grinned as she gave it a hearty kick from below, sending the mug flying. Deftly he caught it mid-flight and handed it back, and she pulled a face behind her hair as their fingers brushed. There. Again. She'd started out all spiky but after they'd talked in her garden the other day, he was almost sure he'd detected a spark of something else. That *spark* was something he hoped he'd been imagining. The last thing he needed was another woman looking at him all googly-eyed because of how the network portrayed him—they'd cut out most of his words and focused instead on long shots of his body and close-ups of his muscles as if he was nothing more than a gym rat—which he was, to some degree, he supposed. Keeping strong was imperative, plus it kept his mind from going into dark corners it would do best not to revisit.

But there was something different about Sage, too. As if she was looking beyond all that. As if she had the capacity to reach places he'd barriered shut for a reason. Good thing he wouldn't be here long; he'd fix up this horse and be out of here in no time. Back to his father, who needed him.

Sage took her coffee outside, and this time he didn't leap over the fence as he had a few times now. Force of habit. It was just what he did back home. She seemed as conflicted as Billy when he walked towards Storm's stall. They both stood behind him as he flicked the latch again, but soon they disappeared somewhere into the silence on the periphery, as people usually did when it came to the horses.

He'd always been this way, so deeply connected to the animals in a way most others couldn't understand. Except Dad, who'd done it all his life, too. This horse had been growing increasingly restless. He heard Billy whisper as much to Sage, but Ethan hoped his presence would offer some kind of solace to the creature. As it had the first time, right before Storm had reared up and almost taken their eyes out.

'Easy, boy,' he said, holding out a steady hand so the horse could see he meant no harm. Slowly he approached Storm, and noticed the animal's ears flicking back and forth, his nostrils flaring with every breath.

'What made you this way, boy? Or who?' he murmured softly, stepping closer. He allowed Storm to sniff his palm before gently stroking the horse's velvety muzzle. Sage held her breath behind him, but this time he didn't break his focus. That was what had happened before, he realised. It had kept him awake for a good hour extra that first night. For the first time in a long time while dealing with a distressed horse he had looked away, distracted. By Sage. She'd asked if he was a wizard.

There *was* something about her that unsettled

him, more than just her likeness to Carrie. He'd
seen it increasingly these past few days, watching
her going about her business, a faraway look in
her eyes. They had as much pain locked behind
them as this horse sometimes. Like looking in a
mirror, he thought, not looking away from Storm.
He was still stroking his snout—this was some
form of success at least. To his relief, Storm's
eyes softened further at the touch, and he let out
a quiet nicker as if to say thank you.

'I can tell he trusts you. At least he's starting
to, mate,' Billy said behind him. Sage immediately asked him to be quiet.

It wouldn't be smart to push things, he thought.
This was enough for now. 'The exam can wait,'
he told them, backing out of the stall again. Billy
left to answer a call. Sage watched intently as
Ethan reached an arm over the railing and gave
Storm another soft stroke, along his chestnut neck
this time.

'How do you…?' Her voice, before she cut
her question short, was tinged with a kind of be-
grudging respect that tickled him.

'I don't know, Sage, you tell me,' he said, biting back a smile. He led her back outside. It was
getting warm already and he removed his hat
to tighten his hair in the band at the back of his
sticky neck. He didn't miss Sage's eyes trailing
down the front of his shirt, all the way to his belt,
where they hovered for just a moment too long.

'My dad, his father, and his before that,' he said, by way of further explanation as her gaze flicked back up to his. He locked his eyes to hers as he adjusted his belt. He didn't need to. It just felt tighter after having her look at it. 'They're communicating with us in their own way. We just have to tune in to what they're saying, like finding the right frequency on a radio. They harbour fear and pain just like we do. And they can be blissfully peaceful. So calm and tranquil. Which humans are not, generally speaking.'

'You're intuitively understanding their pain from the signals they transmit.'

'Kind of.'

Sage studied his face again thoughtfully, waving a fly away from her face, then fanning her white shirt, which was open just enough at the neck to reveal sun-tanned skin and freckles. There was a flicker of hurt in her voice now, a hint at whatever pain she harboured herself deep below the surface. 'Well,' she said quickly. 'Whatever it is you're doing, it's working.'

Ethan watched her run a brief exam on Karma. There were five horses here, considerably less than his herd of twenty-plus, give or take, depending on the equine patients who stayed for variable lengths of time. Billy had explained this morning how three of them were his, including Karma. He worked in the stable and grounds here to subsidise their upkeep. Sage was the chief vet and, as far as he could see, she had a limited staff on the rota. Ellie and…that was it. It seemed like a lot of work for a skeleton crew but he wasn't about to question or judge.

He had got the impression, that first day in her garden, that she had poured all her efforts into this place because it was more than just a job to her. This was her entire life. No wonder she hadn't wanted some strange vet waltzing into what she'd built and upending it all. He also got the feeling that this was her whole life for another reason too. He knew better than to push, though. There was the matter of his own internal scars; he'd hate to be forced to discuss all those. Losing Mum to cancer three months after her diagnosis was one thing…two years on and Dad was only just starting to come out the other side. Then there was the ultimate gut-punch on top, knowing his best friend and his ex-fiancée were probably happier than they'd ever been now that Ethan's own grief and his horses were no longer in the equation, living their city dream in wedded bliss.

He could still hear Cam's words to Carrie. It was far too easy to picture himself standing right outside the door of that hotel suite all over again, the blood from the cat he'd just done emergency surgery on still fresh on his shirt.

'How can you stand Ethan when he does all that weird horsey stuff? You know he'll never

love you as much as his animals, right, Carrie?
You won't ever come first for him.'

'Don't be so mean. His mum just died!'

'Is that why you don't want to tell him about
us yet?'

Catching himself, he snatched up a bridle from
the hook on the wall and threw it to her. 'Tack
him up,' he said. Thirteen months and three
weeks since the day he'd found out about their
affair, and it still had the power to stab him in the
gut, as if it had happened only yesterday.

'Now?'

'He's healing just fine.'

Sage stared at him, incredulous. 'I don't ride
Karma. He's Billy's horse. And are you sure he's
ready? He's not long been castrated.'

'He's fine,' he said. 'It'll probably be good for
Storm to see you riding him, too. Show him what
his role's supposed to be. You said the mayor
bought him for his daughter, over the phone?'

Sage shook her head at her feet a moment, and
he realised that despite her growing tolerance to
his presence, and their undeniable attraction,
she still harboured a little scepticism over his
so-called unconventional methods. It wasn't as
though he was the only qualified veterinarian in
the world who knew horses and their minds, but
for people like Sage, who'd gone down a more
traditional path with all her certificates from top
establishments…well, sometimes they needed

convincing. Not that he had the time for all that. If people didn't trust his 'weird horsey stuff', that was their problem. The results spoke for themselves. Karma was clearly well and could do with a ride after his time off.

A call came from beyond the fence. Ellie, Sage's veterinary assistant, was waving a phone at them. 'Sage, it's Lance, down at Redgum Ridge. A kookaburra just crashed into his glass door, and it's in pretty bad shape. He doesn't want to move it.'

'Lance's place is beyond the bridge, the one that's closed,' Sage explained to Ethan, chewing her lip. 'I can't get the ute through.' She cast speculative eyes at him. Before he could even suggest it, Sage was striding back over to Billy.

'Do you mind if I take Karma out?' she asked him, pressing a gentle hand to Karma's silky forelock.

'Not at all. I think he's ready, too.'

'Great. I'll have to take more supplies than I can carry. We're going to need a cage to bring it back.' Then she looked at Ethan again, her gaze filled with the question.

'I'll go with you,' he replied. 'Billy, can you saddle up one more while I grab my bag?'

CHAPTER FOUR

'DR DAWSON?' LANCE, an older guy, maybe late fifties, stood in the doorway of the old run-down house, clutching their injured kookaburra protectively in his hands. 'I was watching TV. Then I heard the crash at the back door,' he explained. 'I thought someone was trying to break in, but when I went to check I found this poor fella just lying there all…wonky.'

'No worries, Lance, you did the right thing, calling us,' Sage said. 'This is Ethan Matthews, by the way. He's working with me for a while over at the clinic.'

Ethan stuck his hand out, noting the dishevelled hair, the crumpled shirt and the beer cans littering the porch. His own dad had gone this way for a while, after Mum died. Luckily Ethan and his sister had pulled him out of it. Jacqueline had been a total rock through the whole thing, though she'd suffered the loss in her own way. She always said she had to be strong for her husband, Mack, and she'd had the kids to think about when their mum had passed, too. He'd always maintained it was better to experience the full spectrum of emotions that orbited grief. Then Carrie had done what she'd done, and he'd blocked the whole damn lot of it out.

'You rode all the way out here,' Lance said, nodding towards the horses tied up out by bushes in the shade.

'The bridge is still out of action, remember?' she said kindly as he directed them inside. Lance furrowed his brow, as though he had actually forgotten.

'He doesn't leave this place much,' Sage whispered to Ethan in explanation as they followed the man inside. 'Not since he lost his wife.'

Ethan nodded. So he'd been right. Poor man.

Despite its old tin roof and weathered exterior, the house seemed quite cosy and well maintained on the inside. A cat unfurled itself lazily from the sofa and crept around Lance's legs as Sage instructed him to place the bird carefully on the small round table in the kitchen.

Together, they examined the kookaburra, gently probing it for signs of injury. Sage inspected its wings and feathers, murmuring softly to it under her breath as she did so. As they worked side by side, her green eyes seemed to glow even more with determination. Her loose chestnut hair fell in soft waves around her face, framing her delicate features. When she wasn't wearing the hat, she looked younger for some reason. She couldn't have been much younger than him though, and he was thirty-five. So much like Carrie, he thought again…only, the more he looked at Sage, the more he could see how different they really were.

Sage had a look that was entirely her own. Besides, being a city girl, Carrie wouldn't be seen dead in overalls. Looking back, she probably never would have ended up moving from Brisbane to the homestead as they'd planned to after they married. It was far too rustic out there, with way too many snakes and spiders for her to feel completely comfortable. Besides, she wasn't all *that* into horses really. They'd been an odd match from the start. She was an actress, fresh from Sydney. He'd met her the same night as Cam in the pub next to the theatre. The three of them had chatted for four solid hours, till Cam had murmured that he felt like a third wheel and left them to it.

Carrie used to love how he and his family had turned the old family cattle station into a successful equine centre and homestead, with plans for an eco-conscious community that would eventually, with all of their help, thrive around it. Mum had always dreamed of off-grid living, creating a hub for sustainable ventures and permaculture initiatives. Carrie had seemed so into it at first, talking about 'learning the bees', as his sister, Jacqueline, had done. His sister's honey was still the best for miles around, and she still came over every Saturday with Mack and his niece and nephew, who buzzed about the place more than the bees.

Carrie had helped Mum and Jacqueline with the bees a lot for the first couple of years, or just read her books and studied her lines in the hammock while he worked with the horses. She'd seemed happy, and it had shaken his world up when Dad had taken him aside one day and asked if everything was OK between them.

Dad had noticed Carrie was spending more time on her phone than she was engaging with them; more time out and about in the city with her friends than honouring plans she'd made to do things with *him*. She'd missed three farmers' markets in a row.

He'd thought if he proposed, things would get better. She'd always said they could wait for marriage—who knew when her latest show would go on tour? He'd agreed; after all, he'd been so busy being a vet, and working out in the fields with Dad and the horses. There had been plenty of time to plan a wedding, really, but he'd figured they would be doing it eventually so he'd asked her anyway.

For a while, things had got better; Carrie had got excited trying on dresses, sending him photos of vineyards and beaches and wine glasses and platters of cheese. Then Mum had died. And afterwards, when neither of them could agree on a date for the wedding—probably because she'd already started seeing Cam—she'd stopped coming to the homestead at all, saying he spent *too* much time with the horses, and that she found it all increasingly boring being with someone who didn't seem to enjoy the same things any more. Maybe she was right. But after several years together, she should have gone to him with all this. Instead she'd gone to Cam.

'Looks like a broken wing,' Sage was saying now, carefully holding the bird still.

'But there must be some internal damage too,' he mused. 'He's not moving much. We can take him back with us for further tests.'

Their hands touched briefly as he helped apply a splint and Sage seemed to be looking at him with a strange look on her face as he wrapped a towel gently around the bird, motioning for her to open the cage they'd brought with them.

'What?' he asked.

'You're good with the animals,' she said, and he frowned.

'Did you think I wouldn't be?'

'I don't know…you never know if what you see on TV is real or not any more,' she answered as he took over settling the kookaburra inside the cage on another fresh towel. 'And I'm not used to having a qualified partner for things like this.'

'Well, I'm here. And I'm totally real.'

'I see that now.'

The vulnerability in her eyes caught him off guard, and he found himself wondering if she'd had any partners at all lately, all the way out here.

'We should get this little guy back to the clinic, make sure he's OK,' she said, breaking whatever moment that had just been.

As they were leaving, Ethan got a glimpse of the bedroom through the hallway. Two broken windows. Peeling paint everywhere. He made a mental note to talk to Billy later about them possibly helping out with some repair work. It wouldn't take long to fix a few new glass panes and run a brush around. Unless that wasn't his place, he thought as he lifted the cage out carefully to the horses, telling Sage he'd carry it back. He'd only been here five minutes—of course it wasn't his place! He just wasn't the kind of guy who could stand around knowing someone might need help, as his dad had needed help; not when he could be doing something about it.

The vast outback surrounded them on all sides as he rode with the cage in front of him against the saddle. The silence seemed charged. 'Is he OK?' Sage asked stiffly.

'He's doing fine,' he replied, hoping it was true. The sun beat down on his back and the horses plodded along steadily, their hooves creating a comforting rhythm that was broken only by the occasional soft whinny. Ethan couldn't help but marvel at the beauty of this wilderness: the rolling hills, the majestic gum trees reaching for the sky. It wasn't home. He could never leave Queensland permanently—his dad relied on him, and his mum's living legacy was still under construction—but despite its ferocious heat and unforgiving terrain, there was something inherently peaceful about it.

Then Sage spoke.

'Does your wife or girlfriend mind all the travelling you do?'

Ethan hesitated, caught off guard by her personal question. How much did he need to reveal?

'Or your husband, or boyfriend, perhaps?' she added with a rare smile.

He bit back a laugh. 'I don't do relationships at all,' he said, keeping his tone light. Neither of them mentioned the kangaroo that bounded away into the distance from behind a bush as they passed.

'Ah, I see,' she replied softly, her gaze focused on the path ahead. Was that a small smirk on her face? Did that sound like a 'typical bloke' thing to say? It wasn't as if he could blurt out why he didn't do relationships, and probably never would again. 'I'm single. And I like it that way…for now.'

He'd only added 'for now' so he wouldn't sound too miserable. That wasn't how he felt most of the time; in fact, he was starting to see a little light through the fog of confusion and anger that had seen him confiding only in his horses, and pouring his grief into working out in his makeshift home gym for the last year. But he'd never get over it completely—who would? His best friend and his fiancée…such a cliche.

'So, what brought you to Amber Creek?' he asked her, realising an awkward silence had descended again.

Sage blew air through her nose and kept her eyes on the horizon. She told him how she'd floated around a lot before landing on this place, working with aboriginal tribes, and cultural and conservation programmes across various indigenous protected areas. She'd even worked at a koala reserve for a while. 'Guess I didn't know where I wanted to be, till I found this place.'

'Why's that?' he pressed, picturing how cute she'd look with several koalas clinging to her.

She told him about her friend, Abigail, the mayor's wife. How she'd helped her a lot. How she'd found it nice to be able to talk to someone about anything and everything. He told her how he used to have a friend like that. Ethan couldn't read the look on her face, but Sage was starting to drift somewhere in her mind again.

'How did she help you?'

'I guess I grew up pretty reserved after…well, after losing my parents. I mostly talked to the animals about it all, you know, like a weirdo.'

He flinched. Being a weirdo who talked to the animals. He knew all about that, too, but all he said was, 'I've met bigger weirdos, trust me.' They had the horses walking slowly, so as not to disturb the kookaburra, but he could feel his shirt starting to stick to his back. This Abigail had probably heard more about Sage's life than she'd ever share with him and it wasn't his job to pry.

'I'm so sorry you lost both your parents,' he couldn't help saying, picturing his mum again, how she'd used to wear a silly hat around the homestead, as Sage did around the clinic grounds. 'How old were you?'

That was OK to ask, right?

'I was ten when they both died,' she replied curtly, pulling Karma to a stop and leaping off. 'Anyway. It's all ancient history, right? Here we are.'

Ancient history? She'd lost *both* her parents at the same time?

Ethan hadn't even realised till now that they were back at the clinic already, and she was un-latching the front gate, sending a dust cloud up around her that swallowed her boots. She reached up for the cage, blowing her hair from her sticky face.

'I'll carry it from here. Can you take the horses back to Billy?' She squinted up at him. Her tone had turned strictly professional again now, with no room or time for personal stories.

'Yes, ma'am. I'll examine Storm now.'

'If he lets you,' she said drily.

Ethan opened his mouth to reply that he was sure Storm would, but decided against it. If she was so determined to be surprised every time he was good with an animal, let her be surprised when Storm let him in.

Ethan watched her walk purposefully up the path, where Ellie met her on the front steps. She stopped, then gave a quick glance back at him over her shoulder, and even from a distance he could see the apprehension in her body language. Sage already felt as though she'd told him too much about herself, but if it really was ancient history, why didn't it explain the lingering sadness he could feel ebbing out of her? What else had she endured? Now he needed to know more.

CHAPTER FIVE

SAGE WATCHED AS Ethan's fingers drummed rhythmically on the wooden fence, his blue eyes narrowed in concentration. He had those damned boots on again. He looked so hot in them. Last night she'd dreamed about them—weren't they on her kitchen floor, along with that denim shirt he was wearing the other day? The details were kind of blurry. In fact, the blurry and not so blurry dreams about Ethan Matthews were getting out of hand now, the more he seemed to crawl inside her skull.

They had retreated to the shade of a nearby tree, allowing Storm some space after his first semi-exam. It was a semi-exam because Ethan had so far managed only to lift one front leg. Three days ago, after rescuing the kookaburra together, which thankfully was now doing a lot better, Ethan had tried to examine the unruly animal and failed. He'd spent an hour on the phone to someone afterwards and later she'd found out it was his father. He seemed to speak with him every day, actually, and she envied that a little. Obviously they were close after losing his mother; they lived together at the homestead. What she wouldn't give to be able to pick up the phone to her biological dad—not that Ken wasn't there for her when she needed him. Her foster dad was amazing.

Even after showing some semblance of normality and trust towards Ethan in the stall, when it came to an exam, Storm just wasn't having it. Almost as if the horse didn't *want* anyone to see inside his head. 'Doesn't it bother you that he's still being so…hostile?' she said now, surprised at herself for actually being concerned that Ethan's methods weren't working—wasn't that what she'd expected, before he showed up? Ethan huffed a laugh, still drumming his fingers as Storm trotted around the perimeter of the paddock, sweeping right past them like a tease.

'We'll get to the bottom of it. I'm not worried yet. It just takes time.'

'Well, I admire your confidence,' she said, pulling her phone out to check the time. Ellie was supposed to be at the clinic by now, but she had called in sick, and there was a long list of animal patients still left to see today. A no-show was not ideal.

She looked up from the screen, feeling his eyes on her face. 'Everything OK?' he asked, sipping from the chipped mug, which by now was pretty much his mug. She had taken to arriving at the stables earlier than usual the last few mornings, just to have a coffee with him. It amused him whenever she kicked and cursed at the machine. The tension between them simmered just below the surface, a palpable undercurrent that seemed to charge the air with electricity every time there was a second of silence between them. Unless, of course, she was imagining it because of her dreams, and *he* hadn't noticed at all.

She explained that she was a little stressed because of her veterinary assistant's absence. 'Could it be something in his diet?' she then asked, steering the subject back to Storm so as not to appear entirely unprofessional. People got sick; it wasn't fair to be annoyed at the inconvenience.

Ethan nodded. 'It's possible. I've seen horses become more anxious when their feed is too high in sugar.'

'Exactly,' she said. 'Only, we've been careful what we fed him.'

Ethan shrugged. 'I doubt diet alone would cause such severe symptoms. I'd bet it's purely psychological but...'

'Until we can get close enough to rule anything out, we can't say for sure,' she finished, and he nodded, pulling out his shirt slightly. Even in the shade, it was hot, and she forced her eyes away from the fine chest hairs peeking out above the neckline. What was wrong with her? She almost wished he'd leave and take his sexy chest with him, but the mayor was paying for him to be here, and here he would stay until he succeeded.

Still, her wild dreams about him weren't helped by the fact that he was so good with the animals, when she'd actually assumed his so-called gift had been staged! He was also a good man in other ways, too. Ethan had rallied Billy to help repaint Lance's place, down at Redgum Ridge, once he knew the man had lost his wife. She knew she'd do well to keep things professional with Ethan, not to get too close, and definitely not let on how he was affecting her! The last time she'd let her barriers down with a man enough to truly make a connection—Bryce, ugh—he'd just disappeared on her, and while she most certainly was not going to be forging any kind of meaningful connection with Ethan in the brief time he was here, how could she not be intrigued by him?

Sage's thoughts drifted back to their conversation out on horseback the other day. She'd told him her parents died when she was ten, which in retrospect wasn't a whole lot of information, but the whole self-deprecating thing about being a weirdo who'd grown up talking to animals... Why had she said that? He was beyond perceptive. He could probably see by now that she was more than a little broken, but she'd gone and admitted her confidence, outside her veterinary skills, was in the toilet.

Still, why didn't he 'do' relationships? She was dying to ask him. Something about his tone and general secrecy had implied there was a pretty interesting reason behind that decision.

'I can help out,' Ethan said after a moment, his gaze not leaving Storm. 'I can't paint today anyway; Lance is expecting a delivery.'

Sage's heart kicked at her ribs. He would do that for her? Could she even handle working so closely with him?

'If you're sure,' she said nonchalantly, realising she sounded quite unsure of herself. He'd already moved in on her own responsibilities with Storm—not that she'd had a choice, and not that he wasn't making more progress than she ever had, annoyingly.

He turned to her, deadly serious, his voice low and gruff. 'Am I really so unconventional that you don't trust I'd obey your every command, Doctor?'

'I do trust you,' she heard herself say, a little too quickly. Gosh, why was she getting so hot again?

Later, Sage was wrapping up the last examination of the day—a cat who'd been struck down with the feline calicivirus—when she heard Ethan greeting someone who'd walked in. She would know that voice anywhere. Abigail, and her kids too by the sounds of it.

Waving off the lady and her cat, Sage felt un-
ease coil in her belly as Abigail, gorgeous as ever
in a long pink sundress, hair in a standard messy
bun, raised her eyebrows out of Ethan's eyeline.
Sage knew exactly what that look meant. It meant
that Abigail also found him astonishingly attractive and was already pairing Sage up with him
in her head!

'It's nice to meet Ethan here,' she said, beam-
ing. 'I brought you some of that pineapple cake
you like. Mum made too much again and you
know it makes Daisy go doolally. Daisy, don't
touch things, please, darling.'

Sure enough, Abigail was clutching her tod-
dler, Charlie, over her bulging pregnant belly. Her
five-year-old, Daisy, was already assessing the
blue teddy bear in the box of toys by the window.
Ethan crouched beside her, holding up a fire truck
while throwing them both a look of his own that
said he'd watch her a second.

'We should, uh, get this to the kitchen,' Abigail
said loudly, holding up the cake tin. Quickly, Abigail pulled Sage by the sleeve towards the back
room and shut the door. 'Oh, my God!' she murmured at her, eyes comically wide.

'Shh, Abi!'

'He's gorgeous!'

'He'll hear you!'

Abigail snorted and deposited Charlie onto the
table, stretching out her back for a second before

hoisting him back up onto her belly. 'So he's the one who's fixing our Storm?'

'Storm is not a car, Abi, but yeah, he's trying.'

'Maybe he can fix you too, if you know what I mean?' Abigail laughed and dodged Sage's play slap, then rummaged in the cupboard above the sink for mismatching plates. 'Seriously, the mayor didn't tell me he was this hot; I would've come by sooner.'

'I still think it's weird you call your own husband the mayor.' Sage sighed, slicing up the delicious-smelling cake, only just realising her stomach was growling. Abigail often fed her here when she worked long shifts, and the kids enjoyed meeting any animals she had in the healing room. Sometimes the thought sneaked in that some day she might like to have kids of her own. It wasn't entirely an unpleasant notion, the thought of raising a little animal-loving tribe to run around here with Abigail's, teaching them the ways of the world. A fresh start, she supposed.

Then she had to remind herself that in order to have kids, she'd actually have to meet a man… which meant opening herself up emotionally. Something she could never quite manage. Her life was the exact opposite of Abigail and the mayor's. It was so adorable how crazy they were about each other, how easy their relationship was. They trusted each other implicitly. When they bickered it always evolved into laughter. It felt inconceivable that she might some day find the same. There were things she probably shouldn't share with a man, and more that she couldn't laugh off. She'd never heard from Bryce again after he'd disappeared on her, and she'd liked him. A lot.

He'd shown up at the koala reserve, all smiles and stories, a bright light, a shiny distraction from Canada. He'd already done another three-month stint at an orangutan sanctuary in Borneo. A real nomad animal activist. They'd bonded, and for a while it had felt pretty real. More real than anything she'd known till then, at least. She'd slept with him, trusted him. He'd even promised to take her to Canada to meet his dog.

He'd vanished one morning. Left without so much as a 'this was nice but I'd better be on my way'. She'd always assumed he couldn't handle learning how and why her family had died. He'd looked horrified when she'd told him, literally the night before she'd found him gone! She'd taken the leap and confided in him, and straight away he'd brought the facts and newspaper articles about it up on his phone. As well as feeling wounded all over again by her parents' death, she'd had to relive the shame of hearing how many dead koalas the environmentalists had found in the following weeks. All the birds.

The story about the bushfire and her parents had done the rounds for months. She remembered her foster parents whispering about it, trying not to let on what they were talking about—but she'd grown to trust Bryce in their short time at the reserve. She'd revealed everything, the way she had disobeyed her parents' request that she leave her phone alone for a whole night while they got back to nature as a family and camped outdoors in their yard. She'd been such a stubborn ten-year-old, waiting till they fell asleep, then sneaking back into the house to grab her phone and text with her friends. She'd completely failed to notice that their smouldering fire was in danger of spreading into their makeshift camp. By the time she'd come back outside, the fire was raging beyond control. A neighbour had called the fire brigade, but it had been just...too late. The bush had burnt for a mile in all directions, taking her sleeping parents, their dog, and their tents with it. Sage had never forgiven herself.

'The mayor hired Ethan for up to six weeks,' Abigail commented now.

'Did he?' she said casually, forcing her focus back onto the cake. 'That's helpful. Ethan has offered to help me out while Ellie's off sick, too.' She realised from the look on Abi's face that, despite her efforts to appear unaffected, she must still sound quite put out about it.

'Listen to you! You sound like you don't want a stupidly handsome and incredibly buff guy walking around looking hot all day, helping you out.'

'I don't!'

'Liar.' Abigail took a huge bite of cake before Charlie swiped at it, sending it flying to the floor. 'Oh, God. Sorry, babe.'

'Leave it,' Sage told her, as the slice slid behind a floor cabinet. Charlie giggled in delight. 'Anyway, he might be hot, but it's not like he'd look twice at someone like me…a lonely spinster who spends most days hiding in a clinic in the middle of nowhere.'

Abigail cocked her head and scowled in the way she often applied to her kids. 'Stop that. You're a rock-star vet and a pillar of the community, Sage. Now, be a good spinster and deliver your hot new assistant some cake.'

Before Ethan could take his third bite of pine-apple cake, having been accosted by Daisy and swept up in a game of teddy-bear-driving-fire-truck-over-cushions-and-books, the main phone shattered the playful reprise, during which Sage had firmly implanted the image of Ethan's future 'Greatest Dad' trophy in her brain. She answered the call, trying to ignore the looks Abigail kept shooting her whenever Ethan wasn't looking.

'Camel sanctuary?' she repeated. 'What's wrong with the camel?'

She could feel Ethan watching her intently throughout the call, his curiosity piqued as he finally got to finish his cake.

'OK,' she said, ending the call and looking up

at him. His eyes remained fixed on hers despite the blue teddy bear being swept across his head. 'There's a camel in distress at the sanctuary down by Cable Beach. They think it might be colic, but they aren't sure. Ellie's still out sick, obviously, so I'll be going alone.'

'Why don't I come with you?' Ethan offered, oblivious to Abigail pulling another dramatic face behind him as she swept up the toys and ushered Daisy through the door, waving goodbye.

'No, thank you, I'll be fine,' she said.

'I've dealt with colic before, and it might be good for you to have a second opinion.'

'Are you sure?' Sage asked, realising she didn't actually have a good reason to refuse him, even though she really could have done with some distance to fight this mounting and deeply unsettling attraction. 'It's been a long day already, and I don't want to impose.'

Ethan just stood with his empty plate, then deposited it dutifully back into the kitchen. 'We should get going,' he called back. 'My ute, or yours?'

CHAPTER SIX

'PRETTY INTERESTING PLACE, isn't it?' Sage remarked, feeling her boots sinking into the soft white sand outside Camel Ride HQ. The afternoon heat shimmered over the beach ahead of them, casting an almost ethereal glow over the surroundings.

'Emphasis on the pretty,' Ethan replied, glancing at her quickly—too quickly to know if he was referring to her or not—before taking in the scene with a mixture of curiosity and amusement. They could already see people on camels, heading out from HQ onto the sand. This company ran tours all day, every day, as well as rescuing camels and orphaned calves and giving them a new loving home.

As he joined her on the path from the parking lot, she picked up on his scent again, the earthy musk of it, almost animal. He hadn't had to join her out here, but he'd volunteered, which felt more exciting than it should; this was getting silly now. Abigail had got into her head too. As if anything was going to happen outside her hot, sweaty dreams.

'Dr Dawson!' A woman in an orange skirt with long strawberry-blonde hair pulled back in a ponytail was holding her hand up, exiting the main building ahead. This was Marleen, the woman who'd called her. Soon they were both being ushered into the long corrugated-iron shed, where twenty or so stalls were bulging with hay and healthy-looking camels. A small crowd was already gathered around one of the enclosures, which Marleen dismissed as they approached. The camel was lying on the ground, its breathing laboured and shallow. Ethan got to his knees in his jeans, back muscles flexed as he murmured to the sick animal, rolling up his sleeves.

The poor creature looked so vulnerable and helpless. It stirred a wellspring of empathy inside her as she knelt beside Ethan with the stethoscope, running her fingers gently along the camel's side. The soft groaning sound the creature made caused her heart to ache as Ethan gently lifted its heavy head, his strong hands cradling it with tenderness.

'Could be dehydration, or even anaemia,' he suggested, and she pressed her fingers to the camel's neck next, feeling for any swollen lymph nodes. The scent of hay and animal musk hung heavily in the air, mingling with the salty breeze drifting in from nearby Cable Beach, and Ethan's scent too. She couldn't get enough of it. He was close now, leaning even closer, feeling along the camel's back as she ran the stethoscope over the smooth fur of the creature's belly and sides. Sage couldn't help but steal glances at him as he concentrated, admiring his strong hands and the way the sunlight was streaming in through the door and dancing off his dark hair.

'Her gums are pale,' Ethan said after a moment. He was peering into the camel's mouth now.

'And her heart rate is elevated,' Sage confirmed. 'Anaemia seems unlikely though, given her diet and environment. She doesn't appear to have any external wounds or lesions.'

Ethan reached for the thermometer and she watched as he slipped it under the camel's tongue. She could feel the animal tremble beneath her touch.

'Temperature's normal,' he announced after a moment, his brow furrowed in concentration. Then he pressed his ear to the creature's neck. He appeared to be listening intently as if trying to discern some other subtle clue from the animal's laboured breaths and she wondered...did this gift he had with horses extend to other animals?

'We'll run some blood tests,' she said to him, worried for a moment that she might be starting to believe he could diagnose an animal without any modern tools at all. He helped her collect the samples, she asked Marleen a few more standard questions and arranged some pain meds, while Ethan mumbled something indecipherable to the camel, still stroking her tenderly. By the time they left the stall, the poor thing was definitely calmer.

On the way out, Ethan stopped promptly at another stall, where a smaller camel was grazing. The gentle creature looked up, focusing its doe eyes on him. Then, to Sage's surprise, it stepped forward and promptly placed its head in Ethan's waiting hands.

What is happening?

Ethan seemed to study the camel in silence, caressing its big soft head, before a smile flashed across his lips. 'I think she's pregnant,' he announced.

Marleen, who was watching in equal fascination, shook her head. 'Nah, mate. No way. We just got her—she's a newbie.'

'It happened before she got here,' Ethan murmured. Sage felt her pulse fire up as he guided her hand to the camel's belly, his warm fingers lingering just a moment too long on hers. 'Do you feel that?'

'Is that…a heartbeat?' Sage looked at him in shock as she felt the unmistakable rhythm of life beneath her fingertips. 'Ethan, you're right.' A quick exam with her stethoscope proved it.

'Really?' Marleen looked confused as he showed her how to feel for the heartbeat, too, without the stethoscope. 'But she's not even showing. How did you know?'

Ethan just shrugged his shoulders and dragged a hand through his hair. It was loose now, free of its usual ponytail, and Sage had to admit she really liked it. It looked wild. Marleen was looking at him in awe. 'How…?'

'It's a gift,' Sage heard herself whisper.

Marleen's eyes widened.

Of course, Sage had looked all this up online, and there were lots of animal communicators out there, lots of proven cases of people diagnosing mystery problems. It still didn't make it any more conceivable to her scientific brain…but it was definitely hot when Ethan did it. She'd known, since before he even drove onto her dusty forecourt, that he had a special gift with horses, but to see it *did* in fact appear to transfer to other animals actually left her speechless.

It wasn't right to feel jealous of him. This was not a competition. But she'd had to work so hard for her qualifications and here Ethan Matthews was, doing everything as easily as breathing. Her envy was quickly merging with admiration, however, the more she witnessed him in action. The attraction she felt to him in this moment was so far off the charts there was hardly a measure for it, she thought, forcing her feet to walk her back outside while Ethan and Marleen discussed the pregnancy. What if he could see inside her head, too? Lord, the shame of what he'd see!

He found her by the ute, watching the ocean. Its gentle lulling waves, the sound of the gulls, all of it was a balm to her frazzled senses.

'Marleen asked us to join the sunset camel safari.' Ethan opened the door and dropped the bag back onto the back seat. 'I said I'd ask you. Are you as confident on camels as you are on horses?'

'They don't tend to move as fast,' she replied coolly, instantly aware of his manly presence beside her; the way her skin and cells stood to attention. 'Sure, we can ride, if you like.'

On the beach, Marleen and her staff were greeting the returning riders and guiding the camels to water. They'd have to wait a few minutes for their turn. The ocean glistened and a fishing boat bobbed in a path of sparkles as she dropped to the sand, letting the warmth travel up through her feet to her bones.

'This reminds me of my dad,' she said aloud without thinking. 'We used to visit the ocean a lot when I was little.'

Ethan was quiet a moment as they studied the sky on the horizon. The sun was already sinking, a huge ball of fire casting peach-amber streaks across the water. 'Losing your parents, at just ten years old, I can't imagine. What happened to you after that?'

'I got lucky,' she said, turning to him. 'I landed

on the *good* side of the foster system. Ken and Arielle treated me like their real daughter, and I love them like one. But you never forget a loss like that. It only takes a little thing, like this view, or a smell, or a song to bring it all back.'

'I know,' he said on a deep exhale that came right from his heart. Of course he knew.

'Were you close with your mum?' she asked.

'Very.'

She bit her lip. There were so many questions she wanted to ask him, still, but he wasn't staying long, and the last thing she should be doing was sharing her feelings, or catching more feelings for someone who'd simply disappear back into the TV in a few weeks…or wherever else he was called to next.

Soon, the sunset tour group was gathered on the sand, and Marleen had Ethan stepping on a small stepladder up to the seat on the camel, which made Sage laugh. Just the way the bulky beige animal lowered to its knobbly knees to let the equally awkward humans on its back was hilarious.

'You next,' Marleen said, gesturing to her. Sage paused. Oh, so they were riding in twos, on the same camel?

OK, then.

Ethan held out his hand and she clasped it tight, allowing him to hoist her up into the seat. She sat in front, with barely a centimetre between her back and his chest, just like the other 'couples' in the group. Maybe Marleen had misinterpreted their relationship...not that she was complaining, exactly.

Just enjoy it for what it is, she told herself, settling into his safe, strong proximity, letting out a thrilled shriek as their camel stood up slowly, as if it was actually being careful not to drop its heavy load.

Ethan's hands landed on her shoulders, steadying her. He kept them there as he pointed at a young couple attempting to coax a stubborn camel into posing for a photo further down the beach. As the sun dipped lower in the sky, painting the horizon and people with deeper shades of orange, Sage found herself relaxing, even though the camel's plod was bumpier than any horse she'd ever ridden. Every now and then her back would brush Ethan's chest and sparks of adrenaline flooded her belly from behind. The salty breeze tugged at their hair and hers was more than likely landing in his mouth from time to time, but he wasn't complaining. Was it weird that she'd never ridden a camel before? She was just about to ask Ethan this question when he spoke over her shoulder.

'You know, I haven't been to the beach in a long time.'

She swivelled her head back to him and bumped his nose with hers by mistake. He laughed, as did she, but his eyes quickly fixed on the setting sun. He'd felt it too—when their noses touched—and he clearly didn't want to address it.

'Why not?' she said, feeling a flash of heat to her groin as her back slid another couple of times against his torso. She should focus on the magnificent view, but the effects of Ethan's muscles swiping her flesh with just flimsy bits of material between them were impossible to ignore.

'I had a pretty big bust-up with a good friend on the beach not so long ago and it brings it all back.' He stopped talking abruptly, his mouth a thin line. Sage's heart was already hammering. She knew she shouldn't ask but it was way too intriguing. This was more than he'd ever said about his life.

'A bust-up?'

'More like a heated argument.'

'What about?' she dared to press. He didn't seem the type to engage in arguments of any kind. But Ethan stayed silent. Then he sighed so hard she felt it ripple through her hair, leaving a trail of goosebumps on the back of her neck.

'You don't even want to know,' he said, finally. His tone silenced her, right until their group came to a stop and they were ordered to dismount for a break and a drink. This was more vulnerability than she'd expected from some supposedly arrogant hotshot celebrity vet. Maybe she'd painted him as that quite unfairly. It was becoming clearer every day that there was more to Ethan Matthews than she'd seen…maybe more than anyone watching him on TV had ever seen. He had layers, and some of those were still tender, still painful, as hers were. She was so caught up in her thoughts about his mysterious bust-up on the beach that she almost missed what was going on around her.

Oh, no.

Already, everyone was settling down around a huge, spitting, burning, roaring fire.

CHAPTER SEVEN

SAGE SLID OFF the camel after Ethan and stepped onto the sand, inhaling air deeply into her lungs. Their guide was handing out small cups filled with sweet tea and she took one gratefully, breathing in the aromatic scent; anything for a distraction. Ethan was taking a seat close to the fire already, where someone had scattered cushions in anticipation of the tour group. This was basic tourist stuff, and she willed herself to calm down as laughter and conversation filled the air, along with the giant sparks from the crackling logs and driftwood.

Don't be a baby. Don't be an idiot, Sage.

Despite her internal pep talk, fear and panic welled up inside her as she closed her eyes. The memories were slamming her now from all directions. Her cup almost crumpled in her fierce grip. She'd stood just like this that night, helplessly overwhelmed in front of the raging bushfire, watching the tents ablaze beyond a flaming row of bushes. She'd stared, unable to move, feet glued to the floor. It was only when the neighbour had arrived and swept her up in his arms and carried her away that she'd been able to comprehend the magnitude of what had happened, what she'd failed to try and prevent, but by then, everything was gone. Everyone had died.

'Sage?'

Ethan was in front of her suddenly. His curious gaze made her shuffle in embarrassment as he studied her distance from the fire. 'What's wrong? Don't you want to sit closer?'

'No, I'm fine here,' she replied, her heart pounding in her chest at the thought of revealing her vulnerability to him, as she had to Bryce. 'I just, uh, I don't like fire a lot. At all.'

'You don't like *fire*?'

She would have to say something. 'There was a bushfire,' she said finally. 'Around our property. That's how I lost my parents.'

Ethan was quiet. Maybe it was the fact that she'd sensed his own vulnerability back there, about the argument with his friend, that had forced her guard down just a little, but his eyes were filled with such empathy and sadness now, she almost felt sick.

'I lost my dog that night, too,' she added. Might as well get it all out. In fact, she was quite prepared to carry on, suddenly, to tell him everything about how she'd failed to save them all, how the fire had spread beyond control past their little makeshift campsite, designed to get the family back to nature and away from all technology for the night, how the house had burned to the ground next along with all their possessions, but her voice got lodged in her windpipe till she could barely breathe, let alone speak.

'Sage.' Ethan was looking at her with such horror now, she was glad she'd stopped talking. 'What happened?' he asked. 'I mean, how did you—?'

'I still think about Juni, my dog,' she interrupted, nervously. 'Maybe that's why I do what I do, you know? If I can save just one animal's life, then I can still make a difference.'

'You make a big difference here every day, everyone knows that,' he said. 'But, Sage, I'm so sorry to hear about your family.'

'Doesn't matter. Enough about me, what about you, Mr Secretive? What was your big argument with your friend about? Does that have anything to do with why you don't *do* relationships?'

Her blurted questions hung in the air like a lead balloon. The laughter around them seemed to fade into the background as her heart slammed in her chest. Abigail would have punched her in the arm right about now; that eager question made her seem way too interested in deep diving into his life history than was acceptable, or attractive, but better to talk about him than her, and all the stuff that she couldn't discuss.

Ethan's eyes met hers again and she swallowed. Suddenly she forgot what she'd been thinking. There it was, plain as day: layers of hesitation and discomfort flickering within their ocean-blue depths. She'd hit the nail on the head. Whatever had happened on that beach was exactly why he didn't do relationships. Taking a step back again, she watched the group over the rim of her cup, desperate for some distance between herself and this burning reminder of her own trauma, and the feel of his eyes burning equally hot on her face.

'I'll get us some cushions,' he said, and she wrestled with the guilt as she watched him collect two from beside the fire, his muscular frame a solid silhouette against the flames and the fading sun. He motioned for her to take a seat beside him away from the flames, and watched her closely, as if she might combust with her grief.

'You sure this is OK?' he asked.

'I'm fine here,' she replied. 'So, you were saying?'

He shook his head and adjusted himself on the cushion. 'It's...complicated,' he muttered as she put down her cup.

'Isn't it always?' she said. It felt as if her cheeks had absorbed the flames as he took her in, as if committing her freckles to memory. Then he cleared his throat and dropped back onto the sand, resting back on one thick, toned arm. The firelight played on the rock of his biceps, a thin sheen of sweat making her lick her lips despite herself. Maybe fire wasn't so bad under the right circumstances. She was fully attuned to him now, and there was no way he didn't feel the same; the air between them was buzzing, even though he was clearly deflecting. Something complicated had stomped on any wish he might have once had for a relationship with someone special and he didn't want to talk about it.

'Look, I didn't mean to make you uncomfortable,' she said softly, hoping her eyes were filled with sincerity as much as the questions that were still jumping about in her brain. 'I understand if it's something you don't want to talk about. I know what that's like.'

Ethan pressed his lips together a moment. 'You're right, I don't normally talk about this stuff with anyone.' His voice was strained with the effort to find the right words. 'I was with someone for a long time. We were engaged to be married, and I very much *wanted* to be in that relationship with Carrie, until she...'

Carrie?

Sage gripped his hand without thinking, feeling the warmth of his skin beneath her fingertips instantly. 'Oh, no, Ethan. Did Carrie die?'

Ethan's eyes grew wide. Mortified for him, she squeezed his hand. It should have been obvious, of course, the pain she'd seen in his eyes, the way he was reluctant to talk about it, just as she still was. It hurt too much. It would always hurt.

'No one died,' he blurted, biting back a humourless laugh.

'Oh. Sorry.' Sage pulled her hands away and hugged her knees to her chest. Great, now he thought she was a total drama queen. 'I just always assume...'

'No one actually died,' he said again, gruffly. 'But I have two people in my life who are pretty much dead to me now and maybe that's the saddest thing about what happened. I miss them even though they're still alive. I miss what we all used to be to one another. We won't ever be that way again.'

'What did they do? I assume the one who isn't Carrie is the person you argued with.'

'On the beach, yes. Palm Cove to be exact,' he finished. 'His name's Cam.' The name came out through slightly clenched teeth before he continued. 'Cameron. I've known him my whole life, since we started school together.'

Sage realised she was staring at him with her mouth open as the pieces started fitting together in her head. Ethan had been engaged once, and then his fiancée did something, and now there were two people he couldn't see. Cam was one. What did his buddy Cam do to cause a bust-up...? Oh, no. He'd stolen Ethan's fiancée! She knew it without him saying; it was written all over his face.

'They're married now,' he confirmed, still looking at the fire. She shook her head, touching a hand to his quickly as he sat back up beside her, cross-legged. 'I hear it was a beautiful wedding.'

Sage pulled a face, and he mirrored it. 'Look at us,' he said, wrinkling his nose. 'We only came to help a camel, and now we're on a beach, which I hate, near a fire, which you hate—'

'Well, at least we're alive.' She smiled, nudging his shoulder with hers. 'And beaches aren't that bad, are they?'

'Not when you're with me, they aren't.' Sage felt the shivers from her fingers right through to her feet as he took her hand and held it tight over his knee. 'I like talking to you, Doctor,' he murmured, without realising he was stealing all the breath from her body.

'How long were you together?' she asked as the heat of his hand seared through her, hotter than the fire.

'A long time,' he replied, looking at their fingers. 'Seven years.'

'And how long ago did you split up?'

'Thirteen months ago. That's when I found out about it anyway.'

'Some friend,' she heard herself say, before she could hold it in. The injustice of it all left a nasty taste in her mouth, and a tsunami of empathy for him threatened to have her say more, but she didn't, equally occupied by the drumbeat throb of her heart now that he was holding her hand. Even as their group reassembled around them, ready for the ride back up the beach, Sage felt suspended by some strange new gravity holding her right here.

So she'd had a messed-up start herself as a ten-year-old orphaned girl, but at least no one had betrayed her as Ethan had been betrayed; not that she'd let anyone close enough to try. She'd started to think she wouldn't know how to be someone's long-term partner anyway, that maybe it just wasn't in her destiny. At the heart of it, she supposed—and as Abigail often reminded her—was her raging guilt. It slammed shut every door she'd ever tried to open, till she'd eventually given up. Why should she be happy when her family never would be again, because of her selfishness?

The silence between them grew heavier, punctuated only by the sounds of the camels' footsteps and the distant laughter of the other riders. The sun had fully sunk now, but the moon was huge and the magnetic pull from Ethan only seemed to intensify every time he looked her way. It didn't subside in the ute either. The whole way back to Amber Creek, it felt a lot as if an unspoken desire to unpick the other's past was simmering between them. Unless it was all her, she considered, stealing another glance at his profile in the moonlight.

What was his ex-fiancée like? Was she pretty? Of *course* she was pretty. Ethan wouldn't have been with anyone *not* pretty for all those years.

'Look,' Ethan said suddenly, gesturing towards the paddock. They were back at the clinic already, where they'd planned for him to drop her off before he drove on back to the guest house. She turned to where he was pointing, but he was sprinting from the ute already, making for the gate. Sage's heart swelled as she watched him vault over it with one leap again.

A momentary reprieve from the intensity of her thoughts was promptly replaced by slight alarm. Storm was lying down in the grass, cool as a cucumber under the moon, calmer than she'd ever seen him. He was lying right next to Karma and, contrary to all of their previous encounters, the two horses seemed entirely comfortable with each other.

She gasped as she reached the gate and watched Ethan kneel slowly in front of them. Karma snorted and got to his feet, trotting off merrily, but Storm, to her total surprise, stayed put, and lowered his head, as if bowing to him. Even from where she was, she could tell that this was progress. Storm had never been this welcoming or appeared this placid before, and he barely flinched as Ethan started running his hands gently along his neck and back.

'He's going to let me examine him,' Ethan said,

and the look of victory on his face made her grin,
it was so infectious. 'I'll wait till the morning,
first light,' he followed, striding back over to her.
He met her on the other side of the gate.

'It was only a matter of time,' she heard herself say, through her own smile. Why did he have
to be so gorgeous, on top of being a bona fide
equine wizard?

Maybe it was having the gate safely between
them, but a quiet confidence overruled her com-
mon sense. Before she knew it, her fingers were
reaching out for his face, brushing off a small
fleck of ash from his left cheek that had been
bugging her since the beach. He caught her fingers deftly, and held them against his face, and for
a moment neither of them moved as he scanned
her eyes. An almost tortured expression hovered
in his gaze that made her pulse thud, before he
reached across the gate and cupped the back of
her neck. Butterflies exploded in her belly.

Oh, my Lord...he's going to kiss me.

Sage closed her eyes and prepared herself as
her heart started bucking like an unbroken horse
in her chest.

Don't move, she willed herself. *You do deserve this, just one kiss. One little kiss to keep
you floating from someone who's just passing
through. That would be OK, wouldn't it? That
would be enough.*

He was inching closer over the gate, she could

feel his breath warming her face, smell his earthy scent mingling with heat and hay. He was going to kiss her, she knew it. Any second now…

Ethan pressed his lips to her cheek, and then dropped her hand. In a beat he scaled the gate, landing with a thud beside her as she blinked her eyes back open, mortified.

Her senses screamed in unison—*What about the kiss? The proper kiss!*

'I should go. We have an early start tomorrow,' he said, striding ahead of her towards the car.

Reeling, Sage hugged her arms tightly around herself as he gave her a final look over his shoulder, then drove away. OK…so that was weird, she thought, straightening up and composing herself. They'd been so close to kissing, but he'd backed off. Probably for the best, she thought with a wince, seeing as there was no point starting up anything with someone who was leaving as soon as Storm's issues were fixed, but still… hmm. Something must have been going through his mind to have pulled away like that, though. Was it Carrie? She frowned down the drive, now devoid of any sign of him. Perhaps he wasn't over Carrie.

CHAPTER EIGHT

ETHAN KEPT HIS hands steady as he aligned the splint against the koala's fragile leg. All the while his heart thrummed an erratic beat that betrayed the calm of his practised movements. Sage was close, too close, her own hands mirroring his with a deftness that spoke volumes about her compassion and skill, both of which he'd had the pleasure, and the torture, of observing up close since volunteering to help her out at the clinic. He'd almost pressed his mouth to hers last week. What the hell was wrong with him?

Ellie had come in briefly to share some patient files, despite her sickness, and before Sage had sent her away again to rest she had eyed him in that usual awestruck way. He was used to women like her, looking at him as if he were something amazing, something to be devoured with a gaze alone.

A woman like Sage, however, who grasped at the broken shards of his soul and loosened the reins on his heart, and made him want to talk about things he would rather usually not talk about…that was something else entirely. He had never felt so drawn to anyone so inexplicably before. It was as if her wounded soul called out to him—and it was why he'd almost kissed her. But also why he'd swiftly backed off. There was no way he was going down the road Carrie had taken him on again, where a woman had bent his universe so out of shape that the loss had altered his DNA for ever.

Still, with Ellie still sick, here he was. How could he have kept his distance knowing they were running out of hands to attend to all these animals? There was so much to do. And now that Storm was finally responding to him without galloping off a mile each time, it was imperative he stay close, vital he make sure the horse didn't do a one-eighty and backtrack on the progress he'd made in the week since conducting that first physical exam.

'Good, just like that,' Sage murmured now, her voice soft but authoritative as she secured the bandage. The air between them was charged, thick with the words they hadn't spoken since that…what had it been? A mistake. It *should* have felt like a mistake, but every time he watched her mouth move now, the slow burn for her went from a smoulder to a full-on inferno till all he could think about was pressing Sage Dawson up against the stable wall, running his hands over

the curve of her hips and claiming her lips and…
healing her, like one of his horses? As if he could.
He hadn't even been able to heal *himself* enough
after his mother had died to notice Carrie was
slipping away.

'Ethan?'

'Yeah, it's secure,' he said.

Focus, man. What was it now, just seven days?
A week of wondering if he just should've kissed
her and been done with it.

Ethan kept his attention on the tasks at hand,
trying to ignore how the scent of her—wildflowers and something uniquely Sage—overwhelmed
his senses. His ego didn't quite know how to handle looking in a mirror like this, seeing someone
else so fragile, someone else he didn't know how
to fix. She'd been keeping her distance, too.

'Steady there, mate, we're almost done,' he
whispered to the fidgeting koala, who blinked
up at them with trusting, glassy eyes. The animal's quiet resilience struck a chord with him. In
the face of its obvious pain, it was clearly letting
them help. If only his own efforts to maintain his
composure weren't so flimsy around Sage. Every
time he so much as brushed against her acciden-
tally, that moment in the paddock the other night
flew back into his brain, as well as the way he'd
exited stage left as if she'd threatened him with
a cattle prod!

But after everything he'd spilled to her on the

beach, after showing that level of vulnerability it was hard to place the feelings he was starting to experience for someone who didn't even live in the same Australian territory as him. Why start up anything with someone like her, who'd be incredibly hard to get over? The dreams he was having were torture enough.

He used to have regular dreams about walking in on Cam with Carrie. They had tortured him for months, and he'd barely dared to think about sex as anything other than something *they* were doing together, which had repulsed him. Now, though, his suddenly revived libido was roaring back in spades, taking those dreams to new places, mostly steamy midnight rides with Sage, and not always on horseback…

Sage stood back, running a gentle hand over their brave koala. 'Thank you, Ethan,' she said on a sigh, brushing a wisp of hair from her forehead. 'I couldn't have done this without you. We're so short-staffed.'

Ever the professional attitude now, he mused.

'Any time,' he replied gruffly as she snatched her gaze away again and turned to the sink, visibly flustered by his closeness. She'd told him some pretty personal things on the beach, and he'd reciprocated. At least, he'd told her the necessary details. And then he'd turned away from her. She hadn't brought it up since, or the almost kiss, and neither had he, but it still hung between them in the silence.

'What's next for today?' Sage's question cut through his inner reverie.

'I'm just thinking about Storm out there,' he lied, offering a tight smile. He *should* be thinking about Storm—he and Billy were planning to try and saddle him later—but now he was thinking about Sage, yet again.

'He's already doing so much better; the mayor said so this morning, didn't he?' she said, before going on to the subject of the new food and troughs Ethan had suggested, and then the weather. Her brow creased slightly, and she diverted her eyes the whole time, as if she was just filling the air with words for the sake of saying something, anything. He watched her shift the koala gently on the table, motioning for him to open the cage. 'Could you bring it a little closer?' she said.

Ethan picked it up easily and placed it closer. Her sleeve caught for a second on the cage door, and he freed her deftly, then drew his hand back quickly this time, before she could retreat from him again. 'Sorry,' they both muttered simultaneously. Then they shared an awkward smile over the koala's head. Why did he feel like a fake all of a sudden? As if he was lying about not wanting to rip off her clothes, press his mouth to hers and kick the door shut behind them.

'Looks like our friend will be OK,' he said about the koala. It seemed to be quite comfortable now, if a little dozy.

'We're a good team,' Sage replied. More words to fill the silence, from both of them this time. Then she busied herself folding up some towels while he filled in the animal's file. The little marsupial's leg was neatly splinted now. She was right, their team was a good one for the most part. He watched her cross the room, putting significant distance between them again as she put away instruments and bottles.

'What?' she said, somewhat nervously from near the window, brushing another tuft of fallen hair from her eyes.

The air between them was charged with that thick, hot, electric buzz he knew should be defused. Every rational thought screamed at him to keep his distance, yet his hands and his body seemed entirely disinclined to obey right now. Sage was the first person who'd made him forget the extent of the pain Carrie and Cam had inflicted on him, but at the same time, this thing had just as much potential to mess with his head, more than it already was. Talk about being blindsided! The very last thing he'd expected to find when accepting this gig was a woman like Sage bringing his libido back to life, most inappropriately!

'What?' she said again as he looked at her. She

sounded so conflicted, as though his eyes on her made her feel things she didn't know what to do with. Same as him, then.

'You…' he started.

Sage lowered her head slightly, then looked up at him through her eyelashes. This mad chemistry was not going to go away. Maybe he should just address it? Drag it out into the open so they could laugh about it.

As if he would laugh about it.

'Me?' she said, finally, searching his face through narrowed green eyes.

He opened his mouth. The words formed on his tongue: *You are driving me crazy.*

He stepped forwards, all efforts to resist this gone, out of the window.

As if on cue, the shrill ring of the clinic's phone shattered the bubble. Sage cleared her throat, lifting the receiver. 'This is Dr Dawson.'

The caller's frantic voice spilled through the line; something about a bird, rare and injured, found miles away. With each detail, Ethan's professional focus snapped back into place. What was he thinking, almost letting that craziness consume him again?

'Got it. We're on it.' Sage hung up and turned to him, her expression grave. 'It's a black-throated finch. Someone up at Koorabimby Nook's found one, but it's badly hurt.'

Ethan frowned. He had no clue where Koorabimby Nook was, but the black-throated finch species was in a precarious state, almost extinct, in fact.

'What's the plan?' he asked, and she bit her bottom lip thoughtfully, pacing the room while the koala looked on.

'It's too far by road. We won't make it in time,' she calculated quickly, making his mind race through alternatives. But Sage was already on the phone again, dialling someone.

'Mayor Warragul, it's Sage Dawson. We've got a situation with a black-throated finch,' she said. 'I need a huge favour.'

Ethan watched, admiration warming his chest as they talked. Her decisiveness was one of the hundreds of things he admired about her—her ability to switch modes and take action under pressure, her drive to save any creature, no matter the odds. It had started with losing her dog, she'd told him that, which made sense if it died in the bushfire, but there was so much he didn't know; not that he would be asking. Getting too personal had never been part of his plan when he got here... In fact he'd made up his mind to get the job with Storm done as fast as he could and get back to rebuilding the second beehive with Dad, the one his niece and nephew wanted to keep as their own. And he was losing his train of thought about what mattered most, more often

than was safe. He'd almost kissed Sage already.
Twice.

'We should pack a field kit,' she said now, and
he helped her gather supplies.

'How are we going to get there?' he asked her
on their way out. He'd failed to hear exactly how
Amber Creek's mayor was planning to help them
in this situation.

Sage turned to him, her expression a blend of
determination and hope. 'The mayor's going to
fly us out there in his chopper.'

The whirr of the helicopter blades grew louder as
they approached, the rhythmic chopping sound
slicing through the air.

'Thanks for doing this, Mayor,' Sage said as
they climbed aboard, her voice barely audible
over the din. Ethan watched them make brief
conversation, admiring this multifaceted mayor
who clearly had a soft spot for Sage. She'd been
close with his wife Abigail since she moved here,
he remembered as the helicopter lifted off and
Billy and the horses and Sage's rock garden grew
smaller and smaller below. In fact, Sage had been
to their house a few times since he'd joined their
small team at the clinic. They loved her, and she
loved those kids. It was nice to see. He wasn't
so great with kids himself, with the exception of
Jacqueline's kids, Kara and Jayson—the horses
had always been easier to understand, and qui-

eter too—but sometimes he imagined a tribe of his own: little people who he could teach to ride and read and take over the plot some day. Carrie had wanted all that, initially. She'd probably get it too, with Cam.

'I hope we're not too late,' he heard Sage say, and he stopped himself saying anything. There was no point in giving her false hope. Who knew the extent of the bird's injuries? It was moments like these, however, that reminded him why he'd become a veterinarian himself—to save and protect animals in their natural environment, to give a voice to the creatures who couldn't speak for themselves. The rare finch had been mentioned in a lecture at a conference, just the other month, about endangered species, and now here he was, with Sage in a chopper, on a mission to save one. Dad would get a kick out of this story.

Sage sat next to him now, her face pressed against the window as she scanned the terrain below. Her eyes filled with concern, and maybe a little annoyance too as the massive coal mines started dominating the landscape below. The stark contrast between the untouched wilderness and industrialisation was even more unsettling from up here. So many creatures had perished and would perish with all this overdevelopment. It only strengthened his resolve to do everything in his power to protect and preserve this fragile ecosystem, as well as get the homestead running as sustainably as they could back in Queensland.

He found himself staring at her mouth, thinking again about their almost-kiss, when she turned to him and found his eyes on her. It was too late to turn away. Busted. She quirked an eyebrow and shook her head.

'It's not a good idea, Ethan,' she murmured over the rotors. Ethan's pulse spiked but he kept his expression in neutral.

'What isn't?'

'You know what,' she said, sweeping her hair back to a rough ponytail and holding it to the nape of her neck, like his. He said nothing; what could he say? It was not a good idea, and of course he knew it.

She released her hair, letting the chestnut waves loose till they were catching the gusts from the open door and billowing around her face. Wild strands whipped against his cheek, daring him to question the validity of these claims.

Oh, so that's how she's playing this.

She was freaking out, because, yes, it had almost happened again, and she knew it shouldn't because they were colleagues? Who knew why, really? But she was making excuses. She wanted him as much as he wanted her. Just by saying *this* she was confirming it. He couldn't fight the smile from his mouth at the look of pure tortured desire in her eyes.

'Stop it,' she said again, pretending to thump his shoulder.

'Stop what?'

'Looking at me like…that.'

Then her face seemed to scrunch up in front of him before she pressed her face into her hands quickly, as if she was trying to erase her last words. 'I shouldn't have said anything, should I? You weren't going to. Forget I said anything?'

'I can barely hear you anyway,' he lied loudly, pointing at the roof, mouthing, *The blades are too loud.*

She pulled another face and shook her head at the window, and he busied himself with double-checking the contents of the field kit, pulling it between them on the seat, creating a necessary distance between them. OK…so the small talk was killing him, but if she thought him kissing her for any reason was a bad idea, he'd respect that, of course. He was here to work, after all. There was no point getting swept up in this… thing. She'd obviously been thinking about their situation as much as he had, so much in fact that she'd blurted out an attempt at resistance, to push him away. He almost asked her why she'd done it, but did it matter, in the end? What could come of it? Best to keep things professional, however hard it was going to be.

The noise of the chopper felt like a fitting match for the turmoil he could feel building inside him though, every time he considered how much he was kidding himself, trying to imagine it would be fine for the rest of his time here ignoring the obvious sexual tension between them. They should talk about this. It would hang over them otherwise. He'd promised to work the weekend on the drip irrigation system outside her house and she'd agreed. Why had she done that, if she didn't want him getting too close?

She wasn't looking at him now, she was talking to the mayor again, and he weighed up his options, watching the curve of her shoulders in her billowing white shirt. He could simply tell her there was no room in his life for romance either. In truth it wasn't what he was looking for at all, at least, not a *relationship*. But anything else would end badly, not just because of the distance between their home lives. He could never leave Dad, and the horses, and all of Mum's memories, the same as she could never leave her practice. This was probably just his libido rebooting after months of being dead and dormant, that was all.

Also, Carrie and Cam had a point. His work would always come first, he would always be considered a solitary enigma, and any good self-respecting woman would tire of that eventually, as Carrie had. And Sage's life was here. It was hard to measure how much he admired her for pulling her life together, for providing this selfless service to others: How could anyone go through losing both their parents in a bushfire and come out so strong and seemingly self-assured?

On the *outside*, he reminded himself quickly. Sage appeared strong on the outside, to most people. But now she was showing him her vulnerabilities too. He was one of them. For that reason, he would stay well away from her.

'It's over here!' The towering, big-built lady in knee-high rubber boots raised a trowel at them as they reached the path, metres from the chopper. The mayor had landed in a eucalyptus field and Ethan noted the Koorabimby Nook sign by the slatted house. Ah, so it was part of a farm. Llamas and a solo horse were looking at them curiously. There, beneath a scrubby bush, lay the finch, its delicate plumage ruffled, one bloodied wing hanging at an unnatural angle. They crouched down beside it and Sage held a hand up, instantly protective of the rare bird.

'Careful,' she instructed, as if she needed to, as he gently scooped up the injured creature, cradling it in his big hands. Blood soaked his fingers. Sage's gaze turned sad. 'It doesn't look good,' she told him. She was right, it didn't. Some kind of animal attack? It was definitely a predator of some sort that had done this much damage.

'I think it probably had a disagreement with a cat,' Sage said with a frown, confirming his thoughts.

'I think he had a run-in with one of mine, yes,' the woman told them sadly, blocking the sun from their faces with her generous frame. Sage communicated her sorrow with him via another look, her fingers gently probing as he held the bird steady. It was hot, still, in the afternoon sun. Its low-hanging intensity scorched the back of his neck as he watched a bead of sweat trail down Sage's cheek. Why did he want to touch her so badly, even in moments like this? It was completely unprofessional and unnecessary, and it was damn well not helping his resolve to keep his emotions out of working with her.

'Fractured wing, possible internal injuries,' Sage was noting now. 'We'll get some pain meds ready. We can't do a proper analysis until we get it to the clinic.'

'Will it survive that long?' the woman asked in concern. 'They're rare, you know.'

'We know,' Sage said after a lingering pause, flashing her eyes to his. Ethan got the distinct impression she wanted to tell the woman to lock up her cats. There wasn't much you could do about natural instinct, though. He should know; his was building the longer those beads of sweat trickled down Sage's cheek…and onto her neck. All he wanted was to touch her, wipe them away with his lips, as if that were likely to cool her down. Or him.

Back in the chopper, the mayor was ready to

take off the second they'd both buckled up their seat belts. Ethan carefully laid the injured bird on the foldable table and prepped a bandage, while Sage pulled out a syringe and vial from the field kit for the meds. Neither of them spoke but he could read her face. She was determined to save this bird.

Everything she did lately, after what she'd told him on the beach, spoke volumes about why she'd chosen this profession. She was obviously haunted by losing her parents in that fire, and her dog too. What the hell must that have been like? Unimaginable. Her love of animals ran deep, her need to care for them and save them when no one else could. He would do everything he could to make her job easier, he realised as she raised the syringe and the chopper bumped around mid-air. And that involved not kissing her.

'Sorry, guys, the wind's getting up,' the mayor's voice echoed from the radio.

'Steady now,' Ethan murmured, holding the bird gently on both sides of its fragile body as Sage administered the medication slowly.

'I'm always careful,' she said through gritted teeth, taking the bandage from him and getting to work while he continued to steady the finch and ease some water into its dehydrated mouth. The medication had to be enough, but what if it wasn't? Its breathing was laboured, its eyes were closed, the poor thing could barely move.

His gaze lingered on Sage, the furrow of concentration between her brows. He itched to tell her that it would be OK, but it wouldn't be fair, so he didn't. In truth, the bird didn't look at all good now. Each breath from its fluffy chest seemed more difficult than the last, and the towel on the table was blood-soaked, its colour growing increasingly darker. The mayor was doing his best to avoid more bumps, but Ethan's instincts were on red alert; none of this was making much of a difference.

'That cat did a real number on him,' Sage cried. This time he didn't pretend he couldn't hear her. They were both watching the bird's chest rise and fall with less vigour, even as he held the oxygen to its beak. Sage's hands faltered slightly.

'Come on, little one,' he encouraged, hoping to be a mantra of hope against an encroaching shadow of inevitability. This bird's life was ebbing away between them. Sure enough, all too soon, the heartbeat beneath his fingertips stilled. Sage's shoulders slumped and her fists clenched.

'Damn it,' she muttered, not looking at him. Her voice was a heavy growl of anger and sorrow that tightened Ethan's throat. When he put a hand to her shoulder her green eyes brimmed with resignation and sent a chill up his arm— they'd failed. They hadn't even made it back to the clinic.

'I'm so sorry, Sage—'

'I suppose it was a long shot, considering the injuries,' she said, swiping her damp forehead. Any sparks he'd felt before felt smothered by the finality in her tone. He'd seen death before in a hundred innocent creatures, the end of suffering, the quiet exit from pain that was often as beautiful as it was distressing for those left behind, but somehow the loss of this rare bird felt personal, tied to the woman beside him and everything she had already lost. Sage turned to the mayor and told him what had happened. Ethan wrapped the delicate bird carefully in a clean towel, watching her body language. Her posture was telling him more than words ever could; she was definitely taking it personally.

'Hey,' he said. 'You did everything you possibly could.'

Her gaze flickered to him. For a second, Ethan thought he saw the walls she'd built around herself tremble, but she squared her shoulders and sniffed. 'Sometimes it's just not enough though, is it?'

The silence returned, heavy and oppressive as they descended over Amber Creek. When the helicopter touched down in the adjacent field and the blades wound down, Sage didn't even wait for the rotors to stop turning before she thanked the mayor and disembarked with the bird in the towel, her steps hurried as she made for the clinic.

Ethan made to jump out after her but the mayor was faster. 'Ethan. Make sure she's OK, yeah?'

He paused with the supplies, his gaze tracking her as she made for the gate to the property. He was about to ask the other man what he meant, but he decided it was pointless. You could tell a lot about Sage Dawson by how she walked or held her head, the things she wasn't saying. He'd picked up on that already but the mayor had known her longer. She was putting on a brave face now, but they could both tell she was shaken.

'She goes out of her way to do these things, and we all want to help her, knowing what she's been through, you know?' the mayor said, looking over his sunglasses at him, as if inviting him to reveal he knew exactly what she'd *been through*.

Again, Ethan almost asked how he was supposed to know what Sage had been through, but again, it would have been pointless. Sage was best friends with this man's wife—she'd probably told Abigail about their conversations…and their almost kiss… The mayor would likely know he'd been getting closer to Sage than to Storm since taking on this project.

'I'll keep an eye on her, make sure she's OK,' he reassured him.

'Good man, take her out or something, make her laugh. She needs it.'

Ethan nodded resolutely. 'Yes, sir,' he said, remembering this man was the one who'd hired him, and trusted him, and who'd *also* dropped everything to try and help save a rare bird. He would do it for the mayor as well as for Sage, he decided, because taking Sage out, feeling the way he was starting to feel about her, was the last thing he should be doing, really.

CHAPTER NINE

THE RHYTHMIC KNOCK on the flimsy wooden door
of her cabin startled Sage from her reading. She
glanced up at the clock—six minutes past eight.
She moved the plate of half-eaten toast from the
duvet, her heart racing as she folded the corner
of the page in her book, and flicked the needle
off her vintage record player. She wasn't expecting company.

'Hey, Sage? You OK in there?'

Ethan's deep voice carried through the thin
barrier with an undercurrent of concern at the
sudden absence of her jazz music, and she stood
up too quickly. She'd seen him through the windows before settling down to read, his muscular silhouette moving around the paddock with
Storm. He and Billy had finally managed to saddle him but she'd forced herself not to watch, to
mind her own business. The day's events had
taken their toll, another almost-kiss that had
freaked her out, an unpreventable death, all of it

confusing and sad and now she wanted to hide away from it on her own.

She opened the door to find him standing there. The moonlight cast long shadows across his angular features. His blue eyes searched her face.

Oh, Lord, why do you have to be so gorgeous, Ethan, and why did I tell you this wasn't a good idea...?

'What can I do for you, Ethan?' she said instead.

'It's been a tough day,' he confessed with a weary smile that melted some tiny frozen-over part of her. 'I could use a drink. What do you say we go out somewhere?'

Sage clutched her book to her chest. That look in his eyes was unnerving. The way he'd said *'You...'* earlier at the clinic, before they'd been interrupted by the call about the finch, had been playing on her mind. *'You...'* As though he'd been about to confess something she was doing to unnerve him. It had turned her inside out.

This chemistry between them was undeniable, and after their first almost-kiss it had started to affect her concentration—it was why she'd done her best to undo it all in the chopper. Why start something up that would just go wrong and leave her worse off than she was, thinking even *worse* things about herself? He'd pretended not to hear her.

'Actually, I was about to go see some friends.'

Sage stepped aside, inviting him in anyway. How could she not? The walls felt as if they'd closed in tighter with Ethan's broad shoulders moving past her in the confines of her small living quarters. His scent caught her nostrils, mixed with soft hay, and she tried not to groan.

'Some friends?' he asked now, with a small smirk. She rolled her eyes at him.

'Yes.' Did he think she didn't have many friends, except Abigail? He was right, though. She really needed to get out more.

'You can come too, if you like,' she said, trying to keep her tone even while her mind buzzed with questions. Why did she just invite him to the only place she ever went at night besides Abigail's? What did he think of her home? Too humble, too cluttered with all her veterinary journals and second-hand furniture? 'Sorry about the mess, by the way.'

'This isn't a mess,' he said, casting an eye over her record collection before perching on the corner of the tattered leather couch and picking up the book she'd just put down. 'You should've seen the chaos at Jacqueline's house last Christmas.'

'Jacqueline?'

'My sister,' he said, flicking absently through the pages. 'My niece and nephew, little terrors... Kara's six, Jayson's eight, they're like a tornado of toys. One day when I was there, they decided it was the perfect time to test out their theory that the ceiling fan could carry their weight and help them fly.'

Sage raised an eyebrow, her earlier tension giving way to a grin. 'And you stopped this… experiment?'

'Caught them red-handed, chairs stacked on tables, tinsel everywhere. I had to channel my inner negotiator to get them down.' His laughter was infectious, so rare from him, but clearly coming from a place of deep love and affection and, for a fleeting moment, Sage felt a lightness she hadn't known she'd needed. He had come here on a mission to make her smile, she realised. Because of the dead bird. Or maybe he just felt sorry for her, she thought suddenly, now she'd told him how her family died. Did he think she couldn't cope when things got tough? She frowned. Maybe she was overreacting… Ugh—too many confusing emotions, it was hard to know what to think around this guy, but she'd invited him out with her now, so she was stuck with the consequences, whatever those might be.

She crossed to the corner where her shoes lay scattered, her well-worn slippers now seeming embarrassingly inadequate. 'Just need to change out of these.'

'I've got a pair just like them,' Ethan told her, with a nod to her slippers. 'Comfiest things ever.'

Sage smiled, feeling another shard of ice thaw inside her at the thought of sharing something so trivial with this man. She couldn't really imagine someone so masculine and active sitting about the house wearing slippers, stopping kids from attaching themselves to ceiling fans. And she hadn't known he had a sister, and a niece and nephew. Seeing how comfortable he'd been with Abigail's children, she'd bet he was a great uncle to them.

Beneath this new warmth and appreciation, tension coiled tight in her belly. The proximity of him in the small room magnified every breath, every shift of movement. As she bent to slip on her boots, she felt him watching her, but, standing up, she caught his gaze lingering on an old photograph of her with her mum and dad. The pride in her parents' eyes was immortalised right there in the picture, all three of them standing by the swimming pool after she'd completed her one-hundred-metre race and come in first place. The medal around her neck was so huge it covered her stomach.

'I was nine,' she said, looking at the photo with him. Then she felt his eyes on her again. Did he see the way she ached so badly to turn back time? She waited for him to bring it up, to ask more questions about her parents, but he didn't.

'Ready?' He broke the silence that had stretched too thin between them and she opened the door for him to walk ahead.

'Sounds like you're quite the uncle,' she remarked as they stepped out into the balmy evening air. Somehow she hadn't pictured him with anyone else from his family besides his dad. He always seemed so solitary, as if all he did outside working with his horses was hang out even more with his horses.

'I love the little monsters,' he quipped, making her laugh. He was pretty good at dissolving tension when he wanted to, she thought, gratefully. Also pretty good at making her forget she should be staying away from him.

The sky above was a canvas of ink around the moon. It hung like a solitary lantern amongst the stars as Sage clutched the straps of her backpack. Thank goodness it was cool out now. They walked side by side along the dusty path that curled behind the clinic, and she tried not to think about the fact that his presence out here in the silence was already sending a stampede of horses to her chest in place of her heart.

The mayor had almost certainly put him up to this, told him to check on her, and stupidly she'd invited him further than her doorstep, where she probably should have just thanked him for his well wishes and closed the door. It was hard, though, to resist this softer side of him. To think she had once assumed he was more style than substance, only good for posing for the cameras! The more she got to know him, the more he proved he was actually a really decent guy and a great vet.

The crunch of gravel underfoot was the only sound now, and the rhythm seemed to pulse with unspoken words. She was already turning this into something it wasn't.

So silly! Just calm down, Sage.

She glanced at Ethan, his handsome, way too kissable profile etched against the night sky, and felt that familiar pull, the one that tied her stomach in knots. He was close enough that she could see the contours of his face soften in the moonlight, but he wouldn't try to kiss her again, she'd made sure of that. Surely she had done enough to keep him at arm's length, at least as far as a romance was concerned. He was only here now because of the mayor, anyway.

The possibility that he might not be interested in her after all caused her thoughts to spiral, her confusion mingling with the cool night air.

'So, where are we going?' Ethan's question sliced through her reverie.

'You'll see,' she told him, but her voice came out distant and distracted. She wrapped her arms around herself. Why had she invited him along? This was something she always did alone. Maybe she *did* want a fling…maybe she should just stop being a wuss and kiss him! But flings led to feelings and she knew her heart couldn't handle someone else she admired and cared for disappearing on her.

She stopped just short of the familiar tree, her eyes tracing the constellations in the sky above them as she slid the backpack from her shoulders. Ethan stifled a smile.

'I thought you were seeing friends?' he said, his voice low and curious.

'And here they are.' She didn't look at him as she pointed skyward. 'Up there,' she whispered, spreading out the soft pink blanket she always brought with her, and dropping to the ground. He was here now, so she might as well reveal her secret.

'That bright one, that's my mum, Caroline,' she said. 'And next to her, that's my dad, Anthony. The little one that sparkles a bit differently? That's Juni, my Australian Shepherd.'

Ethan lay beside her, his body a solid presence. His silence instantly comforted and unnerved her at the same time. He probably thought she was completely crazy. 'What do you talk to them about?' he asked instead and she felt the heave of relief lift her heart. Of course he wouldn't judge her; he knew what it was like to lose loved ones.

'Everything. You mean to say *you* don't talk to the stars yourself?'

He smirked, shook his head. 'No, but I might have to start. At least they don't talk back.'

'Neither do animals,' she reasoned.

'Which is exactly why we like them, stars and animals. Peaceful beings. Mostly unargumentative.'

'Exactly.'

She stole another glance at him, at the strong line of his jaw, the faint stubble that was growing on him, and her too. He was more than what people saw on TV. So much more than what she had expected to see, when he'd first shown up in his sexy jeans and boots with enough charisma to charm a nation. With her he was both open and closed, revealing these small parts of himself to her piece by piece, only to withdraw again, protecting himself.

A lot like she was doing, she realised now. He'd been through enough himself to warrant him being a little cautious when it came to their obvious chemistry. But he did feel it, with her—it was pretty much undeniable when the panic and confusion around her own feelings subsided. Should she kiss him now? It would be so easy.

No. Sage, what are you doing?

'So you come here all the time?' Ethan said.

'I do. Always alone,' she added.

He nodded. 'Well, thank you for introducing me to your family.'

His gaze followed hers as she stared at all the sparkling celestial bodies she'd assigned to her loved ones, and various other animals she'd lost over the years.

'What happened that day?' he ventured gently after a moment. 'The fire?'

Oh, man, here we go.

Sage drew a shuddering breath as her chest and every bone seemed to tighten inside her. 'I should've helped them...' Her voice trailed off, choked by the weight of it like always, heightened by the loss today. That poor bird.

If she said too much, he'd find an excuse to leave, he'd link her to the stories that had done the rounds when they were kids, that still resurfaced now sometimes, thanks to the Internet. Bryce had loved all animals, just like Ethan. Bryce had turned his back on her and Ethan would, too.

Ethan shifted, propping himself up on his elbow to look at her. He seemed to see the battle in her eyes and for a second the whole story formed on her tongue, but she willed herself to keep quiet.

'What do you mean, you should have *helped* them?'

She bit her tongue.

'Sage?'

She released a small sigh through her nostrils. 'I was looking at my phone, in the main house,' she said eventually. 'That night. We were camping out front—my dad loved us all to do that. Campfires, stories, hot dogs on the flames, no technology. I needed the bathroom in the house, so I went inside, and then of course I sneaked a look at my phone and got distracted chatting with my friends, and when I came back, the wind must have changed direction and…the fire was… everywhere. I hadn't noticed on my way into the house that our campfire was starting to spread outside the pit we'd dug.'

Ethan was still studying her closely. Sage's mind spun. Any moment now she would stop talking, if only her head weren't processing it all over again and sending it straight out of her mouth into his understanding, way too hypnotic eyes.

'They couldn't get past it. It just kept spreading,' she continued. 'My phone was back in the house. I *could* have just run back there but I didn't. I completely froze.'

'You were just a kid,' he said, putting a hand over hers softly.

She sighed. 'I wasn't a *stupid* kid, Ethan. I could have done something. Instead, my family died, and the fire spread out of control and all those poor animals in the bush… I can't ever forgive myself for any of it. If I hadn't been so selfish, and absorbed in my phone, if I just hadn't gone behind their backs to check it in the first place, I would have got there in time to—'

'Sage!' He sat up straighter now, reached for both her hands. She was looking at him through a blur of tears, as if it had all happened yesterday. Great, she was already way too emotional because of the bird's death. It had brought everything roaring back to the surface. 'What happened wasn't your fault,' he pressed. 'Please don't tell me you've been carrying this guilt around all this time. Fires spread, that's what fires *do*.'

Sage's throat tightened around her next words. She turned away, ashamed of the tidal wave building up in her chest, and the tears he was bringing out of her.

'Tell me, sweetheart,' he urged gently, stroking the backs of her hands with soft thumbs.

'Everyone says there was nothing I could have done,' she confessed, her breath hitching, 'but I failed them all, I know I did. I should have seen—'

'You didn't fail anyone,' Ethan insisted, his tone firm and compassionate all at once. 'You were only a little girl.' He squeezed her hands in reassurance and she watched his hands tightening around hers, big hands, safe hands. Did he even know how she had wanted someone to understand all this, to talk to someone other than Abigail about it?

'You're making a difference every day, Sage. That counts for something. I'm inspired by you. Look what you've done here, for the people and for the animals. And for yourself.'

Sage's fingers curled around his now, grounding her in the present, in Ethan. It was such a relief, feeling as though someone truly saw her. Then… 'Did you just call me *sweetheart*?'

The word cut through her suddenly. Bryce had called her that once, before he'd changed his mind about her and disappeared from her life completely.

Ethan was studying her mouth now in silence, tracing the lines of her face with those all-seeing blue eyes again, and she swallowed, drawing strength from him. He was still here, he wasn't getting up to leave. 'The last person I told about the animals couldn't handle it at all,' she said before she could think straight. 'It was a guy, actually.' She glanced up at him, checking for a reaction, but he was unreadable. 'He broke things off with me. Well, actually he didn't even do that. He just disappeared without ever speaking to me again.'

Ethan shook his head gravely, and gave her hands a final reassuring clasp before rolling to his back again. 'Well, maybe he had a different reason for going,' he said, looking up towards the southern cross while her heart continued to pound at his closeness and everything she'd just spilled out after telling herself she wouldn't. What was it about Ethan that made her want to talk? She was just like one of his horses already, responding from a place deep inside her that she couldn't fathom.

Then he turned his head to her. 'Did this man

actually *say* he was breaking things off with you because some animals died in a fire that wasn't even your fault?'

Sage opened her mouth to talk, but nothing came out, so she closed it again.

'Who was he?' he demanded gently.

Sage swallowed, measuring the seriousness in his eyes. 'A Canadian man I was seeing, called Bryce.'

'And Bryce just *disappeared*, right after you told him about that night?'

She nodded slowly, cringing. 'It was the morning after,' she admitted. 'And nobody else knew why he left the koala reserve, because he didn't tell anyone he was leaving.'

Ethan was nodding to himself slowly, still looking at the sky. 'Which koala reserve was it?'

She told him, and his eyebrows drew together. 'I've heard about that place. It's notorious for not paying people who show up without work visas and still expect to be paid.'

Sage combed back through her memories. Come to think of it, Bryce had once said something about not getting the money he'd been promised for the work he'd done there. Being an Australian citizen herself, she had never had a problem getting paid, so she'd forgotten about it. Also, she'd had a lot going on at that point, namely opening herself up to a man for the first time since vet school. She'd been a recluse, pretty much, till Bryce, aside from a couple of brief flings that had gone nowhere. Her work had been far more important to her, and she'd let everyone know it.

Her mind reeled; she must have zoned out because when she came back to herself, Ethan had changed the subject already.

'Did you know that Alpha Centauri is actually three stars, not one? And it's the closest star system to our own,' Ethan said, nudging her out of her reverie. 'And over there, that's the Carina Nebula…'

'The Carina-Sagittarius Arm of the Milky Way galaxy, I know. Almost nine thousand light years from Earth. Can you imagine how long it would take to get there?'

'Or what we'd find?' he added. 'I see I'm not about to impress *you* with my star facts.'

'You can try?' She shrugged. Was she flirting now? How did they get here from what they'd just been talking about?

Sage's heart pumped furiously as they talked about the stars and veered onto the subject of the cosmos and the probability of aliens and the intricate connections that bound humans to each other and to the world. For a while she forgot about Bryce entirely—who cared why he'd left at this point, anyway? She was distracted by the fact that she could talk to Ethan about anything, she realised as they lay there on the ground, side by side. But then, she couldn't quite muster the courage to ask any more about what had happened with his ex-fiancée and his best friend, and he didn't bring it up. Had he had a relationship since Carrie, of any length? A fling, maybe? If she asked him now, would he think she was sizing him up as more than a colleague and friend? Were they even *friends* now?

They were barely touching but somehow they were still travelling the world together tonight. It had been so long since she'd had a conversation like this with a man. Being friends with Ethan would be OK. A friend like him was welcome. If only she didn't still want to rip his shirt off and get inside his bed as well as his head!

In no time at all two hours had passed and they were both fighting back their yawns mid conversation. Ethan walked her back to the front door, told her it had been a pleasure meeting her friends, and Sage waited a few seconds longer than she should have, gazing into his mesmerising eyes before realising he most definitely was not planning to kiss her this time. He seemed different, as if he'd drawn a line under the whole idea, and once again she cursed what she'd said to him in the chopper.

'Goodnight, Sage,' he reiterated.

I liked it when you called me sweetheart more, she wanted to say.

But she let him go.

She groaned to herself as she listened to his ute pulling away. Who was she kidding? She could never make Ethan her friend. She'd never wanted to be with *anybody* as much as this in her life, but she couldn't have him. He was going to disappear out of her life, just as Bryce had, eventually. And there was no way she was going through that again, whatever the reason.

CHAPTER TEN

THE UTE'S ENGINE ROARED, cutting a furious path through the dense bushland. Sage clung to the dashboard, her knuckles white as the vehicle lurched over another unseen dip in the rugged earth. Beside her, Ethan's hands were steady on the wheel, his jaw set with determination. 'How much further?' he asked her.

'Should just be over this ridge,' she said, squinting at the coordinates on her phone against the glare of the sun. It was doing its best to blaze through the canopy overhead.

'Are we sure it was caught in a trap?' Ethan asked, his voice mirroring the unrest inside her, not least because they'd left the clinic at the speed of light after a local hiker had sent coordinates to them, telling them a dingo was stuck. Sage replied, her gaze not leaving the rough track ahead.

'Yes. She said the poor thing didn't look too good, but she couldn't stay with it, because she was out of water herself, and then she had to search for a phone signal.' As she said it, she noticed the bars on her own phone were fading from five right down to one. 'It's all alone right now, the poor thing.'

'We'll find it,' Ethan assured her, pressing his foot to the gas again.

Sage tried to focus on the dusty path, hatching a plan to help free the dingo whatever state it might be in, but her thoughts kept drifting back to the other night, last week, the last time they'd sat alone talking, under the stars. He'd helped her at the weekend with the irrigation system as promised, stopping only to answer a call from his dad. They'd chatted as they'd worked, but only on the topic of sustainable gardening practices. Nothing deep. Nothing personal. It was killing her.

It was almost as though that whole night alone with him under the sky had been a dream, and he'd closed off again, deeming her too broken maybe, as Bryce probably had? Ethan had made her think for a moment that maybe there had been another reason why Bryce had disappeared on her, but she couldn't figure out what that might have been. Why hadn't he just talked to her about it before he'd left?

The stars had been the only witness to her and Ethan's conversation that night. Now, as they drove deeper into isolation, surrounded by the twisted trees and sprawling scrub, the memory of Ethan's hand in hers that night, how nice it had felt, how safe and reassuring, wove itself so stubbornly around her heart she knew she'd be able to recall it fifty years from now, even if they never saw each other again once Storm was healed. Was it wrong that she was starting to wish Storm would never recover fully, that Ethan would have to stay here for ever and start doing more than just holding her hand?

'Here!' Ethan braked hard. The ute skidded to a stop. As they stepped out into the dust, the silence of the bush greeted them both like a living entity. They found the dingo just beyond a thicket of mulga bushes.

'Oh, you sweet thing, look at you.' The creature's furry leg was firmly caught in the grip of a rusted steel trap. 'The farmers just don't know what they're doing when they set out to get kangaroos,' she told Ethan. The dog-like animal's eyes were wild with pain as it lay panting, its coat matted with dirt and blood.

'Don't get too close,' Ethan warned her as she got to her knees. 'He's scared.'

'I know,' she told him, approaching slowly while he grabbed the bag from the ute. She crouched over the wounded creature, murmuring soothingly, even as it snarled in self-defence. Its teeth were tiny razors and Ethan put a hand to her shoulder, warning her to let him try something. At first, she ignored him, determined to do things her way. It was still so frustrating that he was here, on her turf, working his methods with

more success than she was having with hers…
but when the dingo snapped at her again and she
narrowly missed a sharp bite she stood back in
resignation and let him take over. She watched
him lay his hands on the animal, how it immediately stilled beneath him.

'Easy there, mate,' he whispered, his voice
low and soothing as he slipped a muzzle over its
mouth as a precaution. The dingo had already
stopped trying to bite. Sage just swiped her hot
forehead and let him assess the damage to its hind
leg. Their closeness, with bare arms and knees
in their respective T-shirts and shorts, shot bolts
of awareness through her bloodstream, though
she tried to concentrate on the mission at hand.

That night, after she'd told him about Bryce…
after he'd got her thinking about what really might
have happened to make Bryce leave… Ethan had
walked her back to her door like a gentleman, and
left her to think about it some more. Only now,
the more she thought about why Bryce left, she
couldn't help but think that maybe he just hadn't
been that into her…not in the way she'd wanted
him to be, after trusting him with all her secrets.
Maybe she'd just been a brief holiday romance
for him, and she had turned it into something
more. He'd seen his chance to make a break for
it, and like a coward he'd taken it without even
talking to her first. For whatever reason, Bryce
was long gone, and now Ethan was here. For a

while at least. She could have invited him into her home. This time, if she got the chance, she would accept it for what it was, a fling, a bit of fun, and she wouldn't get attached.

I should have just invited him in...

'Pass the bolt cutters,' he requested. Sage did so without a word and he concentrated on the task with fierce intensity, his muscular forearms glistening with sweat. With gentle, precise movements, they worked in tandem to free the dingo and soon the nasty trap was cast aside. She tossed it into the back of the ute, where it couldn't harm anyone else, and felt Ethan's gaze on her as she carefully applied iodine to the animal's injured leg. She continued with her soothing words, although it had stopped trying to lunge for her too now, as if it knew they were trying to help. She was even able to apply dissolving stitches and an antibiotic shot and she knew that together they were giving it the best shot at survival they could.

Ethan's admiration for her—or for her work, at least—was evident even without words. It felt nice when he looked at her so approvingly and worked with her like this. It made her feel guilty for not wanting him here at first and for not trusting in his methods. His methods worked for him, and by proxy they were working for her too. Ethan knew that every creature was of equal importance to her: a dingo was no different from a rare, endangered bird. Losing either was another heartbreak, to her at least. He knew that now and he knew why she felt that way, because she'd told him everything. And now the air around them crackled with an electric charge as another shared mission brought them closer, beyond the physical.

Sage allowed herself a fleeting glance up at him, her pulse quickening as the sunlight played across the angles of his handsome face. He'd shone a new light on the whole Bryce thing, making her wonder if she should gain closure by looking him up and finally *asking* him what had happened. Ugh, why couldn't she just get over it? It was as if, as soon as she decided to try, the guilt crept back in and stopped her. Despite Ethan's reassurances, nothing would *ever* make her feel differently about the way she'd let her family down. How could she ever shake the guilt over what had happened? How would she continue to live if she lost anyone else she cared about? That was the biggest reason she hadn't initiated anything with *this* man.

Ethan told her to stand back and she obeyed, watching him unclasp the muzzle. The dingo limped away, and a rush of pride blocked everything out for a moment. She turned to him, and before she knew what she was doing she'd held her hand up ready for his. Their palms met in an awkward high-five that somehow morphed into something resembling a clasp.

'Nice job, boss,' Ethan said.

'I'm not really your boss,' Sage huffed, swigging from her canteen, trying to ignore the hum of awareness that zipped along her nerves as his thumbs brushed the back of her hand. 'You're on the mayor's payroll, remember.'

Ethan's eyes held hers, and she found herself lost in their vivid blue depths for a heartbeat too long, trapped as the dingo had been. She knew why he called her boss, really. Because it was better for him to see her like that, an illusion of safety.

'It suits you, being a boss lady,' he said, thoughtfully, motioning her back to the truck.

The drive back began in silence along a different route. Sage focused on the landscape unfurling outside the window—a tapestry of greens and browns all punctuated by the brilliant blue sky above. None of it was enough to distract her from the fact that Ethan knew everything about the night of the fire, which had formed the very backbone of her existence, yet she still knew next to nothing about him really; not when it came to matters of the heart. Maybe it was too soon after Carrie for him to feel right about initiating anything with her, someone who would soon be operating tasks like this alone, thousands of miles away from him. Torture. Maybe he really did still have feelings for his ex, despite how she'd betrayed him with his best friend?

The pull towards this man, who hadn't judged her in the slightest, was getting impossible to ignore.

'Watch out for the—' Sage's warning came about three seconds too late. A jolt threw her against her seat belt as the ute's front wheel caught on something. Ethan wrestled with the steering wheel, his jaw set in determination as he tried to manoeuvre out of whatever was ensnaring them, but it was no good. Each attempt only seemed to dig them deeper into the earth. He cursed under his breath, throwing the ute into reverse. It still wouldn't move.

'Here, let me try,' Sage said, unbuckling her seat belt. As she stepped from the vehicle with him the issue was immediately apparent. They were ensnared in a network of tree roots that would be a pretty impressive work of nature if it didn't mean their vehicle was totally stuck. They swapped places and she gripped the steering wheel with the familiar surge of adrenaline that came with a challenge. The engine growled as she tried to manoeuvre them out, but the roots held fast.

'Stubborn thing,' she muttered in frustration.

'Like someone else I know,' Ethan teased through the window, a half-smile softening his features.

'Ha-ha, I had to try,' Sage shot back, though secretly she appreciated the lightness in his voice.

It was rare to see this side of Ethan—the same one he'd revealed when he'd been talking about his sister and his niece and nephew that night under the stars and, later, all the speculation about aliens and the cosmos. It was impossible to think there was nothing else out there when you lived under skies like this. The thoughtful philosopher was yet another facet to him that wasn't at all like the larger than life, sometimes arrogant personality the TV had portrayed, but still, the revelation did nothing to free the trapped tyre.

'Looks like we're going to be stuck here for a bit,' he said, his gaze meeting hers.

'Seems so, yes.' The tension flew back in between them and wove itself through her frustration like a fine thread, till she stepped back out of the ute into the dust, shutting the door behind her with a sigh. Her thoughts were in a frenzy, trying to come up with a solution while also avoiding the intense energy that seemed to surround them as he approached. She nervously watched him move around the car opposite her as they circled it together, inspecting the tangled mess of roots once more. Sage fumbled for her phone, her heart sinking as she swiped the screen. No bars. Not even a flicker. She met Ethan's expectant eyes and shook her head. 'Still no signal,' she reported. The isolation enveloped them like a second skin.

'Maybe if we dig around the tyre?' Ethan suggested, and she shrugged. They might as well try.

Sage's hands were caked with red dust as she clawed at the earth, her fingers aching from the effort. Ethan was beside her, his body bent in exertion as he dug around the trapped tyre with a piece of sturdy wood. The sun bore down on her shoulders, relentless in its late-afternoon fury.

'Almost there,' Ethan grunted, his voice threaded with dogged resolution. 'Just a bit more leverage and we should be able to rock it out.'

Sage wasn't so sure, but she didn't like to say it. She watched him swipe at his brow with the back of his hand, leaving a smear of dirt in its wake, and continued digging. She knew she really shouldn't be looking at Ethan's muscles bunching under his sweat-dampened shirt at the same time; her mouth was already dry enough as it was. But who would be able to help it?

'Ready?' he called out as she finally positioned herself behind the wheel yet again.

'Ready,' she echoed, finding him in the mirror. He braced himself against the ute's frame and started to push, straining against the metal beast, willing it to break free. The vehicle groaned, a low, protesting sound, and soon it lurched, once, twice, and again before settling stubbornly back into its earthen prison. Ethan swore softly, kicking at the stubborn root that was holding the wheel captive. Checking her phone again, she felt dread settle in.

'Still nothing. We're completely cut off.'

A heavy silence settled over them. It felt compounded by the vast, lonely wilderness that stretched endlessly in every direction. It was just them—the bush, the fading light, and all their unfinished business hanging in the air like ripe fruit. The thought of spending the night out here in the open wild sent a shiver down her spine despite the heat.

'Someone will be along soon. If not, it could be worse,' Ethan noted, scanning their surroundings. 'At least we've got that one water canteen, and some supplies…'

'We have trail mix,' she said, and he pulled a face, making them both smile for a second.

'It'll be fine.' She sighed, clinging to the practicality of the moment. But the sun wouldn't be up for much longer, its descent already painting the sky orange and pink. Maybe *someone* would realise they weren't home yet, and be along soon?

Ethan's silhouette cut through the dwindling light as he stooped to pick up another branch. 'We don't *need* a fire, you know,' he called over his shoulder, but the growing heap of wood beside him belied his words. She wished she could be as enthusiastic and as useful as he was, but they'd been out here an hour and a half already with no hope of rescue and she was hot and exhausted.

'Are you going to keep the wildlife away with your bare hands, then?' she retorted, and he flexed a biceps at her playfully. It was meant as a joke, but instead it made her insides flutter. He had no idea what his strength and physique, on top of his talents—not to mention his *eyes*— could do to a woman.

'Seriously, I've seen your "no naked flames" signs,' he said, tossing a bunch more sticks onto the pile. 'And now I understand why.'

'I'm fine with it, really,' Sage said quickly, gathering a smaller, more manageable stack for herself. The scent of eucalyptus rose from the bark and mingled with the earthy fragrance of the cooling ground. 'We need to save our phone batteries,' she added, trying to ignore the thrum of her heart that had started along with his concern. They were pretty close to the bush. But Ethan was here, and she couldn't let her old fears control her for ever. More to the point, she couldn't act like a fool in front of him when it was her fault they were stuck out here anyway. There had been warnings on the radio and from locals about the tree-root system. It was because of the drought— the ground was just too dry. What with the dingo, and her head being full of Ethan, she'd clean forgotten.

Ethan located the cigarette lighter from the ute

and coaxed the first flickers of life from the dry
wood. Sage forced her feet not to take three steps
backwards, instead inching closer. He shot her a
look, as if to ask if this was *really* OK with her,
and she nodded her silent consent. Thank goodness he was with her, really. Being out here alone
would have been terrifying, and there was no way
she'd have lit a fire on her own.

They'd pulled bags and a couple of spare towels from the ute to sit on, and soon the last of the
dusk had faded from above them and the flames
were curling up into the sky, spitting at the stars.
What would her parents think if they could see
her now? she mused, feeling Ethan's eyes on her
again. He was picking at the last of the trail mix,
which was all they had to eat.

'I'd murder a bowl of pasta right now,' he said,
scrunching up the empty packet.

'Are you a good cook?' she asked curiously.
She had never seen him cook a thing in the clinic's small kitchen.

Ethan nodded slowly. 'I can heat things up in
saucepans, put pizzas on a rack, boil water in the
microwave… That's what you mean by cooking,
right?' he teased.

They started to talk about their favourite
foods and Sage realised she was imagining him
in a silly apron with boobs or something on the
front, in a cosy kitchen with sunshine streaming
through the windows. She was there too in this

imaginary kitchen, stirring something in a pan on the stove. He was coming up behind her, coiling his arms around her waist, nuzzling her neck...

She chastised herself silently. *Sage, you are being totally ridiculous.*

'Here, drink some of this water,' Ethan said, handing her the canteen.

'Thanks.' Her fingers brushed against his as she took it, and a timely, inappropriate jolt attacked her core. She took a sip, busying herself with arranging the towel underneath her, trying to focus on the practicalities of settling into a night out here in the bush, rather than the warmth that lingered from his touch, or how much she wanted to sleep pressed against him. They talked about their favourite restaurants, his in Brisbane, hers mostly in Perth, and she tried to ignore the ache to ask him anything too personal, even though she was dying to.

'The fire feels nice,' Sage murmured without thinking. Ethan just raised his eyebrows and smiled, resting back on his elbows. It had actually grown a little chilly now that the heat of the sun was completely gone. She hugged her knees, the silence around them deep and full of unvoiced thoughts the second they stopped talking. Ethan swigged careful rations of the water, muscles shifting under the fabric of his shirt, shadows playing on his cheekbones. Sage couldn't concentrate any more. She also really had to pee.

'I have to go…' she told him, making to stand up.

'Need me to come too?' he asked her, sitting up straight. She laughed and shook her head, looking around for the non-existent bathroom.

As if.

'I can manage, thanks.'

'Well, take your phone for the torch, at least.'

'OK.'

The second she left the heat of the fire, the vastness of the sky and the shadows closed in. Silently she wandered to the nearest line of trees and crouched down close to the earth. What a situation this was. People were probably wondering where they were by now, but it was highly likely that no one wanted to take the path they'd all been warned about in the dark.

Sage was just doing her business when something sleek caught the corner of her eye. She turned her head slowly, her heart rate quickening as she flashed the phone's light around.

Where are you? What are you? Oh, my God.

Suddenly, she was frozen in a crouch. Just a couple of metres away, coiled among the underbrush, was a huge snake. It was hard to see its length exactly, but its scales glistened under the faint moonlight, reflecting a dangerous mix of black and deep red. She knew this one—a red belly. Highly toxic.

Sage's breath caught in her throat. This was not ideal—she'd been mere steps away from this creature while she'd just relieved herself! The gravity of the situation sank in, right as the creature decided to move again. A scream instinctively clawed its way up her throat, but she bit it back, not wanting to alarm Ethan. She had to stay composed.

Calm, calm, calm...

Careful not to make any sudden movements that might provoke the snake, she rose slowly from her crouched position, her heart pounding against her chest like a trapped bird.

Calm, calm, calm...

Her mind raced as she weighed her options, right as Ethan appeared from behind the tree. She almost jumped out of her skin as she fumbled to do her buttons up, eyes darting from him to the snake. She couldn't see it any more, it had moved. 'Ethan...'

'Sorry, sorry,' he said, shielding his eyes. 'You were just gone too long and I was worried.' He went to move towards her but she held up her hands.

'Snake,' she hissed.

He froze on the spot, just as she had. 'Where?'

'It was just here!'

'I don't see it. You must have scared it off.'

Even so, he shone the torch around as a warning as he led them both back to their makeshift camp. The fire was blazing now, its crackle deafening in the hush of the evening. The flames leaped and twirled and she forced herself not to move further back, to embrace it. It was a good thing tonight, keeping all the bad things at bay. Ethan's features had hardened, the lines of strain around his eyes more pronounced as he sat closer to her than he had before, shoulder to shoulder, alert and aware, as if he'd assumed guard duty on the lookout for snakes on attack.

Sage had dealt with snakes her whole life, but she'd let him protect her, she decided. Ethan was quiet for a few moments, contemplating the fire. Then he turned to her and out of nowhere he asked: 'So, that guy Bryce. Was it serious between you two?'

CHAPTER ELEVEN

ETHAN WAITED FOR her reply, studying her lips close up in the firelight. Maybe he shouldn't have asked such a personal question but, after hearing everything about the fire that killed her family, he was still putting the pieces of the Sage puzzle together. She'd tortured herself over what had happened that night, completely unnecessarily he was sure, and that guilt had affected so much of her life. As it had with Bryce; the way she'd just assumed he'd left because of something she'd done or hadn't done as a child.

She chewed her lip, looked at him sideways. 'It was just a little fun, I suppose,' she told him warily, fidgeting on their makeshift blankets.

'How long did you have fun for?' He looked over her shoulder for the snake, before focusing on her eyes again.

'Why do you care?' she asked, digging a stick into the dirt between her feet.

He studied her brown boots, the way one of

the laces was coming undone, and nodded quietly. He'd asked for that.

'You're right, it's none of my business.'

She sighed. 'It was just a few months, and, looking back on it now, it was nothing serious. I mean, I'm like you, I guess. I don't really *do* relationships.'

'Is that right?' He couldn't help the smirk that crossed his mouth.

'I'm pretty good at self-sabotaging my own happiness, in case you hadn't noticed,' she said tartly, straightening her shoulders. 'I suppose I always just assume...'

'That you don't deserve anyone's love or attention,' he finished. 'Which isn't true, by the way. I've said it before and I'll say it again. What happened to your family was not your fault. I really hope you know that.'

She pursed her lips but didn't answer.

'You were just a child. Would you really still be blaming anyone else for something that happened when they were ten? You're thirty-five, right? I saw your driver's license.'

Sage's eyes widened, before her brow furrowed into a deep frown, and he had to wonder whether anyone actually ever reminded her of this, whether she even talked to anyone about it, besides Abigail. She looked as if she was going to argue with him for a second, but then she tossed her stick into the fire and deflected away from her family. 'I don't know if I was ever really in love with Bryce anyway. I don't think I've ever really been in love with anyone.'

He didn't ask why, even though her quick glance at him made him acutely aware she was attracted to him. Her survivor's guilt, and her fear of letting someone in, only to lose them as she'd lost her parents, had dictated her whole life…the same way losing his mum, Cam and Carrie had dictated his. This was all dangerous ground, but here they were, and he wasn't just going to sit here in this weird silence.

'The more I think about it, I know I haven't,' she followed. 'I've certainly never wanted to marry anyone.' Sage's voice caught as her fingers twisted the edge of the towel. Ethan stared into the flames. Her hesitance to continue plunged them into another heavy silence.

'I proposed to Carrie because things hadn't been that great between us for a while,' he admitted after a moment. Sage pulled a face, and he grimaced. 'I know, I know. I just thought maybe it would keep us together—we always said we'd do it one day. It was the longest engagement anyway. Four years…'

'Four years?' Sage looked incredulous.

'We got engaged three years in, but we could never agree on a wedding date,' he explained, realising how silly it sounded now, even to his own ears. 'Looking back, I guess neither of our hearts had been in it for a long time. Carrie even stopped wearing the ring. It started when she lost interest in my life, in my horses and my family, everything I loved, you know? Everything she used to love about me...or said she did. Then I lost Mum and had to care for Dad and I guess it all just got too much for her. I was blindsided... or just blind, I suppose. I let my grief take over everything for a while, and I didn't even see her slipping away till she was gone.'

Sage listened closely, not interrupting. It felt strangely therapeutic to talk about it, even with her. 'How did you find out about the affair with Cam?' she asked.

Ethan scowled into the flames. He was saying things he'd never said to anyone but Jacqueline, but then, keeping it all stacked up inside him was toxic and he loathed small talk more than anything. Their crumbling communication had been the death of him and Carrie.

'I booked a hotel on the beach for Cam's birthday,' he said eventually. He explained how it was something they always did for each other on their birthdays, a guys' night away somewhere. Fishing, motorcycling, surfing, all that stuff. That year Carrie had really wanted to come, and he frowned to himself as he recounted it all, remembering how much Cam had advocated for her being there that year. 'We had dinner booked for seven, but a cat was knocked down by a car outside. I went to see if I could help. By the time I got back from the local vet I'd missed dinner. I heard Cam and Carrie talking in the suite...'

'They went to a suite together?'

'I'd booked the suite for Carrie and myself,' he said, explaining how he'd thought it was a little strange that they'd gone there instead of staying in the restaurant, or the bar. 'I was about to walk in but then I heard what they were saying.'

Sage touched his arm gently, her expression gently inquiring.

'It doesn't matter,' he said, his voice a low rumble. It really didn't matter; besides, there was no way he was telling her the exact conversation he'd overheard about his 'weird horsey stuff', and about how Carrie had dragged the wedding plans on because she didn't have the heart to break things off after his mum had died. How he'd then heard them kissing, convinced they were doing great at keeping their secret. 'I heard all the proof I needed that I was about to be given the boot, one way or another,' he said instead.

'What did you do?'

'Nothing, for a while.' He poked at the smouldering logs with a stick. 'I took myself down to the beach to clear my head. That's where Cam found me,' he said. 'I had it out with him, but Cam went on the defensive, telling me I hadn't been paying enough attention to Carrie, how she'd come to *him* and he'd fallen in love with her, and he hadn't been able to control it. I went and faced Carrie next,' he continued. 'She was angry...but more angry that I'd found out, I guess. Then she said she just didn't love me any more. That she'd tried to, but I wasn't the same person any more. Simple.'

'Seven years together—that doesn't sound simple.' Sage looked furious on his behalf all of a sudden, and while his own burning anger had turned to a mild, albeit perpetual simmer months ago her solidarity made her all the more attractive, all the more deserving of the truth that had driven him away from wanting another relationship.

'You lost your mother; how could you be the same person after that?'

'I'm fine,' he said quickly, even as the humiliation tore through him like a lightning bolt. It was true, he'd retreated, but Carrie hadn't been there for him either. 'It wouldn't have lasted anyway, me doing what I do, her doing what she does.'

He told her about Carrie being an actress, travelling city to city, party to rehearsal to late nights on the town with different casts and crews. His head and his heart had always been at the homestead, and now he was working towards making his mum's dreams a reality and making sure his dad never felt alone.

'You were just doing what you love, what you were born to do,' she reasoned kindly, and he ran his eyes over her lips, wondering why he was saying all this to her, while he could barely imagine Carrie's face any more.

'They're not like us,' he said. You're not a city girl, Sage, no more than I'm a city guy.'

'That is true.' She sighed. 'Cities have way too many people in them.'

'And you can't always see your friends when all those other lights are blinding you.'

'My friends?'

He pointed up at the sky and she smiled. 'Oh.'

The silence had shifted now into something comforting. 'I'd be lying if I said I didn't like it remote and quiet. Even though, tonight, I would have planned more of a dinner if I'd known we'd be out here *this* long.'

Sage was still smiling to herself. 'Sounds like a date, Ethan.'

Their eyes met and he knew they both felt this unspoken acknowledgment of the bond between them growing stronger, and tighter. It was a kind of quiet understanding he hadn't felt with anyone human in a long time. Only the horses.

'She'll never know what she's missing, you know,' Sage said next. Her tone was laced with so much sympathy and longing it drew the flames from their fire into his blood. He'd been cleansing himself of the pain of what Carrie and Cam had done to him just by talking about it with Sage and now he couldn't stand it any longer.

Ethan reached out, his hand brushing hers tentatively. She turned her palm upward, allowing their fingers to entwine as they'd done before, and his body responded in the exact same way, as though her touch was grounding any swirling emotions, pulling all his focus back to one place—her. He leaned closer, slowly, checking if she'd push him away.

The kiss was soft at first, exploratory, but it soon deepened as they both gave in. His heart thundered in his ears as he drank in the sweet taste of her mouth, and he let out a low moan that was swallowed up by the crackling of the fire. She felt so good in his arms. Sage's heart was racing against his chest as she pressed closer, her knees in the dirt as she straddled his lap, hips to his. Moving the way she was now… It turned him on so much he could hardly think. Their tongues danced together, teasing each other's mouths eagerly.

'Sage,' he heard himself groan, before she silenced him with another kiss. Her hands travelled up his chest and wrapped around his neck, holding him tightly as she deepened the kiss even more. Her breath was warm and ragged against his skin when she pulled away slightly.

'You taste like trail mix.' She smiled against his lips before sliding her tongue back into his mouth again. Their bodies swayed together with every passing second. He was lost in her now, they were lost in each other, and the rough bark digging into his backside as she writhed on top of him only seemed to add to the intensity of it all. It was almost as if nature itself were encouraging them onward and he groaned again with anticipation.

He lay back on the ground and brought her with him; they were wrapped up in each other, still kissing furiously. Every touch, every taste of Sage consumed him. The warmth of her breath against his skin, the sound of the crickets, the heat of the flames and the sensual urgency of her touch all made his blood rush around his body. He couldn't actually remember an encounter that could match this one. This woman was made from something different. He'd sensed it the first day they'd met. So what if this was a bad idea? It didn't have to be serious or complicated...just a fling. She didn't do relationships either—wasn't that what she'd said before?

'Ethan,' she moaned against his mouth, clearing his head again of everything but her.

Just enjoy this, he told himself, allowing his fingers to travel softly down around the curve of her waist, circling her navel. It was so hot when she shivered underneath him.

Sage's body was on fire. Ethan's tongue claimed her mouth over and over, dancing with hers as though he was trying to bury every thought that might be advising him against this, as though she was already his. His big, strong hands stroked her skin, sending shivers of butterflies round her belly and down her spine despite the fire. She gasped his name, pressing her eyes shut, losing herself again in the sweet sensations so her brain wouldn't get the better of her.

Stop worrying too much, she told herself. *Focus on the now a bit more, the things about this that are so good.* Right now, she felt more alive than she ever had.

'Ethan...' Her voice came as a breath against his mouth.

Just enjoy this, be in the moment, feel him... his fingers on your waist, curling around your hair, so soft, so gentle... God, I am shivering...

They'd rolled over and her back against the roughness of the ground felt deliciously wicked. The blankets and towels they'd set out were somewhere else entirely now, they'd pushed them away, and the root system dug into her flesh as if it wanted to keep her there too, with their vehicle. He lay on top of her, propped up on his elbows, arching into her, letting her move them both together.

Every tiny touch and caress and kiss drove her deeper into him. *So* connected, even without him inside her. This connection was everything, she thought to herself as her skin warmed at the friction, at his kisses.

'Do you want this?' Ethan whispered against her neck, his breath hot against her skin.

Yes, yes, yes, never stop, she said in her head, but any vocal response was lost the second his lips were on her throat, kissing softly, sensually up the column of her neck.

The trembling started again, from her toes this time, right up through her core. His kisses grew more focused, more passionate, harder against her mouth, harder and harder, and harder.

His thighs around her waist pinned her, till she felt herself biting back a laugh at the sheer absurdity of herself like this, being here with him, pinned between these legs, deep diving into his soul, feeling with a non-refutable certainty that he wanted her despite what he knew she'd done. His fingers traced the line of her shoulder blades, following the gentle curve to the small of her back, then back up again.

His hands on my body feel so good. I love the way this feels when he's pinning me down.

Her eyes raked his muscled chest as he lifted his arms and slid off his shirt, tossing it aside to refocus all his attention on her, arching beneath him, locked between his rock-hard thighs, like a trapped animal. She sat up beneath him, letting his hands slide down her body, catching her breath as he slowly unbuttoned her blouse while trailing more soft kisses along her exposed skin. She had never felt this way before, completely and utterly surrendered to the kind of desire that was consuming them both in this moment.

He pulled away then, his gaze still burning with intensity as he looked down at her, his eyes searching hers for any sign of hesitation or uncertainty.

I want this, she confirmed with her eyes, and her hands, and another urgent kiss that felt as if it were binding his soul to hers.

Seemingly satisfied with her silent consent, Ethan trailed his fingers down to the waistband of her shorts, and he inched it down slowly, savouring every bit of skin that was revealed with another stroke of his thumb, or a groan that made her feel like more of a woman than she'd felt since…since when? It was actually hard to remember. Sage moaned into his mouth as he moved back between her thighs. She tangled her fingers in his hair and arched against him, wanting even more, all of him.

How is this happening?

His eyes were dark, full of desire and longing, making her start to perspire in places she hadn't been too aware of for a while. The firmness of him against her thigh was insistent, and huge.

Oh, my.

She could feel every inch of him now, with only their underwear between them, and the trembling, the anticipation, was too much to take.

She made to reach a hand into his boxer shorts, preparing herself.

Ethan stopped suddenly. Pure torment took over his face as he groaned in dismay and pulled away, sitting up on the ground beside her. Her heart lurched at her ribs as if a truck had slammed on the brakes a millisecond before hitting her.

'What's wrong?' she asked him breathlessly, sitting up beside him, suddenly self-conscious. She was more exposed than she'd ever been, and not just physically—her brain had just been somewhere else, dancing in a whole other universe, and they hadn't even had sex yet! If that was foreplay with Ethan, what the heck would the real thing be like?

Ethan looked at her with regret, making her insides swirl with dismay. 'We shouldn't do this, not right now,' he said with a growl.

'What?' Sage was confused, more than a little disappointed, and also... *What the heck?* 'Why not?'

Ethan shook his head. 'We don't have any protection,' he told her, tying back his hair that had come loose in their fit of passion.

'I have a coil,' she explained tightly, suddenly feeling silly. It was true, it helped calm her ridiculously heavy periods, but she hadn't expected to have to spell it out; she wouldn't be initiating sex if she wasn't protected against pregnancy, would she? Especially out here. He must know that.

'I'm sorry, I don't know what I was thinking. It's not you, OK? I just, I got carried away in the moment, but it's not fair to you.'

Sage nodded again. Not fair? This felt an awful lot like rejection. In fact right now she didn't trust herself to even speak. Her soul could not retract that fast, even if his could. Maybe sensing her disappointment and confusion, he took her hand again and kissed her palm gently. 'It doesn't mean I don't want you, trust me,' he followed, tracing a finger across her cheek in a way that made her breath catch.

OK...so he seems like he's telling the truth.

'I want you, Sage, more than you know.'

That same tortured expression came over his face again, and her heartbeat felt like a thousand kicking kangaroos all over her body.

But?

He was wrestling with emotions he was not going to talk about. Was it too soon for him after Carrie? After seven years of being with the same woman? How could she not think that, after everything he'd just told her? But she wouldn't mention her name, not after everything they'd just done.

Ethan shook his head at himself, and she couldn't help it, she reached for him again and kissed him, and for a moment, as he responded, all traces of uncertainty disappeared as she melted into him again. All right, so they didn't have to have sex right now, it was probably smart not to, what with there being a snake and God only knew what else on the loose that might bite them…but when they were home again, some-where safe, she was not going to allow any ex-cuses. They'd started so they'd finish. Seriously, it had been so long since she'd felt this good, there was no way she'd deny herself an extension of this…so to speak.

Sage pulled back and turned over on the ground. Ethan draped a protective arm around her body, pulling one of the giant towels over them both. It felt like a shield against the night, and everything else she'd been carrying around that had been keeping her in this bubble of self-defence and denial. Why on earth had she been denying her own needs, her right as a woman to feel this way, even if it was only for a little while?

She had to remember what he'd been through with Carrie though, she thought, watching a shooting star scurry across the sky so fast she didn't even have time to mention it to him. It was hard to believe he'd just shared all those awful memories with her, and that he was here, holding her close, leaving her in no doubt that he wanted her. Maybe there was a side of Ethan only *she* had been able to coax back out into the open. Imagine that.

The thought made her smile as she snuggled into him as his little spoon. The warmth of his body curled around hers, his heart beating steadily against her back, the scent of the outdoors mingling with the lingering, delicious scent of his own personal sweat... This was enough for now. They lay there, wrapped up together, as Ethan's hand moved gently over her hair, his fingers trailing along her scalp in a soothing touch.

Ah, that feels so wonderful... I wish this night would last for ever.

'Sage, wake up!'

Ethan's voice broke into her dreams. Sage blinked her eyes open to the light of dawn creeping through the trees behind him. He'd already started scrambling for his clothes and she caught a brief glimpse of his impressive muscles before he yanked his jeans back on over his boxers. The sound of an engine hit her ears. How long had she been asleep?

'Oh, no!'

'Hurry,' he urged her, half laughing as he threw her shorts at her. The engine had been distant at first, but now it was growing steadily louder. Sage buttoned her top up wrong, and then hurriedly rebuttoned it, scanning the horizon.

'I think rescue is on its way,' he said, folding the towels up haphazardly and then much more carefully scattering the remains of their fire across the dirt. He'd left his shirt open and now

she was fully awake, looking at the flexing of his
six-pack in the early morning sunshine, all she
wanted was to kiss him again.

CHAPTER TWELVE

THE UTE EMERGED over the ridge, and she recognised it instantly. 'Abigail!' Her friend's dusty old truck had seen more of the bush than most locals combined; she and the mayor knew these roads and everything off-grid around them for miles. The sight of her best friend coming for them should have brought unadulterated relief, she thought as Abigail and the mayor pulled to a stop and got out, but as Ethan shook the hand of the mayor, who quickly assessed the situation and started pulling tools out, Sage's emotions were a train wreck. She drew a deep breath, then another and another, closing her eyes, trying to find her equilibrium.

Abigail took her aside, her deep blue sundress swishing around her ankles, her giant sunglasses hiding her expressive eyes.

'Did you do this on purpose to get him alone out here?' her friend asked with a wicked smile.

'Of course I didn't,' she replied, a little too haughtily, watching Ethan sliding under the stuck ute with the bolt cutter. She rolled her eyes at herself, turning her back to him and facing Abigail head-on so her eyes wouldn't be forced to linger on Ethan's sexy body.

'I think I'm in big trouble,' she admitted with a sigh.

Abigail pushed her shoulder playfully. 'Have you gone and done the unthinkable, Miss Dawson?'

Sage cringed at the ground. 'Not quite. Almost.'

Abigail just grinned. 'I don't blame you,' she swooned. 'I mean, have you ever seen such a stunning specimen of a man?' Her gaze followed Ethan as he expertly manoeuvred the cutter around the tree's roots. 'I love my husband, but, really, possessing those arms and abs should be a criminal offence.'

Sage merely nodded. What could she say? Her head was still full of the warmth of his touch, the comforting rhythm of his heartbeat, everything they'd shared in the quiet darkness. Her heart ached at the thought of losing that connection with him so soon after she'd discovered it. Sage couldn't help the pang of loss overriding her thrill at having spent the night in his arms. Sex or no sex. The intimacy of it, all that shared vulnerability. It had felt so right, and so real. But now it seemed as though it was slipping away from her already. He'd said something like it wasn't fair to her. It wasn't fair of him to sleep with her? That had to mean he still had feelings for Carrie, didn't it?

'You're beating yourself up over this, I can tell,' Abigail observed quietly.

'He didn't want to, you know, he didn't want to have full sex with me,' she muttered, creasing her nose.

'Sage, look at where you are!' Abigail gestured around them as a tumbleweed floated past. 'It probably wasn't the time or the place. Maybe he's got some stuff going round in that big old handsome head of his, too. Am I right?'

She was pretty spot-on there, actually. 'Don't say anything, Abigail, keep it quiet, OK?' Before Abigail had a chance to say anything more, a holler from the guys told them the mission had been a success. The adventure was over; finally she could get home, and take a shower...with or without Ethan in it with her. Already she was flushed just thinking about what might happen next.

Sage and Ethan unloaded the gear from the back of the ute, while Abigail hurried inside to the bathroom and the mayor padded over to the stables to see Storm. 'I'm hoping I can saddle him up again, show the mayor how much better he's doing,' Ethan said as his hand brushed hers over the empty water canteen. The move sent a trail of sparks right up her arm and she gripped the canteen, its cool metal a stark contrast to the scorching morning sun. Or was she hotter because of Ethan, and last night? She took a deep breath, resting for a moment against the back of the truck.

'Everything OK?' Ethan's ocean-deep eyes searched her face. The intensity in them left her feeling more exposed than she had last night. She'd had to do a quick check in the ute to make sure she hadn't buttoned anything else up wrong—not that Abigail didn't know exactly what had gone on. Why had she told her what had happened…or what had almost happened? Now the mayor would know, and there were no secrets in Amber Creek, ever. The last thing she wanted was for poor Ethan to think everyone was talking about them.

'Of course I'm OK,' she said anyway, tucking a stray curl behind her ear. The memories of what they'd shared last night were clinging to her harder than the dust on her boots and he was throwing her thoughts off track the more he looked at her.

Ethan took the canteen from her hands gently, his gaze not leaving hers. 'You've been quiet since we left. If I crossed a line—'

'I wanted us both to cross a line, Ethan. I thought I made that perfectly clear.' The words were out before she could stop them. Again. She watched his eyes widen in amusement a second before they narrowed in speculation.

Oh, great, so now he thinks you're desperate for sex, Sage. How attractive, well done.

Ethan scratched at his chin. 'I'm sorry if I made things weird,' he said finally. 'I guess I got lost in my head after everything we were talking about and seeing you so…'

'So what?'

He growled to himself, low in his throat, and shook his head and she willed her hands not to reach out and touch him. 'I did think that maybe you're just not ready for that level of intimacy with someone else after—I mean, you were with her for years until pretty recently. And that's OK,' she lied.

'It's definitely not that,' he confirmed, and the incredulous look on his face made her cringe inwardly.

'Then, what is it?'

'You're making me kind of nervous here, Sage.'

Her heart lunged right for her throat again. She swung her head around. No one was watching or listening. Ethan's eyes were fixed on hers. 'You do the same to me,' she confided.

He sniffed, glanced sideways. 'The things I told you, I've never told anyone other than my sister.'

'Well, that makes two of us, only in my case it was Abigail,' she said.

Oh, Lord... Sage swallowed against the tightening of her throat as it threatened to choke her. He just kept looking at her as if he were scanning her brain, his jaw moving side to side as if he were chewing on his next words. Was the fact that she made him nervous a good thing, or a bad thing?

When he spoke, his voice was laced with a kind of knowing that sent shivers along her arms and between her thighs. 'I don't think we had a choice anyway, back there. What happened between us was always going to happen.'

Gosh, it was hot already. Sage reached for the bundle of towels to stop her hands from touching him again. The fabric unfurled slightly in her grasp. In an instant, the smile fell from her face. 'Yeow! What was that?'

Snatching her hand away, she sprang back from the ute, clutching her arm against her chest.

'What happened?' Ethan asked, his eyes flooded with concern.

'Something sharp, I don't know...' Her wrist was turning red already and the markings sent her blood cold. Two tiny punctuations, set close together. Then she saw it; a flicker of black and red slithering out from the folds of the towel she'd just dropped to the ground.

'Snake!' she cried out, stumbling backwards again. Her heart pounded against her ribs as if it wanted to run even further, but she sank to her knees in shock. 'It got me.'

Oh, no...no, no, no! This isn't happening.

Ethan leapt over the snake as it writhed on the ground as though it wasn't sure what was going on either, and he was at her side in a heartbeat, his hands examining her wrist with urgency. 'We need to get you into the clinic—now.'

Too late. A flash of pain seared her arm. The red-bellied black snake's poison was already doing its job, working its way into her system. Soon it would paralyse her. She watched, horrified as the creature slithered away and vanished into the brush. Shock morphed into ice-cold fear as reality sank in. It was the same snake that had watched her pee last night; it must have sneaked past their warm fire and up into the stationary ute while they were sleeping. And now it had sunk its fangs into her.

'Can you walk?' Ethan asked, his brows knitted with concern.

'Y-yes,' Sage stammered, fighting the dizziness that was threatening to consume her already. Could she? She wasn't sure. They had to move fast. The world was already swaying around her.

Seeing her rapid deterioration, Ethan scooped her up into his arms as if she weighed no more than a new-born foal and stepped up the pace. Cradled against his chest, she felt herself shrinking as somewhere in her periphery she saw the mayor sprinting towards them. Everything was moving in slow motion. Sage gritted her teeth against the pain, willing herself to stay conscious.

Do not pass out, Sage, do not pass out.

'Stay with me, Sage,' Ethan urged as if he could read her mind, and she held onto his voice like an anchor, fighting for something to make sense in the chaos of her thoughts.

That stupid snake...what did it want with me? Why did it do this? Oh...everything's so floaty...

'Sage, you're fine,' he stated with a confidence she couldn't quite believe. She was clutched tightly against his chest for all the wrong reasons, and a part of her mind that felt as though it existed outside herself replayed the warmth of him last night, as she'd snuggled into the protective circle of his arms.

It would be worth it, if she died like this, she thought groggily; at least she would go knowing nights like that could happen to her. And he'd just admitted he still wanted her...that he'd been processing everything, how nervous she made him feel because...because why? Had he actually given her a reason?

They burst through the door of the clinic. Abigail was on the way out from the bathroom. The mayor was right behind them now and somewhere she heard Ellie, back from sick leave, hurrying a customer out with their animal patient. She vaguely heard Ethan barking out orders, his years of experience evident even to her, in her state, in the way he took charge.

'Antivenom, now!' he commanded, sweeping whatever was on the long metal table to the floor with one hand and laying her down gently. It was hard to force herself to focus on him, but he squeezed her hand and she clung to him like a lifeline, her body trembling with shock and pain. Searing pain. It was snaking from her arm to her lungs, and her blood, it was on fire. How was this happening? One moment everything had been fine, and the next, she was here on her own cold, hard operating table, fighting for her life.

'Ethan,' Sage said hoarsely as her eyes focused in and out on the vial of antivenom he now had in his hand. Abigail clutched her other hand, while the mayor hovered behind on his phone. Who was he talking to? Their childminder?

It doesn't matter, Sage. Am I really dying?

'You're gonna be OK, my darling, just hold on.'

Ethan took her arm, which she couldn't even really feel at this point. He injected the serum and Sage winced, waiting for another sharp sting that never came. From somewhere that might have even been from outside herself again she saw Abigail's eyes flash to Ethan, then back to her, and she had the distinct impression one of them had just said something she'd do well to remember. But she was woozy…so woozy…

He mumbled something and soon she was fluttering in and out of a dreamy sleep. Moments later, or maybe it was an hour, it was hard to tell, she could feel the effects of the antidote taking hold. The world around her began to sharpen into focus again, and she realised with a start that Ethan was still holding her hand, his piercing narrowed eyes searching her face for any sign of distress.

Gosh, you're so handsome.

'Is she going to be all right?' Abigail's voice was laced with genuine worry beside her.

'I won't let anything happen to her,' Ethan replied with a conviction that made Sage's heart thud erratically all over again. It wasn't just the snake venom causing her pulse to race now. What was it she should be remembering? She tried to sit up on the table, causing a makeshift pillow under her head to fall to the floor. This was so embarrassing.

'Easy, Sage,' Ethan ordered, supporting her weight suddenly and urging her back down with an arm that felt like an iron band around her waist. Her senses slowly righted themselves, and she felt the warmth of his breath against her temple, real and intimate.

'Thank you,' she whispered into his eyes. Her voice was barely above a whisper. Her head was light, a residual venom-induced haze clouding her perception. But even through the fog, the expression on her best friend's face was clear as

day. Abigail and Ellie had both seen Ethan's un-
guarded emotions out on show, his raw concern
totally stripped of any professional facade. And
so had she.

'We should get her to her cabin,' Ellie said
just as Mrs Dalloway, one of their regular clients, walked in with a cat basket.

'I'll take her,' Abigail and Ethan said at the
same time. Then Abigail relented, placed a soft
hand to her cheek. 'Fine, you're stronger than me,
Ethan. You can carry her.'

Embarrassment flooded her veins like a new
serum. 'Thank you, Ethan, really, but…' She
paused in her efforts to get up again, swallowing hard against a tidal wave of nausea. 'You need
to be out there, helping with Storm. I'll be fine.'

'I'll see to Storm later.' His eyes were brimming with an emotion she couldn't quite name.
Concern, yes—but there was something more
now, something deeper.

'If you're sure,' she said with a feeble smile.

Ellie ushered a bewildered Mrs Dalloway and
her cat through to the other room, insisting *she*
would help with the patients and that the mayor
could come back tomorrow. The short journey to
Sage's quarters behind the clinic was a blur. All
Sage could register was the rhythm of Ethan's
movements and the sound of his voice reassuring her.

'Here we go, this is better than last night's cold,

hard ground,' he said as he located her bedroom, and gently laid her down on her bed. The cool pale-blue walls and bedsheets were a small comfort against the heat that was radiating from her skin. She still hadn't showered. This was a nightmare… Was her bedroom tidy? Had she put her laundry away or were her clean knickers still in a pile on the armchair? Was any of this suitable for a guest to see? It wasn't exactly how she had envisioned bringing Ethan here, or why.

'Please, Ethan, the others…' Sage began, her voice trailing off as another wave of dizziness hit her.

'All right,' Ethan conceded, though his blue eyes darkened with worry. 'I'll check back in with you really soon.' He put her phone down on the dresser. 'Call if you need anything.'

'Will do,' she managed to say, though the words felt like stones in her mouth. Maybe the snake bite had been fate stepping in, telling her not to get ahead of herself, not to sleep with him the moment he was ready, not to make whatever this was between them into something that would destroy her once it ended and he went home.

Ethan stood up, hesitating for a moment as if torn between duty and desire. He looked as if he was about to say something, but decided not to. Then, with one final, lingering look from the doorway, he left, closing the door quietly behind him.

Alone now, Sage closed her eyes, trying to

steady her breathing. Then she opened them and checked her chair for the laundry pile. Small blessings, she had at least put her knickers away. But Ethan's big, steady presence in her humble, small home still lingered like a tangible thing, wrapping around her in the quiet.

Now that the drama was over, she had had time to consider other things. *Ethan*. What was blossoming between them was real, wasn't it? Everyone had seen it now. He hadn't said it in so many words, except for when he'd called her darling... yes, that was it, that was what she'd forgotten! He'd called her darling, in front of everyone. Not Doctor, not even just Sage. *My darling*. Did that mean Ethan truly cared about her? She already cared about him, and that was even scarier than the thought of that snake, still out there somewhere, lying in wait for its next target.

CHAPTER THIRTEEN

ETHAN'S FINGERS TRACED the coarse hair of Storm's mane. The animal was standing calm and collected beneath his touch in the early hours and he'd watched the dawn break like this, the air cool and the paddock quiet, save for the occasional snort from the horses. His eyes locked with Storm's, a silent conversation flowing between them. Trust was not given freely in this world, he mused, especially not by an animal with a past shadowed by mistreatment like he suspected this one had dealt with. The more he worked with Storm, the more he figured the guy the mayor had bought him from had not been completely honest about his history. But Ethan sensed another definite breakthrough. They'd been coming more frequently. He and Billy had even managed to saddle him the other day, though Storm hadn't liked that much and had taken off around the paddock pretty quickly afterwards, snorting angry little snorts from his nostrils while the other horses looked on in amusement.

Ethan's eyes moved over Storm's back to Sage's quarters, just visible beyond the tree line. Her small cabin wasn't much but she'd made it her home and he'd been to visit her over the last few days, while she'd been resting. He'd forbidden her to work, as had Ellie, and as such he'd taken on more responsibilities around the place. The grass had even been mown, the irrigation system was well under way, and a new surprise would be arriving soon that he was pretty excited to share with her. He didn't mind the work, but the way he cared about it all with ever-increasing depth and passion was starting to unsettle him. He was doing it for Sage. It was all for her, and that indicated that he was starting to like her more than even he thought he did. But he had been down this road before and it scared the living daylights out of him.

'We can't help our feelings, though, can we, boy?' he said to Storm, who grunted indifferently, making him smile. He wanted that woman so badly. He'd wanted her that night out in the bush, but seeing her so vulnerable, after letting himself be so vulnerable in front of her, had pushed a barrage of what ifs into his brain that no amount of kissing or burying himself inside her would ever diminish. She was making him extremely nervous, and that was the truth. Terrified, in fact. This was a dangerous road to go down, but he couldn't deny that he wanted to, even more now.

'Morning,' a voice called out, pulling Ethan from his constant thoughts about Sage. She was walking towards him in the flesh, her footing steady but cautious. The vibrant green of her eyes seemed muted in the early morning light. It was a testament both to the ordeal she'd been through with that damn snake bite, dulling her light in general and keeping her laid up for the last few days, and to how he made her feel, which was clearly equally nervous. They wanted each other. And they were going to have each other.

And then he was going to miss her for a very, very long time, because, even if she came to Queensland for a visit and loved it, this was her home. After everything she'd lost, she'd bravely built a new life here with her practice and her small staff, the local community, and her found family—Abigail, the mayor and their children— and she wouldn't want to give it up any more than Carrie had wanted to give up her life for him. Grasping for a future with Sage would probably end the same way as *that* had, with him feeling less than what she really wanted or needed, and her chasing after something better.

'Hey,' he replied, watching her come closer. 'How are you feeling?'

'Better, thanks.' She stopped at the fence, leaning against it. 'I've been going stir-crazy in that bedroom.'

'Can't keep a good vet down, huh?' He smiled,

but he could hear the undercurrent of concern in his own voice, even as he fought the sudden uncharacteristic urge to make an ungentlemanly quip about what he could do to make her bedroom more exciting.

Not the time, not the place.

Sage's snake-bite incident had been drifting into his mind unasked-for ever since; the way her body had gone limp in his arms, her face ashen, the terror that had gripped his heart like an iron vice. Just seeing her like that had been hell. Pure torture. He was surprised his mind hadn't gone completely blank, that he'd managed to somehow stay calm and administer the antivenom, but in that crystallised moment he'd understood the depth of his feelings for her. The revelation was still churning around in his mind, as worrying as it was exhilarating.

'Those flowers you brought me, they're beautiful, Ethan. And the vinyl records...' She trailed off, her gaze flicking back to him. 'I didn't realise you knew I liked vintage jazz.'

'Your record collection gave you away,' he confessed, feeling his cheeks colour just slightly as he caught the hint of a smile on her lips. 'I figured you could use some company, even if it was just more Coltrane and Fitzgerald.'

'Just some of the most influential voices of their era,' she replied. 'Very thoughtful.' Her voice came out slightly strained, her eyes narrowed at the floor for a beat, as though she was struggling with the meaning of his gifts, as he was, he supposed. He'd gone to the tiny cafe in town, which doubled as a record shop, and the guy in there had known Sage, of course; he'd shown him what she didn't already have in her collection.

Ethan's hands stilled on Storm's mane, the weight of his thoughts growing heavy as hay-bales on his shoulders. He hadn't kissed her since their rescue from the dingo adventure. The urge had almost overwhelmed him, especially when he'd come by with the gifts, rearranged her pillows, made her tea.

They'd been pretty safe while she'd recovered. Her weakness and vulnerability had been every excuse not to lean in and pick up where they'd left off, but they were still perilously close to the edge. Whatever was growing between him and Sage was something that would not just go away, he knew it, as certain about that as he was about the trust growing in Storm's eyes. Even as he warned himself not to pursue it.

'Thank you, for everything you've done around here too. It means a lot to all of us,' Sage said now, breaking the quiet tension.

Longing and reminiscence tormented his senses as he nodded and pulled his eyes from her legs in those jean shorts—legs he remembered wrapped around him on a night that was probably best left forgotten. She was so near now, he could hear the soft rustle of her shirt against her skin as she moved. How could he forget how her shirt had come off that night, how she'd revealed herself so willingly? Sage was beautiful, inside and out. He cleared his throat.

'Any time,' he replied, before turning to study Storm's eyes. The horse's ears flicked back suddenly as Sage inched closer. The ghosts of this horse's old fears were still there. He could totally relate, he thought ruefully.

'You can tell, can't you?' Sage asked, stepping backwards again, her voice low and steady beside him. 'You know what's wrong with him.'

'Every time I touch him. It's like he's decided to let me in,' Ethan said, his fingers tracing a faint line along the horse's flank as he met her eyes. They were standing close enough to feel the warmth of each other's bodies without touching, and he willed himself not to move even closer or he'd have to give in and make love to her right here. 'He's been traumatised by humans. It's in the way he flinches at sudden movements, how his eyes constantly dart around searching for an escape.'

Ethan caught a glimpse of pride on her face as she looked at him, which was not how she'd looked at him before, when she'd clearly been wishing he'd never shown up at all. She ran a hand over Storm's soft neck. 'Is there anything we can do to help him recover fully?' Her question held hope, but the shadows beneath her green eyes told Ethan she understood their limitations. 'Or will he always be like this?'

'Time and patience,' he murmured. 'He's getting better. Trust doesn't come easy, not when it's obviously been shattered before.'

'Like with some people we know,' Sage agreed, and Ethan felt her words like a gentle accusation. He knew she was talking about him. Or maybe both of them?

'Sage, listen—' he started, stepping around the horse. But the moment was interrupted by a call from his dad. Oh, man. Dad had the kids and Jacqueline over. He quickly explained to Sage how Kara and Jayson were collecting honey and probably wanted to show him on a video call, and she nodded encouragingly, though he didn't miss the flash of despondency in her eyes as he spoke to his family, *oohing* and *aahing* over their finds, pretending he'd never seen any of it before, to amuse the kids. No sooner had he hung up than the sharp ring of the clinic's emergency bell sounded out. Without another word, both of them broke into a run.

Ellie was still caught up with their first patient in the treatment room, and Ethan recognised the kindly Barbara from the guest house, or Babs as everyone in Amber Creek called her, standing over her terrier. The dog lay whimpering on the examination table. His paw was swollen, and a thin line of blood seeped worryingly through his fur as Sage hurried to pull a white coat over her shirt and shorts.

'Marley jumped off the porch again,' Babs explained as Ethan pulled on his own coat. The woman who had been so kind to him at the guest house was wringing her hands, her usually warm face etched with worry.

'Let's check for fractures,' Sage directed. Her professional demeanour had kicked in again, full throttle. She went for the X-ray machine as Ethan moved to calm Babs.

'Marley's strong, Babs. We're going to take good care of him,' Ethan assured her, his hand firm on her shoulder. He didn't miss the look on Sage's face as she looked up; was that an expression of slight despondency on her face, the same as he'd seen outside? No time to think about it now.

Ethan helped Sage manoeuvre the terrier onto the radiography table. The machine hummed to life, casting a pale blue light over Marley's form as they positioned him gently. Ethan watched the rhythmic rise and fall of Sage's chest as she leaned over the operating table, her focus unwavering. The marks on her wrist were uncovered, healing well just as she was, but the sight of them only reminded him of how it had felt when she'd been lying so weak in his arms. She operated the controls while Ethan held the dog still, his hands firm yet comforting against the terrier's quivering body. So small and defenceless…as Sage had been that night, when he'd rushed her into the clinic after the snake had got its fangs into her.

'Good boy, Marley,' Sage whispered now, eyeing the animal as the X-ray did its silent work. Sage couldn't stand to see any animal in pain, especially dogs. It was like this for her every time, he imagined. And it would be after he was back home with Dad, and the bees, and his own horses.

The image soon appeared on the screen, revealing a minor fracture. Sage discussed the treatment plan with Babs, explaining the need for a cast and pain management. Ethan prepared the syringe with expert precision, his movements conveying the quiet confidence he knew would help ease Babs' distress.

'Will he be okay to walk on it?' Babs asked, her voice concerned.

'Absolutely,' he answered, before Sage narrowed her eyes slightly and continued before he could.

'But he'll have to take it easy for a few weeks. No more jumping up, or chasing sheep.'

As Sage applied the cast, Ethan observed the gentle way her fingers smoothed the edges, and how she spoke softly to Marley, reassuring the animal with every touch. Even so, she was annoyed about something now. It was plain to him, even if Babs wasn't picking up on it. Was she starting to resent him again, for befriending all her clients? he wondered suddenly. Amber Creek was so small, of course he'd got to know a lot of people here, and he'd showcased methods that had worked as well as hers, if not better sometimes. It didn't mean he was trying to take over.

'Thank you, both of you,' Babs said, relief flooding her features as she finally scooped Marley into her arms, the newly applied cast a stark white against his ruffled brown fur.

'Any time, Babs,' Ethan said, offering her a smile that he hoped had reached his eyes. When she left with Marley cradled close against her chest, he turned to find Sage watching him, a set of unspoken grievances lingering between them.

'You called her Babs,' she said, perching on the edge of the desk, pulling off her gloves slowly finger by finger.

'That's what everyone calls her,' he reasoned. What was the problem?

'Well, Babs loves you. Everyone knows you round here now,' she said. 'They all know you're leaving again soon, though. Once Storm is better. Which he is…he's almost better.'

He felt his eyebrows knit together. 'So *that's* what this is about,' he said sharply. 'Me leaving.'

'Well, you will be, won't you?' she said, standing up and tossing her gloves into the bin a little too hard. He heard her voice crack. The tension hummed between them like a charged circuit. 'Storm is like a different animal already.'

She crossed to the sink and turned the tap on full, as if she was trying to drown out the noise in her head. Ethan watched as the water cascaded over Sage's hands, the droplets splashing against the stainless steel. He knew she was struggling, her emotions churning beneath the surface as his had been for days. He stepped forward, the linoleum floor creaking quietly beneath his boots. With each step, he felt his heart beat louder in his chest, till he was right behind her. He reached out and turned off the tap, silencing the rushing water.

'Sage,' he said gently. Slowly she turned in his arms and looked up at him. Her green eyes held a mix of vulnerability and sadness that tore at his heart. Without hesitating, he closed the distance left between them and gently cupped her face in his hands. To his surprise she turned her head away, even though her lips trembled at his touch.

'No. This has to stop,' she said, her voice weak and shaky. She drew a hand across her mouth, as if she was intent on stopping him from even so much as looking at her lips.

'We didn't do anything,' he replied, feeling the weight of his unvoiced confession heavy on his tongue. God, he wanted her so badly, even if it was only one time. One delicious, thrilling, beautiful time. The guilt over these exact thoughts didn't sit well—she would never go for a one-time thing, and nor should she be expected to. But he had stopped what they'd started before this. And yes, he had then gone on to buy her gifts, sat at her side, folded her clean towels, ordered her a new coffee machine…which still had not arrived. No wonder she was as confused as he was.

'Yes, we *did* do something,' she said, running her fingers over her lips, meeting his eyes. 'It's not just about sex to me, Ethan. You've made me feel things I haven't felt before…for anyone.'

She screwed up her nose then, and stepped out from between his arms, moving to the other side of the room. 'You bought me books, and flowers…'

'OK, well, sorry?' This was confusing as hell. And ridiculous. He needed to confront this, whatever 'this' was between them. He couldn't leave with regrets, with what ifs haunting him across the miles.

'I don't know what's going on either,' he admitted, crossing to her again. She inched against the closed door, pressing her back to it, and he placed his hand gently on her arm, feeling the warmth of her skin beneath his fingertips, even through her lab coat.

'You know what you do to me—you've seen it. But I don't want to hurt you,' he said.

Which was true, even though the voice in his

head was screaming, *Liar! It's you who doesn't want to get hurt.*

'I'm not staying here. I can't—my life is in Queensland,' he heard himself say anyway. Maybe it *was* too soon after Carrie to trust someone else with his heart.

'And mine is here,' she said sadly, so close to his mouth he could feel the heat of her breath on his lips. 'So I guess that's that. It goes no further, Ethan.'

He studied her mouth in silence. Stuff that. It had nothing to do with Carrie being the last woman he'd been intimate with. It had everything to do with falling for Sage, plunging him straight back into a deep, dark funk that he'd only just climbed out of. *Coward.* Fear should not, and would not, dictate his choices any more.

Ethan closed the remaining distance between them, this time with an urgency that made her gasp as he finally captured her pink lips with his own. Their breathing grew heavier as they lost themselves. Moving one hand to his neck, Sage trailed it down to his chest as their tongues danced, no doubt feeling the pounding of his heart beneath his skin. Tugging her coat undone with one swipe, he pressed his body against hers, pinning her to the door with a new urgency that sprang from nowhere.

Sage folded against him in surrender, moaning softly into his mouth. Her breath hitched with anticipation and he leaned into the kiss, cupping her backside, squeezing it gently, then possessively. Her kisses and lips rained over his face, exploring every inch, and his hands roamed to her thighs, pushing them further apart as he grasped at her shorts, pulling them gently but firmly down to allow him access…

A knock on the door behind them made him shudder. Sage sprang out from under him, pulled up her shorts, and started buttoning up her coat. 'Coming!' she called, sounding delightfully flustered.

He felt himself grin. 'Really? I wasn't even close,' he whispered. She pretended to slap him, casting her eyes to the bulge in his jeans. He caught her hand and pressed his mouth to hers again hard, and she laughed under his kisses before letting her tongue dance seductively around his once more.

'I have to go,' she whispered frantically, pressing both palms flat to his chest. 'You should get back outside to Storm. The mayor will be here again soon.'

She made to open the door, first smoothing down strands of her hair that had fallen from her ponytail in their passion.

'Hey, Sage,' Ethan called after her, his heart hammering against his ribs with the adrenaline. Sage turned, a question in her green eyes as she touched a finger to her lips. There was no stopping this thing now, judging by the hope that flickered in her gaze, and the way he heard his own voice soften whenever he spoke her name. He was gone. A lost cause.

'Come riding with me, this evening,' he said. 'There's a place I found the other day I want to show you.'

He watched her expression shift through surprise, joy, and something akin to fear, before she took a deep breath. 'Sure, Ethan,' she answered, her smile finally reaching her eyes. 'Why not?'

CHAPTER FOURTEEN

THEY GALLOPED IN SILENCE, apart from the thundering hooves that broke the stillness of the night, sending up mini dust clouds that threw Ethan into a sandy blur ahead of her. Sage couldn't help grinning as the world was reduced to the wind's rush in her ears, and the magnetic pull of this incredible man riding beside her. She tightened her grip around the reins as her horse picked up speed, racing alongside Ethan on Karma.

The pale glow of the moon bathed the land around them in a silver sheen, turning the rugged landscape into an ethereal dreamscape that felt all the more surreal because she knew, at the end of this, that she would be making love to Ethan, if they still had the energy after last night. They'd shut themselves into her cabin, listening to the rain again, and he'd reached for her, pulling her closer as the jazz filled the air in her tiny living room, his hands moving with the gentleness of someone who was treating a wild animal with care. His touch still made her shiver, sending goosebumps spreading across her skin. She could feel the desire for him coursing through her veins every time, as if she could never get enough.

Night-time rides had become their unspoken ritual for the past couple of weeks, even in the recent rains. It could have been something to do with being out with him in particular, but Sage felt that the wild pulse of the land had started to call her: *Don't work so hard, get out of your head, come and be happy!*

The way he looked at her, the softening of those guarded blue eyes, told her she had helped take a battering ram to some of the walls he'd built around himself, and he had definitely brought something else out in her.

The part of her that had always been so capti-vated by nature and these beautiful, rugged land-scapes had been shaken fully awake. There were new reasons to breathe now, more space in her tired lungs to sync with her surroundings, and Ethan Matthews. Less time to tie herself to the past, and fewer reasons to feel trapped in the cage she'd locked herself into all this time. In Ethan's arms she was discovering parts of herself she hadn't even known existed.

'Where are we going?' she called to him now.

'You'll see. If you can keep up.'

Sometimes she could feel her heart swelling, as though it were learning how to adjust to being so full after so long. She caught another glimpse of Ethan's profile, determined as they started to race. When the moonlight hit him just right she could have sworn he was from another planet. Oh, Lord, this was completely crazy. This big, huge, all-consuming feeling for him had sprouted from a tiny seed of reluctant admiration into something she couldn't even define. There weren't enough words to express how she felt.

'Too slow!' he teased her now, kicking his heels to Karma and speeding on ahead, even faster towards the horizon, daring her to follow. Their first ride, he'd taken her to a waterfall she'd known about for a while, but she'd pretended she'd never seen it before. He'd known she was pretending, of course. So the next night, she'd shown him a special place she'd known he wouldn't have seen: a circle of earth-red rocks still boasting aboriginal art in red and black markings. After each escapade they would have sex…a lot of sex, everywhere, anywhere. It had started out as just sex anyway. The last couple of nights had definitely felt more as if they were making love.

The word felt so strange, even as it grew in her own head. Love. It was more like a kaleidoscope, constantly changing colours and patterns in her mind, leading her thoughts down different paths she hadn't dared to travel in a long time. It was overwhelming, but the world seemed different now, as if with Ethan at her side in work, and pleasure—a lot of pleasure—she was seeing everything through a different lens. Colours were heightened and vivid, details were clearer, her patients seemed to smile more around her because she was smiling more at them, and everything was tinged with a sense of wonder and magic.

With Ethan, she felt truly seen, and not just for the compassionate veterinarian she had come to be known as in Amber Creek's small community. He made her feel as if she could do anything. This profound connection they seemed to share had almost stitched the fragmented pieces of her heart back together. If only she could summon the courage to tell him she wanted him to stay.

If she said that, she might ruin it all, she thought now with a stab of fear, watching his broad shoulders as he took the lead again, the way the trees seemed to bend in the wind to welcome him. She would probably hear, 'I can't stay,' or, 'Don't talk about that now, let's just enjoy the moment,' and those words would cement the end of the spell for good. Obviously, this was too perfect to last. She knew he'd have to go back to Queensland. It was just something she was trying not to think about right now.

The fear of people disappearing without notice from her life had kept her life pretty small. Yes, she'd been successful with her career, but life had to be about more than making money; what was it for if you couldn't share any of it? She'd blocked out her need for companionship, stubbed it out like a cigarette by keeping herself busy, but the loneliness and emptiness had a habit of sneaking up on her anyway. Her empty home had echoed with it, till now. Now her humble cabin at the back of the clinic was filled with laughter and all the secrets she and Ethan shared in the dark.

Because of it, and because of him, she had even found the courage to reach out to Bryce. Wouldn't it be good to get some closure after all this time, confirmation that Ethan was right—that he'd left so suddenly because of some discrepancy or altercation over outstanding pay, or purely just because he wasn't into her, instead of because he'd taken offence over all those animals that had perished because she hadn't put the fire out in time?

'Woah!' Ethan's deep booming voice broke through her thoughts. They'd ridden to where the sands met the rainforest, but she couldn't quite figure out where they were exactly. Good thing she trusted Ethan, although since the last time they'd found themselves stuck somewhere for the night she had been careful to bring a spare two-way radio, just in case.

'We're here,' he announced as the horses slowed without another word from either of them. Sage realised her heart was pounding from more than just the exhilarating ride. In awe, she drank in the sight before her. The relatively hidden glade seemed to pulse with an alien glow under the moon. A ribbon of water reflected its beams, creating a desert oasis that felt as though it had been created just for them.

'I've never seen this place,' she said in wonder, following him forwards on her horse. It was as if they'd stumbled upon a secret that had somehow been kept for centuries.

'Welcome to Star Creek,' Ethan announced, his voice brimming with pride as he slid off Karma with ease. 'I found it when I was tracking that herd of wild horses the other day.'

Sage dismounted, her legs shaky not just from the ride but also from the pure beauty of the place. How was it possible she had never seen this before?

'I've never even heard of Star Creek,' she confessed as they both moved to tie up their horses, giving them a rest and a chance to drink from the creek. He looped his arms around her and pulled her close, dropping a soft kiss to her forehead that still sent sparks flying from her head down to her feet.

'That's because I named it myself. I think the recent rains must have helped it form,' he said. And she kissed him again because she could, and because, of course, this hot wizard had managed to find something out here in the nothingness that she'd never seen before. Together, they explored along the bank of the creek, their footsteps quiet on the soft earth. The air was alive with the sound of crickets and cicadas, and other nocturnal creatures. The serenade to the night was a living pulse, and her heartbeat matched its thrum as Ethan's hand found hers, their fingers intertwining naturally.

They settled near the edge of the oasis and Ethan pulled a bottle from his saddlebag. It was wine, he told her, aged and apparently special, saved for a moment such as this. 'Where did you get it?' she asked.

'Babs brought it over, to thank us for looking after her dog. You were with another patient so I thought I'd surprise you somewhere special.'

It felt as though she was the only woman in the entire world he'd ever looked at like this. Then he leaned down and drew her into a kiss that made her insides fill with balloons that threatened to float her up into the sky. He uncorked the bottle with a flourish and whipped out two glasses that he'd carefully wrapped in towels, handing her one so she could take the first sip. The wine was rich and full bodied, and as the taste of it filled her mouth, she let her head rest softly on his shoulder, looking up at the stars. This was perfection. Having him here with her was perfection. Maybe she should risk it and ask him about his plans after this—ask him to stay longer? Or would that seem too needy? Maybe she should just relax and leave it to fate and the stars, and see what unfolded naturally?

'Look at that,' he said, pointing upwards, and

she smiled as she caught the particularly bright star he meant, twinkling above them. 'That one seems new to me, what do you think?'

'It could be a UFO,' she teased.

He smirked. 'Take me to your leader.'

'Let's name it anyway,' Sage said, caught up in the moment. There were lots of them like this, filled with a kind of childlike excitement that Abigail declared was disgusting, even though she said it with the utmost affection. They suggested different names for the star as Ethan's fingers trailed softly along the back of her neck in slow movements that made her shiver with desire. They kissed for a long time before refocusing on the star.

'I want to call it Hope,' she said after a while.

'Hope,' Ethan echoed, his thumb brushing over her knuckles. 'I like that.'

'It used to be a pretty alien feeling to me,' she added with a sigh. There was no way she was going to tell him, but she really *hoped* he wouldn't decide he'd had enough of her company once Storm was fully recovered. She was filled with so much hope she was bursting with it some days, but somehow she couldn't bring herself to put him on the spot and ask him what this was exactly. What *were* they? It felt like more than just a fling, more real than anything she'd ever experienced in her whole life. It was unprecedented and had sprung up from nowhere and now that it was here, she couldn't imagine living without it. No one had ever made her feel like this, as if she could face anything.

With the taste of the wine lingering on her lips, she felt the confession bubbling inside her. It was no good, she couldn't keep it from him. 'I reached out to Bryce the other day,' she said finally, her words coming out slowly as she gathered up the courage.

'Bryce?' Ethan's hand stiffened around hers. Suddenly his expression turned impenetrable.

'I felt I needed to know why he really left the sanctuary, why he left…me. To give me some closure.' She watched him carefully, searching for any sign of understanding in his deep blue eyes.

Ethan released her hand and looped his arms around his knees, picking up his wine glass again and twirling the liquid in it around. 'And did he reply?' he asked neutrally, his voice level but distant. He was acting as though he'd retreated behind a wall all of a sudden.

'Not yet,' she admitted, a twinge of regret making her shuffle her boots. Did he think she was a bit silly for doing this, for reaching back into the past like this, looking for an affirmation that probably wouldn't even come? The silence stretched between them, her unspoken thoughts turning into heavy weights.

'Closure is important,' he said quietly, though

his eyes didn't meet hers. 'Unless you want him back, of course.'

What? Sage snorted in indignation. 'Why would I want him back? That was just a fling. It was nothing like what we have…'

Ethan tightened his lips.

Oh, no. Why did I say that?

She heard him release a deep breath through his nose as he studied the water, as if he couldn't risk meeting her eyes now. The words had just fallen out of her, she'd blurted them at him before she'd even had a chance to rein them in. Great, now she'd gone and admitted how obsessed she was with him, that she thought being with him was more than a fling, when he'd never mentioned it being anything at all.

'Do you need him to remind you that what happened to your family and the bushland around your home wasn't your fault, or are you ever going to start believing that for yourself?' he cut in quickly.

What? Sage's heart dropped into her boots. Why was he changing the subject away from him, and them?

'Because I've been telling you that for weeks,' he continued, 'and I'm sure Abigail has reminded you of it too. I would hope that, even if I'm not here, you'll at least remember that, Sage.'

Even if I'm not here… OK, then. Now she knew. She chewed on her lip, rocking on the spot as she hugged her knees. The words sounded so final, like a message he'd been waiting to clarify at the first chance he got. The silence grew louder and louder, until it rang in her ears and made her head hurt.

'I don't know what I want Bryce to say,' she said finally, realising it was true. She'd found the confidence to reach out, but she supposed it really didn't matter what Bryce said or did in response. His opinions of her had ceased to matter a long time ago. It was herself she'd always had issues with; her crippling fear of people entering her life and then leaving her again with nothing but ashes.

Ethan drank his wine quietly, and she wanted so badly to ask him what was on his mind, to ask if this was a fling or if it *could* possibly be more, if they both found the courage. But no... the mood was totally ruined now. He looked as if a storm was going on between his temples. Like Bryce, he *was* going to leave her. It was probably what he'd been thinking ever since they'd started whatever this was: that they'd just have sex and keep each other warm at night until he finished the job with Storm.

He'd never deceived her; he didn't do relationships. He'd told her that himself. He also had to go home; he'd warned her about that, too. He had a successful, thriving equine centre on prime, lush land, a million memories of his mother, and a father who still counted on him. She'd been so wrapped up in him, she'd conveniently forgotten all that…or more like chosen to ignore it.

Don't say anything, you'll just make it worse, she warned herself.

Instead, she took another sip of wine, letting the flavours distract her momentarily from the questions that had started to claw at the edges of her new-found confidence. This was going to end badly, so it would probably do her good to back off a bit, before it really was too late.

CHAPTER FIFTEEN

ETHAN STOOD, ARMS CROSSED, in the shadow-dap-pled stables, the sound of hooves stamping softly against the hay-covered ground blending with the distant hum of the bush. Mornings were quiet, peaceful. He was starting to enjoy them too, es-pecially the part where he woke up with Sage in her bed. He watched her now, unboxing the deliv-ery. It was finally here; it had taken ages to arrive. Mind you, he thought, everything did out here.

'Ethan, what did you do?' Her brow furrowed in puzzlement that quickly melted into surprise as she pulled off the last of the brown paper and got down to the giant square box.

'Is this…?' She trailed off, pulling the sleek new coffee machine from its cardboard confines, gasping in surprise.

'Don't drop it,' he said, swiping it from her quickly, biting back a smile. He loved nothing more than seeing this woman happy, even though he should probably get used to not seeing her smile, and not hearing her laugh, and not waking up next to her hair tickling his face on the pillow next to him.

'Figured we could use a decent shot of caffeine around here that we didn't have to kick something to get,' he managed, his own voice sounding gruff with attempted nonchalance.

'You're the best.' Sage's green eyes met his, and he caught them with his gaze. He knew her eyes by now, in every kind of light. He knew when she was genuinely happy, like now, and when she was retreating, holding something back, as she had been for the past few days, since he'd taken her to Star Creek.

'Thank you, Ethan. This means more than you know. The rest of the staff will be so thrilled!'

I did it for you, he wanted to say, but he didn't because she already knew. Well, she *should* know. Things had been a little weird recently, though, and if he was honest, her gratitude, simple and sincere, was perforating the tension that had been hanging between them like a heavy curtain.

They'd been close in the most physical of ways over the past weeks, their bodies moving and talking without words, and that had started to make him feel infallible. But even as their mouths and hands and limbs found their way under the sheets, or in the hay right here—clichéd as it was—he knew it would soon be his last night here, and the longer he tried to delay the inevitable, the more painful saying goodbye would be.

He couldn't move out here, he was too embedded in his homeland, in his business and his family, and why would any feelings she might have for him override her need to be where *she* belonged? He was not enough. As he hadn't been for Carrie.

'I thought you'd like it,' he said, stuffing his hands in his pockets to keep from reaching out to her. 'It's a good one, right?'

'Definitely a good one,' she agreed with a smile that didn't quite reach her eyes.

She turned to examine the machine, and Ethan's gaze lingered on the wavy chestnut hair falling like a sleek horse's tail down her back. There were so many questions now. They'd been coming at him for days like barbed hooks waiting to tear open the worst of his wounds.

Maybe she would find someone else soon—possibly even Bryce, if she listened to his explanation for leaving, understood it and forgave him. She'd have every right to, seeing as he himself didn't do relationships. This was the rock and the hard place.

He just didn't know if he could ever trust another woman with his heart. Carrie had been so thrilled when he'd slipped the ring on her finger, as if nothing could ever be more important than them or their relationship and their plans, and look how *that* turned out. Carrie could be barefoot and pregnant with Cam's baby by now, for all he knew.

The past kept clinging to him like a ten-tonne koala, strangling any ounce of courage he mustered when it came to really talking to Sage about what came after this. Dad and Jacqueline had both said he should ask her to come and visit Queensland, to try it out, to see if she might like it there. But his walls had shot back up that night at Star Creek, brick by emotional brick, and he still hadn't really let them down. The second she'd clammed up on him, he'd done the same. What he wanted, what he needed, really, was to not get in any deeper.

Damn it, man, you're always overthinking things. Just ask her to visit Queensland!

'Hey,' he heard himself say, the word slicing through the silence. 'So, I've been thinking…'

'About?' Sage prompted.

'Queensland.' The word felt like a stone in his mouth, heavy and hard.

She flinched. 'Ethan, I—'

The moment shattered with the jarring ring of her phone. Sage glanced at the caller ID, her expression shifting into something unreadable. 'Hold that thought,' she said, before she excused herself and stepped outside to take the call.

'Right,' Ethan murmured to no one, watching her go. His heart thudded in his chest. He had only managed to utter one word, with no context around it at all, and already his insides felt as if they were being mauled by jackals. Later, he would just put an end to this misery and initiate the conversation. He would ask her to come and visit him in Queensland. Maybe some form of long-distance relationship might work, while they figured this thing out?

'Please! She's been attacked by a croc!' Ethan's hands clenched at the sound of frantic footsteps rushing into the clinic. He turned from the guinea pig he was placing back into its basket as a middle-aged man burst through the doors, his face etched with panic. He was cradling a bloodied Blue Heeler in his arms.

'Help my Belle,' the man cried again as Ethan hurried with the guinea-pig cage. Sage was close behind him and he caught the flicker of panic on her face as the man gasped with fear and exertion. The dog, a sturdy, strong animal built for the terrain of the outback, lay limp, its breathing shallow and laboured. Deep gashes marred its side and leg. Raw flesh on show made a stark contrast to the dog's dusty fur, which was matted with blood.

'Get her to surgery!' Sage barked, and Ethan led the way, the man following close behind, their footsteps echoing down the small corridor and into the next room. Ellie met them at the door, her eyes widening at the sight of the wounded creature.

'This is an emergency, cancel my next appointment,' Sage directed, her voice steady but her eyes betraying the swell of emotions he knew must be breaking inside her. Another badly injured dog. There were a lot of dogs coming in and out of here, they were the most popular pets, of course, but he'd never seen one this badly injured before.

'Easy, Belle,' he muttered, catching for the briefest second a look of such profound fear and pain in her eyes that he had to swallow back a cry of his own. Together, they transferred the dog onto the stainless-steel table. Its surface seemed extra cold and unwelcoming, even to him, as the traumatised owner stood back, wringing his hands. Gloves snapped against skin, and tools clinked as they were laid out with careful precision despite the pounding hearts in the room.

'We have multiple puncture wounds and lacerations,' Sage observed, her brow furrowing as she assessed the damage. 'We need to stop the bleeding, fast.'

Ethan helped elevate the animal. With deft fingers, he began applying gentle, steady pressure to slow the bleeding while Sage worked to clean around the wounds so they could judge the severity of the attack. The dog whined softly, her body twitching with pain despite the sedatives they had quickly administered. At least she was alive, and breathing on her own.

'Easy, Belle, you're going to be okay,' Sage murmured soothingly, working on another deep cut with a concentration that bordered on reverence. Her hands moved with an expertise honed across her years spent dedicated to healing animals. He could feel how each of her movements and whispers and treatments was a silent promise to end the suffering before her, and, as it always did, his mind went to Sage as a kid, watching the flames of the bushfire, knowing her parents and her dog were dying right in front of her.

He'd been through hell, but nothing compared to what she had... How could he inflict any more suffering on her, asking her to come to Queensland, starting something he already knew would probably end badly, one way or another? Was that the kind of life she'd want, living off-grid with him and his dad, and the horses? Without the small support network she'd gathered around her? He could move here, he supposed... but then it wouldn't be fair on Dad, Jacqueline and the kids, or his mother's legacy, which they'd vowed to honour at the homestead. The equine centre he'd established wouldn't thrive here either, not on this dry soil. His heart sank.

'Scalpel,' Sage requested, without looking up. Ethan placed it firmly in her waiting palm and watched as she carefully excised a piece of embedded tooth from the dog's hind quarters. 'Got it,' she announced, holding up the jagged remnant triumphantly before dropping it into a metal tray with a clink.

How the heck did the crocodile's tooth end up there? he wanted to ask. It must have been an old croc, or maybe a really young one? The man didn't know, he'd been so panicked at the sight of his dog in its mouth that nothing else had really registered.

'Well done, boss,' Ethan said, and her eyes softened at the genuine admiration that laced his tone. 'Let's flush these wounds and get her closed up.'

Sage reached for the saline. Together, they irrigated each and every wound meticulously once more, making sure that no trace of infection would remain and put this creature on course for any more suffering. It was a dance they knew well by now, moving around each other with a synchronicity that made him wonder sometimes if he'd ever work with another vet this well again.

What might they do if they did make something work, if she wound up moving to Queensland with him? They could open a surgery there, as his father had always planned. Dad had been pretty disappointed initially, when he'd ended up with an actress from Brisbane as a future daughter-in-law instead of a qualified veterinarian who could help mould the family business into something beyond horses. Mum's dream of a self-sufficient life, and eco-conscious activities for the community, had only just started, really. There was so much still to do, and he would do it there, with Dad, while Sage remained here, honouring her own commitments.

They continued to work seamlessly, anticipating each other's needs, passing instruments back and forth without needing to speak, and the man looked on from the corner, his face a shade of grey Ethan recognised. A special shade that seemed to be reserved for the owners of beloved animals who were fighting for their lives.

Belle's breathing steadied as they worked. As Sage finished the very last suture, a palpable sense of relief flooded the room and he removed his mask. It felt as though he hadn't drawn a breath this whole time.

'She's going to be OK,' Sage said, peeling off her gloves and giving Ethan a tired smile.

'I can't thank you both enough.' The man's voice choked as he ran his hands along the dog's head and ears, tears glistening in the corners. They told him they'd have to keep her in to monitor her, and as the man slunk off in relief and exhaustion Ethan watched Sage watching Belle. Her dedication to her work, the way she fought for each life as if it were the only one that mattered, still stirred something in his soul. It was more than professional admiration; it was a growing affection and appreciation and happiness he felt around her that he couldn't compartmentalise. It was so soon after Carrie, though, how could he trust this was even real?

'So, that was Bryce on the phone in the stable, earlier,' she said suddenly into the silence.

He turned to her, feeling the muscles in his jaw tightening. Her attention was already shifting to the paperwork that needed to be filled out.

'What does he want?' Ethan asked, guarding his tone. He should feign indifference; besides, he had nothing to be jealous of.

'He wants to visit me,' she said coolly.

'Right.'

He watched as Sage's shoulders stiffened, her body language telling him how much she hadn't wanted to divulge this information, but had decided to anyway.

'It's OK, if you really still need him to visit you,' he said. 'But what do you want from him?'

Meeting her eyes, he encouraged her silently. She was free to tell him the truth, if she wanted. She could tell him how she still deemed herself responsible for the fire that killed her parents and all the animals, and that despite everyone reminding her it wasn't her fault, including him, she was rewriting the story in her own head where she was still guilty and undeserving of forgiveness.

'Why do you still need reassurance that the bushfire wasn't your fault?' he probed. Her eyes clouded over as she looked to the side and sniffed. 'Why didn't you talk to me before you contacted Bryce?'

'I don't know what you mean.'

'Talk to me, Sage, I'm right here,' he urged. Then he realised how it sounded and backed off as her eyes narrowed. She was like Carrie right now, refusing to talk to him, or even acknowledge that she wasn't happy, despite him asking her to just be honest with him. How many months, even years, had Carrie been sleeping with Cam before he'd found out? Their communication had broken down so slowly he'd barely noticed, till she was admitting the affair.

This was supposed to be different. He'd thought, despite the challenges they faced, that what he had with Sage was a world away from anything he'd had with Carrie. But right now Sage was shutting him out on purpose, edging him off the cliff while he was blind, and he was right back where he'd started.

CHAPTER SIXTEEN

Sage chopped carrots with rhythmic precision, watching the sky cloud over. Each slice was pretty much a futile attempt to silence the cacophony of shrieks and laughter that were echoing through Abigail's kitchen. The kids darted around them like wild spirits, their energy the total opposite to that of the quiet, calm horses the mayor was tending to outside the window. Bad weather was coming, and already she could feel the tension in the atmosphere…although maybe some of that was of her own creation.

'Bryce called me,' Sage confessed over the din, her knife pausing mid-motion. She'd been storing up this information since that phone call and yes, OK, she was nervous. Abigail always told her things how they were, no messing. 'He wants to come to Amber Creek, to talk.'

Abigail glanced up from where she was seasoning the chicken, her brow furrowed in confusion under her fringe. 'Are you going to let him?'

'I don't know,' she said, pulling a face.

Abigail tutted. 'Why would you even consider it? Didn't he walk out on you, never to be seen again?' She made a 'poof' motion over her own head with the oregano jar.

Sage sighed, pushing a loose strand of hair behind her ear. The weight of her thoughts pressing down on her was worse than last night without Ethan in her bed. At least she'd had Belle. The Blue Heeler was good company, and it was also easier to keep a close eye on her there. She'd have been pretty much alone in the kennel in the clinic.

'Ethan's been…different since I told him. He didn't even stay over last night. He just went back to the guest house.'

'*Why* did you tell him?' Abigail said, skewering a chicken breast with a sharp look in her eyes. 'What are you doing here, Sage?'

Sage let out a long sigh as her hands faltered. Setting the knife down, she turned to face her friend, admitting she wasn't even sure. Abigail accused her of trying too hard to protect her heart, and also of thinking she didn't deserve something real, like she seemed to be building with Ethan. She said Sage was deliberately inviting in drama that would push him away. That drama, of course, being Bryce.

'You're also freaking yourself out over the chance that something will happen to Ethan and he'll leave you one way or another. Sage, these are old demons of yours—we know them well.'

'Wow.' Abigail was so wise, as well as pretty beyond measure, and successful. For a moment Sage had to laugh at how much they must have shared during all those nights they were getting to know each other, drinking wine, confessing their sins and their darkest moments. Abigail was right, of course.

'Let it go,' Abigail said, clutching her hand and pressing it to her heart. 'Let all of that go, Sage, please.'

'I know I should…'

'Please. Ethan might be guarded, but you two have something special. I've seen it. When that snake got you, I swear I saw that man's heart working overtime. Ethan is head over heels in love with you. How did you do it, by the way?'

Sage absorbed her friend's words as Abigail stirred pots and picked up shoes and reminded her kids that this wasn't a zoo and that they were not animals. Whether she was right or not about Ethan's feelings, Abigail saw through all Sage's excuses, the crazy stuff inside her own head that had been holding her captive since the fire. It was true, she sabotaged everything that threatened to bring the slightest trace of upheaval into her life, the good as well as the bad, sometimes.

'Would you move to Queensland if he asked?' Abigail's question pierced through a fresh round of screeching by the kids.

Sage held the knife suspended as the gravity

of the question sank in. 'But he hasn't asked. He did once briefly mention Queensland but then dropped it.'

'Ah.' Abigail hummed, reaching for the pepper grinder, adding a twist to the pan. 'Well, this could get awkward pretty fast. He'll be here any minute.'

Sage almost dropped the knife. 'Ethan's coming?'

'Jarrah invited him, to say thanks for everything he's done with Storm.'

Sage drew a breath that was mostly pepper. A twinge of annoyance at the mayor's impromptu decision flitted through her mind—this was supposed to be a quiet, no-stress dinner between friends—but then she couldn't blame Jarrah; Ethan had charmed him as he had everyone else. Before she could probe any further into the sudden dinner arrangement, the sound of hooves on gravel told her he was here already. Her chest tightened on the spot as she saw him through the window and Abigail gasped.

'He's riding Storm!'

Sage took a moment to process that Ethan was actually here, arriving on the back of the horse that up to this point hadn't let anyone ride him. Storm was finally healed? She wiped her hands on the apron tied around her waist, suddenly more than conscious of her flour-dusted jeans and basil-scented fingers. Not that anyone was looking at her. Ethan was the man of the moment now, Charlie and Daisy, and even the eleven-year-old Lucie were all busy cheering and whooping at his arrival.

Finally, the back door swung open. Ethan stepped inside followed by everyone else. Sage held her breath as his eyes found hers immediately.

'Hi,' she said. The intensity of his gaze magnetised her. Her feet somehow moved across the floor without her knowing. She leaned in for a kiss, her cheeks warming just attuning to his presence. It was almost instinctive now, this greeting they had shared countless times in private. She almost couldn't have helped her body's reaction to him, even standing in her best friend's kitchen, covered in flour. But as the family scattered around her, all talking at once, Ethan's hand came up gently and rested on her shoulder.

'Best not,' he said softly, so only she could hear. 'I'm still working for the mayor, remember?'

Sage stopped short. 'But Jarrah knows about us,' she protested quietly, searching his face for clarity. Was this because of what she'd said before, about inviting Bryce here?

Ethan's jaw tensed. A flicker of something unreadable passed through his eyes before he composed himself. 'It's about keeping things professional in public,' he explained, his words measured but firm.

'Right.' Sage stepped back from him, panic gripping her heart. Abigail asked her to get the plates out and help her set the table and she got to the task, head whirring. She'd helped serve a hundred meals in this house, but now she felt clumsy, opening all the wrong cupboards. He was being weird. Because of Bryce, probably. She needed to apologise, tell him how ridiculous she was being, still needing any kind of closure from her ex. Abigail was right. Bryce was just another barrier she'd erected quickly to make sure Ethan couldn't hurt her. What if they made something work, she and Ethan, something incredible, but then Ethan decided he wasn't over Carrie, and that *she* had always been a rebound? Or what if he was thrown from a horse and died… God, it was just too much for her heart to cope with, all these boomeranging emotions.

'We made chicken,' she heard herself say as she placed a plate down in front of him at the table. Her fingers knocked a fork and Ethan caught it in his lap. His eyes went to hers for a brief hot second and the look in them made her hands tremble more. Wanting him. More, now he was being so different around her. More, now that she could lose him in a hundred different ways. Storm was finally healed and he was back where he should have been weeks ago, with his family, ready to be the horse Lucie had dreamed of. Which meant Ethan would be leaving.

Sitting next to Ethan, she tried to compose herself, feeling his body heat meld with hers even though he wasn't touching her. She could be the professional veterinarian she was, the one he wanted her to be right now, but he knew her now, he knew how to tune in. He could probably tell that just by doing what he'd done, refusing a kiss, he'd made her long for him all over again…

'So, bees, huh?' Abigail started talking about the honey he'd told them about, asking Ethan all about the permaculture project and the rain-collection system he and his dad had built.

What was Ethan's father like? Sage wondered. Would she ever know? What they were trying to achieve in Queensland sounded interesting too. More than interesting, it sounded like building a sustainable future in every sense of the word. There was no possibility of anything like *here*, it was too dry and dusty for most things to thrive, whereas her practice could, in theory, be moved anywhere. OK, she would have to start again, make new friends, new relationships, new clients, but she could do that, couldn't she?

Yes. You would move to Queensland if he asked you to. You would go anywhere with him. Because you love him with your whole heart!

She watched as Ethan sliced through the tender meat, his movements deliberate and controlled. He could barely seem to look at her, except for the occasional sideways glance, like a wolf checking in on its prey. Sage's mind was drifting now, zoning out, stealing more glances at Ethan. Maybe he *was* over Carrie, but he was worried about their whirlwind romance. He just didn't want his world to be smashed to smithereens again, any more than she did.

'Ethan,' she whispered, trying to catch his hand under the table.

He pushed her away gently, but firmly.

The longer they sat there, talking about horses and bees and farmers' markets, the further away she drifted, and the more she felt him letting her. It was like a light going out between them, with Ethan operating the dimmer switch. He was tired of her already, all of these emotions that she was only half sharing. If she didn't start being totally honest with him, as his ex hadn't been, he would go and he wouldn't come back, and who would blame him?

Sage heard a toy drop to the floor above their heads. Abigail and the mayor were now upstairs, doing their best to put the kids to bed, and the warmth had all but evaporated from the room. Ethan's eyes were on her, watching her when he thought she wouldn't notice. They were alone.

'Great dinner,' he said, leaning against the doorframe across the room.

She nodded, unsure how to articulate the feeling of being on the edge of a confession that could turn her life around. He had no idea what he was doing to her, all these emotions buzzing through her, but she'd invite herself to Queensland if he didn't do it first.

'Your parents would be so proud of everything you've achieved here, Sage,' he said, his voice low. 'But, look, I didn't come here looking for anything serious.'

What?

His words hit her ears first. Everything felt hotter as the statement hit her brain, and then got at her heart, stones hurled onto glass. Ethan watched her, his expression guarded.

'What do you mean?' she stammered.

'I mean, I'm not here to start a relationship with you,' he said plainly.

His face was so dark now, and he wouldn't look at her.

'Is this because of Bryce?'

'No. Let's not forget our reality,' he said. 'This was always going to be temporary.'

The word 'temporary' echoed through her and hollowed out her belly. Temporary felt the same as worthless, as if he was off to better things already. Her heart clenched tightly, as if his actual fist had squeezed it.

'Is that truly what you want?' she asked numbly. Ethan's eyes would still not find hers. The ground felt as if it were opening up beneath her, as if everything he'd given her physically till now, the safety, the comfort, the reassurance, the love, was being retracted slowly but purposefully, as if he were pulling what was left of the snake right out of her. 'Is this because you're scared I'll run away with someone else, like Carrie did?'

'It's for the best.'

'I don't believe you.'

His face was set, his cheek turned slightly, but she stood there in silence until he was forced to look at her. Holding his gaze, she projected what she hoped was loathing and anger and disappointment, but the more he held her stare and worked his jaw, and curled his fingers to his sides, the more she knew she was only telling him she loved him. Daring him to break first. Daring him to tell her he wanted her. The more he ignored her silent confession, the harder she projected it, and the harder he rejected her.

Then he turned his head away and the slight almost sent her collapsing to the floor.

'I read you all wrong, Ethan.'

'I just wanted to make it clear, before I go,' he murmured. 'I don't want there to be any misunderstandings between us.'

Sage nodded, walking to the window and fixing her eyes on Storm, chomping on grass in the floodlit yard. There was no way in hell he was getting the satisfaction of seeing her break down and beg him to take her with him.

'Sage… I'll be leaving first thing tomorrow.'

'Go,' she said, her back still turned, where he could only see her legs shake, and not her face. Her eyes had crinkled into wet slits and her stomach was threatening to make her sick. 'Go then, Ethan. I'll tell Abigail and Jarrah you had an emergency.'

She heard his feet shuffling on the floor for a moment.

Do not turn around. Do not give him the satisfaction. Do not call out that you love him.

He left without another word. The sound of the front door closing behind him punctuated the end of their conversation, right as Abigail appeared on the stairs.

'The mayor's doing story time—' she started.

Sage slumped into a chair. Abigail rushed to her side, urging her to explain what had happened. How could those words have just come from Ethan's mouth? Abigail told her all the right things, like he was probably just freaking out and pushing her away because men were incapable of processing their emotions in a way that actually included open communication. She told her to go after him and tell him how she felt.

'I tried to, already!'

'Did you? Did you say those actual words? I love you, Ethan?'

Sage growled into her hands. He knew, he knew what she felt without her saying it. So why couldn't she just say it for real?

'You don't think you deserve him,' Abigail observed. 'But what if you're what *he* needs, Sage?'

This was ridiculous. She needed to be brave for once. Ethan had as many walls up and blind spots as she did. She'd been so focused on her own woes that she'd forgotten his. Just being around Ethan had been like opening a door she hadn't even known was there—one that had all the happy things hiding behind it. There was no guarantee that Ethan would reciprocate her feelings, or even talk to her if she followed him to the guest house and sat on his suitcase to stop him packing it. But there was no peace left in the 'what ifs' and 'maybes' any more. Things had gone well beyond that.

CHAPTER SEVENTEEN

ETHAN STOOD AT the window, his gaze fixed on the horizon as the first drops of rain on the guesthouse balcony started tapping against the plants. Telling Sage he didn't want a relationship—why had he done that? Even the word relationship did not sum up what he'd imagined he'd have with her. It had been the same story the entire time he'd been here, knowing he wanted her, but knowing what had happened the last time he'd felt like this. Going through that again could hollow a man out.

He glanced at the caller ID on his buzzing phone. Jacqueline. 'Hey, sis.'

'Ethan—did you book your return flight yet? The kids are asking when you're coming to finish that game of Jenga with them. You know, they haven't touched it since you left.'

His tone was nonchalant, bordering on dismissive as he told her about the flight delays and the storm, but she saw right through it. 'OK, what's wrong?'

There was a softness to Jacqueline's prompt that loosened his tongue. He explained what he could, how he'd blown something small out of proportion in his head. She asked if he was feeling overwhelmed because it was happening so soon after Carrie, and he stopped himself saying, *Yes, everything is because of Carrie,* because what was the point? He said nothing and Jaqueline, who knew him, told him he wasn't giving things a fair chance, because Carrie was not Sage.

He bristled at the comparison, unsure how to articulate the fear of being vulnerable again that had rooted itself so deeply in his bones. Instead he paced the wooden floorboards and kicked at a fallen coat hanger.

'It was just a bit of fun, you know, and I took it too far, and now… I have to forget about her.'

'Ethan. Why don't you just give her a chance?'

'I don't want to give her a chance.'

Jacqueline sighed deeply and he almost felt her eyes roll. 'Well, you're an idiot, even though I love you. Sounds like you love *her*, too. Just remember the love, brother, and you'll be fine. I gotta go.'

Ethan clenched his fist as she hung up, the phone still tight against his ear. His breath hitched. 'It's not love,' he muttered into the emptiness, as if he could possibly convince the walls— or himself at this point. 'I do *not* love Sage.'

The words fell flat. The lie felt like a physical ache in his chest as he paced the cramped space between the bed and the window. 'Sage doesn't need someone like me. She's better off alone.' Even as he said it out loud, he was picturing her laughter, all the times she'd caught him kicking the old coffee machine. When Sage forgot herself and the pain and guilt she wore like a badge of honour, she had the kind of laugh that stopped time. *All you want to do when you hear a laugh like that,* he thought, *is keep it going, and lose your own dark thoughts in the light.*

As long as he lived he would never stop seeing the way she'd looked just now when he'd hurt her with his words. She'd looked as if she'd never laugh again, as if he'd stolen something new and precious and irreplaceable, something maybe he'd gone some way to providing, right out from under her. And he loved her even more after he'd done it, because no one had ever looked at him with that much love, especially when he was taking it away.

All the times he'd told himself he didn't want a relationship bucked at his insides; it wasn't true, not when it was Sage. It was just…impossible… to know for certain that she wouldn't come to his home and be with him, and his father, and his horses, and promise him for ever, and make him want to have her babies, and then do the same thing Carrie had done. Not that she would do that—she wasn't Carrie—but how could he really be sure something else wouldn't go wrong, and take him right back to square one? He just had to trust that she wouldn't. He *could* trust her not to hurt him, he realised. But now he'd gone all out to ruin what they had on purpose. If she never forgave him, he wouldn't be surprised.

He tried to call her. It rang off. Of course, why would she pick up the phone to him now? She was probably fuming. He knew she didn't really want Bryce here. And instead of sympathising with her attempts to protect herself, and giving her the reassurance that she still needed, or fighting for *them* and telling her to forget Bryce and come and see his home in Queensland instead, where she could make love to him in the study, and the cabin and the greenhouse, meet his horses, meet his sister…instead of doing any of that, he'd shut her down.

Dialling her again, he bit his nails and waited. And waited.

She's clicked off again!

'Tomorrow,' he growled, eyeing the fierce storm. The word felt like less of a promise to himself and more like a lifeline right now, some remaining tiny tether to the kind of life he could have with her if he'd just get out of his own damn head and reach for it.

Tomorrow he would find Sage and mend what

he'd smashed to pieces—or, at the very least, try and explain to her why he'd felt the need to break it in the first place.

Sage was seething. She'd been seething when she'd gone to sleep after getting back home in the rain, and now, waking up after only an hour to the ominous skies overhead, she was even angrier.

How dare he humiliate me like that? But I still love him.

'Come here, girl,' she said to Belle, putting a plate of kibble down close to the Blue Heeler on the bed, so she wouldn't have to walk for it on her bad leg. Realistically it probably wasn't right to have the dog on the bed, but she'd been such good company last night after what she'd overheard from the other side of that guest-house door.

'It was just a bit of fun, you know, and I took it too far, and now I just have to forget about her... I don't want to give her a chance.'

Sage pressed her face into the pillow. It smelled of him, his scent, the animal and the gentle lover, taking turns to savour and worship her, giving her space and time to explore him in return. She'd seen inside him. Let him inside her.

How could I have been so stupid over this man, so many times?

'I went there to make things right,' she said, tossing the pillow to the floor. Belle swiped her hand with her hot tongue in understanding. 'I mean, I actually thought I would hear him say he wanted me to at least go with him to Queensland. I thought he was going to say we should try. As if men just change like that!'

Thinking back to the tone of his voice through the door, it had struck her more than his words. He'd made it very clear that whatever had been between them, it wasn't what she'd thought. '*I do not love Sage*,' he'd said, definitively.

To think how determined she'd been, marching to the guest house earlier this evening…then realising she didn't know his room number. And she didn't have a key. And she'd left her phone at Abigail's. It was still there, probably tucked down the sofa on silent mode. She'd set it that way in case Bryce called back; she would have to let him know she didn't want him to visit any more, but it was too much to deal with now. What a mess.

After Babs had let her into the guest house and pointed to Ethan's room, which weirdly she had never been to this whole time, she'd raised her hand to his door and prepared herself to show him exactly why it would be a crime not to see if this connection could be something worth salvaging…and expanding…for a little bit longer. Or for ever. This kind of emotional roller coaster was a sign that the path was right for both of them, but obviously the way there was always going to be rocky, considering the challenges that faced them.

But then, Ethan had been on the phone, probably to his father or sister. Oh…what an idiot she'd made of herself going over there. He was probably at the airport now, counting down the minutes till they started rescheduling the flights. Her heart burned till the anger turned to tears that threatened to soak poor Belle's head.

A crash of thunder. Sage sat up and blinked in shock. Great, a storm was definitely on its way. 'Stay here,' she ordered Belle. 'I have to go check on the other animals.'

The isolation pressed in on her as she checked on the few animal patients they had—a tortoise, a cat and a wallaby. It wasn't unusual for her to be alone in the clinic, her patients often kept her at work long after the others had gone, but now, on top of everything with Ethan, the solitude felt a lot like abandonment. The air was thick with electricity, too, a tangible intensity that put her even more on edge.

Another crash, closer this time, sent a jolt of dread to her bones. It sounded too close for comfort. She whipped around, her eyes landing on the window. The sight rooted her to the spot.

No, no, no, not again!

A bolt of lightning must have struck her cabin. Smoke was curling out from somewhere she couldn't see. Fear knotted in her stomach. Not again, she couldn't face this again!

Then… 'Belle! Belle is in there.'

Somehow, Sage forced herself to the phone and called in the emergency. They'd take too long to get here, though. The flames were erupting from the roof now, greedily devouring shingles and wood with an insatiable hunger as her legs propelled her outside. The cabin was fully ablaze and poor Belle was still trapped inside. The world seemed to pitch and toss as Sage took a step forward on trembling legs.

'Belle!' she called out, as if the dog might appear through the closed door. The flames before her eyes were dancing with an eerie familiarity. She was back to that night again, when the same orange tongues of fire had greedily licked at the tents and trees and sky and robbed her of everything she'd known and loved. The sheer magnitude of what she was about to do settled in her chest like lead. The same terror rendered her immobile as a frightened child, clawing at her insides and threatening to paralyse her again.

But… Belle. The thought of the poor dog, trapped and afraid, spurred her forward. She wasn't a child any more. And she could finally see, through adult eyes, that what had happened back then had never been her fault. She had let the guilt and fear eat her up, and now she'd lost the love of her life to Queensland. But there was no way she was letting Belle die today. Belle needed her.

Sage dashed towards the cabin, the heat radiating off the structure, pushing back against her advance. Miraculously the front door was still clear; the lightning must have struck at the back.

Come on, Sage, you can do this.

The door was a barrier of heat, but she forced it open with both hands. Smoke billowed out to greet her and met with the dust in the wind. Her vision impaired, she coughed, her eyes stinging as she searched for the bedroom door through the haze. The glow of the fire crept under the door to the kitchen and painted monstrous shadows on the walls like a gallery of all her worst fears coming to life.

You can do this.

'Belle!' Her voice was a desperate plea, hoarse and cracking. Smoke cloaked her as she staggered over the threshold, her lungs screaming for clean air. She could barely see a thing, but she wasn't backing away this time. She would not let history repeat itself. There was no way the fire was taking anything else from her, not if she could help it.

But before she could move any further, a firm hand clasped around her arm, wrenching her back. Ethan stood there on the porch, solid and unyielding, his deep blue eyes boring into hers with an intensity that matched the heat. His ute was behind him, the engine still running.

'Sage, what are you doing?'

She shook her head, wild and frantic. What was

he doing here? 'Belle is in the bedroom, Ethan! I have to—'

His expression shifted as he coughed, something like understanding softening the hard lines of his face. 'Stay here,' he ordered her. Without another word, he released her and sprinted past her, the muscles in his back flexing beneath his shirt as he propelled himself towards the bedroom.

'Ethan!' she screamed after him.

Her heart lurched into her throat as she watched him disappear into the smoke. She screamed his name again, but it turned into a cough. Reluctantly she stood back. Sirens wailed somewhere in the distance and her hands clenched into fists at her sides. The possibility of losing him strangled her with every second that ticked by with her pulse hammering in her ears.

Why had he come back here anyway, after everything he'd said to whoever it was on the phone? Unless she'd missed a piece of the puzzle somehow. She'd been rattled and upset; she could have been creating another narrative, as she'd probably done about Bryce! That fortress Ethan had built around his emotions—he'd just smashed that completely to pieces by coming back here despite the fierce storm, obviously to see her. And now he'd dived into the blaze for her, for Belle.

'Ethan!' Her voice was a raw, guttural cry as she sank back into the depths of terror. The clinic behind her felt like another world, safe and sterile, while she stood here, heart thundering against her ribs, literally on the precipice of her worst nightmare. He had gone after Belle, for her, without a second thought. What if he didn't come out? His selflessness was a blade to her heart suddenly— what if she lost him, too?

The sirens grew louder. She imagined him struggling against the smoke and heat in there and desperately tried to hold onto her belief in his strength and resourcefulness. He was the strongest person she knew! But doubt crept in just as fast, whispering that maybe she was wrong. Maybe he wasn't strong enough. Fire took everything away and she knew it. Seconds felt like hours. Her mind conjured images of him overcome by smoke, succumbing to the heat, and she shook her head fiercely, trying to dispel the thoughts. No, he *was* strong, he could do this.

'Please, Ethan,' she whispered, her voice breaking. 'Please.'

How long had he been gone? Thirty seconds? It felt like a lifetime. The heat pushed against her as if warning her back, but she took a step forward, then another, her body moving with a will of its own. She couldn't let fear paralyse her again, not when it mattered most. She was about to go in after him, when a silhouette forged through the smoke. 'Ethan!'

He was grey from the ashes, arms cradling the limp Belle. 'Get back!' he commanded, his voice rough with smoke but edged with an iron-clad resolve as he urged her away from the door, back to the forecourt. Sage turned to see firefighters jumping out of their truck, unravelling hoses and yelling commands to each other as their battle with the blaze consuming her home began. The urgency of the scene, and the fact that her home and everything in it were being destroyed, barely registered with Sage; all that mattered in that moment was the man in front of her now, leading her through the doors to the smoke-free clinic. The phone was ringing off the hook.

Belle squirmed in Ethan's grip, coming to life as the fresh air filled her lungs. The relief was overpowering as he laid the dog down carefully. With the chaos unfolding outside, Sage reached up and pulled him into a kiss that she hoped held all the words she'd left unspoken, and could barely have uttered if she'd tried.

'Ethan,' she choked out eventually, hands in his ash-filled hair, her voice croaky from smoke. 'I would never have survived losing you! What are you doing here?'

Ethan's expression softened as he put one large hand to the back of her neck and drew her against him. 'You were about to run into the fire,' he

said in awe, stroking her cheek with his thumb.
'You! Sage, do you realise what could have happened to you?'

'I couldn't let Belle die.'

'And you would have done the same thing for
your parents, if you could have. If you hadn't been
a terrified child back then. Do you see that now?'

She closed her eyes, pressed her forehead to
his. 'I know, I do know that.'

'I was talking to my sister about you,' he admitted, his voice carrying over the tumultuous
sounds of gushing water and men shouting, and
the phone still ringing off the hook. 'She kindly
reminded me I was in denial…but I love you,
Sage. I do. I've fallen in love with you.'

Sage's heart hammered against her chest as he
kissed her again, and Belle sat up, confused but
perfectly fine apparently.

'I overheard you talking,' she said, her lips still
an inch from his. 'In the guest house… I came to
talk to you after you left Abigail's. I thought—'

'You thought what?' Ethan's brow furrowed,
his concern palpable.

'I thought you said you *didn't* love me. That
we were just having fun or something.' A bitter
laugh escaped her lips, and she shook her head.
'But I only caught part of it, didn't I?'

Ethan cupped her face, his thumbs gently wip-
ing away the ash that must have been coating her
cheeks as much as his. 'You heard the fear talk-

ing, Sage. My fear of admitting what I really feel for you. But I want you to always talk to me, always tell me everything, OK? We can work anything out, as long as we talk about it.'

She saw it then—the way his eyes shimmered with intensity, the way his hands trembled ever so slightly as they held her. It was raw vulnerability, and it struck at the very core of her being. She hadn't been honest about why she'd really considered asking Bryce here—as if she needed to hear anything from him at all when she had Ethan right here, painting a picture of the truth, plain and simple.

'I've been pushing you away, Ethan, I have, because I was scared,' she confessed, 'of losing someone I love all over again. And you—'

'Guilty as charged,' he said softly, tipping her chin up to meet his gaze. 'I think you should come to Queensland. What do you think?'

Sage felt a shift inside her that felt like chains falling off. She could hardly help her smile as his hands found hers. 'I hope you're not just saying that because my house just burnt down,' she teased.

'I'm saying it because I've fallen madly in love with you,' he replied, a grin tugging at the corner of his mouth. 'How many more times do you want me to say it?'

'As many times as you like, don't ever stop,'

she said, kissing him again. In that moment she knew she would go anywhere with him, and for him. Everything was going to be just fine.

EPILOGUE

SAGE PERCHED ON the edge of the veranda, her feet barely grazing the sun-warmed wood beneath them. She took a slow sip of the honey lemonade they had made together yesterday with Kara and Jayson, and some of the other kids from the local school, loving how the sweetness of it danced on her tongue. Ethan sat beside her, his gaze scanning the horizon where the new horse with the limp would soon appear.

'When does it get here?' Sage asked, breaking the comfortable silence that had settled between them as he sat at the long wooden table, addressing a file of paperwork.

'Soon. I'll have my work cut out with this one, but we'll get there,' he replied, his tone reflecting the calm certainty that always surrounded him when it came to his equine patients here at the homestead.

'You always do,' she told him. There was always a steady stream of horses coming in and out and most days Ethan spent his time outside with them. Occasionally he would fill in at the small clinic they'd just opened on the property, but that was her project really. Setting up a whole new practice in Queensland hadn't been too complicated in the end. Of course, she missed her regular patients, but Ellie and Billy had a new chief vet now, with the fees coming out of Amber Creek's budget, and the community was thriving even without her. And now she had a growing rota of even more regulars and wonderful connections, with both the local animals and people. She had also joined a book club and a swimming club in an effort to socialise outside work; something she hadn't dreamed of doing before, when she'd been too busy judging herself in her own head to make many friends.

The dogs, a ragtag crew of rescue mutts, were sprawled out in contentment around their feet. Their tails thumped in lazy acknowledgment any time one of them was addressed. Their presence was a comforting constant to Sage these days, a reminder of the simple pleasures that life on their little homestead had brought her since the move, although, as hard as they tried, they would never add as much comedy value as Joey.

Sage glanced over to the paddock, where their rescue kangaroo was engaged in his own brand of morning exercise. With each buoyant leap, Joey seemed to defy the very notion of gravity, and a chuckle escaped Sage as she watched him dart after a bird. It was impossible not to find him funny; the kids all loved him.

'You know, he can hop off anywhere, whenever he wants,' Ethan said, catching her eye with a shared sense of amusement. 'But he chooses to hang out around here. Because you rescued him as a baby. You're his mother now.'

'I hope he never leaves,' she told him, her laughter fading into a softer smile. Her hand drifted instinctively to her stomach, resting gently on the curve that had only just begun to show. Three months along, and already the life within her stirred a protective love she hadn't known she possessed.

Ethan stood, and in seconds his big hand was covering hers, the strength in his fingers a reassurance. 'How are you feeling? Any more morning sickness?'

'Better today,' she admitted, more than grateful for his unwavering support in what would have been a somewhat jarring experience without him, feeling her body grow and change day by day. His fierce protectiveness had been a surprise at first, especially when he'd refused to let her ride anywhere alone, but now she knew it was all born from his love for her.

'Remember, no overdoing it,' he said, his thumb brushing across her skin in a tender caress. 'That includes worrying about our new arrival.'

Sage smiled. 'Promise,' she whispered, watching a bee hover over the plants she'd just potted along the edge of the veranda. The new irrigation system was a success, and they'd even given a workshop the other day in town, teaching others how to harvest greywater and rainwater, as she and Ethan had done in Amber Creek before bringing the new skills here with them. Sometimes she thought about that place, how it had all been rebuilt after the fire. Only her record player had been salvaged. Abigail and the mayor had brought it over when they'd come to visit, and she kept it here now, in what was going to be the baby's nursery.

She inhaled the scent of eucalyptus from the surrounding trees, letting it steady her nerves. Ethan looked up, his deep blue eyes reflecting a curiosity that told her how attuned to her he was. 'What's going on?' he asked.

'I've been thinking,' she began, 'about names for the baby.'

'Have you, now?' His lips curved into an expectant smile, lemonade forgotten.

'Actually, I already have one in mind.' She watched his face, seeking assurance, needing to know if he agreed with her. 'I was thinking… about naming him after my father if it's a boy. Or my mum if it's a girl.'

Ethan's reaction was immediate, his happiness sending butterflies swooping through her. 'Anthony or Caroline. I love that. Your parents would be honoured,' he said, and the excitement in his tone gave way to a warmth that wrapped around her heart.

'Really?' The doubt in her voice was a whisper of her old fears, but she let it wash away as he dashed his hands through his hair, grinning before kissing her and lifting her from her feet.

'Absolutely,' he affirmed, pulling back just enough to meet her gaze again. 'It's perfect.'

The creak of the veranda gate made them both look up. Ethan's father, John, emerged from his part of the homestead, a basket of eggs in one hand. He offered a knowing grin as he caught the tail end of their intimate exchange.

'Morning, you two,' he called out, approaching with a stride as familiar as Ethan's. 'Fresh eggs for breakfast.'

'Thanks, Dad.' Ethan shifted his stuff to make room for his father at the table.

Sage studied John's face. It was etched with the wisdom of years and the kindness that he always seemed to bestow on her when she needed it most. Living with Ethan's father on the property was great. Not only did the two of them seem to have endless topics to discuss whenever it was just them, but he'd brought an unexpected kind of solace too. While her adopted father and mother had visited several times already and always made the place feel more like home, in a way, John was filling a void left by her own biological dad's absence. It wasn't the same, of course—nothing could be—but it was a comfort that further dulled the edges of her loss, and she knew without a doubt her own parents would have loved him too. They would have loved this whole place.

'Any special plans for today?' John asked. The twinkle in his eye suggested he knew more than he let on.

'Just taking it easy,' Sage replied, sharing a glance with Ethan. Sometimes she wondered if they'd ever been caught making love; it was impossible to always keep quiet, and John had a habit of pottering about the place on his chores in the yard. Luckily he was pretty relaxed about that sort of thing. Ethan had said before now that his dad was different now, less shrouded in grief, and more like he used to be. He insisted they had Sage to thank for bringing a new lease of life to the property, but Sage knew Ethan was probably different too. They were both a work in progress, but somehow they made things work. Communication was everything. And their love.

'I was thinking I might make some calls today, tell people about the baby,' she said.

'Good, good.' John nodded. He glanced at Ethan, his voice softening. 'You know, I'm so proud of the family you're starting, son. It's going to be good for you, for all of us.'

Sage's heart swelled. Ethan reached under the

table and gave her hand a squeeze. 'Let's call Abigail first,' Ethan suggested. His blue eyes sparkled with the kind of anticipation that made Sage's heart do a somersault. The news they were about to share was big, life-changing and, oh, so gossip-worthy. Abigail was going to flip out, not least because this had happened so soon after the wedding.

Sage had only just come off birth control when the faint blue line on the pregnancy test had had her weeping with both joy and fear in the toilet cubicle of a Brisbane shopping centre. Fear because she hadn't the faintest idea how to be a parent. Ethan had soon taken that fear away though. He always liked to say that they could handle anything together, and she knew just by looking around this place that he was right.

Sage watched him dial, her fingers absently tracing the rim of her lemonade glass. 'Abigail? It's Ethan. Could you put me on speaker? Sage has something to tell you.'

The line crackled slightly before Abigail's familiar voice filled the air, bubbling with warmth. 'Hey, you two! To what do I owe the pleasure?'

'Hi,' Sage chimed in, her pulse quickening. She took a deep breath, feeling Ethan's supportive gaze upon her. 'We wanted to tell you first… I'm pregnant.'

There was a moment of stunned silence before Abigail erupted into squeals that could have woken the entire countryside. 'No way! Are you serious? Oh, my goodness, congratulations!'

Sage laughed, relief flooding through her. Sharing this secret with her best friend had just lifted a weight she hadn't realised she'd been carrying. 'We're over the moon,' she confessed.

'I wish I could hug you right now!' Abigail cried, and the longing in her voice travelled across the miles, making Sage blink back a sudden tear.

'Us too,' Ethan agreed, his strong hand finding Sage's again.

'Remember the wedding, Sage? When the kids chased the chickens around the coop and collected eggs like they were treasure? They'll have a little cousin to teach them all the farm tricks too, soon,' Abigail mused aloud, sending Sage's mind drifting back to that day five months ago.

'It was a great day.'

'It was magical,' Abigail agreed as they reminisced. 'They've been asking to help sort the recycling and throw coffee on the compost heap ever since. I don't know how you did it. They want to visit you again soon.'

'They're always welcome.' Sage smiled, picturing her friend's children's faces all lit up with wonder...dirt smudged on their cheeks despite their best smart outfits for the wedding.

'Speaking of warm welcomes, we should let you go. We've got a new horse coming in today that needs some love and care,' Ethan interjected, mindful as always of their responsibilities.

'Of course, you busy bees,' Abigail said playfully. 'Take care of yourselves, and that little miracle too. Love you both.'

'Love you too,' they echoed before hanging up.

Sage leaned back in her chair, the lightness in her chest spreading through her entire being. She glanced at Ethan, who was already lost in his thoughts, watching the gates for the horse. She could barely believe she'd got so lucky. How had it happened to her? Soon they'd be nurturing more than just animals here; they'd be raising a child of their own.

'Are you going to be OK here for a while, Mrs Matthews?' Ethan asked as the horse and its owner appeared ahead. He reached across to tenderly brush a strand of hair from her face, then bent to drop a kiss to her belly.

'Always, Mr Matthews,' she replied, her eyes locking with his. Sage knew without a trace of doubt that she was home, and safe, and for as long as he was with her, she always would be.

* * * * *

An Irish Vet In Kentucky

Susan Carlisle

MILLS & BOON

Susan Carlisle's love affair with books began when she made a bad grade in mathematics. Not allowed to watch TV until the grade had improved, she filled her time with books. Turning her love of reading into a love for writing romance, she pens hot medicals. She loves castles, travelling, afternoon tea, reading voraciously and hearing from her readers. Join her newsletter at susancarlisle.com.

Visit the Author Profile page
at millsandboon.com.au for more titles.

Dear Reader,

It's with great pleasure that I wrote this book. I have attended the Kentucky Derby and enjoyed it so much that I wanted to share those moments with you. The fact I had the opportunity to revisit that exciting time was fun. I hope you enjoy Christina and Conor's love story against the backdrop of Churchill Downs and the greatest two minutes in sports.

I love to hear from my readers. Please contact me at susan.carlisle@ymail.com.

Happy reading,

Susan

DEDICATION

To Thomas

I'll love you forever.

CHAPTER ONE

CONOR O'BRIAN STEPPED into the dim stable hall to a view of a female behind encased in dusty jeans, raised in the air and swinging back and forth. For the first time in a long time, he took a moment to admire the well-developed lines of a woman's firm bottom.

He cleared his throat to gain her attention and adjusted his focus. "Excuse me, but I'm looking for the owner."

The woman straightened then shoved the pitchfork she held into a pile of loose hay. With a swift practiced move, she flipped it off the fork over a stall wall. Dust floated around her in the stream of light coming in through the doors.

"Hello," he said louder.

She whirled, making her rust-colored ponytail whip round her head, the pitchfork held like a weapon. With a slim build, the plaid shirt, jeans and boots covered the curves he'd admired earlier. What caught his attention was the sparkle in her brilliant green eyes. Ones that reminded him of the countryside at home after a rain.

"Ho. Ho." He threw up his hands and stepped back. She stood almost as tall as he did. "I'm just looking for the person who owns the stables."

"What?" She leaned the handle of the pitchfork against the wall then pulled white speaker buds from her ears. "Can I help you?"

"I'm looking for the owner." How long was this non-conversation going to go on? He was tired, having traveled all day.

She placed her hands on her hips and glared at him. "You found her."

His step faltered. This woman he hadn't anticipated. She looked more like a farmhand than the veterinarian he had been told she was. "I'm Conor O'Brian. I understood you would be expecting me."

Her eyes narrowed and her brow wrinkled. In a sweet Southern drawl she said, "I'm sorry. I don't recognize that name."

Had he been sent on a wild-goose chase? He had no desire to make this trip to begin with, but William Guinness, Liquid Gold's owner, had insisted Conor come with the horse. Someone who knew the animal well enough to see about him in the weeks leading up to the Kentucky Derby. Conor's siblings had encouraged him to make the trip as well. Now this.

"I was told that Gold would be stabled here for two weeks before moving to the racetrack barns."

The woman's face brightened. Her body relaxed. "Liquid Gold. Yes, the horse from Ireland. I wasn't expecting him until day after tomorrow. I should've guessed from your accent who you might be." At least she had expected the horse if not him.

She stepped forward and offered her hand. "I'm Christina Mobbs. Welcome to Seven Miles Farm and Stables."

He liked the name *Christina*. But they were not friends, so he settled on calling her by a more formal name. "Dr. Mobbs, I would really like to get Gold settled. It's been a long trip. The flight, then three days in quarantine in Indianapolis, then the three-hour drive here. I think he needs something stable under his feet."

"Certainly. I have a stall ready." She walked farther down the hall and opened a stall door wide, then returned to him and moved beyond.

Conor stepped outside just behind her. He glanced at the countryside. It reminded him of home with its green trees and grass-covered rolling hills. At least that much he could appreciate about being here. Except he'd rather be in Ireland in his own home, being left alone.

Conor had pushed back about coming here but the knowledge that his brother and sister were worried about him had made him agree. They feared he had become too insulated and removed from life because of his loneliness and anger over losing Louisa and his unborn child. They had said they even feared for his mental health. Their idea was that with a change of scenery he might snap out of his depression. He didn't share the idea that a trip to the United States would change his mindset, but he had been left with little choice but to make the trip. After all, it was only for three weeks. What could happen in that amount of time?

Christina put out a hand as if to touch the large white truck and kept it there as she walked beside the matching horse trailer. "Nice rig."

"Not my doing but I agree it is nice."

"I'm going to need to see some papers before I let you unload him. Do you have a health certificate, import permit and blood tests?"

"I have them right here." He handed her the papers he had pulled out of his back pocket.

She flipped through the sheets, running a finger down each page. "Looks good. The training and racing certificates are even here." She handed them back to him and continued to the rear of the trailer.

Conor joined her there. Inside, he could hear Gold shifting his weight, making the trailer creak. After opening the back door wide, he pulled the ramp out and stepped inside. "Easy, boy. We're done traveling for a while. It's time to rest and get ready for the big day." Conor spoke softly, running his hand across the Thoroughbred's neck. "You have a nice stall waiting. Just for you."

Only with his equine patients had Conor felt like himself since his wife had killed herself and their unborn baby. Working with the horses eased his pain, or at least let him forget for a few minutes. With the horses, he dared to care.

"Let's get you out of here." He untied the halter rope from the bar in the trailer. Turning Gold, Conor led him out and down the metal ramp. He looked at Dr. Mobbs, who stood beside the driver, to see a look of pure pleasure on her face.

"What a fine-looking horse." Awe hung in each of her words.

"He is a handsome fellow. And fast, too." Conor could not help but speak like a proud parent. "I've been taking care of him since his birth."

"I would like to examine him before you put him in the stall." She stepped toward them.

"Why?"

She looked directly at him. "Because this is my place and if something is wrong with such an expensive piece of horseflesh, I want to know about it. I'm a veterinarian. I know what I'm doing. I also need to know Gold isn't carrying anything that might make the other horses here ill."

Conor straightened his shoulders. He wasn't used to anyone questioning his care of Gold or any other animal for that matter. "I assure you Gold is in fine health."

"Still, I must insist if he is to stay at Seven Miles."

She walked to the front of the horse, lifting his head with a hand under the horse's chin. "You are indeed a handsome fellow."

Conor watched as Christina looked into Gold's eyes, pulled up his lips to study his teeth and then ran her hand over his shoulders and back before doing the same to his legs.

She had a gentle but firm touch. Gold didn't take to just anyone; that was part of why William had wanted Conor with Gold, but the horse seemed content with Christina's attention. Did she have that effect on all males she touched? He pushed away that uncomfortable idea. What had made such a foreign thought flash through his mind? He hadn't thought of a woman that way since his wife died. Hadn't wanted to.

"I understand he was the highest point earner in the Europe seven-race circuit." She continued around to the other side of the horse.

"That is correct. That's why he was issued an invitation to the Derby race."

"You know no visiting horse has ever won

the Derby." She looked at him from under the horse's neck.

Conor shrugged. "There is always a first time."

She grinned, taking his breath for a moment.

Christina had to admit the horse was in prime condition. Not unlike the man assigned to handle Gold, despite a sadness that shrouded him. It particularly showed in his blue eyes that held a hollow, haunted look. She had instated a look-but-don't-touch program after her no-good ex, Nelson had pulled his trick last year. After that horrible experience she didn't allow herself to trust anyone. She had considered herself a good judge of character until she'd been proven wrong in a very painful way.

When she stepped away from the horse, the Irish man said, "Now it's my turn."

She watched as wide, confident fingers repeated what she had just finished.

The horse's muscles rippled beneath his administrations. The animal stood still, obviously used to the man's hands.

All the while Conor spoke in a soft, low voice. His deep Irish baritone washed over her.

It made her think of the warmth of a fire on a cold, snowy night, pushing all the drafts away.

She hadn't had that in her life for too long.

What did she have to do to keep him talking so she could bask in that feeling just a little longer?

Instead of finding an answer to her internal question, she stood there looking at him as if she'd never seen a handsome man before. Shaking herself figuratively, she redirected herself to the thoughtfulness he gave the horse's legs. He spent more time on them than he had other areas of the animal's body, giving them a thorough assessment. She watched, mesmerized. It always amazed her how so much weight and strength could rest on such thin supports. A racehorse full-out running was pure majesty.

Once again, Christina's consideration fell to the man doing the exam. The thick, dark waves on his head captured her interest.

A tense, blue-eyed look snagged hers, held. "He fared well for such a long trip."

"I would agree." She managed not to stammer.

The man squatted beside the horse. He reminded her of a Thoroughbred, slim and moving with slick, easy motions.

The driver of the truck stated he had to go if he was no longer needed. Conor removed his bag from the backseat and shook the man's hand. Minutes later they watched the truck and trailer rattle down the drive.

"Let's get Gold in his stall." She turned and entered the barn.

He followed with Gold on a lead.

A half an hour later they had Gold settled in a stall.

Conor stepped back from the stall gate. "It's always tough on a horse when it travels."

"Yes, and horses that are good enough to run the Kentucky Derby tend to be rather high-strung."

"Exactly. That's why Mr. Guinness's trainer wanted Gold to come a few weeks early. It gives him a chance to settle in. He can spend the time acclimating to the weather. Kentucky's humidity alone is far different from Ireland's."

"I imagine it is." One day she would love the chance to visit Ireland.

Conor continued, "I, on the other hand, am worn out. Could you show me where I will be staying? It's been a long day and the time change still has me out of sync."

Her head shifted to the side. What was he talking about? Her mouth twisted in thought. Dr. Dillard, the head veterinarian of the clinic at Churchill Downs, had said nothing about someone staying at her farm. She boarded and cared for horses. Not men she didn't know. "Uh... You're expecting to stay here?"

"Yes, I understood I would be staying near Gold." He looked around. "It doesn't look like there is a hotel on every corner, so I assume I'm to stay in the house."

"That isn't what I understood." But Dr. Dillard might have failed to tell her.

"I'm afraid that isn't going to work. I don't know you and it's just me here. I wasn't expecting to board you as well."

Dr. Dillard had asked if she would be willing to board Gold for two weeks. She needed the money and the doctor's goodwill since she wanted to work the Derby week at Churchill Downs. After what Nelson had done to her, she needed to prove to her peers she was nothing like Nelson and wasn't involved in his drug selling. The Derby only took the best veterinarians, and she wanted that seal of approval. She'd been working for the invitation to serve all year long.

"I will pay you twice what a hotel would charge me. Make it three times."

"You really want to stay here."

"Gold is my responsibility. I take that seriously. I need to be close by."

Christina liked a man who felt that kind of concern for those he cared about. Even a horse. She imagined that translated to people as well. Nelson had felt none of that in regard to her, and they had been together for four years. In fact, he had thrown her to the wolves to protect himself.

Along with Nelson had gone her dream of a

husband and children as well. He'd destroyed all her business and personal dreams.

She didn't want it to get back to Dr. Dillard she hadn't been a team player. Enough that she wouldn't make any ripples by insisting he stay elsewhere. With her work at the Derby, she could make great contacts that would help her rehabilitation program grow. If Gold won the Derby it would also put her farm on the map just because he had stayed there.

And she could use the money. She was trying to build her business. That money could be put to good use. Part of her rehabilitation program was the water program she had developed and invested in. The heated pool for horses had put her back financially but it would pay for itself in a few years. Or at least that was the plan. She hoped one day Seven Miles Farm and Stables would be synonymous with the best place to take horses for rehabilitation and rest.

"Okay, but only twice the amount. Three times makes me feel dishonest."

He huffed.

They exited the barn into the afternoon sunlight.

Conor stopped and looked around the area.

She rested her hands on her hips and squinted against the bright spring afternoon sun. Did he see what she did? The beauty of the long tree-lined drive. The emerald green of the grass. The brilliance of the white wood fences. She loved the area around Versailles, Kentucky. For her, there was no other place in the world.

"It is pretty here. More than I imagined it would be."

Christina heard the sadness in his voice. "But you're already missing home."

"Something like that. This wasn't a trip I wanted to make." She had the distinct feeling his perceptive look missed very few details.

"You don't have to be here long. Only three weeks. It will pass fast. Especially Derby week."

"I'm counting on that." His face remained a mask, showing none of the emotion his tone indicated.

For some reason his attitude made her sad. But it wasn't her job to see about him; it was to board Gold. That was what she should focus on. She shouldn't see much of him. Her job had her keeping early mornings and late evenings. There was also her regular practice to see about. For the trouble there would be great gain. What could go wrong?

Conor watched the expression on Christina's face change from shock to thoughtful to acceptance.

He had Gold stabled, and he was ready to get some rest as well. All the traveling had left him tired and irritable. "If you don't mind, I really am exhausted. If you'd just point me in the direction of where I am to stay, I'll head there."

That shook her out of whatever was running through her mind and started her toward the barn's open doors to the outside.

Conor was quickly running out of good humor. He opened his mouth to say he would stay in the barn, but he thought better of it. "I assure you I am not an axe murderer. You are safe with me. I promise. I'm too tired to attack anyone."

"I wasn't thinking—"

"Look. I have no car. Until I pick up my rental tomorrow. I don't know anyone in the US. I don't know my way around."

She rolled her eyes. "I'm not scared of you. I want you to know I'm putting you in the extra room off the kitchen. It's little more than a storage room."

"That sounds fine. At this point I don't care."

Indecision flickered in her eyes.

What had made this woman so scared of men? "I promise I'm a good guy. I'll stay out of your way."

"Then come on up to the house. I'll show you your room." She walked in the direction of the one-level sprawling brick house.

A black truck with supply boxes built on both sides of the bed had been parked near the back door. Conor followed her up the two brick steps into the house. They entered a pale green kitchen. There were dishes in the sink of the same color. On the wood table that looked well-worn lay a pile of envelopes. On the green countertops were the usual appliances such as a coffeemaker, mixer and toaster.

Somehow, this retro look suited her. Yet, he had the idea it wasn't intentional. More like modernizing the kitchen fell low on her to-do list.

She turned down a small hall off the kitchen and entered a room. "This way is your room, or that might be an exaggeration. It's more like a large closet with a bed."

He joined her.

She was busy stacking boxes against the wall so there was a path to a bed. "Sorry about the mess."

A small bed of sorts sat in a corner. There was also a desk and chair. The only item that leaned toward modern was a flat-screen TV on a stand.

"I'm sorry there's not more to it. I just didn't realize that I was gonna be boarding a horse as well as a man."

For someone who didn't want him staying with her, she apologized a lot. The room was so small he could smell the sweetness of hay and lavender on her. The scents of home. "I appreciate it." Conor dropped his leather bag to the floor.

"Thanks. Beggars cannot be choosers. I'm not going to complain."

"The bed is made but I'll have to get you some clean towels." She brushed by him.

His body tensed. The reaction strange yet familiar. It had been a long time since he felt anything for a woman. Conor didn't want to now. He wouldn't be unfaithful like his father had been. She needed to leave. He forced out, "Thanks, I appreciate it."

Christina grabbed a couple of towels from her bathroom closet and returned to the small room. She slowly approached, listening. "Conor?"

Hearing no sound or movement, she stepped to the door. She found him sprawled on the too-small bed, facedown. A soft snore came from him.

It had been over a year since there had been a man sleeping in the house. Until today, she had intended for it to stay that way forever. Nelson had made her hesitant about trusting anyone. Conor wouldn't be around long enough for it to matter. His money would be worth the chance.

After placing the towels on the desk, she took a blanket from the end of the bed and draped it over him. Apparently, he had had all he could take for the day.

Christina headed out the back door. There were still chores to do. Feeding the horses and securing the barn for the night must happen no matter what.

Who was this Irish stranger with the sad eyes now staying in her home?

The next morning the house was still quiet when Christina went out the back door at daylight to take care of the horses. Her guest had not arisen yet. She quickly scribbled a note stating, *Make yourself at home*. Then she left.

A bitterness that hadn't eased much over the past months filled her. She wouldn't be in this position of having a houseguest if it hadn't been for Nelson. Because of him, she was fighting to regain her good reputation and her aspirations and bank account. As if that hadn't been enough, Nelson had almost been the cause of her losing her veterinarian license.

One piece of paper had saved her, or she would have been working elsewhere. Not doing what she loved. That paper had proven she hadn't been the one stealing the drugs. She had to give Nelson kudos; he had been good at covering his problems. She'd no idea what he had been doing behind her back.

Worse, she'd believed he would be her future. Even the father of her children. Which she desperately wanted.

She had been deeply hurt once, and had no intention of letting that happen to her again on a professional or personal level. She kept any relationships on a superficial plane. She wouldn't permit another man to crush her like Nelson had. The fact she had managed to salvage her practice and her business was the only thing that had saved her sanity.

Even worse still, when she was down, all her mother could say was how disappointed she had been in Christina's judgment. Her mother reminded her in detail that Christina didn't dress like a lady or have a job where she could have pretty nails. That she lived in a man's world, and the list went on. That if Christina had tried harder, Nelson wouldn't have had to turn to drugs. All she had wanted from her mother had been her support, and there had been none.

Enough of those thoughts. She needed to get moving, there were chores to finish, then horses to exercise and more horses on her schedule to see. She finished feeding the horses and spoke to Gold on her way out. She would let Conor handle him. He really was a fine-looking horse. She couldn't afford to have anything go wrong with him in her barn.

Breakfast for her came before exercising the horses. Closing the kitchen door behind her, she inhaled the smell of coffee. She toed off her boots and left them lying beside the door. She padded across the kitchen floor with nothing but thoughts of her morning cup of coffee.

She pulled up short. Conor stood in front of the range with a fork in his hand. His hair looked damp. Apparently, he had found the bathroom. A worn jean shirt covered his wide shoulders, and the same type of jeans his muscular legs. His feet were bare. As enticing as he looked, she didn't care for how comfortable he appeared in her personal space.

He glanced over his shoulder. "I took you at your word and made myself at home. I haven't eaten since yesterday morning. I made enough for you as well."

"I'm surprised you found anything to fix a meal with." She moved to see what was in the pan.

"It was pretty slim pickings, but I do like a challenge."

Shame filled her. "I'm not much of a cook but I'll try to get by the grocery store today, tomorrow at the latest."

"If you'll tell me where the store is, I'll take care of that after I pick up my rental. It's the least I can do. Especially since you weren't expecting me."

Who was this man who just showed up and cooked her a meal then agreed to buy groceries? He wasn't like anyone else she knew.

"You have about ten minutes before it's ready. You might like to take a look in the mirror."

Christina's hair was a mess. That sounded too much like her mother. "I've been working in the barn, and this is my house. I'm sorry I don't look like I came out of a fashion magazine."

His hands came up in a defensive measure. "Ho, I didn't mean to insult you. I just thought you might like to know you have dirt on your face."

She stomped to the bathroom and looked in the mirror. A large black smear went across her left cheek. Conor's statement had been a nice way of keeping her from going out on her rounds looking foolish. Most people wouldn't have been as considerate. She owed him an apology.

Conor looked up from where he was placing a mug of coffee on the table. "You look neat and tidy."

"I'm sorry I overreacted. Thanks for telling me. I'd have hated to spend all day with dirt on my face."

"No problem," he said as if he had already forgotten it happened.

She glanced around the room. "Talk about neat. You've made a difference in here in a short amount of time."

"I hope you don't mind. I wasn't always tidy. My wife made me learn."

Of course, he had a wife. A man who looked as good as he did, liked animals and was kind enough to help someone out and cooked wouldn't remain unattached for long. A woman would be quick to snatch him up. "I'm sure she misses you."

Clouds filled his eyes and he looked away. "I'm sure it's more like I miss her. She died three years ago."

"Oh, I'm sorry."

"She was a good woman who died far too early. I miss her every day."

The pain in his voice said it was more like every minute. What would it be like to have someone care that much about her? To feel that love and connection so deeply it would still bring sadness to his eyes after you had died.

Nelson had professed that love but in the end they were just words. Their relationship had turned one-sided. His largest interest had been himself. Once she would have liked to have an unbreakable connection with someone, but the chances of that happening were gone. Now she didn't trust her judgment enough to let a man into her life.

CHAPTER TWO

CONOR COULD NOT believe he had just told an almost perfect stranger about his wife. It was the most he had shared about Louisa in years. Yet, he thought of her daily. Remained devoted to her even after she had done something as selfish as committing suicide. But he could never talk about the loss of their child.

That was something his father never gave his mother. Devotion. When his mother had been alive or dead. Conor had watched his mother slowly drift away, become a shell of herself in her humiliation over his father's public infidelity. As a boy, Conor had vowed to remain true to his wife. He had kept that promise even after her death. That conviction drove his personal life. When he made a commitment, it stood for something.

He had tried to keep his pain and thoughts over Louisa to himself. In an odd way it had felt good to let go of even one detail about her. Maybe that was what his family had been wanting him to do for the past few months. They saw what he needed even if he couldn't. But guilt rose in him. The worst was he had noticed Christina as a woman, causing the guilt to swamp him, but he could not help himself.

Like now, as he watched her move around the kitchen. Her actions fascinating him. He had missed that part of being with someone the most. Having another person around. The peace of knowing someone was nearby. Maybe that was it, the reason he had been comfortable enough to tell Christina about Louisa. He had nothing to worry about. It had nothing to do with attraction and everything to do with his needing someone to talk to.

"I must exercise the horses and then I've got some rounds to make this afternoon."

Christina's statement brought him out of his perplexing thoughts. "Mind if I get a ride to the car rental place? I understand it's not far from here."

"Sure." Having finished her meal, she pushed back from the table. "Leave the dishes. I'll clean up later."

"I'll get them today."

Christina shrugged. "I appreciate it."

"I'll be out to check on Gold in just a few minutes."

She set her dishes in the sink. "Thank you for breakfast."

"You're welcome." She headed out the back door as if she was already thinking about what she had to do for the day.

Conor wasn't sure he liked being dismissed or why it bothered him that she did so.

Fifteen minutes later he had finished tidying the kitchen as much as he could without invading her personal space. He pulled on his boots and walked to the barn.

Outside he took a deep breath, bringing the fresh spring air into his lungs. He scanned the countryside. If he couldn't be in his beloved Ireland, then this part of the world must be the next best place. He continued to the barn. Gold would be glad to see him. He had agreed to fill in as groom as well.

Gold's trainer would arrive by the end of next week in time for Gold to move to the barns on the backside of Churchill Downs. The trainer had other horses he worked, and he could not be away for weeks. Gold's trainer intended for the horse to have a couple of weeks' rest before he started serious workouts. The idea was to have Gold eager to race.

Christina walked one of the other horses back into a stall as he entered the barn. "That's a fine-looking animal."

She patted the horse on the neck and closed

the gate between her and the animal. "Yeah, this is Honey."

The horse did have a coat that reminded Conor of warm honey.

"She's staying with me because of a torn tendon."

"That's pretty difficult to repair." Conor was surprised she was even trying. It was an expensive and long process, if it worked.

"It is, but that's what this farm is all about, or at least it will be."

He walked over to pet Gold's nose hanging over the stall gate. "I thought you just boarded horses."

"No, I'm working to build this into a rehabilitation farm for racehorses. I'm just boarding Gold as a favor for the track vet."

"I understand." He opened Gold's stall and entered.

Christina went to another stall. She walked the horse out of the barn.

Conor fed Gold before leading him outside to the padlock where Christina was circling the horse on a lead rope. As the horse went around the space so did she. Her movements were easy and graceful.

She glanced in his direction.

Had she caught him staring? He continued to the mechanical hot walker. After attaching Gold to one of the arms of the merry-go-round-looking contraption, he started the motor. Gold was led around, getting his exercise. Conor returned inside to muck out Gold's stall.

Christina entered the barn, tied the horse to the gatepost and proceeded to brush the horse.

Conor became caught up in her actions once again. Each stroke was smooth and careful. She made long ones across the horse's back that had him bowing his back. What would it be like to have her do that across his body?

Was he losing his mind? He hadn't had those type of thoughts in years. Why this woman? Why now? Maybe she should be afraid of him.

Conor held himself back from rushing out of the barn. He took his time returning with Gold. Thank goodness by the time he did Christina was nowhere in sight. He groomed Gold in peace, but still glimpses of Christina's attentions flashed in his mind as he worked. Was it wrong to be jealous of a horse?

For lunch Christina put out bread and sandwich meats. She ate at a desk on the other side of the room while on the computer. He sat at the table reading an equine magazine he was not familiar with.

She turned in her chair. "I'm leaving in about twenty minutes if you want a ride to the rental car place."

He closed the magazine. "I'll be waiting by the truck."

* * *

She asked as he climbed out of the truck at the rental place, "Can you find your way back?"

"Yes, I've been paying attention and I have GPS." It was the first concern she had shown him.

She nodded, a slight smile on her lips. "GPS doesn't always work well around here."

"I'll keep that in mind. Thanks for the ride."

Christina wasn't home when he returned. He spent the rest of the day getting settled into his small office slash make-do bedroom. He stacked boxes around and cleaned off a space on the desk for himself. Would Christina mind him doing so? She was so different from Louisa, but for some reason he found Christina interesting. He wasn't sure if he was comfortable with those feelings or not.

The next afternoon Christina pulled up her drive and circled into her regular parking spot behind the house beside Conor's red rental truck. She had been gone all afternoon doing rounds and hadn't seen him all day. He'd already left by the time she had returned to the house after seeing to the horses that morning. Her breakfast waited on the table. A carafe of hot coffee sat there as well. Where he had gone so early in the morning she couldn't imagine, but that wasn't any of her business. Yet, that didn't keep her from wondering.

She climbed out, immediately noticing the barn doors were open. She had closed them securely that morning. Maybe Conor had gone out there and failed to secure them since then.

She walked to the barn, entering with the late-afternoon sun streaming in from the other side.

Wind, one of her boarded horses, stood in the hallway tied to the post of a stall gate. Conor was squatted down on his haunches, looking at the horse's leg. He ran his hand along the leg, pausing at the knee joint.

Her concern turned to anger. What was he doing? This horse had been entrusted to her. He had no business touching him or having the horse out of the stall. Some of her boarders were temperamental and could easily run. What if one of them got away?

She started toward him.

He looked up. "Hello."

"What exactly is going on here?" She heard the bite in her voice. Did he? She stepped closer.

"He has a wound. I brought him out because the light is better."

"You could have just waited to tell me. This horse is in my charge. The owners don't like just anyone touching them."

Conor stood to his full height and squared his shoulders. "If I was the owner, I would appreciate help where I could get it."

"These horses' owners want a veterinarian seeing to their animal. Pardon me but not a trainer or groom."

Conor's eyes bore into hers as if he were speaking to a simpleton. "Many trainers and grooms are better equine caregivers than a veterinarian. That being said, despite your lowly opinion of me, I am a veterinarian."

Her brows went up. He was? She had assumed he was a groom sent over to see about Gold. It had never crossed her mind a veterinarian would have come all the way from Ireland with a horse.

"I am here at the request of the owner. I've taken care of Gold since he was a colt. His owner wanted me to travel with Gold since he can have a temper, and this is a new environment for him, but he knows me. I assure you I'm more than capable of taking care of Gold or any other horse you have in your stable."

"I'm...uh...sorry. I didn't mean to insult you."

"What about grooms and trainers?" His look chastised.

"Or them, either. It's just that I'm responsible for these horses and I can't afford for anything to happen to them on my watch. I guess I'm pretty proprietorial."

"I would say you are." His attention returned to the horse's leg.

That didn't sound like a compliment.

"But that can be a positive or a negative." He softened his earlier words. His deep Irish brogue went a long way toward easing her frayed nerves.

"Back to this horse." He touched the horse lightly. "The wound on his foreleg needs to be debrided and cleaned then wrapped."

"Let me have a look." Christina went to one knee and examined the leg. "This is pretty deep. I think stitches are required."

"I disagree. You are too quick to add something that isn't natural. A good cleaning with antiseptic and a bandage should do well. It isn't that deep. Let nature take its course."

She stood. "I should be the judge of that. I'm the one responsible for the animal, not you."

"Yet, I have some knowledge in these matters."

She placed her hands on her hips. "And you're saying I don't?"

"I'm not saying that at all. I'm just saying you might be overtreating."

His calm words only irritated her. "I don't agree. I would appreciate it if you would step away and leave me to this."

"What can I do to help you?" He coolly watched her.

She huffed. "I'm going to need some heated water. You can go to the house and see to that."

"Sending me off to get me out of the way?"

"Just pretend you're preparing for the delivery

of a baby." Christina didn't miss the darkening of his face before he swiftly turned and stalked out of the barn. What had she said to upset him?

She would have to worry about his attitude later. There was work to do now. She went to the large enclosed room in the barn where she stored all her medical supplies and tack for the horses. After entering, she gathered bottles of saline, bandages, a tube of anti-infection cream and placed them in a cardboard box before going to the locked box that held her injectable medicines.

This was one part of her world she kept in order by the alphabet. And kept a count of. What was an S drug doing in the Ws? She must have knocked it out of place. Those types of occurrences she'd never questioned until Nelson's stunt. Now she found problems everywhere.

Had Conor been in here for some reason? He didn't even have a key. With a shrug, she returned the vial to its correct position and took out a vial of antibiotic. She also grabbed a syringe in a plastic cover. Picking up a bowl, she headed back to Wind.

Wind stomped as she set the box down to retrieve a four-legged stool and placed it nearby. "Easy, boy, this will be over soon."

Christina found the suture kit and opened it, removing the scissors. "I'm going to cut away the skin. Hold still and it'll all be over soon." She snipped pieces of dead skin off.

Conor entered the barn with a pan in his hand, but she didn't slow her work. Wind shifted to the right, but Christina held tight to his foot.

With a quick movement Conor placed the pan on the floor and came around her to hold Wind's head. He whispered to the horse in a low, smooth voice. Conor's gentle brogue rippled over her as well.

She did like his accent. What would it be like to have him whisper in her ear? She shivered just to think of the possibility. Where did that bizarre thought come from? It was not something that would ever happen, but still a girl could dream.

She'd had dreams but they'd been shattered. At one time, she had believed that there would be a forever-after between her and Nelson. They'd made plans to marry, and then she learned of his duplicity. At least this time she had been smart enough to put the house and farm in her name. Nope, she was better on her own. She would keep it that way.

Finished with the skin removal, she brought the pan close and dipped a rag into the warm water and washed the area around the wound, removing a piece of hay, dirt and grit. All the while she worked Conor spoke to the horse, keeping him distracted from what she was doing.

Christina patted the front thigh of the horse then picked up the bottle of saline and opened it. "This next bit might not be too much fun but hang in there, Wind."

Conor changed his stance, taking a more secure hold on the horse's head.

"There we go, boy," she spoke to the horse. Turning the bottle up, she let the fluid flow over the wound, washing any debris away. She continued until it was all gone, then looked carefully for anything in the wound. There couldn't be any chance for infection.

"You want a second set of eyes?"

"Yeah, sure. I could use a leg stretch, too."

"Then change places with me." He offered his hand to help her up.

She hesitated a moment, then placed her hand in his. A shock of electric awareness went through her. She quickly let his hand go. He moved closer to take her seat. Conor smelled of citrus, hay and grain. Like the countryside.

He handed her the lead rope before he stepped away from her. Lifting the horse's foot, he braced it on his knee.

Christina watched the top of Conor's head as he looked at the wound. Her fingers itched to touch his thick hair, but she resisted. Setting the foot on the floor, he took a seat on the stool and picked up the tube of ointment. "Nice job. The trimming and cleaning are excellent work."

Christina couldn't help but glow under his praise.

He glanced at her. "I'll finish if that's okay with you."

"I'm still not convinced that it doesn't need to be stitched."

Conor's look met hers and held. "Trust me."

Trust wasn't something that Christina gave easily, if at all. Nelson had destroyed that ability. "I'm just supposed to trust your word on this?"

"Yes." His tone didn't waver.

She couldn't have him messing around with her horses. "Their owners trusted me. If something goes wrong, I'm the one with her name and business on the line." What she didn't say was she had already had that happen and that one time had been enough. She was having to re-earn her good name.

"I'm telling you that nothing will go wrong. In fact, my way is easier on the horse. You try my way for twenty-four hours and then you can do it your way."

He made it sound like he was the one calling the shots. "If there isn't improvement by the morning, I'll be stitching him up."

Conor said nothing. He pulled on plastic gloves

and smeared antibacterial ointment on his finger and applied it to Wind's leg.

The horse flinched, its skin rippling. Christina held the halter snugger. "Easy, boy, it's almost over."

Conor sat the medicine aside and picked up the paper-covered gauze and began wrapping the leg in a sure neat manner born of practice. He worked with swift efficiency.

"That should do it." He stood and stretched, raising his hands above his head.

Despite her best effort, Christina couldn't help but watch.

He finished and his look met hers.

She had been caught staring. Why he interested her, or why she even cared about him knowing she'd been watching him, she didn't know. Still, a tingle shot through her, and she looked away. "I'll give him a shot and put him in the stall then clean up. Thanks for your help."

"I don't mind putting things away. See to Wind." He patted the horse on the neck. "You are a good patient, boy."

"That you are." She ran her palm down the horse's nose then tied his lead rope to the post. She drew up the liquid from the vial.

"What're you giving him?"

"Trimethoprim sulfa."

Conor nodded. "That antibiotic should work well."

At least they could agree on that. She injected the needle into the horse's hip. "Before you go back into the stall, I need to see if I can find what caused this."

She went to the tack room. After finding a hammer and flashlight she entered the stall, searching for a nail or piece of metal sticking out. In a methodical order she searched for what might have wounded Wind.

"Got it." A small piece of metal that secured the bottom of the feed trough stuck out. "Wind," she spoke to him over the wall of the stall, "how in the world you managed getting your leg near this I'll never know, but it's the only place I see where you could have gotten hurt."

Conor joined her. "Show me."

She pointed to the spot.

Conor shook his head. "Horses never cease to amaze me."

Christina hammered at the metal to flatten it but it didn't lie against the wood as it should.

Conor put out his hand. "May I?"

"Sure. You're welcome to give it a try." She watched the muscles in his back and arms flex and release as he worked. Were they as hard as they appeared? These thoughts had to stop. Conor was her guest, not on her farm to ogle.

"How's that?"

"Uh…yeah, that looks good. I'll get Wind."
She stepped into the hall, glad for the soft breeze
blowing through it. Tonight it would rain. Taking
Wind's halter she said, "Come on, big boy, I'll get
you tucked away for the night."

Conor had the surgery items cleaned away,
leaving a small bag of trash neatly tied up on the
ground beside the stool and the pan on top. It was
nice to have such an efficient man around.

"Anything I need to do?" he asked.

"I need to put the antibiotic in the refrigerator."
She went to the tack room and placed the vial in
the small refrigerator she kept there for just this
reason. On her way out she picked up a folding
chair and carried it with her.

She unfolded it near the gate to Wind's stall.

Conor stood behind her. "What are you doing?"

"I'm going to sit up for a while to make sure
no heat sets in around the wound."

"You can't take the bandage off until the morning. The more you open it the less likely it is to
heal well."

She cut her eyes at him. "I know that."

He lowered his head, acting contrite. "Sorry.
I'm sure you do. I'll take the pan and trash in."

Twenty minutes later he returned with a basket.

"What're you doing?" She turned in the chair,
putting the paperback book she kept in the tack

room for these occasions across her knee not to lose her spot.

"I brought us something to eat since we missed dinner and I will not let you sit up alone with our patient." He placed the basket on the floor beside her. "I hope you have another chair put away somewhere."

"In the tack room behind the door."

Conor set up the chair beside her. Picking up the basket, he removed a thermos. "Tea. Hot." He placed that on the floor. "And ham and cheese sandwiches." He handed her one covered in plastic. "Can I pour you some tea?"

"Sure. Thanks for this, Conor. It's very nice of you."

The smile he gave her made her stomach flutter. "You're welcome."

They sat in silence for a few minutes before Conor asked, "Will you tell me what made you decide to become a veterinarian? A large animal veterinarian at that. We don't have many female large animal vets in Ireland."

"We're about fifty-fifty here. As to why, I imagine it was the same things as you. I love animals. I just gravitated to large animals and then horses in particular. Look where I live. It would have been hard not to care for horses."

"I guess it would have."

"Did you grow up on a farm?" Conor watched her face. He liked how expressive her features were.

"Nope. In town with one small dog. Much to my mother's chagrin, I loved horses."

"She doesn't like them?"

Christina rubbed her booted heel in the dirt of the floor. "It was more like she wanted me to be a girly-girl and I was more of a tomboy. Let's just say I didn't always measure up to her expectations. In fact, I still don't."

He took a moment to digest that information. Conor knew well the feeling of disappointment in a parent.

She put her cup down near the leg of the chair. "How about you? Did you grow up on a farm?"

"I did. But I didn't know what I wanted to do until I went to work during the summers, just to have a job, at a local veterinary clinic cleaning out cages. That's when my love of veterinarian work began." It also got him away from the ugliness between his mother and father.

"So what brought you on this trip? I've never known the horse's vet to travel with it and do groom work as well."

"My family encouraged me to come when I was offered this opportunity and Gold's owner insisted. He wanted somebody he could trust with Gold. What I did not expect was not to have a place to stay. I appreciate you giving me a room here. Actually, I have liked doing some physical work. It reminds me of when I worked at the clinic."

She grinned. "You're welcome. Please feel free to muck out as many stalls as you wish."

Conor chuckled. "Thanks for reminding me about what it is to do real veterinarian care."

For the next three hours she checked on Wind at least ten times. More than once, she entered the stall to study the bandaged area for any seepage. Placing her hand on the leg to see if there was heat in the skin caused by infection. He had volunteered a couple of times to do the exam, but she had refused.

They turned quiet and Conor watched as Christina's eyes slowly lowered after she leaned her head back against the chair. She would have a crick in her neck if she remained like that all night.

He studied her. She really was a pretty woman. Not in the goddess-or-movie-star-beauty way, but in the simple, fresh and natural sense. What really made her appealing was her caring heart for animals, her quirky, haphazard way of keeping house and her drive to go after what she wanted. What confounded him the most was that he even noticed those characteristics.

It had been forever since he had sat with someone in a simple setting and been satisfied. Even thoughts of Louisa were not hurtling through his mind. For once, he had to bring her up instead of her always being there. The idea made him both uncomfortable and relieved. He wanted to hang on to Louisa while at the same time it was past time to let her go. Was that how his father had felt about his mother?

He gave Christina's shoulder a shake. "You better go inside or you're going to fall out of the chair."

She mumbled, "I need to stay here and keep an eye on Wind."

"I understand that, but I think we can go inside now. Get a few hours of sleep. He will be all right until morning."

"I better not…"

"If it will make you feel any better, I'll check on him in a couple of hours. You need to get some sleep." He helped her stand. She swayed on her feet, and he placed an arm around her shoulders, pulling her against him. "You are dead on your feet."

"It's my job."

He started her toward the door. "That may be so but I can help. Now, stop arguing and let me get you inside to bed."

"To bed…"

The way she let the words trail off made him

think of a fire, a soft bed and a warm woman against him. He swallowed hard. The guilt. He did not want that. Could not want Christina. More importantly, he wouldn't allow himself the chance of the pain that caring again might bring.

Christina took a moment to look at Wind. "You promise?"

"You have my word. Now, come on, sleepy-head." Conor guided her, arm around her shoulders, to the house, inside and down the hall to her bedroom. He'd never been in there. At the door, he flipped on the light.

She squeaked. "Turn it off. That hurts my eyes."

He did as she said. "Good night, Christina. Get some rest."

Christina murmured something and moved into the room.

Conor grinned as he walked to his little office bedroom. He shook his head. At the brief glimpse of her room, he saw clothes strewn everywhere. A pile of veterinary magazines beside the bed. It hadn't been made, and the covers looked pushed over to one side, as if she had been in a rush when she woke. The woman might be a great veteri-narian, but she needed a housekeeper like no one else he knew.

Taking just his boots off then setting his alarm for two hours, he lay on his bed. He had a horse to check on. A promise to keep. The first in many years.

A buzzing sound went off sooner than he wished. He pulled on his boots and headed out the kitchen door to the barn. Fifteen minutes later he was on his way back to the house. Two hours later, after the sun had brought light to the day, Conor entered the barn again.

Christina was there in Wild's stall on her knees. Conor went to his haunches beside her. "What do you think?"

"I think it's better."

His voice took on a teasing tone. "Then I will not tell you I told you so."

She glanced at him, a gentle smile on her lips. "Thank you for that. I would've hated to hear it. We don't go in for the old methods much around here. Little patience or time. Thanks for reminding me that sometimes time helps more than anything."

Had that been true for him? Or had the passage of time just closed him further off from life? He stood. "You are welcome."

She picked up a roll of gauze and began wrapping the leg once more. "This reminder will come in handy when I plan rehabilitation for horses in my program."

He stepped to Wind's head and stroked his

nose. "What type of horse issues are you planning to concentrate on?"

"Any that are leg related. I hate to see a horse put down when there's a chance that they can be saved. Maybe they won't race again but they still have value." She stood and patted Wind on the neck. "Just like this guy. He's worth the time and energy."

Conor patted the horse's neck as her hand passed. She stopped her movement, and he did, too. She quickly pulled hers away.

"I hate to see the waste of such a majestic animal." She picked up a feed bucket and moved to the trough.

"You know you can't save them all." He continued to stroke Wind while he watched her.

"Maybe not but I can try." She poured the feed into the trough.

By the tone of her voice, she believed deeply in helping the horses. Yet, the reality he well knew. "An admirable goal."

Done with the feed she picked up the trash.

Conor smiled and shook his head. Christina might not be a housekeeper, but he could find no fault in her care of the horses, her supply room, or the barn's cleanliness. "Come on. I'll fix us a hot breakfast."

They stepped out of the stall.

"Did you cook when you were married?" Christina asked.

"No. I had to learn after she was gone. Now I enjoy it."

"You know you don't have to cook for me all the time." She went to the gate and pushed it closed, locking it.

He started down the hall beside her. "I know but you're letting me stay here when you had not planned to have company, and I've got to feed myself so I might as well feed you, too."

"I have to admit your cooking is better than cold cereal but I'm gaining weight." She chuckled.

"From what I have seen you'll be just fine with a few extra pounds." He glanced at Christina, who met his look.

"Thanks. That's nice of you to say."

CHAPTER THREE

CHRISTINA WOKE TO the sun shining through the window of her bedroom. She jerked to a sitting position. She never slept this late. The horses would be starving. After being up late two nights ago, her lack of sleep must have caught up with her. The horses were no doubt stomping in their stalls to have their morning feed.

She flipped the covers off and popped out of bed. She didn't bother to remove the T-shirt she wore. Jerking yesterday's jeans on, she zippered and buttoned them and headed for the door. She would dress for the day later. The horses came first.

Not slowing down, she ran into a solid wall of warm, damp flesh. Strong fingers wrapped her upper arms, preventing her from falling backward.

"Umph."

She grabbed Conor's waist to steady herself. That only made the quiver running through her worse.

"Where are you headed in such a rush?" His sexy Irish brogue had deepened despite the spark of humor in it. The warmth of his breath whispered by her ear.

"Morning chores. Running late," she managed to get out.

"All taken care of. I saw to them all this morning when I checked on Wind and Gold."

"How is he?"

"Doing much better. I removed the bandage and checked him and reapplied it. He seems to be comfortable."

Unlike her. Christina stepped back, putting space between them. She now had a clear view of Conor's well-formed bare chest. He must have just finished his shower. She had been better off standing closer to him. She swallowed hard.

"I appreciate the help, but I'll just go out and check on him." She was used to doing everything by herself. She hadn't had help in a long time. Even then it hadn't turned out she could trust it.

"They've all been well cared for but I'm sure you'll want to see for yourself."

At least he didn't sound offended. More like impressed.

He shifted to the side, giving her clear passage. His look dropped lower. He cleared his throat. "I'll see to breakfast."

It wasn't until she pulled on her jacket, she realized he could see through her thin shirt. Even now her nipples remained at attention from being so close to him. Great. She couldn't do anything about it now. With a tug, she put on her boots. In the future she would be more careful.

In the barn she found everything just as it should be. Each animal looked well cared for.

She returned to the house to find Conor sitting at the kitchen table with a cup of coffee in front of him. At the chair to his right waited her coffee. There was also a bowl of oatmeal with toppings sitting on the table. He spoiled her. This attention she would miss when he left.

"I should get a shower before I eat." She stepped toward the door.

"Then your oatmeal will be cold." He sounded disappointed.

"Ugh, I'm not exactly adequately dressed."

His gaze lingered at her chest then came back to meet hers. Her nipples tightened. "I'd say you look just right."

"I still believe I'll change. I'll warm my coffee and oatmeal up."

He wore that slight grin she found so sexy. "If that's the way you want it."

She shivered. Should she be concerned about whatever was not being said between them? Yet, he had never once been anything but a gentleman. In fact, he looked irritated, she noticed. Maybe she was wrong. Her judgment could be off. Nelson had proven that. Still, Conor had been good to her and the horses.

Christina hurried down the hall to the bathroom for a quick hot shower and returned to the kitchen a short while later.

Conor still sat at the table, nursing his cup of coffee, with an *Equine* magazine she had received in the mail the day before open in front of him.

While she warmed her meal he asked, "What are your plans for today?"

"I've some patients to see." She pulled the food out at the beep.

"Mind if I tag along and see how it's done over here?"

Could she spend the entire day with him? She didn't say anything as she sat down to eat.

"This babysitting job is not quite as intensive as it could be. Gold is doing fine."

How could she say no? "I imagine it will be rather dull for you. It's simple basic veterinarian work. But you're welcome to come along if you want."

"I bet I will learn something. I'll straighten up here and be ready to go when you are."

"I've got to load supplies into my truck. I'll be about twenty minutes or so." She started toward the door.

"I need to collect my wallet and jacket." Conor went to his room.

Christina finished her breakfast and hurried out to the barn to get her supplies together. She was inside the tack room looking at the medicine box when Conor walked up.

"Is something wrong?" He came to stand beside her.

"No. I'm just doing my daily count."

"Daily?"

"Yes. I like to keep a close eye on my regulated medicines." Especially after what Nelson did. She couldn't take a chance on anyone ever stealing from her again.

"I also check the truck daily." She closed and locked the metal box attached to the wall.

He stepped into the hallway. "Why such vigilance?"

Christina joined him. "Because I can't afford any controversy. I've been working too hard to get my reputation back."

His brows came together and created a furrow. "What do you mean by that?"

"I'll tell you in the truck. I need to get going if I don't want to work late into the night."

They walked out of the barn.

"Stealing drugs is a real problem. Offenders are good at it." Nelson had been getting away with it for almost a year before she realized what he was doing.

"In Ireland it's the same. We watch ours closely as well. Those days of it just sitting on the shelf unattended are long gone."

She put the few items she needed away in one of the supply compartments on the truck.

He stood at the front of the vehicle. "Anything I can do to help?"

"No. I got it." She stored the medicines and IV needles in a locked bin. "Let me check the horses once more and I'll be ready to go."

"I now understand why Gold was boarded here. You are careful."

Her look met his. "I take what I care about seriously. Don't you?"

Conor did. To the detriment of his heart. Three years later he still honored his marriage vows. Something his father hadn't done. Conor believed in keeping his promises. Would Louisa have wanted or expected that of him for this long? Hadn't it been her choice to leave him? If he stepped out and had interest in a woman, would that be bad? He was tired of being lonely. He had not realized how much so until he'd started staying with Christina. But wouldn't that make him no better than his father? That, Conor wouldn't accept.

Conor climbed into the passenger side of her large truck. What had possessed him to request to go with Christina today? He wasn't sure if it had been out of boredom or being truly interested in the type of veterinary practice she had, or worse, the fact he just wanted to spend more time with her. That last thought gave him a prickly, panicky feeling.

Christina settled in behind the steering wheel. "I have a rather long day today. You're sure you want to go?"

Was she trying to encourage him not to go? "I am. How far do we drive to the first patient?" He buckled up.

"What I like to do is start at my farthest appointment and work my way home unless there is a serious case that needs to be seen right away. About sixty miles is my radius."

"That's half the distance across Ireland in some places. That can make for a long day."

She glanced at him. "Would you like to change your mind?"

"Are you trying to get rid of me?" He made a show of getting comfortable.

Christina started the truck. "Not at all."

She still hadn't relaxed enough for him to question her about the medicines more. He watched the countryside, glancing at her occasionally. She drove with determination.

Before midafternoon, they had stopped at three different farms all with long driveways and miles of wooden fence. At each, the owner or trainer was there to greet Christina when she stopped the truck outside the barn. She grabbed her bag and hopped out, ready to go to work each time.

With a wave of her hand in his direction she would say, "This is Conor O'Brian. He is visiting from Ireland." Her attention would then return to the problem with the horse.

Her efficiency amazed and impressed him as she went about the care of the horse, all the while talking and touching the animal as if they had been friends forever. Why did she insist on hiding all that tenderness behind gruff toughness?

They finished with one farm and were driving to the next. Christina hadn't said more than what was necessary the entire day. Being a veterinarian could be a solitary job but this was ridiculous. "Are you mad at me? Did I do something wrong?"

"Why would you think that?" She tilted her head in question.

He turned in the seat to see her better. "You haven't said over ten words to me in the last three hours."

"I've been thinking."

About what? "Maybe if you talk it out it would be better."

"I don't think that'll work." She slowed and

made a left turn down a tree-lined country road with fenced green pasture.

"Try it. You never know." He looked at her profile. At least her jaw didn't appear as tight. Either way, Christina appealed to him. What would she look like in something feminine? He had certainly been aware of her breasts in the thin T-shirt that morning. More so than he'd been in years. Why Christina and why now?

"I almost lost my license a few years back."

He shifted in the seat, sitting straighter, his attention completely on her.

She glanced at him. "You aren't going to say anything?"

"No, I figured you'd say more when you were ready."

A small smile came to her lips. "I was stupid. Too trusting, really. I should have been doing the inventory of the medicines since it was my name on the line. But my then live-in boyfriend of four years, who I believed I would marry, had been stealing drugs. He was a vet tech and planning to enter veterinarian school. Then the authorities caught him selling and everything blew up. I barely retained my license. I'm still trying to build my good name back."

"So that's why you count the medicine daily. You blame yourself for his mistakes."

"That's pretty close to it."

He could hear the shame in her voice. "I'm sorry to hear that. It must have been hard to have believed in someone and have them let you down." How many times had he watched his father do that to his mother?

"It was."

Christina pulled into a small roadside park. Horses stood in the field surrounding them, swishing their tails in the bright sunlight. She faced him.

"I had just gotten the idea for opening a rehabilitation farm for racehorses and had started to look for funding. All the banks had gotten the word about what happened, so that was a no-go. Nelson, that was my ex, had not only destroyed my regular world but had managed to do the same to my dreams. That's why I agreed to take Gold so I could get in good with Dr. Dillard at Churchill Downs. I want to be one of the veterinarians on duty during the Derby. That's a prestigious position. It will look good on my vitae. I can also make contacts with those who might use my farm for not only rehabilitation but for horse holidays." She pulled two protein bars out of the pocket of the driver's door, handing one to him. "Break time."

His brows rose. He took it and unwrapped it. "Horse holidays?"

Her first smile of the day. "You know, a place to stay during downtime."

"That's sort of what this trip has been for me."

"How's that?"

Conor took a bite out of his bar and chewed slowly, trying to stall having to answer. Why had he said that about coming to America? After Christina had shared her own story, he owed her at least part of his. But he couldn't give her all. That, he wouldn't talk about. The loss of his baby was too painful.

"You have heard most of it. About my family wanting me to be here. Because they don't think I'm moving on after my wife's death."

"Are you?"

He'd never really thought about it. How like Christina to cut to the center of the problem. He would like to say he had started moving on but he couldn't. "I don't know."

She studied him a moment. "I bet you do."

"They thought I kept to myself too much. They wanted me to visit old friends, go to the pub, or come to their house for parties."

"But you didn't, did you?"

He shook his head. "Mostly I saw my patients and stayed at home. Then it became one patient. Gold. That might have ended if William Guinness had not insisted he wanted me taking care of Gold." Even to Conor that sounded sad. "I've been around more people since I came here than I have been in a year."

"I guess them pushing you to come worked."

He gave her a wry smile. "I guess it did."

Christina's phone rang and she clicked the hands-free speaker in the truck. "Doctor Mobbs."

"This is Dr. Dillard at Churchill Downs. I was wondering if you could come by and see me sometime today at the clinic."

Christina's eyes widened. Maybe this was what she'd been waiting on. "Sure, I can be there in about thirty minutes."

"I will expect you then."

She hung up. To Conor she said, "I hope you don't mind a trip to the racetrack. I need to obviously have a conversation with Dr. Dillard."

"I don't mind at all. Do you know what it's about?" His eyes held concern.

"I hope it's about me being on staff during Derby week." Christina pushed down her excitement.

"Why does that matter so much to you?"

"For one thing it's an honor. It also says that I'm a good enough veterinarian to be a part of that group." She started the truck.

"And you doubt you are good enough?"

"No, but others might." She wanted to move off that subject. She wasn't ready to go into why working at the Downs was so important to her.

Instead, she shared the reason she could utter. She wasn't ready to go into how she had disappointed her mother. How her mother had thought Christina had dragged their name in the mud with the business with Nelson when it made the news. "It's a golden opportunity for me to tell other veterinarians about my new program. They will hopefully refer our horses to my farm."

"I get that."

"The Derby is the greatest event in Kentucky each year. It's like the English have Ascot. Hundreds of thousands will be there in person, and millions will watch it on TV."

"I had no idea it was so big. The racetrack is massive."

She glanced at him. "You've been to Churchill Downs?"

"Yes. I had to go see about a stable for Gold. Check out where he would be staying. I made arrangements to have him examined and tested before he could be boarded there. I also checked in with the vet clinic to make sure I knew exactly what was expected testing-wise."

Before now she hadn't thought much about what Conor had been doing with his days. "You've been a busy guy. And here I thought you spent your days planning my meals."

He grinned. "That doesn't take me hours."

She smiled. "I'm glad because then I'd feel obligated to feel guilty."

They took the wide highway out of the rural area into the large busy city of Louisville. She entered the Churchill Downs grounds and drove around to the backside.

"You've been here before?"

"Numerous times." She pulled into a parking spot near a large building.

"Do you mind if I come in with you?"

"No, that's fine." Christina didn't wait on him before she headed toward the door of the Churchill Downs Equine Medical Center.

"I want to check out the facilities up close." He caught up with her and followed her into the building.

"Then I'll see you in a few minutes," she said over her shoulder before she spoke to the woman behind a desk just inside the door. "I'm Christina Mobbs. I'm here to see Dr. Dillard."

"Give me just a minute. He's seeing a horse right now." The woman walked down a hall toward the back of the building.

Christina took a seat in one of the two plastic chairs against the wall in the small reception area. Conor sat beside her.

She clasped and unclasped her hands. She couldn't help being nervous.

He said softly, "Hey, you have no reason to be so nervous. You'll wear the skin off your hands."

She narrowed her eyes.

"From what I've observed of your work you're as good as anyone I've ever seen. You're excellent with the horses, and your veterinarian work is superb. Don't ever let anybody make you feel any differently. It'll be fine." He placed his hand over her wringing hands for a moment.

That tingle she had when he touched her shot through her again. She gave him an unsure smile. "Thanks for that vote of confidence. It's been a long time since someone encouraged me."

A barrel-chested doctor walked toward them. Christina quickly stood. "Doctor Dillard, it's good to see you again."

"You, too," Dr. Dillard said. He glanced at Conor.

She turned to Conor. "I understand you've met Doctor O'Brian."

"Yes. Good to see you again." The two men shook hands. "Doctor O'Brian, please feel free to observe wherever you like while I speak with Doctor Mobbs. Doctor Mobbs, if you would come with me. We'll meet in my office."

Conor gave Christina a reassuring smile before she walked away with Dr. Dillard.

Christina appreciated Conor's encouragement. She'd had little of that in her life and even less in the past few years. Now that she could look back at it realistically, Nelson hadn't provided that, either. She had been the one who kept the farm and their relationship moving. Nelson rarely offered her help or encouragement. She'd wanted marriage and children. He dragged his feet. Why she'd waited until he almost destroyed her entire world to distance herself from him, she would never know.

She certainly hadn't looked to her mother for praise. Her father said little to contradict her mother. To Christina's surprise, Conor's kind words were the most she could remember hearing in a long time. It took a stranger from halfway around the world for her to start believing in herself again.

"This is more a closet than an office but it's the best they could give me out here," Dr. Dillard said as he led her through a doorway.

"It's not a problem." Christina entered the room.

"Doctor O'Brian seems like a good fella. Thank you for being willing to board the horse he's overseeing."

"My pleasure." Conor really had been a good houseguest. She couldn't stop herself from enjoying having another person around. And he wasn't hard to look at, either. It was nice to have someone in her corner, too. A surge of pleasure went through her at the memory of his supportive smile. "Gold is acclimating well. Doctor O'Brian has been good help as well."

"When I spoke to him the other day, he said he was pleased with staying at your farm. I'm glad to hear that." Dr. Dillard cleared his throat. "Why I asked you here is to speak to you about joining the vet team during Derby week."

Christina's heart beat faster. "I would appreciate the opportunity."

He nodded. "You'll be doing different assignments leading up to the race days and on those you'll be stationed along the racetrack."

"I look forward to helping out." At least she would get a chance to watch the races. Some veterinarians would remain in the barn area, unable to see anything.

Dr. Dillard's eyes turned concerned. "Will you be able to handle your practice and farm while being here for a week?"

"I'll make that work."

"You'll need to be here before daylight and you'll be staying until after dark." Dr. Dillard wore an earnest look.

She straightened. "That won't be a problem."

"There'll be over forty veterinarians here on Friday and Saturday. We'll have a big responsibility here."

"I'll be glad to be one of them." She meant it.

"And we'll be glad to have you. By the way, next weekend on Saturday night my wife and I are hosting a cookout at our place for the team of veterinarians working at the Downs during Derby week. You should get an invitation in the mail this week. Why don't you bring along Doctor O'Brian as well?"

Christina wasn't sure she wanted to show up as a couple at Dr. Dillard's party but she really didn't have a choice. "I'll be sure to ask him."

"And I'll see you for the party and then on the Monday morning afterward for an orientation meeting here at the Downs." Dr. Dillard smiled at her.

She returned it. "I'll be here."

Christina left the office with a light step. She could hardly wait to tell Conor. She reached the front to find him talking to the woman behind the desk. He left the woman with a smile and joined Christina. She continued out the door and stopped out of sight of those in the clinic.

"Well, are you going to be working the Derby?" he asked, facing her, anticipation in his eyes.

"Yes." She threw her arms around his neck. "I am."

Conor's arms came around her, holding her tight against his hard chest. She absorbed his heat and strength for a moment before she realized what she had done. Letting go, she placed her hands on his shoulders and stepped back. He let his hands fall to his sides.

Her face heated and she looked at the tips of her boots. "I'm sorry. I didn't mean to do that. I was just so excited to tell someone."

"Don't be. That's the nicest thing that has happened to me in a long time."

She glanced up. Conor watched her with a warm intensity that made her belly flutter. "Doctor Dillard wants me to bring you along to a party at his house next Saturday."

He hesitated and looked away before he put more space between them. "Let me think about it."

She hadn't realized until then how much she had liked the idea of their going to a party together, despite her own reservations. Did he just not like parties or was it that he didn't want to go with her? Either way his answer shouldn't have bothered her as much as it did.

"Are we headed home now or out to more stops?" Conor looked everywhere but at her.

"I'm going to stop in and see if my cousin is here. She sometimes helps out at the human clinic." Christina turned toward a small white building down the dirt and gravel road that led farther into the backside. "It's been a while since I've seen her."

He fell into step beside her. "This is really some

place. The spires are impressive. You told me it was large, but I had no idea."

He acted as if nothing had happened a few minutes earlier. If Conor could do that so could she. "I love this place. My cousin's parents used to bring me here occasionally. Not on Derby Day but on weekends just to watch the horses run. I am still amazed by the beauty and majesty of the Thoroughbreds' movements."

"You make it sound like poetry."

She looked at him. "Isn't it?"

"I've never thought about it, but now I have I couldn't agree with you more. One thing we do share is the love of a good horse. There's nothing like watching a morning stretch."

"We call it the Breeze. That's one of the many reasons I can't just let old racehorses go. I want them to have another life after racing. We all deserve a second chance."

His eyes met hers. Admiration filled them. "I think it's a very admirable thing you're doing."

She stopped. "Thank you for that. I needed to hear it."

"You're welcome. You should be praised more often. You are a great vet. You really care about your patients." He grinned. "The only thing I can find you fail at is cooking. And housekeeping of course."

That didn't even begin to hurt her feelings. She laughed. "Yes, I fail at both. Much to my mother's chagrin. She would like me to be a homemaker and mother like her. I don't care much for the homemaking, but I would like to be a mother."

His eyes shadowed over and he looked away for a moment before he asked, "Your parents live close by?"

"No, actually in Florida. They retired and moved down there. But my mother stays in touch with her friends here and seems to know all the gossip before I do." She stopped in front of the medical clinic, a building with the door in the middle and two windows to each side. She opened the door. "Callie works here."

He followed her inside.

"Hi, is Callie around?" Christina asked the man behind the desk. At the sound of a squeal Christina looked down the hall. Callie hurried in Christina's direction with her arms open wide.

"To what do I owe this nice surprise?" She wrapped Christina in a hug.

They separated.

"I've been over to see Doctor Dillard."

"And?" Callie looked at Christina with an anxious expectation.

Christina straightened her shoulders and smiled. "I'll be seeing you around on Derby weekend."

"Well, good for you. I'm not really surprised. I think you're more concerned about what happened than others are."

Christina huffed. "Tell that to the licensing

commission. They seemed pretty uptight about it last year."

Callie waved a hand as if she could brush it all away. "That was then and this is now." She looked past Christina to Conor leaning casually against the wall. "Can I help you?"

"He's with me. Callie, this is Conor O'Brian. He's visiting from Ireland. He's staying at the farm seeing about one of the racehorses."

Callie's brows rose as she studied Conor a moment. "Hello."

"Hi." Conor stepped forward but stopped behind Christina.

"Staying at the farm." She had made it a statement instead of a question. Callie studied Conor keenly for a moment.

"Just while Gold acclimates to the weather and settles from the trip over." Why did Christina feel she had to justify Conor's presence? Because it had been over a year since she had anything to do with a man. It was time to get Callie's mind on something else. "How're you doing?"

"Well. Just getting prepared for the onslaught of people for the Derby. As much as I love the races it's super busy around here."

"This isn't even your place to oversee anymore," Christina said.

"I know but I help out when I'm needed. You're

lucky to catch me here today. Langston is running a test today or I wouldn't be here."

"Langston is her husband, who works with preventing brain injuries," Christina explained to Conor.

Callie said, "I can't believe we live so close and don't see each other more."

"We'll have to do something about that. I hear you and Langston are really doing some innovative things with horse-and-rider safety." Christina liked Callie's Texas husband and appreciated his life-changing work.

"I like to think so. Only problem is we seem to work all the time, but we love it."

"Y'all are supposed to be on your honeymoon." Christina couldn't prevent the wistfulness from entering her voice. At one time she believed she'd be married by now. Maybe even have a child.

A silly grin formed on Callie's lips. "Sure, we are."

What would it be like to have someone act like that just at the thought of her? She looked at Conor, who stood with such patience, waiting on her. That wasn't a direction she should consider.

Callie spoke to Conor. "I hope you're enjoying your stay in America."

"I am."

"I'm sure it's quite different from Ireland," Callie said.

"That it is, but it has its appeals just the same."
He glanced at Christina.

Callie's eyes brightened and she studied Christina a moment. "It does now."

Her face heated. Callie had fallen in love with her husband a year ago and she thought everyone should be in love.

A man holding his hand in the palm of his other one hurried into the clinic.

"I got to go." Callie stepped to the man and led him down the hall. "Be sure to pop in and say hi during the Derby."

"Will do." Christina pushed out the door.

Conor walked beside her on the way to her truck. "Did you and Callie grow up together?"

"We saw a lot of each other. Back then she was determined she was going to be a vet but changed her mind and now she does medical research with her husband on sports-related head injuries."

"That sounds like something beneficial to the industry. I do know there are too many head injuries."

They walked toward her truck. "They're doing some really great innovative work. I'm proud of them."

He reached for the passenger door. "I'm sure they are proud of the work you do or plan to do. Your plan for horses is to be admired as well."

How did this man manage in a few words to lessen the self-loathing she had felt for so long?

CHAPTER FOUR

CONOR APPROACHED THE BARN. He'd thought more than once over the past two days about what Christina had said about everyone deserving a second chance. Wasn't that what he needed, too? His siblings had accused him of not moving on. For so long he hadn't felt he could or even wanted to, but since coming to stay at Christina's a week ago, that had slowly been changing.

Conor wished he had a better idea of what caused Christina distress. He might be able to help. But why did it matter? This was someone he hardly knew, and he would be leaving in a couple of weeks. He had no investment here.

He entered the barn and walked through to the other side and out the doors into the sunlight. He found Christina bathing a horse. He stepped up beside her. "I figured I'd find you here."

She jumped and turned. The water hose she held soaked him from middle to his knees.

Horror flashed over her face. She dropped the

hose and pulled the earbud from her ear. "I'm so sorry. You scared me. I didn't hear you."

He gave her a thin-lipped smile.

Then she doubled over in giggles.

The sound filled him with something best called happiness. He loved the tinkling sound. "Did you do that on purpose?"

Christina took control of her laughing and straightened. She looked at him and busted into giggles again.

Conor reached for the hose, but her booted foot came down on it before he could pick it up. She held it to the ground. He pursed his lips and glared. With a swift movement, he lunged. He would show her. Christina's eyes went wide seconds before he wrapped his arms around hers and secured her against his wet front. He held her there letting his damp clothes seep into hers.

"Stop. You're getting me wet." She wiggled, trying to get away.

His manhood reacted to her struggle. Something he'd experienced little of in the past few years until he had met Christina. It both thrilled and worried him. Yet, he didn't release his hold. He teased, "Who got who wet first and then laughed at them?"

She continued to squirm. "I didn't mean to."

"But you meant to laugh at me," he goaded.

She went still. Her gaze met his. He held it,

watching her eyes shift from determination to awareness to questioning. Did she realize how aroused he was?

The need to kiss her had grown with having her so close, touching him; the days of being near her had compounded themselves into a need to taste her.

She blinked. "I did do that." The giggles bubbled again. "I'm sorry. You should have seen your face."

"I was too busy feeling my clothes being soaked." He tugged her closer.

Mischief filled her eyes. She said with complete innocence, "I didn't mean to."

His look held hers. He made himself not focus on her lips. "Maybe not but I'm still wet."

And desiring her. The feeling had been building for days. He'd pushed it down, shoved it away, but there it had been every time he was around Christina. Maybe if he got the unknown out of the way it wouldn't return.

Would she let him kiss her? What if she refused him? She had her own ghosts holding her back. Did he dare take the chance she would reject him? How would he know if he didn't try? He might regret it for the rest of his life if he didn't. There was enough of those in his life already.

His head lowered. His lips touched hers. He released her arms, his hands moving to rest lightly on her hips. Making her captive was not what he wanted. He needed her to want his kiss. Her hands ran up his chest to settle on his shoulders. An electric thrill shot through him at her touch. Christina wasn't pushing him away. She wanted it, too.

He deepened the kiss. Christina returned it. He pressed her closer.

Conor understood then how he had been fooling himself about not needing a woman. How quickly Christina had made his excuses lies. Every nerve ending in his body hummed with awareness of her. She made him feel alive once more.

She sighed and wrapped her arms around his neck, pressing herself into his throbbing length. Conor slowly kissed the seam of her lips. His tongue traced it, requesting entrance. Pleasure washed through him when she opened her mouth. He savored the warm moment, then plunged forward, eager for more. She welcomed him. His hands caressed her hips and circled to cup her behind, lifting her to him.

He would take all she would offer him. His body hummed like it hadn't in too long, in ways he had forgotten existed. Christina had managed to make him push past his pain.

The whinny of the horse nearby broke them apart.

Christina looked as shocked as he felt. He had to straighten this out. Say something. Reassure her he wouldn't take advantage of her. "I'm sorry. That was inappropriate. I shouldn't have done that. Excuse me."

Disbelief turned disappointment filled her eyes. A flicker of hurt flashed in them before he turned and walked off, guilt washing over him.

Christina watched Conor stalk away, stunned. What had just happened? With him. With her. This wasn't something she'd seen coming. Or had she? Wasn't she attracted to him? She would be lying if she said she hadn't noticed his wide shoulders, his beautiful eyes, or how supportive of her he had been. And that list didn't include his accent that sent shivers down her spine any time he spoke. That had her thinking things she shouldn't. Before going to bed and in her dreams.

Still, she had never expected him to kiss her. Apparently, he hadn't anticipated it, either. Conor acted disgusted that he had kissed her, that he had made the first move. She didn't appreciate that at all.

Having been used before by Nelson and not measuring up to her mother's expectations enough in her life, Christina had no intentions of feeling that way again. Then along came Conor and she had opened herself up once more to rejection. He had slipped through a crack of crazy loneliness, and she'd welcomed him, basking in the feeling of being admired.

She picked up the hose and ran the water over the horse's back. Picking up the sponge, she soaped the horse down.

Maybe their interaction had been a bad idea but the kiss had been amazing. Perfect, in fact. His lips had brushed hers gently then he had crushed her to him as if he might never let her go. In a brief amount of time he had made her feel wanted, desired—necessary. It was as if he sensed what she needed and had agreed to gift it to her.

Then he had abruptly left her. Lost and alone. And not sure all she had felt had been true.

She took in a deep breath of air and let it out slowly. Conor hadn't been completely unaffected. His arousal had been evident between them. That gave her some sense of satisfaction.

A few minutes later she heard the sound of his truck being cranked then the tires over the gravel of the drive. He had left.

He did not return by that evening. She saw to Gold when she made her nightly round.

She had the light off in her room, but she wasn't asleep when Conor returned.

Conor came in quietly, went to his room. He must have taken his boots off because she heard his padded feet in the hall outside her door. His footsteps stopped there.

She held her breath. Would he knock on her door? Was he hoping she was still awake?

Long, lingering moments later, the shower in the bath came on.

Christina rolled her face into the pillow and moaned.

The next morning before breakfast Conor went looking for Christina. It was no surprise he found her in the barn. As he approached, she continued to brush the horse's leg.

From the tension in her shoulders, she was aware he stood nearby. He swallowed hard being fully mindful that she deserved an apology for his actions, during and after their kiss. He shouldn't have done it to begin with and he shouldn't have treated her like she was a mistake.

"Christina?"

"Yes?"

"Can we talk? Clear the air." He stepped closer.

"There's nothing to talk about." She didn't even bother to look at him.

"You know there is."

She faced him. "I've been kissed before. No big deal."

Conor wanted to take her by the shoulders and shake her. Of course, it was more than a kiss. He could still feel the sweetness of her lips beneath his. Had dreamed of doing so again. He cleared his throat. "I shouldn't have walked off like that. I didn't mean to hurt you."

"Don't worry about it. I get it." She didn't look at him.

Conor didn't see how she couldn't worry about it. He had hurt her. "I said some things I shouldn't have. It's just that I promised to be true to my wife."

Her chin dropped and her eyes narrowed as she looked at him as if he had two heads. "I thought she had died."

"She has but I promised to be true."

A compassionate look came to her eyes. Her voice sank low. "Conor, she would want you to go on living. A kiss doesn't mean you're desecrating her memory. It doesn't mean you loved her any less."

He had made a promise he would always be true to Louisa. Not be like his father. But hadn't he used that to build a wall to protect his heart? If he let it down, he might get hurt again. He wasn't sure he could live through that again. Even for Christina.

Christina untied the horse from the post and led it out of the barn.

He watched as she released the animal into the pasture. She slapped the animal on the hip. "Go and have a good day."

The horse ran into the field with his tail in the

air. Wouldn't it be nice if he could do that? Feel free for just a little while?

Conor came to stand beside her. "You care for them like they're your own."

"While they're here, they're my own." She looked at him as if that included him as well.

A lump formed in his chest. "Thank you for caring for Gold last night."

"Not a problem." She made it sound as if it wasn't. Is that the way she saw him, too?

"I know what I do with Gold is important but I'm thankful to you for reminding me of what it is to be a vet again. I've been babysitting one racehorse for so long I've started to forget what it's like to do the dirty part of vet care. The part that makes you feel alive."

"Well, I have plenty to do here to make you feel alive."

Conor chuckled. How like Christina to take him literally. "Let me check on Gold and give him a good walking and I'll be at your service. Are we good, Christina?"

"We are good."

She sounded like it, but he still couldn't be sure. He would just have to let time tell.

He spent the next hour seeing to Gold. Every once in a while, he caught sight of Christina swinging her hips as she listened to music and worked around the barn. She sang to the horses as well. He couldn't help but smile. Something he'd started to do more often since coming to America.

When it started to rain he brought Gold inside and put him in his stall. With that done he joined Christina in cleaning out stalls and replenishing hay. Every once in a while, she would remind him of something he'd missed. Still, he enjoyed the companionship, which he hadn't had in a long time.

Maybe now was the time to take a step forward. To move on with life. Couldn't he be friends with a woman and be true to Louisa at the same time? His family and friends, even Christina, had said it was time for him to move on. To have a second chance. Why shouldn't he start now? Christina had the kind heart to understand. He enjoyed her company. He couldn't think of anyone he'd rather spend time with.

He cleared his throat. It had been years since he'd done this. And after yesterday he wasn't sure she would agree. "Christina."

"Yes?" She turned to face him.

"I was wondering if you would like to go out to dinner this evening?"

Christina took a moment before she spoke. "I uh…don't think that's a good idea."

She had turned him down. He couldn't blame her after he'd stepped over the line. "Dinner. Nothing more."

"We shouldn't." She returned to using the pitchfork to spread hay.

"Probably not. But I'm asking you to dinner between friends. Something to repay you for letting me stay here. It would also give me a night off from cooking." All of that was true but he still couldn't help but want more. He liked her. Couldn't seem to stay away from her.

She turned. "I'm sorry. I shouldn't have assumed."

"Not a problem." Apparently, his statement about not cooking caught her attention.

She confirmed that a second later. "I'm sorry. I should have thought about all the time you've spent in the kitchen. I imagine you'd like a night off. Thank you. I would like to go to dinner with you."

The knot of anxiousness between his shoulders eased. He had no idea until then he had been afraid she might say no. Tonight he would try to make up for mistreating her the previous evening.

That evening Conor waited in the kitchen. He forced himself not to pace. He was out of practice when it came to going out with a woman even if she was just a friend. He had not been out alone with a non-family member in years. But this wasn't a date, he reminded himself. Yet, it felt like a date.

Christina entered the kitchen dressed in a floral sleeveless dress with a V-neck that showed a hint of cleavage. The fabric hugged her breasts and fell in waves around her hips. Conor's mouth went dry. He forced a swallow. She was lovely like a new filly in the field.

Her auburn hair flowed around her shoulders. Pink touched her cheeks as she ran her hands down her dress. "Too much?"

"Not at all. But you look like we might have to call this a date."

Bright spots of red formed on her cheeks. "I don't get many chances to wear a dress, so I thought I'd wear one tonight. My mother would be proud of me."

"I'm glad you chose a dress." His gaze went to her legs, which were trim and muscular. Just perfect.

"Thank you."

"After you." He directed her toward the door.

As they exited through the back door of the house, Conor took a moment to appreciate the soft swing of her hips. *Not a date*, he repeated to himself. "I'll drive."

"You're one of those guys."

"I guess I am." He opened her door and waited for her to settle inside his truck.

"That was nice of you but not necessary."

"You work hard day in and day out. You deserve to be treated special on occasion." He went to the driver's seat and slipped behind the wheel. "You smell nice."

"Not of manure and horse?"

"I have no problem with the smell of barn, but this suits you better." He needed to slow down, or he'd be right back where he was yesterday if she would allow him to kiss her.

She clasped her hands in her lap. "Are you going to spend the entire evening embarrassing me?"

"I just might if you continue to blush."

She pushed at her cheeks. "I've always hated the way my emotions show on my face."

"I rather like knowing how you're feeling." He enjoyed knowing where he stood with her. Where was the guilt he had been feeling over the kiss? One look at Christina in a dress had him thinking of other things.

"Conor, this is a friendly outing."

"You're right. We're going to be two people enjoying each other's company over dinner." He turned out of the drive.

"Where're we going to do that?" she asked when he pulled onto the main highway.

"I went through Versailles the other day and did not have time to stop. I thought we would go there if you had no objection."

She hesitated a moment then said, "That sounds fine."

He glanced at her. "If you'd rather go elsewhere, we can do that."

She placed her hands back in her lap. "No, Versailles will be nice."

Twenty minutes later Christina walked beside him down the main street of the quaint town with its brick courthouse in the middle of an intersection. The 1940s storefronts had been maintained with care. Hot pink flowers hung in baskets from the lampposts. A rosy glow fell over everything as the sun lowered.

Christina had covered her bare shoulders with a sweater while he enjoyed the warmth with his sleeves rolled up his forearms. He resisted putting his hand at her back. Yet, he remained close but not touching. He had already gotten in over his head where she was concerned. Was it from his forced proximity to Christina or was the attraction that strong?

He remained conflicted over his feelings for her, yet he couldn't keep his distance from Christina.

Christina, to his knowledge, had never made a movement he could have called a stroll. Tonight was no different. It was as if she were a horse pulling on the reins to go faster.

"If we don't hurry up, there might not be any tables. Then we'll have a wait."

"I'm enjoying the stroll with you." He wanted

to spend as much time as he could with her. That way maybe he would better understand this temptation between them.

"What?"

"It's about slowing down and appreciating life. Something you find difficult, I know." He had learned to do that. Having lost someone special, he knew about appreciating time. He would be leaving Christina in another week and a half, and he wanted what time he could have with her. His footsteps faltered. That idea hit him like a kick in the chest. Since when did spending time with Christina become so important?

What about Louisa? Christina was right. Louisa would want his happiness.

From what he understood the week of the Derby would be busy. He would be lucky if he saw Christina at all. Sadness fell over him. They didn't have much time to explore what was between them. Did she want to?

"What makes you think you know me that well?" She sounded irritated by the idea he might see something she didn't want others to see.

"Because I've watched you over the last week and I've gotten to know you pretty well."

Her eyes widened.

Conor took her elbow to gently move her out of the way of a group walking toward them. "Now, where would you like to eat? It can be anywhere."

"There's a nice restaurant right down here on the corner." She pointed ahead of them.

"Then that is where we will go." It was the first time he'd used a firm tone with her, but he was not going to let her change her mind. The woman really did need to take time to enjoy life some.

She huffed. "You're not the boss of me."

"No, I am not, but you are my dinner date…uh friend. I like them to have a smile on their face when they eat with me."

"Says the man that showed up at my farm a little more than a week ago looking like a thundercloud."

He smiled. "My brother and sister said something like that before I left."

She patted his arm. "With good reason."

They paused in front of the restaurant. It had matching front windows on either side of the dark wooden door. On both the windows was etched the word *Thoroughbred*. Above that was the figure of a horse stretched out in a run. In the corners were filigrees. Light from inside spilled out onto the sidewalk.

He held the door open for Christina. She balked at entering. "Maybe we should go somewhere else."

Was this about the same thing that had her hesitating on the ride over? Did it have to do with him or had she seen someone she didn't want to face?

Her expression said she might be uncomfortable with the idea but she quickly recovered.

She inhaled a breath as if bracing herself before she stepped inside.

"Hey, Christina," the woman behind the hostess desk said.

"Hello, Jean. Do you have a booth available?" Christina asked with a note of forced brightness.

The woman smiled. "Sure. Just take a spot wherever you like."

"Thanks." Christina didn't wait on him but headed toward the far side of the room away from the door and traffic. She slid into a booth constructed to look like a barn stall as if relieved to get there.

Who was she hiding from?

He ran a hand down the smooth pieces of wood that made their booth. "These look like the real thing."

"They are from an old barn that was torn down near mine." She looked at the table.

"I like it. This old-world work reminds me of home." He took a seat on the red cushion and settled in front of her. "This is an interesting place."

A teenage waitress stood at the end of the table and handed them a plastic-covered menu.

During their meal a number of people casually spoke to Christina as they were coming to their tables or leaving. Each time she acted unsure when they approached then pleasantly surprised at their greeting. Just what was her problem?

Conor settled back in the booth watching Christina. "Apparently, you are well-known around here."

Her eyes flickered up to meet his look. "Yes. I grew up in Versailles. But that can have its disadvantages."

Those would be...? "True, but I bet it can have advantages as well."

She crossed her arms on the table, looking directly at him. "Have you lived in the same spot most of your life?"

"Yes."

"Then you must know what it's like for everyone to know your business good or bad."

"I do." His home was a place where everyone knew his pain. Like that his wife didn't love him enough to stay alive. That his father cheated on his mother. These memories walked daily with him. The expressions on townsfolk's faces held pity. The ones he hid from. Yet, it was home. "I've lived in the same village my entire life except for when I left for school." He needed a change in subject. "This is the kind of place that reminds me of a pub back home. But only quieter."

She looked beyond them. "It'll get noisier later. I've never been to a pub."

"Never? Our pubs are where the whole community hangs out. You couldn't live in Ireland without finding your pub. Have you ever thought about visiting Ireland?"

"No, but I've always wanted to travel. With the farm and horses to care for it's hard to get away. Maybe one day."

He turned the water glass in his hands. "I guess it doesn't ever let up. If you do come let me know and I'll show you around."

"I doubt that will happen any time soon. I'm trying to build up a business." Her voice held a wistful note.

"Why are you trying to do that instead of just having your regular practice? I would think it would be enough."

Christina let out a breath slowly. She leaned back against the booth. "Well, I sort of just fell into it. My ex-partner had the idea. When he left, I just couldn't close it down."

"But that doesn't mean that you don't need a life outside of here." He looked around the room.

She leaned back and pinned him with a look. "Is this the man whose family had to force him to come to America?"

The woman didn't mind hitting hard. "You have a point."

She smiled. For once that evening, she looked relaxed. "Tell me about Ireland."

He smiled. "I think you would like it. It reminds

me very much of Kentucky with its rolling hills and green grass. The people are friendly. We've got stone walls, where you've got all these wooden fences, but we love our horses. We've got cooler temperatures."

She grinned. "You love the place as much as I love here."

"I do love it." But oddly, he hadn't missed it like he had when he had first arrived.

Christina stepped out of the restaurant to the streetlights burning. She had enjoyed her dinner with Conor more than she'd imagined. She had gone to extra trouble dressing and his reaction had been worth the trouble. Then to have his complete attention focused on her had heated her skin. More than once her heart had skipped a beat when his hand had brushed hers as they walked down the street or reached for something at the same time at the table.

She had to stop herself a couple of times from staring at his lips.

The only negative of the evening had been her reaction to going into the Thoroughbred. She had misjudged her strength in being able to handle returning. It had been a regular place for her and Nelson to join friends. Those who disappeared when she had been in trouble.

She'd had a choice to admit that to Conor or make herself hold her head high. The latter won. Being with Conor gave her extra reassurance. She was with a handsome man who would support and protect her.

How did she know that? Because he'd done nothing but show that since she had met him. She believed he was a good man. But hadn't her judgment been off before?

"A few people I've met have mentioned there is a small racetrack around here and that there is racing tonight. Would you like to go?"

She couldn't go there. The urge to shake her head wildly filled her but she didn't do it. What would she do if someone said the wrong thing in front of Conor? She would die. "I don't know. I should really get home and make sure the horses are settled for the night."

"I can help you do that when we get back. I'd like to see how a race is run before the Derby."

She quickly released a sigh. "Okay, we can go for a few races."

In the car he said, "How about giving me directions."

"Turn left. It's only a few miles out of town. There's a large sign on the highway." They were walking toward the racetrack when she said, "These are the horses that didn't make the Kentucky Derby cut or probably never would but the locals coming here have fun watching the horses race. It's also a good place for the jockeys to learn and get experience."

She led Conor to the entrance where a woman sat at a portable table with a metal box at hand.

"Hi, Christina. We haven't seen you around in a while." The woman took the money Conor offered her.

Christina stiffened. She was surprised Emily sounded genuinely glad to see her. "Hello. It's nice to see you again."

They continued toward the stands.

Conor walked beside her. "Apparently, they know you here, too."

"Yes, I used to work here on the weekends." She led the way to a seat in one of the two metal bleachers going to the second row from the top. "I like to see. I love the horses, but I also love coming to the races. I've always enjoyed the small track. Sometimes I think they're more fun than the big races. Here you can really see the horses. And the crowd likes watching them instead of being seen themselves."

Conor sat beside her just out of touching distance but close enough she could feel his heat. Her skin tingled with his nearness.

"Tell me about your races. I understand they're different from ours."

"There will be several races tonight but lots more on Derby Day, including the Derby. The horses run ten furlongs, or about one and a half US miles. Only three-year-olds run on a dirt track. These tonight will be very similar to those at Churchill Downs on Kentucky Derby Day."

"Do you bet much?" Conor looked toward the betting boxes.

"Almost never. When I'm working they don't allow it. Therefore, I make it a practice not to do it." She had already had a close call with the law once and she wouldn't give the racing commission a reason to question her behavior again.

"Christina." A woman called her from the aisle of the stands.

"Hi, Lucy. It's good to see you."

"You, too. How have you been?" Lucy sounded sincere.

"Just working a lot. How about you?" Lucy had been her friend.

"Busy, too. I was sorry about what happened to you. I haven't had a chance to tell you that. I should've been a better friend and believed in you." Lucy's look didn't waver.

"Thank you for saying that." Even now it was nice.

Lucy smiled. "Well, I better get back to work. I hope you come around more often."

Christina said to Conor, "Sorry I didn't introduce you. Lucy runs this racetrack."

* * *

She had been Christina's best friend, but Nelson's lies had fractured that as well. That, Christina didn't plan to dwell on. She'd been enjoying herself tonight. Conor had been a wonderful dinner companion. She didn't want to talk about the past and ruin the time they had together.

Conor looked out toward the track. "This reminds me of our local course at home."

Christina followed his gaze. There weren't any barns just horse trailers hitched to big trucks in a large lot off in a distance. The track was grass. It had been cut and trimmed. There was a well-used horse gate stationed across the track.

"Really? How is that? I understand your races are a cross between a steeplechase and a regular race."

"Some of them are." He leaned forward, resting his elbows on his knees.

"I have seen horses jumping on TV but I have no idea what happens in your races. I bet it makes for an interesting experience with the combo of jumping and running."

"It does." Conor intensely watched the activity in the area. He was a man who looked at the details.

"That certainly adds an element of danger to the event."

"It does but it also adds to the challenge." He commented without looking at her.

"I could see your point there. It sounds rather exciting." She would like to see one someday.

"We like to think so. We don't have such a large spectator area as Churchill Downs. Our seating is simpler. When the horses come up to the starting line people pour to the outside, and when they're not racing, they go inside under the stands to the bar and to place their bets."

"That's interesting. Our attendees pretty much live in the stands. You'll be amazed on Derby Day the number of people there. The pomp and circumstance involved, the traditions."

He looked at her and grinned. "I look forward to it. And Gold winning his race."

She had to admit she would be pulling for the horse. "Wouldn't that be exciting? You'll enjoy the Oaks race on Friday when the three-year-old fillies run. The stands will be almost as full and it's all day as well."

"But I guess you'll be busy."

Conor sounded disappointed she wouldn't be sharing it with him. It was nice to have someone want to share her company.

The announcer called over the microphone. "The horses are in the gate." Seconds later he announced, "And they're off."

The crowd stood. The horses ran around the first curve.

Christina went up on her toes in an effort to see better. When she wobbled, she grasped Conor's forearm so she wouldn't fall. His arm went around her waist when she climbed on the bench to stand on it. She spoke to Conor without looking. "Sorry, I can't see. I do miss having a large television screen like they have at Churchill Downs. I can't tell how they're doing on the backside."

Even in the distance the thunder of the horses' hooves could be heard. The horses came around the second back turn.

Christina stretched to see. She registered the tightening of Conor's arm. He wouldn't let her fall.

The crowd grew louder along with the pounding of hooves. The horses made the front curve and entered the part of the track in front of them. Unable to help herself Christina started jumping.

"They're coming down the stretch," the announcer said.

The crowd cheered as the horses thundered across the finish line.

Christina whooped then threw her arms around Conor's neck. His arms wrapped around her waist and held her. He grinned up at her with amazement sparkling in his eyes. Reality struck her. She pushed away from him and stepped down from the bench, pushing her dress into place. "I'm sorry. I should've warned you I get carried away."

He chuckled. "I have no problem with that. My arm may be bruised in the morning but it will have been worth it."

What must he think? After yesterday's kiss and her reaction and then she throws herself at him. She needed to put some distance between them. She patted his upper arm. "I'm sorry. I didn't mean to hurt you."

His arm squeezed her closer. "I enjoyed it. It's nice to see you happy."

During the next race she tried to restrain herself but didn't manage to do much better than she had earlier. Conor grinned then offered his hand to help her up on the bleacher and supported her once more. She looked forward to his protection with each race. Apparently, she wouldn't be successful in keeping her distance.

In the last race the horses rounded the last turn toward the finish line, one horse bumped another then another stumbled into another before two horses went down.

Christina held her breath. She didn't see something like this often, but she had seen it before. It didn't end up well.

The jockeys moved quickly to get away from the horses. Jockeys still in the saddle continued for the finish line. The fallen horses kicked to stand while the racetrack staff ran onto the field. One staff member ran out from the sideline and grabbed the reins and tugged the most active horse's head, encouraging him to his feet. With one swift movement he stood.

The other horse lay on the ground, unmoving. In less than ten seconds a large blue screen had been placed so that the crowd couldn't see what was happening.

CHAPTER FIVE

CONOR ALWAYS HATED to see a screen go up. It didn't bode well for the horse.

Christina brushed behind him on her way down the bench toward the steps.

"Hey, where are you going?"

She pointed down.

It was then he saw her friend Lucy with her hand in the air, waving Christina down to the track. Conor didn't hesitate to follow. He made his way around people who had stepped out into the stairs.

He joined the women just as Lucy said with panic in her voice, "I could use your help."

She didn't wait on Christina to answer.

She followed, keeping pace behind Lucy. Conor was behind Christina as they hurried toward where the accident had happened.

Lucy said over her shoulder as they moved. "Our vet for tonight had an emergency and just left. The replacement is on the way but isn't here yet. It's a blessing you were here tonight."

They reached the track. There they went through a gate and loped across the grass track to where the screen stood. The need for it meant the horse would probably be put down. Unfortunately, accidents were part of the sport. An ugly part.

He followed Christina behind the screen to a scene he had expected. Christina went immediately to her knees beside the horse. She patted his neck. Fear filled the animal's large dark eyes. "Easy, boy, help is here. Easy."

Conor dropped down beside her. He ran his hand over the horse's back legs. Christina did the same on the front.

"I can't find a break here." She continued her examination.

Conor finished his. "I don't find one here, either."

Christina patted the horse's neck once again. She moved her hand over the horse's shoulder and along his back. "No obvious broken bones. Let's see if we can get him up on his feet."

"Let me get around on the other side so I can help push him." Conor moved opposite her.

Christina took the reins and stood. The horse kicked his feet. "Okay, boy, let's see you stand."

A couple of grooms joined Conor. "We're ready."

"Easy, boy. Slow and easy." She tugged on the

reins. Conor pushed the horse. The men beside him did as well.

All the while, Christina continued to talk to the scared animal. Suddenly, the horse kicked and rolled and came to its feet. Conor stepped back to where he could see the horse's movements. He did not see a problem.

"Conor, do you see any issues?"

"No. He looks good to me."

"We'll give him a moment for his head to quit spinning." She stroked the nose of the horse, who settled before their eyes. "Now we're going take a little walk around," Christina said to the horse then led him in a circle.

While she did, Conor watched every movement the horse made for a limp or hesitation. With the next slow turn he saw it. "There it is. Right fore-leg."

Christina stopped the horse. She handed the reins to a groom. "Slow walk."

The groom nudged the horse forward.

She stood beside Conor. "I see it now. Let's get it wrapped up and secure. Then he'll need X-rays."

An older man ran around the screen. He came to an abrupt stop. He demanded as he looked at Christina, "What are you doing here?"

Christina stiffened beside Conor. Who was this guy? Why was he speaking to Christina that way?

"Lucy asked me to help."

"We don't want you here. The racetrack doesn't need any more trouble because of you." He glared at her.

"I understand how you feel about that, but that's not the case here. I was vindicated."

Vindicated? What was she talking about? Conor stepped closer.

She glanced at him. He stopped. "Doctor Victor," she said to the man, "I'll go but first you need to know that the horse has an issue with the right front foreleg. It is barely detectable to the eye. X-rays will be required."

"I can handle this. Thank you." Dr. Victor turned his back to her.

Conor felt her tremble. "Christina, I think we're done here."

Her attention didn't leave the horse and the movements of the man, but she didn't argue. Conor took her hand and led her away. They walked out the gate to the parking lot. At the car she got in without saying a word.

He didn't start the car. Instead, he turned to face her. "You want to tell me what that was all about?"

"Not really."

He watched her a moment then nodded and started the car. He knew from experience that if someone didn't want to talk, he couldn't make them. He had been the same with his siblings. He pulled out of the gravel parking lot.

"You aren't going to try any harder than that to find out?" She almost sounded disappointed.

Conor glanced at her. "You'll tell me when you are ready."

"I guess you deserve some explanation."

She made it sound as if she wasn't convinced he did.

"It's not a nice story."

He looked at her again. "I've heard ugly stories before."

She started slowly. "About a year and a half ago all those people who spoke to me this evening had stopped doing so."

"Why?" That had to have hurt her.

"Because they thought I had been stealing and selling drugs. In fact, I almost lost my license. If I hadn't had the paperwork to prove I had followed the rules, I would have had the racing commission on me. Doctor Victor, the man who just came up, was on the board then. I came closer than I ever want to again to losing my license."

Now Conor understood the interaction between them. "So what happened?"

"My ex. Who lived with me for four years. Who had access to my medicines. Who said he loved me but pointed his finger at me when the authorities started asking questions."

Conor wanted to punch something on her behalf. The pain in her voice made her ex a prime candidate. "What was he doing with the drugs? Taking them or selling them?"

"Both. To make matters worse he gambled on the horses, which is a no-no and was stealing to pay his gambling debt. What made it worse was I thought he loved me. That we were going to get married and start a family."

He winced. Marriage and family. What he had once wanted. But no longer. "I get why working at the Derby is so important to you now. It's your way of proving you aren't the person everyone said you were."

"Yeah. Regaining my good reputation is important to me in general but to my work with horses as well. People need to trust me. Horse racing is a small world. And to start a new business in it is difficult. What made me really mad was I was too stupid to see what he was doing. I trusted him. I can't trust my judgment anymore."

"I can see why. I'm sorry that happened to you." She had endured more than she should have.

"Things are better now. Even as hard as it was to walk into the racetrack tonight, it felt good to have people speak to me. I'm starting to rebuild my reputation."

"I haven't known you long but I think you are doing just fine. It takes time." He certainly knew that well. Three years later he had just started working through his wife's death. He took Christina's hand and squeezed it. "I know I would have missed out if I'd never met you."

Christina appreciated his warmth. Conor's words felt like a hot drink flowing through her. He made her want to believe him. She looked at his handsome profile. He was a nice man.

Conor continued to hold her hand. Gently, he rubbed the top of it with the pad of his thumb. "You have to be true to yourself. You know you are honest. You can't carry others' mistakes as yours."

"To say that is one thing. To live it is another." She relaxed in her seat, appreciating his reassurance.

"You shouldn't have had to deal with all that."

"I was the one that should have noticed or maybe subconsciously I did, but didn't want to know."

"Nor can you be perfect and all-knowing."

Her mother had certainly expected that of her. Do it better, be better, do it just so. Christina hadn't ever felt like she measured up. The thing with Nelson just proved she never would. Here Conor was telling her that she didn't have to do more than be herself. "Thanks for the vote of confidence. You have no idea what the means to me."

"Now I understand why you are so particular about counting your medicine cabinet."

"Yeah, I keep a strict count now. I take no chances." She wouldn't be put in a position of explaining herself again.

"Being super vigilant isn't a bad thing. What isn't healthy is obsessing over it. It's past time for you to move forward."

"You don't think I already know all of that?" Her words had a sharp note to them.

"Oh, I'm sure you do but you need to be reminded of it." He grinned.

They remained in their own thoughts the rest of the way home.

Conor pulled behind the house and shut off the car.

"I need to check on the horses." She was out of the car and at the back door before he caught up with her.

He called, "Hey, wait a minute. You're not running from me, are you?"

She looked at him, her eyes watering. "I don't know. Maybe I'm running from myself."

He cupped her cheek. "You have no reason to be afraid of me. I'm your friend, Christina. You can trust me."

And she knew she could. Christina loved the feel of Conor's skin touching hers. She wanted to lean in to his warmth and reassurance. But if she did, it would soon be gone. She couldn't let herself need it. "I know. Come on, we need to see about the horses."

He sighed, letting his fingertips trail across her cheek. "Yes, the horses."

It had rained while they were gone. They changed into their rubber boots and walked out to the barn. Conor went to see about Gold while she went through her nightly routine. He waited at the barn doors when he finished.

Christina flipped off the inside lights. Conor helped her close and secure the doors. The outside security light formed a subdued glow around them.

"You know, you're doing yourself a disservice. You have to know how amazing you are."

"Thank you. That was a nice thing to say. I'm the one who should be thanking you for your support tonight. For a moment there I thought you were gonna pick up a sword and shield. Maybe I should move away from here so I can leave it all behind."

"Take my word for it, it doesn't work like that. I've left a country behind and it is still here with me."

"You miss your wife, don't you?" Christina couldn't help asking.

"Every day."

What would it be like to be loved so completely? To know that another person had your back no matter what. That you were enough for them.

"I can say that it eases. But you do carry it

around with you all the time. Coming here helped. I didn't think it would, but it did."

"I'm glad. I just don't want to forget what can happen if you trust too much and mess up again."

Christina stopped, watching him. She had been so embarrassed in front of him tonight but instead of turning against her he'd stepped forward as if he would fight for her honor. More than that, he had listened, really listened to her. For that, she could kiss him. "Thank you for being a nice guy."

Placing her hands on his shoulders, she went up on her toes and gave him a soft kiss on the lips. She stepped back.

Conor looked at her a second before he pulled her against him. His lips found hers. She leaned in to him. As his lips applied more pressure, his hands moved over her back. Her muscles rippled under Conor's touch just as the horses did when she caressed them. The man had a tender touch.

His mouth released hers. Placing his forehead against hers, he whispered in a reverent tone, "Christina."

She liked the way her name rolled over his lips in his Irish brogue.

"Yes?" The word came out breathy.

"I know after yesterday I don't have the right to say this but I want you. Something I've not felt in a long time."

"Kiss me."

* * *

Conor didn't make her ask twice. She didn't have to ask. He gathered her into his arms and pulled her firmly against him. His mouth slanted across hers with more pressure than before. Her arms wrapped around his neck as she leaned closer. His hands circled and tightened on her waist.

"I don't know what you've done to me." He kissed her temple. "I've been in this fog for months, years, and all of a sudden around you it's sunshine." His mouth moved over her smooth skin to her ear. Taking her earlobe, he gave it a gentle tug. Christina made a soft noise of pleasure in her throat. The sound fed his desire. She tilted her head, giving him better access. He kissed along the long column of her neck.

This time she purred. Lifting her shoulder, she kept his lips against her skin. She ran her hands across his chest then up and over his shoulders as if memorizing his body with the tips of her fingers.

His mouth found hers once more. He kissed her deeply. She returned his kisses with enthusiasm. Conor loved her passion. He tightened his hold. She pressed against him as she ran her fingers through his hair. If he'd known Christina could kiss like this he would have kissed her sooner. She made his body pulsate. Like a horse waiting for the starting gate to open.

At this rate she'd drive him crazy. He had said he didn't want this. But he did with every fiber of his being. He feared he might be taking advantage of the fact Christina was there and available. No, everything about Christina urged him on. Pulled him to her. He was powerless to turn away. Her special appeal was part of who she was. A tiny feminine woman wrapped in dirty jeans and boots had awakened a craving only she could satisfy.

This lusty fervor for Christina he liked too much. He found her plush mouth again.

A drop of rain hit him on the forehead. It didn't dampen his attention or desire. He continued to sip on her lips. The rain turned steady and he broke away. "I need to get you out of the rain before we're both soaked."

"Like you were yesterday." She giggled.

He kissed her hard. "I will get you for that." He reached around her and opened the door. "In you go."

"Promises, promises." Christina stepped into the kitchen where the only light came from the hall. She moved to the kitchen counter. Her back remained to him.

He sucked in a breath until his chest hurt. "About promises."

She looked over her shoulder. "Don't worry. I don't expect any. I know you can't give them."

Conor released the air but found the pain had

not eased. "I don't want you hurt. I will be leaving after the Derby."

"I know it."

Had Christina started second-guessing what had been happening between them? Maybe that was just as well. He wanted her but what she wanted and deserved he couldn't offer. For so many reasons. The least being he lived thousands of miles away.

"Coffee? Tea?"

What he wanted was her back in his arms, but he wouldn't say that.

The rain had turned heavy and lightning shot across the sky, making the dark room bright for a moment.

Christina jerked.

He made a step toward her.

"I'm fine. The thunder always gets me, but I love the rain. Which is good because I need to go check on the horses. That lightning will not have made them happy."

"Let me do that. I need to check on Gold. He can get wild-eyed quickly."

She started toward the door. "You don't have to do that."

He gave her an earnest look, his gaze fixed with hers. "Let me do something nice for you."

She stopped. "Okay. Thank you."

Walking to the door he said, "I enjoyed my

evening with you more than I have anything in a long time. Thank you."

"Same for me."

Before he closed the door behind him he said, "Good night, Christina."

"'Night," she said so low he almost missed it.

Conor hunched his shoulders against the cool wind and rain as he hurried across the yard to the barn. He was grateful for the weather for bringing the temperature of his body back in line after kissing Christina.

The horses whinnied and shifted as he walked down the hall, checking inside each stall. Satisfied that all was well, he returned to the house. Inside again he turned off the porch light, leaving darkness. The hall light no longer glowed. He removed his boots and padded in socked feet to the bath.

"Are they okay?" Christina stood in her bedroom doorway with the light from her bedside table behind her. She wore a short, flimsy nightgown that the glow made transparent.

Conor swallowed. Those breasts he had been treated to a hint of days before were visible through the fabric. His blood flowed faster. His length had hardened. Why hadn't she gone in her room and stayed? He was torn between being glad she'd been waiting on him and fearing he couldn't stop himself from reaching for her.

Is this what his father faced when he'd been

unfaithful to his wife and family? No, this wasn't the same. Louisa was gone by her own choice. He shoved his hands into his pockets. Even now his body vibrated with the desire to taste her, touch her, experience her. "I didn't mean to disturb you."

Her gaze met his, held.

The air turned thick. The rain pounded on the roof as his heart hammered in his chest. This was one of those crossroads in life where if he said or did the wrong thing he would live to regret it. So he waited.

"Uh…about a while ago… I…" She ran her fingers through her hair.

That made her nightgown flow around her. He could see the lines of her sweet body. "You… what? Tell me, Christina. What do you want?"

"I want you."

His heart kicked into overdrive. "I'm right here. All you have to do is reach out."

She took his hand, turned and led him into her room. Stopping beside her bed, she said, "Make love to me, Conor."

"Are you sure that's what you want?" He wanted no regrets for either of them in the morning.

"Yes."

"No promises. No tomorrows. Just now. Just feeling. I haven't felt in so long. I want to again. With you." He needed that so desperately, he hurt with it.

She looked toward the bed and nodded. He cupped her face in both his hands. Her eyes watched him, wide and unsure.

"We are going to take this slow and easy." He lightly brushed her mouth with his lips.

Her hands came to his shoulders.

He continued to kiss and caress and tease her mouth until her fingers bit into his muscles. His hands didn't leave her face as he deepened his kisses. He reveled in the soft, erotic sounds Christina made.

She returned his kisses. He ran his tongue along the seam of her lips and she opened for him. Greeted him. At first, she hesitated but with one brush of his tongue she joined him in the dance. Even leading at times.

His manhood stood thick and ready. He wanted her now but giving her pleasure won out. Too much had been taken from her. She deserved to feel how special she was.

Her hands moved down over his chest, bunching in his shirt as his tongue stroked hers.

The fingers of one hand traveled along her neck, brushing the tender spot behind her ear then moving across the ridge of her shoulders to cup her bare arm. The other hand followed its lead. He ran the pads of his thumbs beneath the material of her nothing pajamas to touch the swells of her breasts.

Christina shivered. Her hands moved to his waist. She pressed into him.

His manhood throbbed, needing release. He swept a finger over her nipple. A burst of heat flashed through him when he found it stiff and tall, begging for his attention. His mouth left hers to travel over her cheek, down her neck. Cupping her breast, he lifted it and placed his mouth over it. Even with the material barring her from his mouth he continued to suck and tug at the tiny expressive part of her body. He looked at the material sealed over her beauty.

His fingertips touched her thighs. She trembled. His hand crawled under the short gown and over her hips, gathering the material as he went.

Christina stood still, only the rise and fall of her chest visible. Occasionally, there was a lurch and jump in her breathing. He revealed her breasts as if removing a silk drape from a famous piece of artwork with great anticipation and reverence. Unable to stand it any longer, he placed his mouth over a nipple.

Her breath hissed through her lips. Her fingers threaded through his hair, caressing him as he ran his tongue around her nipple to pull and suck. He held her at the waist with one hand and moved to the other breast, giving it the same administrations. His other hand found the edge of her panties and teased the skin there.

Christina quivered, her hands now resting on his shoulders. He left her breasts to kiss the hollow between them. From there his mouth kissed a line to the band of her bikini panties.

"Conor, it's my turn." Her words drifted around them, they were so soft. She tugged him upward.

He stood, his hands still exploring as he went.

The moment he reached his height, Christina's hands went to the top of his shirt. Their mouths met once again. All the while, her fingers worked the buttons from their holes. She pushed the material over his shoulders. He released her long enough for the shirt to drop to the floor. Before he could touch her again, she placed her palms on his chest, keeping the space between them.

Her fingertips dragged over his skin, sending tingling heat throughout his body. His nerves bunched and released as she went. He reached for her, and she moved his hands away.

"I'm not done admiring you. I've been thinking about nothing but touching you since I ran into you in the hall the other morning."

"That was days ago."

"Uh-huh." She kissed him just over his heart.

She had covered up that need well. "You never let on."

"I couldn't." She looked at him and grinned. "I didn't want to look like I was taking advantage of a houseguest."

This time he didn't let her stop him. He took her in his arms. "Take advantage of me any time you wish."

Christina giggled.

"I love that sound."

"What?" She gave him a perplexed look.

He grinned. "The sound of you happy."

Her hands came up his chest and circled his neck. "It's nice to feel that for a change."

He gave her a couple of quick kisses. "You should have that all the time. Now, enough of the talk. I want to explore you more." His hands found the hem of her gown and pulled it over her head. He let it go to land on his shirt.

Cupping her breasts in his hands, he kissed one then the other. He backed her to the bed, laying her on it, then joined her.

She pulled him to her. Pressed against her smooth skin, he found utopia. He rolled to his side and placed his hand on her stomach. Her skin rippled. His manhood twitched with need. Leisurely, far more so than he felt, he moved his hand down to her pink panties, slipping a finger beneath. His reward was the hitch in her breathing.

"These need to come off," he said before he kissed the dip where her neck met her shoulder.

She pushed at the panties then wiggled until she could kick them off her foot.

It might have been the sexiest thing he'd ever

seen. The knowledge that what had been revealed would be his made him hotter than ever.

Christina pulled him to her, giving him a searing kiss. Her hands flowed over his back, causing his muscles to ripple.

His hand caressed the silkiness of her inner thigh before traveling to where her legs joined. He brushed his palm over her curls then went in search of her center. He found it warm and wet. Waiting for him. Slipping a finger inside her, he earned her whimper. Her hips flexed in greeting. Behind the zipper of his pants, his manhood ached for relief.

He continued moving his finger inside and out.

Christina lifted her hips, stiffened and keened her pleasure before she shivered and relaxed on the bed.

Satisfaction filled him. He wanted her to have the best pleasure he could provide. Conor kissed her lips, cheeks, eyes, tenderly giving her the attention and care she deserved all while holding her close.

Moments went by then she brushed his hair back from his forehead and looked into his eyes. "It's past time to take off your pants. I want you. All of you."

CHAPTER SIX

CHRISTINA COULDN'T BELIEVE what had just happened to her. She still basked in the waves of pleasure from her release. This was a new experience. Sex had never been as powerful between her and Nelson. And Conor hadn't even been inside her. Doubts rushed in. Would she be enough for Conor?

He stood and started removing his clothes.

She watched as his hands went to his belt. "Would you like us to get under the covers?"

His gaze remained on her. "I would like whatever you do."

"I didn't plan on this or I would have put on clean sheets."

"I don't care about the sheets," he all but growled. He removed his wallet and placed it on the bedside table then lowered his zipper.

Her mouth gaped at the size of him. She watched in anticipation as he pushed his pants down. Her mouth went dry. "Do you have a condom?"

He grinned. "I do."

"Are you always so prepared?"

"I try to be." He looked directly at her. "It has been a long time for me."

"Me, too." But he was worth waiting for.

When he shoved his boxers to the floor she sucked in a breath. He was all beautiful male.

He stepped closer to the bed. "Why all the sudden chatter?"

"I'm nervous."

"What do you have to be nervous about? You're beautiful and desirable." He pushed her hair off her cheek and cupped it.

"You're just saying that so I don't run off." The temptation to get under the covers grew.

His knee rested on the bed as he looked over at her.

She looked away. "I don't want to disappoint you."

"Just what makes you think you would disappoint me?"

"It's been a long time for me. I may not be any good." She just couldn't fail this man who had just given her so much pleasure. If this would be their one and only time, she wanted Conor to remember her.

He looked into her eyes. "I can't imagine how that would ever be true."

"More than one person has told me I don't measure up. Or I could be better." Her mother. Nelson. "It makes you doubt yourself."

He gave her an incredulous look. "At having sex?"

"At anything. My mother told me that. My ex stole from me, and I had no idea. This may be another area where I'm lacking."

"I tell you what. We will go slow. It's been a while for me also. We are in this together unless you would like me to leave."

"No. Please don't go."

"I'm not going anywhere unless you tell me to." He gave her the same gentling caress along her back she'd seen him give a fearful animal. He spoke her language. "I don't see how you could disappointment me in bed or out—ever."

He stopped her next words by sealing her mouth with his.

She ran her hands over his ribs, enjoying the firm male feel of Conor, to the expanse of his back. His hand cupped her breast, kneading it, teasing it. Her center tingled, and heated. His manhood pressed against her stomach. She wiggled.

Conor broke the kiss. "You keep that up and I'll be done before we get started."

She teased him with the movement of her hips. "I thought we had started some time ago."

Conor rolled away and picked up his wallet.

He removed a little square package, making short order of opening it and covering himself. Returning to her, he took her into his arms again, giving her gentle kisses that had her wanting more and more.

She opened her legs in welcome. He settled between them. Rising over her on his hands, he entered her. She closed her eyes focusing on each movement of him inside her. He filled her and stopped.

Daring a look, she found Conor's face tight in concentration as if he were absorbing every second of their joining.

He pulled back, making her fear he would leave her, before he returned. His movements continued with deliberation until he had her urging him forward while she clutched the sheets and her legs trembled in desperation.

Heat coiled low in her, tightened, folded on itself and burst. She was flung into the air and slowly drifted on pleasure. In a dreamlike trance she drifted back to reality.

Conor increased his pace, pumping into her like his life depended on it.

She wrapped her legs around his waist, pulling him closer. He groaned and sank into her with force. She joined him in the push-pull moments. Conor stiffened, holding himself steady and roared his release.

If she wanted confirmation of her ability to please a man, she had it.

He came down, covering her with his hard, warm and relaxed body.

When he became too heavy she squirmed, and Conor rolled to his back. He pulled her close as their breathing returned to normal.

Conor listened to the rain with Christina's soft, warm body snuggled against his. Disappointment hadn't happened. Christina had been everything he'd ever dreamed a lover should be. He had missed this type of connection with a female. He'd not allowed himself the pleasure of a woman in so long. And to have this special big-hearted female next to him made his heart open again.

Christina sighed heavily.

He gave her a gentle squeeze. "Am I boring you?"

"No, I was just trying to figure out if I should ask you something or not." She ran her hand across his waist.

"You can ask me anything. If you are planning to ask if you were a disappointment then don't bother. You should have been able to tell I thought you were amazing."

"Thanks for that." She turned so he could see her face. "It wasn't that. I wondered if you would tell me about your wife. What happened to her."

Conor tensed. He didn't talk about that. The real story hurt too much. Christina waited. "You want to talk about her now?"

"Yes. I want to know about the woman so special you spent years in sadness after losing her."

It hadn't been just her. But he couldn't even tell Christina about the baby. The pain was still too great. He'd never said the words to anyone. Not even his brother or sister. He didn't want Christina knowing what he had done to his child. He wasn't sure he ever could tell her. He feared he would double over in agony just as he had when the doctor had said, "I'm sorry about the baby as well."

Conor cleared his throat and gathered his fortitude. Christina deserved his trust. She had earned it. "We had a little house in the village. A place we all grew up. Family and friends, and a busy social life. My practice was thriving. But one thing was missing. She always laughed and said she was the perfect childbearing wife. She would pat her hips."

Christina moved so she could look down at him. "Do you have children?"

He almost left the bed, but he forced himself to stay where he was. He would get through this. "No. It wasn't from the lack of trying. Sadly, we never conceived. Even after going through the medical system. As time went by, she became mired in sadness over the situation. Not emotionally strong to begin with, she took our problems particularly hard. She slowly disappeared on me. Becoming a hull of who she was because she wanted children so desperately. It became an issue in our marriage."

Christina's eyes turned sad with concern. "I shouldn't have asked you, but I understand her wanting them so much."

He could imagine Christina as a mother. She would be a wonderful one. Yet, their time together wasn't about creating a family. It was only for the here and now. Still, something nudged him to talk to her. To have her understand what happened between him and Louisa. "We had a horrible fight. I told her I couldn't live like we were anymore. Something had to change. Because of me, the ugly things I said, she went out and saw to it by driving her car into a rock wall."

"Oh, Conor. How awful. I'm so sorry." Christina placed her head on his shoulder and wrapped her arms around his waist and hugged him tightly. "It wasn't your fault."

He wasn't convinced that was true. He'd said all those horrible things to Louisa, yet she'd carried the baby he had given her. Then killed herself because she didn't know. How could that not be his fault? For years he had lived with the conviction he should have known, should have seen the damage he had been doing to Louisa. Why hadn't he seen the mental state she was in? He should have noticed.

He'd helped to create it. Just by saying the words *I will leave you.* He hadn't meant them. He'd made a vow to stay with her in good times and bad. He had been and still was determined he would be better than his father. Threatening to leave hadn't been the answer.

Despite his carrying those doubts and guilts, Christina's tender reassurance made a difference. His load had eased by sharing his past with Christina. She had a way of making him think the future could be different. He started to believe that open wound might heal.

They stayed like that for a long time. Then slept.

Conor woke to Christina kissing his chest. Her hand brushed his chest hair lightly. He returned her kiss. Their lovemaking was silent and tender this time as if she wanted to heal his broken heart.

Conor woke with Christina still beside him. He watched the morning light slowly creep into the room. Soon, Christina's internal clock would have her up, ready to feed the horses. She would push him aside to care for them. He would soak up holding her while he could. Right now, the idea of letting go of her soft, placid body made him want to squeeze her tighter.

He sensed the moment she woke. She gave him a soft smile before her eyes widened and she rolled away from him. "It's daylight. I have to get moving. The horses will be stomping in their stalls."

"I think they can give me two minutes." He couldn't believe he thought they could discuss something as amazing as last night and cover it in two minutes.

"There's nothing to talk about. You're a grown man. I'm a grown woman. We had a nice night together. We didn't plan it. It happened. Let's leave it at that. I enjoyed it and I hope you did, too. We both know that can't happen again."

Her detached attitude made him think of the time a horse kicked him in the ribs. Painful with a lingering ache. She was pushing him away. It was nothing worse than what he'd planned to do to her. She just beat him to it. Maybe that was how it had to be.

Or did it? He shoved his guilt away. He brushed his palm over her bare nipple.

She moved his hand away. "Don't start that. I've got to get to the horses. I've got a full day ahead."

"Christina, I didn't see you coming."

"Sometimes we don't see what we should and just get caught up in it. Other times we don't want to see it. I've been there and done that. I can't,

I won't, do it again. It's too hard to come back from."

She climbed out of bed and started looking through clothes. Her room really was a mess. Just part of her charm.

"You sound like you're speaking from experience." Was she thinking of the jerk who had stolen from her, damaged her reputation and broken her heart? Conor wasn't him. Or was he?

"We agreed to no promises. Just for fun. We both needed it."

He hated her sounding so flippant and callous. Yet, he understood why she lashed out.

"What's the deal with the promises, Conor? I didn't ask for any."

Did he want to tell her? The words came out before he could stop them. "The deal is my father ran around on my mother and me." He hesitated. "I promised myself I would never do that to someone I cared about."

Her look turned perplexed. "Are you planning to go to another woman tonight?"

"No. I'm talking about being faithful to my wife."

Christina's face softened. "Conor, you were a good husband, and I have no doubt faithful, but she wouldn't want you to be alone. I believe we both need to take a step back."

"But I didn't mean…"

She raised a hand. "It's okay. I'm a big girl. I've disappointed people and they have disappointed me. I just make a point not to get too close." She pointed at him then her. "This is not any different. Let's not get too invested. Put it down to a moment of insanity."

Okay, that hurt. "You do know you spent the entire night with me. There were moments of insanity, but they were earth-shaking ones." Why was he tempted to argue with her? Wasn't she offering him what he wanted without him being the jerk who walked out on her after one night together? "Neither of us disappointed the other."

She blushed and looked away. "You know what I mean. It was good but that was yesterday, and this is now."

He climbed out of bed and took a step toward her. "You don't think it could be good here, right now and in broad daylight?"

Christina's eyes widened. A little puff of breath came from the O her mouth had formed. "That's not what I meant. I thought you wanted the same thing as I. That we had an agreement."

"We did but I refuse to have you diminish what we shared."

"That's not what I'm doing." With jerky steps she moved around the room, picking up clothes then letting them float to the floor once more.

"It sure sounded like that to me." He pulled on his pants, leaving them unzipped.

Her gaze traveled over his chest to the opening of his pants. "I didn't intend for it to."

"Good. I'm glad to hear that. It's a time I will remember with pleasure. I would like to think you will, too."

Her look met his. "Conor, you should have no fear of that. It was everything a woman dreams of. Thank you."

Her words bolstered him but now she made it sound like their time together was an experiment in a lab. No emotion. Maybe that was the point; there had been too much emotion on both their parts. He hadn't been prepared for the connection between them. Had it been the same for her? He needed time to analyze it, adjust to it and accept it. She could need that as well.

"Conor—"

"I've got to see about moving Gold today. It's time for him to start working out where he will be running." The last thing he needed was for her to tell him how wonderful, how perfect, it had been and how it would never happen again.

Her eyelids lowered then rose again. "I understand."

"Will you check on Gold while I start breakfast? It will be waiting."

Half an hour later Conor stepped out the back

door of the house and headed for the barn. Breakfast was getting cold. Christina had been gone long enough. Guilt had swept over him the second her sweet smell left the room. He had broken his vow to himself. His feelings roiled inside him. He couldn't sort them out, even if he wanted to. He shouldn't have taken Christina to bed even as pleasurable as it was. He had done her an injustice.

He wasn't staying in Kentucky. He wasn't any better than the guy who had hurt her. Conor wouldn't be around to support and care for her. He belonged at home in Ireland with his memories and his family.

She wouldn't leave Kentucky. Even if he dared to ask her. She was too firmly established here, in her horses, in her dream of starting a rehabilitation farm.

Bloody hell, he'd really made a mess of things.

To have acted on emotion instead of his brain was unforgivable at his age. He should know better. But her kisses, her body pressed to his…

His actions were so unlike him. He had always been practical, solid, thoughtful, yet Christina managed to make him throw out all his thinking abilities and go with feelings. The desire to live in the here and now became too strong.

Christina sat across the table from Conor. He silently sipped his second cup of coffee as if it was a normal morning instead of the one after an amazing night in her bed. She came close to groaning out loud. It had been she who had invited him in.

He'd come searching for her when she hadn't returned. She reluctantly agreed to the meal, but it had become a tense affair, making the food taste like hay.

Conor had been standing on the back stoop waiting, watching the barn when she had come out. She'd stayed longer than usual, needing to think. The moment she appeared he'd gone inside.

What had she expected? Hadn't she known the score before they made love? She was a grown woman. Hadn't they both agreed to no promises? Just the one night. Then why was she letting the idea that there might be more between them grow? She knew better.

Hadn't her past decisions proven that she didn't have what it took to last? She hadn't been good enough then and what made her think she was now? Could she ever keep a man like Conor?

He wasn't over his wife.

Somehow, her future didn't look as happy as it once had.

"Christina, stop it." Conor's bark jerked her out of her thoughts.

She looked at him over her mug. "What?"

"Thinking. I want us to remain friends," he came close to growling.

"We are friends."

His voice softened. "I certainly hope so." He sighed. "I'm going to Churchill Downs today. Gold will be moved there tomorrow. I have to make sure all is ready for him. He must pass inspection. I need to see if there is something more I need to do. Is there anything you need from there?"

Her chest tightened. She knew the day would come when Gold and Conor would leave. It had been inevitable. What she hadn't expected was for it to affect her so. Maybe it was a good thing. She could start getting used to him not being there. Conor might as well leave for good now. At least she could start getting used to the idea because in a little over a week he would return to Ireland.

"No. I have to go Monday for orientation anyway." By then she would have moved past this dreary mood over Conor. She needed to make a good impression, and showing up looking sad and lonely wasn't going to be the answer.

"I'll be moving into a hotel in Louisville close to the racetrack that Mr. Guinness has secured. I need to be closer than this to Gold. But I still plan to attend the party on Saturday night. Will you pick me up since you know the way?"

"I can do that." She looked into her coffee cup as if it had the answers to why her heart hurt.

"I'll be sure to let you know the information about where I'm staying."

The finality of it all saddened her more. But this was how she'd wanted it. He had agreed. It was for the best. She pushed back from the table, leaving half her breakfast on her plate. "Okay. That sounds like a plan. I need to get to work now."

That was what she should be worried about. Focused on. Her new business. She needed to make that her priority, and not worrying about Conor. Still, the thought of his kisses and caresses made her shiver. If she could force them into a box in her mind and close the top, she'd be better off. With some determination she'd get through the next week and then he would be gone.

She picked up her plate, cleaned it off and placed it in the sink. "Thanks for breakfast. I'll see you later."

Half an hour later she heard Conor's truck go down the drive. Her shoulders sagged. Why did she feel relieved and lonely at the same time? How had the man managed to matter so much in such a short time?

Conor drove toward Louisville and Churchill Downs thinking less about where he was going and more about Christina. What had happened between them last night hadn't been something he had imagined or planned for when he came to America. That might be the case, but he couldn't say he hadn't enjoyed being with Christina or that he wouldn't like to repeat the pleasure.

He wanted to respect the distance she had requested while at the same time he wanted to shake her and tell her they could figure something out. Maybe the problem was she had been the one to beat him to placing the boundaries.

Until recently, he would have said he would never be interested in another woman. That had changed because of Christina. Still, he couldn't give her what she wanted. A family. He couldn't go there again. But surely they could find a compromise because she had done the impossible, made him care again.

With little more than a week before the Kentucky Derby, the racecourse was already buzzing with more activity than it had been on his last visit. In just a few days, he would be a part of that. He would miss the calm, slow life of Seven Miles Farm and Stables. And Christina.

His work would really step up when Gold arrived tomorrow. The next day the trainer, along with his grooms and barn hand, would be there. It was Conor's job as the lead man on the scene to see that Gold was safely moved and checked into a barn. Today he would have a look at Gold's stable, but first Conor needed to check in with the clinic. It was time Gold really exercised. He needed to run and flex his muscles. The horse needed to get on the Breeze schedule.

Entering the clinic, he found the place busy as well.

Dr. Dillard came around the corner. "Hello, Doctor O'Brian. I was wondering when you would be in. It's about time to move into the barn, isn't it?"

"The plan is to do that tomorrow. Well over the hundred-and-three-hour limit for the horse to be on the premises."

"Indeed. Tell me, how has it worked out being at Doctor Mobbs's place?"

"Great. Gold seems to be in fine shape, and it's a quiet place to settle in." Conor did really love Christina's farm. If he lived in America, it would be the type of place he would like to have.

"Good to hear. Good to hear. I was wondering about sending others if necessary."

"I can't think of a better place." Conor meant it.

"How did you make out personally? I know the farm is a little farther from here than you would have liked."

"I made out fine." Was the man fishing for more than general information? Too fine, in fact. He had started to feel like it was home. "She was kind enough to rent me a room when I realized there was a misunderstanding about how close I needed to be to Gold."

"Well, I'm glad it worked out. I'm a little surprised she agreed. Christina has had a difficult time during the last couple of years. I'm an acquaintance of her uncle, who is also a vet. I felt the need to help her where I could."

"I know she appreciates it. She is an excellent veterinarian. I believe you will be pleased to have her on your staff."

"I believe you are correct. That's why I suggested her place and have given her a position working here during the week. The man she got hooked up with dragged her name through the mud."

If Conor ever met that guy, he might do something he wouldn't be proud of.

"The program she is starting is worthwhile," Dr. Dillard continued, "I would like to see it flourish."

Conor would, too. "She has a wonderful place for it and she is excellent at that type of work."

"So I understand. Well, is there something I can do for you?"

Conor shook his head. "No, I just need to check in and see if there is anything required that I haven't already covered, then I'm on my way to check out the stall."

"I'll have someone call for a golf cart to take you to the barn. You'll need to plan to walk back."

"I can do that." He shook his hand.

The man nodded. "I'll see you Saturday evening, then."

Conor waited outside the clinic. Soon, a man in a golf cart pulled up. On the ride, he jostled along the gravel road between the barns and past the grassy area where horses were being washed and groomed. The man pulled to a sharp stop in front of a white barn with red flower baskets hanging from the porch. Gold would be installed in the second stall from the right. He got off the golf cart and the driver took off.

Conor strolled over to the barn stall, opened the door and entered. He checked the walls, the gate and feeding trough for any hanging wood, paint or any other material that could harm Gold. It all looked good and was spotlessly clean. Outside lay a strip of grass and a grooming area. Gold should do well here. Everything looked satisfactory.

He started his walk back to his truck. A golf cart came by and came to a sudden stop in front of him, throwing gravel.

The woman whom he had been introduced to as Christina's cousin looked at him. "Aren't you the guy that was with Christina the other day?"

"Yes. I'm Conor O'Brian. I'm staying at her place."

She looked around. "Is she here today?"

"No, I'm seeing about moving a horse I'm responsible for here tomorrow."

A look of disappointment came over her face. "Well, that's good. Do you need a ride somewhere?"

"As a matter of fact, I could use one back to my truck."

She patted the golf cart seat. "Then hop in."

Conor did and she took off like a shot. He grabbed the support bar holding the roof.

"Have you been enjoying your stay in America? At Christina's?" She glanced at him.

"Kentucky reminds me of Ireland. The grass, rolling hills and of course the horses."

"I have to admit I'm a little surprised Christina let you stay at her place."

Conor studied the woman for a moment. Was she trying to get at something? No, she was just making conversation. "Let's just say it wasn't her idea. She wasn't left much choice."

"She's remained closed off for the last few years, unfortunately. To everyone. Especially men."

"I understand she has good reason. I heard he was a real piece of work."

Callie studied him a second. "She told you about him?"

"Yeah, she told me about what happened."

"She must really like you. As far as I know outside of a handful of people, she's never told anyone about what really happened."

Conor couldn't help but find pleasure in that knowledge. Yet, he still held out about the baby.

"I could tell by the way she looked at you the other day she really liked you." Callie made a right turn that almost slung him off the cart.

Christina looked at him a certain way? For some reason that made his chest expand. "I'd say we have become friends over the last two weeks."

"She hasn't let anybody close enough to be a friend in years. You must be somebody special."

He had no idea if that was true.

"I'm glad she has the job on the veterinary team. I know she really wanted that."

Conor was glad Christina was getting something she really wanted, too. "Yes, she puts great stock in working here during Derby week."

"Understandably. She had a difficult time and people were not kind to her, even though she wasn't the one found guilty. That jerk she thought she was in love with didn't do her any favors." Venom filled Callie's voice.

"That's my truck right up there. The red one." He pointed ahead of them.

Callie pulled to a halt beside the truck and he climbed out.

"It was nice to see you again. I'm sure I'll be

seeing you around in the next week. Tell Christina I look forward to seeing her as well." Callie smiled.

"Thanks for the ride."

The visit to the track had been fruitful professionally but more so personally. It certainly had given him food for thought where Christina was concerned. If he'd been trying to push Christina into the background of his life today, he hadn't achieved that.

CHAPTER SEVEN

CHRISTINA WOKE AT the first ring of the phone and picked it up on the second. Truly, she hadn't been asleep. Her night had been spent thinking about Conor on the other side of the house.

She had known better and gotten what she deserved.

Conor was still hung up on his dead wife. He lived thousands of miles away. There was just no way a relationship between them would work. Apparently, he felt the same way. It didn't take him long to freeze her out.

He was a nice guy. But she'd believed Nelson had been, too. Her judgment of character had been way off. What made her think it wasn't the same with Conor? She couldn't afford to put her heart out there again and have it broken.

She ended the call. Scrambling out of bed she quickly dressed. She didn't get many midnight calls, but when she did, she knew it was an emergency. She never questioned whether she needed to go or not. People who owned high-strung horses recognized when there was a problem. Many thought they could handle things themselves so when they asked for her, she took it seriously. It wasn't something that would wait until morning.

She was in the kitchen pulling on her boots when Conor walked in wearing only sports shorts. He pushed his fingers through his hair making it stand up in places. He appeared rumpled and sexy. She looked away and pushed those thoughts from her mind. Now wasn't the time anyway. Later wouldn't be, either. Or she wouldn't let it be.

"What's going on?" His voice was low and gravelly with sleep.

"I have an emergency. I'm sorry. I didn't mean to wake you."

"In the barn?" His eyes turned anxious.

"No, it's one of my clients." She shoved her foot into the other boot.

"You're going off this time of the night by yourself?" He sounded genuinely concerned.

Maybe he did care more than he wanted to admit. "I've done it plenty of times."

"I'm going with you."

A little thrill of heat filled her chest, but she pushed it down. "That's not necessary."

"I'll be ready to go by the time you are." He headed to his room without giving her a chance to argue.

As good as his word, Conor arrived at her truck just as she was ready to go. She climbed behind the steering wheel. "You don't have to do this."

"Sure, I do."

She took off down the lane. They remained silent as she drove through the night.

Finally, he asked, "Where are we going?"

"The Owens' Farm. He has a horse down. He said she has been off her feed. He went to check on her before going to bed and found her on the floor." Christina gave the truck more gas.

"That's all the information you have?"

She glanced at him in the dim light. Even in it she could make out the handsome cut of his jaw. "I know my clients well enough to know when they call it's something I need to react to."

"Okay, that's reasonable. How far is this farm?"

"We're almost there." She made a left turn into the gravel drive.

When Christina pulled up near the barn, Mr. Owen stood under the night-light with his hands in his pockets. He walked toward them. She climbed out and grabbed her bag from the side storage compartment of the truck. Conor joined them with his bag in hand.

"How's she doing?" Christina asked, falling in step with the older man on his way into the barn.

"Like I said, I came out to check on the horses before I went to bed. I found Joy laying on the floor of the stall. She had been kicking something awful. That's when I called you."

"Have you changed her food?"

"No, but I noticed she was off her feed yesterday and circling the stall more than usual. I thought I'd watch her another day, then this. I should have called you earlier."

The poor man looked so distraught she placed her hand on his arm. "We're here to help. We'll do all we can to make it better." She looked back at Conor. "This is Doctor O'Brian. Together we'll figure it out."

She never thought of it that way before, but they did make a good team. They played off each other's skills and experiences well. She enjoyed working with Conor. That was something she couldn't have said about Nelson.

They entered the barn, Mr. Owen directing them down the main hall to a stall on the other end. The horse was still on the floor. Groaning and twitching and kicking her feet.

"Mr. Owen, I need you to hold her head and speak softly to her."

When the farmer had control of the horse, Christina went to her knees beside the animal and placed her hand on the horse's belly. It was distended and hard. Conor came down beside her. He gave the horse the same examination.

"Will you do the general vitals while I listen for stomach sounds?"

Conor rose and picked up his bag. "I'll take care of it."

Thankfully, the horse had chosen to settle in the middle of the stall, giving them working room in the small area. Christina pulled her stethoscope from her bag. After placing the ends in her ears, Christina positioned the bell on the horse's abdomen to listen. The bowel sounds were just as she suspected. The horse had a bowel obstruction.

She put her stethoscope back and then started running her hand along the belly of the horse. "Mr. Owen, this became bad between when and when?"

"I was out here at eight. I came back about midnight. Just before I called you."

She looked out the stall door. "None of your other horses are having any problems?"

The man shook his head. "None that I can see."

Conor's look met hers. "Her face is swollen, and there is bruising around the eyes."

Were they thinking the same thing? As if Conor had read her mind, he nodded.

She took a deep breath. "Mr. Owen, I believe Joy has a large colon volvulus. You may have heard it called a 'twisted gut.' If we don't do surgery right away the intestines may burst. Joy will die if that happens."

Concern tightened the man's face. "I under-stand. So when is this surgery?"

"As soon as we can get ready."

The man's brows rose. "You'll be doing it here?"

She nodded. "Yes, we have no time to get Joy to a clinic."

The man's eyes widened.

"I need you to get me a large sheet that you don't want returned. It will have to go in the trash. Also hot water and soap. I need you to do so quickly."

Mr. Owen patted the horse's neck. "I'll go to the house right now."

"I'll get the supplies out of the truck." Conor moved toward the stall door. "You have this, Christina."

"Thanks. It's been a while since I've had to do serious surgery."

He gave her a tight smile. "I'll be here with you." Then he walked out of the barn.

It was nice to have another competent veteri-narian there with her. In an odd way, Conor made a nice security blanket. She had learned to trust him, at least when it came to their work.

While he was gone she had brushed the hay away from the horse's belly using her boot. After that, she prepared a sedative so the horse would be calm and pain-free while they worked.

Conor returned with handfuls of supplies in a basket she kept in the storage area for such an occasion. "Check and see if I brought everything you need. I'll stay here with the horse."

Christina reviewed everything and found it well prepared. "Conor, talk this through with me. We are going to need to scab the incision site with soap and hot water."

Conor nodded. "The incision will have to be long. This surgery always requires a few more inches than expected just because you need to see so much of the area to find the problem."

At least her and Conor's discussion was calming Christina's nerves. "I need to give a bolus dose of antibiotics before we start."

"Agreed." Conor handed her what she needed.

She drew an amount up in a syringe. "Check me on this. I don't want to have any questions asked."

Conor studied the syringe a moment. "Yes, it looks correct to me."

She then went to the horse and gave her a shot in the hip.

Mr. Owen returned. "Here are two sheets. And the bucket has the water in it." He sat it on the floor and handed her the sheets.

Christina placed one over the wall in reserve. She laid one on the ground at the horse's belly and tucked in under her. Conor set out the supplies nearby. She was thankful for his help.

"Mr. Owen, I'm gonna need you to hold her head." The middle-aged man went down on his knees beside the horse.

She gave Conor a perplexed look when he left. He soon returned with a stool and placed it beside Mr. Owen. Conor was a good guy.

She pulled on plastic gloves then drew up a sedative and administered it to the horse. Soon, the horse had relaxed.

"Conor, will you prepare the incision area?"

He, too, pulled on gloves. He washed the area with soap and water. He then opened a surgical kit and removed the razor. After shaving the surgical area, he scrubbed it with antiseptic.

Conor moved to the side, and she took the space. He handed her the scalpel, and she made the incision.

"Should I go larger?"

"Another two inches. We need to be sure we can see everything." He watched beside her.

Christina did as he suggested. With the horse's abdomen open they went in search of the obstruction. She removed a handful of intestines. "Do you see it?"

"There it is," Conor said. "Down on the left."

She shifted the intestines so she could see. He was right. There was the twisted cord. "Let's get this resected and repaired."

Conor said, "Can you resect it while I hold it?

Clip off on both ends at the same time. We don't need it to build up and burst."

She did as he requested. With that done, she took the scissors from her surgical kit and cut one end below the twist and then the other, and removed the piece of intestine.

"Excellent work."

Conor's praise washed through her. He handed her the needle and thread. She quickly stitched the two remaining ends together.

"I don't know that I've seen nicer stitches."

She smiled.

Working together, they slowly and gently returned the intestines to their place.

"Now, to get her closed up. You stitch and I'll pull the skin together." Conor handed her the needle and thread.

Together they worked until the incision had been sutured.

"While I clean up, why don't you check vitals?" Christina suggested.

"That, I can do." He washed in the bucket and started on the vitals.

By the time she'd cleaned up and he'd finished, the horse was waking.

"Mr. Owen, how are you doing?" Conor placed a hand on the man's shoulder.

"I'm well, and very impressed. You two working together is a show."

"A good one, I hope." Conor grinned.

"Certainly."

Christina had to agree. She and Conor did work well together along with doing other things well. "Thank you. We now need to get Joy on her feet. She needs to be led around for a while. Large animals don't need to lie on the floor. We need to work the anesthesia out of her system and get her organs active. Mr. Owen, you pull on her lead while Conor and I nudge her from behind."

The older man rose stiffly from the stool. She and Conor positioned themselves at the horse's back and pushed.

After a few minutes of encouragement, the horse wobbled to her feet and stood.

"Good job. Now, Mr. Owen, please lead her around in a circle. We need to get her loosened up."

She and Conor backed out of the stall.

The horse staggered but soon found steady footing.

Conor leaned against her. "Nice job, Doctor."

She grinned. "You, too. You know we're going to need to stay here and watch over Joy for a couple of hours."

"I do."

She studied the horse. "I'm sorry I can't send

you home because I might need something off the truck."

"I wouldn't leave anyway." He sounded like he meant it.

She looked at him and smiled. "I guess you wouldn't."

Conor leaned against the stall wall. "We should encourage Mr. Owen to go to bed. He looks dead on his feet."

"I agree." How like Conor to show concern for another. The man got to her.

She entered the stall and took the lead from the man. "Why don't you get some rest? Conor and I have to be here anyway. We can take care of her from here. You may need to give her some attention after we're gone. So go."

Mr. Owen gave her a weak smile. "Thank you. I think I'll take you up on that."

She started walking the horse around the stall. Conor walked out with Mr. Owen but soon returned with a blanket and a couple of folding chairs.

"Go have a seat and let me have a turn." His hand brushed hers as he took the lead.

Her unruly heart jumped at the touch. She had been glad to have his knowledge and help. He had become a fixture in her life. It hurt to think about him leaving. Despite her better judgment, she would miss him.

* * *

Conor grinned. Christina had piled hay in the hallway then laid the blanket over it before curling up on it. Now she slept. This was becoming a weekly event for them to spend one night in a barn. Funny thing was he could not think of anywhere he would rather be except in Christina's bed.

He felt honored she trusted him to watch over the horse. When he had first arrived, she had mistrusted him at every turn. Slowly, her attitude had changed. He found it rewarding. His feelings for her weren't doing him any favors, or her, either. He wouldn't offer her what she wanted. He couldn't go there again. He couldn't take that chance again.

Yet, he smiled down at Christina. They were different, lived in different parts of the world and their lives were damaged. The negatives were too many.

She would be appalled to know that in her sleep she looked angelic. That her tough exterior had slipped and turned vulnerable.

He sat a chair near where she lay and leaned back against the wall of a stall. From there he could clearly see the horse tied in its stall. The animal would not feel like being frisky for some time. He set the timer on his watch to go off in an hour. He would walk the horse a couple of turns, letting Christina rest as long as possible. He would also do the driving home.

He continued to keep watch over her and the horse until light peeked under the doors of the barn. He shook Christina awake.

She opened her eyes and made a long catlike stretch. Which might have been the sexiest thing he'd ever seen.

"I didn't mean to sleep so long. You were supposed to wake me."

He shrugged. "You looked too peaceful."

Her attention went to the stall. "How's Joy doing?"

Conor liked that she had no doubt he would have taken care of the horse while she slept. "I've been walking her every hour. In fact, it's time for a walk now."

"I'll do it."

He watched carefully to see if the horse faltered or showed pain.

Christina smiled. "You know I could've done this without you but I'm glad I didn't have to."

He grinned. "That was a nice thing for you to say. I like knowing I'm needed. It has been too long."

She tied Joy up again. Picking up the blanket, she folded it then hung it over the back of the chair he had used.

"I'm surprised Mr. Owen hasn't been out

yet." She started down the barn hall and in came the man.

"Good morning. How is Joy doing?" He looked toward the horse with concern.

"Great. Conor and I are headed home. You call me if you need me. I'll be back to check on her tomorrow. I'll be gone next week working the Derby but if you need anything you call me and I'll see that you get help."

"That's a big deal to get to work the Derby. I understand only a handful are picked."

"She got it because she is one of the best." Conor's voice held pride.

Christina looked at him and softly smiled, her eyes bright.

"My wife and I don't miss a Derby Day. We look forward to it every year."

"My family wasn't any different," Christina said. "It's an honor to be included as part of the staff."

"It's past due for you. You were mistreated a couple of years ago."

Christina looked down. "Thank you for that. I'm glad to have this opportunity but working ten to twelve hours a day will be tough. Few people realize how much goes on behind the scenes."

"I know they'll be glad to have you." Mr. Owen lifted a bag. "My wife has fixed breakfast for you. Egg sandwiches and a thermos of coffee. You can bring the thermos back when you come again. She said to tell you she would've invited you in but thought you might like to get home to your beds."

Christina took the bag. "Please give her our thanks."

Conor's stomach growled. "Mine in particular."

Christina said, "We'll give Joy one more look then we'll go. It's been a day. I need to get home and check on the horses."

She and Conor did their final analysis and headed for the truck, leaving Mr. Owen with instructions on how to continue Joy's care.

"I appreciate you helping out."

"Glad I was here to help. You were really good in there." He nodded toward the barn. "Impressive, in fact."

"Thanks. That's nice to hear."

Conor studied her a moment. "You haven't been told that before?"

"I didn't get much positive reinforcement from my mother growing up."

"You should be given it often." He meant it. Christina was an amazing veterinarian and equally amazing woman.

"I really appreciate it when I hear it." Christina placed supplies into the side storage bin of the truck. She yawned.

"You're tired. I'll drive home."

On the way to her house, she leaned back

against the headrest and closed her eyes. When her head bobbed, he guided it down until it rested on his thigh. She sighed as she settled in.

Disappointment filled him when he turned into the drive. He would have to give up having her close.

Christina woke to warm, hard muscle beneath her cheek. She'd fallen asleep on Conor. She'd kept a number of long days but staying up all night wasn't her norm. With the Derby week ahead, she needed her rest.

It had been so nice to have Conor along to-night for the help and even the reassurance. She didn't do emergency operations very often and it was nice to have assistance, especially profes-sional assistance. It had also been helpful to have somebody who took turns seeing about the horse.

She felt confident Joy would recover well. It might be touch and go for a few days, but over-all, she would be fine.

When they reached her farm she hopped out of the truck. "I'm gonna go check on the horses. You're welcome to the shower first."

"I'm coming to help you." His firm tone stopped any argument. "I'll check on Gold as well. We're both exhausted and we can both go out there and get everything done in half the time."

In short order they finished caring for the horses and feeding them.

On the way to the house Conor kept pace with her. "Gold will be moving this afternoon. Thank goodness my plans were for later in the day. There is such an influx of horses at the Downs, so this afternoon appointment was the earliest I could get."

Sadness washed over Christina. She would miss the horse. More than that, she would miss Conor. She stepped on the stoop and turned to look down at Conor. "Thank you again for your help last night. I especially appreciate you staying up all night after I fell asleep on you."

"Not a problem. I was glad I was here to help."

She gave him a tight smile when she really wanted to kiss him. "I still appreciate it."

"I was glad I could be here for you."

"You're a really nice guy, Conor, and an excellent veterinarian."

"Thank you for the compliment. I'm not sure I wouldn't like the adjectives to be reversed."

"You are an excellent guy and a nice vet." Christina couldn't help herself. Her lips brushed his.

Conor's hands found her waist. "I think you can do better than that. In fact, I know you can." His mouth sealed hers before he pulled her against him, pressing her tightly against his hard body.

The kiss deepened. Their tongues tangled, searching and giving pleasure.

This is what she'd been wanting and missing since she had given her speech the day before. The one filled with lies. It would still be worth it to have him near, even if it hurt when he left. She would take advantage of what time they had for as long as he would let her.

Christina wrapped her arms around his neck and held tightly. She joined him in the kiss. The heat of desire spread through her. This man was honest and good. She could trust him. It has been too long since she had been able to say that. He'd proven himself.

Conor pulled away. "I'm sorry. I couldn't help myself."

"I'm not sorry at all."

He kissed her again. His need strong between them. "You know if we share a shower we could find a little more time to sleep."

She giggled. "I suspect that we would use it up in another way."

He gave her a deep, wet, suggestive kiss. "I suspect you're right. Let's go inside. I need to touch you."

His hand held hers as she opened the door. In the kitchen they kicked off their boots as if they had done the actions together their entire lives. Finished, she smiled at him. He returned it.

She took his hand again and led him down the hall into the bath. Inside, she turned on the water. Her fingers went to the buttons of his shirt. Slowly, she opened them.

He pulled his shirt from his pants. She pushed it over his shoulders. It dropped to the floor. He chuckled. "I'm not sure this is a time-saving operation. But I do know if I don't take all the chances I'm given to be in your arms, I'll regret it. Forever."

Her hands went to his belt and worked it open. She treasured the intake of his breath when her fingers brushed his skin. Slowly, she unzipped his pants and maneuvered them over his extended manhood. With her hands at his waist she pushed his jeans to the floor.

He stepped out of them.

Her hands went to his underwear, but he stopped her. "My turn to undress you."

Gently, he pulled her T-shirt over her head. With it removed, he kissed the top of one breast then the other while he reached around her and daftly unhooked her bra. He pulled it away and dropped it into the pile of clothing on the floor. His hands made short work of removing her pants. "Honey, we will not make it to the bed."

She relished the deep, throaty sound of his accent as he nuzzled her ear.

"Mmm, that's okay with me."

CHAPTER EIGHT

CHRISTINA STRETCHED HER arm out across the bed. Her hand came in contact with a hard, warm body. A stream of pleasure flowed through her. Conor was there beside her.

She smiled, enjoying him and the sunshine flooding through the window. She could get used to this—waking up next to Conor.

She rolled enough in his direction to sneak a peek to see if he was awake. A blue gaze met hers.

"Good morning. Or should I say afternoon?" He grinned at her.

"It's not afternoon yet but almost. Have you been awake long?"

His hand brushed her breast. "I was just waiting on you to open your eyes."

A tingle flowed through her. "You were?"

Conor's hand moved to the curve of her hip as his eyes narrowed. "I was."

She rolled closer to him. "Is there something I can do for you?"

"Most definitely."

"Did you have something particular in mind?" She ran her hand over his bare chest.

"I do." His lips found hers.

She rose over him to straddle his hips. "Aren't you expecting a truck and trailer for Gold soon? Maybe this should wait," she teased.

His hands caressed the skin of her sides. "No, it can't."

"I should get to work." She moved to climb off him.

Conor held her in place, sliding her over him, filling her. "I don't think so. We both need to take time to enjoy what we have."

He left off *while it lasts*. But she was well aware of it. For a change, she would do just that. Her lips brushed his as she lifted her hips until he almost lost her and she plunged down again.

Conor made a sexy sound of pleasure in his throat.

She said, "I don't disagree."

Later, as they pulled on their boots, Conor asked, "Can we talk a minute?"

The last time that had happened she had said some stupid things, and she didn't want that to happen again. "I thought we had been. In more ways than one."

That brought a wolfish grin to Conor's lips that soon slipped to a wry tightness of his mouth. "I have to move into town. I can't be this far from

Gold and the racetrack. With the security in the backside during the week before the Derby, I'm needed nearby."

"I get it."

He stepped closer. "I have a room at a hotel. Maybe you could spend the week with me there since you must be in town all week. It would make for a longer day to have to drive back and forth."

"I have the horses to see about." Even if she wanted to go, she had responsibilities and a business to consider.

"Can't you get someone to see about them?"

She leaned her head to the side in thought. "Maybe I could for a few days but not the entire time."

"At least say you will find someone for Sunday morning." Conor sounded close to begging. "That way you can stay with me after the party."

"I guess I could do that."

"I wish you would." He gave her sad eyes.

"I'll see what I can do between now and Saturday evening to get some help." She was already thinking of people she could call.

At 2:00 p.m. the truck and trailer to transport Gold rolled up her drive. Conor waited at the barn to meet it. Not soon after the truck stopped Conor led Gold into the trailer. Earlier, he'd collected all of the horse's supplies and placed them in his truck.

They both had examined Gold carefully to make sure he was well and fit. He would not be allowed on the backside unless he could pass the rigid Kentucky Horse Racing Commission list of protocols. Conor reviewed all his paperwork for shots dates and blood tests and how they were handled. All that information must be in order before Gold would be allowed on the property. After the horse was in a stall on Churchill Downs property, he would have limited access to Gold and only when security was around.

With Gold secure in the trailer, Christina joined Conor beside his truck. "I'll see you Saturday evening. Since I know the area better, why don't I pick you up at your hotel?"

"No. Once again, you are my date and I would like to see about getting us there. Please just plan to meet me in the lobby of the hotel at six. I've got it from there."

She started to open her mouth.

He gave her a direct look. "Christina, please do not argue with me."

"Okay."

Conor gave her a quick kiss on the lips as the truck and trailer started down the drive. "I have to go. I will see you Saturday evening. I'll call if I have a chance." He hopped in his truck and rolled down the window. "I will miss you."

She smiled, giving him a wave. A heavy cloak of sadness settled over her shoulders. This was just a taste of the feelings she would have when he returned to Ireland but on a larger scale. Then he would truly be gone.

She had brought this on herself. She'd have to live with that knowledge, but at least she will have had him for a while.

Saturday evening Conor paced back and forth in the lobby of the hotel in downtown Louisville, watching for Christina. He had expected her five minutes ago. Normally prompt, it was not like her to arrive late. Had she decided not to attend? No, she wouldn't do that. She had been working toward this opportunity to become a part of the veterinarian group at the Derby for too long. He pulled out his cell phone and looked at it. There was no text from her.

She must be nervous about being in a group of veterinarians who had judged her just a few years earlier. She worried too much about the past. She had proved herself not guilty and also qualified to care for racehorses.

With a release of fear, he saw her enter through the automatic sliding glass doors. She was a vision of loveliness, and she had no idea. Wearing a simple dark green dress, she appeared confident and dependable. She looked perfect to impress.

Little earrings dangled from her earlobes. The bit of shimmer had him wanting to bite at the sweet spot behind her ears. He had never expected to feel like this about a woman again. Especially for one who did not want him to. Going from not feeling anything for a woman to this intense need made his middle uneasy. Worse, he did not know what to do about it.

The more time they spent together, the greater the difficultly he would have in giving her up, yet he could not stay away from Christina. He kept reminding himself that this situation was temporary. After he left, he wouldn't be able to forget her. The past two nights alone had proved him wrong. He had been miserable without her. He'd quickly learned he would be willing to take any time she would give him.

Christina stopped when she saw him. A smile formed on her lips that had little to do with finding him and everything to do with her being aware of him as a man. His blood heated and his chest swelled. That sparkle in her eyes he would treasure for the rest of his life. She looked him over from head to toe.

Then she stepped up to him. Into his personal

space. "You look very handsome." She ran her hand under one of the lapels of his suit.

He suddenly had no desire to attend a party but to have one just for them in his room. "Thank you. You look lovely, Christina."

"I love the way you say my name. Your accent is super sexy, making it more special." She gave him a quick kiss on the lips. He reached for her, but she stepped back before he could take her in his arms. Apparently, she was more aware of where they were than he. "We better go or we're going to be later than we should be. I had to change a couple of times."

"Was that because of me or the people at the party?"

"Both. Did I tell you how glad I am to have you going with me?"

"No, but I am glad to hear it. When Doctor Dillard mentioned it the first time, I wasn't sure you thought it was a good idea." He grinned.

"Okay, maybe I've changed my mind about you some."

He pulled her close for a moment and kissed her temple. "I'm glad to hear it. You know you really shouldn't worry. You are the most amazing person I know, inside and out."

"Do you say nice things to all the girls you go to a party with?"

He gave her waist a gentle squeeze. "Only to you. After all, I haven't been to a party in years."

"Well, I am honored to be with you tonight." She kissed him on the cheek.

He nudged her toward the door. "We have admired each other enough tonight to create cavities in our teeth with the sugar. We should go."

She grinned. "I was rather enjoying it."

"We can try it again later."

Outside the lobby door, Conor waved his hand and a car pulled up.

Christina looked from him to the car and back again. "What's going on here?"

"I rented a driver for the night."

"That wasn't necessary. You shouldn't have spent all that money."

Conor waved the driver back to his seat and opened the car door for her. "You let me worry about that. I wanted to sit back here with you and enjoy the ride."

They settled into the backseat. She provided the driver with the address as they moved into traffic.

Conor took her hand in his. "I missed you. It's been too long. How are things? The horses?"

"I saw a couple of clients and spent the rest of the time in the barn."

"Did you find somebody to care for the horses tomorrow?" He brushed the pad of his thumb over the back of her hand.

"I made a few calls and found somebody I can trust. He's done it for one night before but he's willing to do it for three or four."

He leaned his forehead against hers. "So you will stay with me tonight?"

She gave him a shy smile. "If you still want me to?"

Conor pulled her hip against him. "Never question that I want you."

The driver pulled the car into the curved drive of a large redbrick two-story home with white columns and a wide porch across the front. The lights were shining in all the windows.

When the driver stopped at the front door, Conor climbed out and offered his hand. She took it. With a gentle squeeze he released it, closed the car door and offered his arm. Christina took it, holding tighter than necessary.

She was nervous about facing her colleagues. He was glad he would be there for her. She must have lived through an emotional ordeal for it to linger this long. But hadn't his wife's death done the same to him?

They entered the house and were directed along an elegant hallway to the open French doors at the back of the house. It looked out into a wide-open yard with a few aged trees. Among them hung white paper lanterns that lit the area along with lights from the house. To one side were four long tables laden with food, and also a man turning beef on a spit in the ground. Other round tables were spread out around the yard set for dining.

"Wow, this is beautiful," Christina said beside him.

"It does look nice, but the smell of meat cooking has my attention."

She smiled. "Always the cook."

"Hey, you haven't been complaining."

She hadn't. In fact, she hated returning to packaged food. "The only thing I can complain about is that I've gained almost ten pounds."

He leaned close. "And every one looks good on you."

"There you are, Christina. Good you could come." Dr. Dillard walked toward them. "And Doctor O'Brian. Nice to see you again."

Conor offered his hand. "Please call me Conor. Thanks for having us tonight."

Dr. Dillard shook it. "You're welcome. I understand you got your horse into the Downs stable without any trouble the other day."

"Yes, with a few hours to spare from those required." Conor took Christina's hand.

His attention went to the action for a moment before his look returned to Conor's. Dr. Dillard smiled. "We do have our rules for a reason."

"Understood. We have ours in Ireland as well."

Dr. Dillard glanced toward a woman waving at him. "My wife is calling. I must greet other guests. Please make yourselves at home. I'll bring my wife around to meet you soon." With that, he strolled off.

They moved to the drinks table and picked one then went to stand under a tree.

"Do you know anyone here?" Conor asked.

"I recognize a few people but most of them I have no idea who they are. People who work the race come from all over the state. It's an honor to do so."

Soon, Dr. Dillard asked for the group's attention. He gave a short welcome and stated that the party would be the fun before the busy week ahead.

That drew a ripple of laugher from everyone. Conor wasn't sure about what that meant but he was confident he would soon learn. By then some of Christina's anxiety had mellowed. For that he was grateful, but he remained close to her anyway.

Dr. Dillard introduced his wife to everyone, and she gave them directions on how to go about getting their food and encouraged them to sit wherever they wished.

Conor and Christina lined up on one side of the long tables. Picking up their plates, they moved through the buffet line. It was some of the most delicious-looking food he had seen since arriving in Kentucky.

"I hope you like barbecue," Christina said over her shoulder.

"I love it."

With full plates, they found an empty table. They settled into their chairs and started to eat. Other couples joined them until there were only two places left. These were soon taken by two men. As each new person joined them, everyone went around the table introducing themselves. Once again, they circled the table with names.

After Christina introduced herself, one of the men gave her an odd look. "Aren't you the veterinarian who was caught selling your drugs a few years back? I'm surprised you were invited to work at the racecourse."

Conor felt and saw Christina stiffen. This could only be her worst nightmare.

"Yes, I'm she, but I was not guilty." Her fork made no noise when she placed it on her plate.

The man poked his companion with his elbow. "Don't you remember that case?"

The other man grunted and continued to eat.

The first man returned to the conversation. "Still, I'm surprised they considered you for this group."

"I assure you I've been officially vetted. And can do the job."

Conor had heard enough. Christina didn't have to sit here and listen to this and neither did he. "I believe you owe Doctor Mobbs an apology."

The man took another swig of the amber liquor in his glass. He huffed. "For speaking the truth?"

Conor stood. "For being rude at the dinner table."

Christina put her hand on his arm. "It's not worth it."

"No, it's not," the man said it. "Especially since I'm speaking the truth."

Christina looked around the table. "If you'll excuse me, it was nice to meet you all."

Conor had to admit Christina held her head elegantly high as she rose, but he knew the willpower it took for her to do so. Inside, she would be a mass of raw emotions. She walked away with her shoulders squared.

He glared at the bad-mannered man. "I know I'm from another country, but I can recognize a drunk ass when I see one. You may not think so but you owe her an apology."

Conor caught up with Christina halfway down a path leading to a large barn in the fenced field behind the house. When he joined her he didn't say anything, he just fell into step beside her. Despite wanting to take her in his arms to comfort her, he resisted.

They continued walking. They were almost to

the barn before she spoke. "I'm never going to live down what happened."

"From what I understand, you don't have anything to live down."

"But it keeps cropping up. My home is here. I don't want to leave. It wasn't even me yet I'm the one that carries the stigma."

"It's not fair. I agree with that. But sometimes life is not fair."

She gave him a troubled look. "I'm sorry. You know that better than I."

"We're not talking about me tonight. We're talking about you. I was proud of you back there. You held your head high and you didn't let it show how much it hurt. And you didn't let me get into a fight. By the way, I'm not sure I could've whipped him."

Christina gave him a weak grin. "You know I do appreciate you defending me."

"It's not hard to defend you because you know what you're doing."

They continued walking, entering the open doors of the barn.

Conor had learned early in his relationship with Christina that being in a barn was where she thrived. She renewed her energy. The barn was where she went when she needed to think. Christina didn't hesitate to enter. They were overdressed for the place but she continued walking and he didn't stop her.

A couple of horses' heads hung over their stall gates. Christina patted the first horse's nose.

The sound of an animal in pain came from the back corner.

Christina hurried down the hall with Conor right behind her. They found a horse lying on its side.

She didn't hesitate to go down to her knees in her dress beside the horse and give it a quick examination with her hands. "This horse is in labor and it's coming breech. We need to get this colt out immediately, or the mare may die."

Conor said nothing.

She looked at Conor. He had gone still as a post. His skin had turn ghostly. A haunted look filled his eyes. He appeared terrified. "Conor? I'm going to need help."

"I'll go get Doctor Dillard."

"There's no time. You'll have to help me. I'm gonna need your muscles if we're gonna get this colt into the world safely."

"I…uh…"

"Conor! Go to the tack room and see what you can find that we might need."

Conor blinked and seemed to rejoin her from wherever he had gone. He hurried away.

While he was gone, she placed her ear to the

horse's bulging belly and listened to her steady heartbeat, hating that her stethoscope was in her bag at home.

Conor returned with an armful of supplies that included blankets and a bucket. His skin had turned to a more natural color, but his lips remained a thin, tight line.

"I saw a water faucet just outside the doors. I'll get some." Taking the bucket, he hurried off.

When he returned to the stall, he sat the bucket in the corner.

She rose and scrubbed her hands. Conor continued to stand there looking at the horse.

"We have to see if we can turn it."

"There are already two legs showing." Conor's words were monotone.

"Still, we have to try. I need your help." Christina didn't know what was going on with him, but what she did know was she couldn't do this without him. He had to focus on what was happening. Whatever problem he had he could deal with it afterward. Right now, she needed his help. "Have you done this before?"

He nodded. "A couple of times."

"Then that's twice as many as I have. I'm going to see if I can turn the colt." She laid a blanket on the hay behind the horse before going down on her knees. She worked to move the colt but made no real progress.

The horse moaned.

"My arm isn't long enough to reach the head." She looked at Conor. His eyes met hers. She watched his stricken look turn to one of determination.

He removed his jacket and hung it over the stall wall, rolling up his sleeves as far as he could then washed his hands and arms before he said, "Let me try."

He helped her stand then he lay down on his stomach. "Watch for the contractions and let me know when one is coming. I don't want my blood cut off."

With relief, Christina placed her hand on the horse's belly and felt. Conor was back with her. "I'll try to give you as much notice as I can."

"If I can use those moments between contractions, I'll have more room. Timing is everything."

"I'll do my best."

Conor met her gaze. "I never doubted it."

Seconds later she said, "Here comes one."

He removed his arm. When the contraction eased he went after the head of the colt. "I need to find the nose. I'm going to shift the head so it's not hung. The colt is still alive. I can feel its heart beating."

"Contraction coming," Christina announced.

Conor removed his arm. "It's still breech, but I believe we can pull this colt out now. During the next contraction, you'll need to pull while I work the head." He put his arm inside again. They waited, anticipation hanging in the air. "Ready? Let's go on my call. You need to make this a steady pull but as quickly as you can."

She looked at him. "I'll be ready. Contraction coming."

"Now," Conor said.

Christina pulled the legs. Conor's face contorted while he worked through the contraction. She could see the behind of the colt.

"Gentle tug. The head is in the right place," Conor encouraged.

Christina continued the pressure. Soon, the colt slipped from the mother. She and Conor were both breathing heavily when they finished. They didn't take a moment to catch their breaths before they were on their knees beside the colt. Christina quickly grabbed a blanket and began working it over the small animal, cleaning its mouth and face.

Conor, more himself than he had been, still looked worried but he joined her in rubbing.

"He's not breathing. We need to get some air in him."

Conor went to work across the colt's middle section using circles.

Christina was busy continuing to clean the baby's mouth and nostrils. She placed her mouth close to the animal's nose and breathed out. After a couple of times, the colt snorted and its eyes opened.

She looked at Conor. Pure relief showed on his face. Far more than she would have anticipated.

"I'll get Doctor Dillard." He went to the bucket and cleaned up then left the stall.

She sat back against the stable wall to catch her breath and watched him go. What was the matter with him? She'd had to force him to help her, which wasn't like him. He'd jumped in when needed when they had worked together before but tonight...

The mare worked her way to her feet before the new colt wobbled its way to her side. The mother licked it in acceptance. It was amazing to see new life come into the world. Would she ever get to have that moment? Conor's face popped into her mind. What would it be like to have his child?

Dr. Dillard rushed up. "O'Brian said you've been busy out here. She wasn't due for another week."

Christina didn't even have the energy to stand. He had to help her.

"I'm glad you two were here." Dr. Dillard fussed over her.

She looked around and didn't see Conor amongst the growing crowd. "It was pretty exciting, but all looks well now."

"I understand the colt was breech. I'm glad you both were here. I really appreciate it. This is my favorite horse. I have high hopes for this colt."

She went to the water bucket. "I'm glad we were, too."

"I heard about what happened at the dinner table. My apologies, Christina. That shouldn't have happened. He's been reprimanded. I put together a team and I expect everyone to work together. Saying stuff like that even when you're drunk isn't acceptable. You have more than proved your worth tonight."

"Thank you. And thank you for including me on the team and for your support."

Dr. Dillard's focus remained on the colt. "I'll see you at daylight Monday morning."

"I'll be there, sir." The crowd opened for her to walk through.

Christina moved away and headed for the house, searching out a bathroom and Conor. She looked everywhere and found him on the front porch. He stood with a shoulder against one of the columns, looking out at the night. What was going on? What had spooked him?

Shame filled Conor at his recent actions. He had failed Christina, his profession and himself. All of his feelings were tangled up in the loss of his baby. He could not think of anything else as he had watched the mare in labor. The horror of knowing his wife had killed herself when she'd been carrying his baby.

"Conor?"

The trepidation in Christina's voice only made him feel worse.

"Is everything all right?"

"I'm fine. Are you ready to go? If not, I'll call a taxi and leave the driver for you."

She went to him and wrapped her hand around his arm. "I'm not going anywhere without you. I'm ready to leave anyway. I'm a mess."

Soon, they were settled in the backseat of the car.

Christina held his hand while leaning her head against his shoulder, yet she said nothing. The driver maneuvered through the traffic. Before long, they were back at the hotel.

After the way he had acted, he dreaded asking when they reached the lobby, "Do you still want to come up? I'll understand if you don't."

She looked unsure for a moment. "I had planned to. If you still want me."

"I will always want you." That was the one thing he felt confident about. He led her to the elevator. "I'm sorry if I made you feel that I didn't."

The door to his suite closed behind them before she said, "I need a bath."

"You were wonderful tonight." He walked to the bar and took out a bottle of liquor. It was the first time in a long time. "I'm sorry I let you down."

"When?" She moved close but out of touching distance. "You defended my honor and helped in a difficult delivery. You have nothing to apologize for."

"I don't feel that way."

"Conor." This time she touched him on the arm. "Talk to me. Tell me what you were thinking back there. What upset you? For a few minutes there I didn't think you were going to help me with the colt."

"I almost didn't."

"Why? I know you're a good veterinarian, so it has to be something else."

He forced the words out. "Because it's too hard to watch a baby being born."

Confusion covered her face and she just looked at him. "I would think you'd be wonderful with babies. Of any type."

"My wife was pregnant when she killed herself."

Christina sucked in her breath. Her eyes watered. "Conor, I am so sorry." She wrapped her arms around him, pressing herself again him.

He returned her hug and pulled her against him, drawing comfort from her. They stood like that for a long time. Saying nothing and taking strength from each other. Slowly, his pain ebbed away.

"The colt brought back what had happened. Reminded me of what I had lost."

"You said nothing." She looked at him.

He cupped her cheek. "The hurt has eased since I met you. You have pulled me out of that dark place and forced me to go to work."

She smiled softly. "I did that?"

"Yes, you did." He kissed her and led her toward the bathroom. "And I intend to show you how grateful I am."

CHAPTER NINE

MONDAY MORNING, AS the sun brightened the eastern end of Churchill Downs, Christina stood at the back stretch of the racetrack. Her hands rested on the rail as she waited for the next group of horses to make their morning exercise run. Excited anticipation that came close, but wasn't quite equal to Conor's lovemaking, filled her. The exception heightened the thrill.

A warm body hers recognized immediately moved in close. She didn't have to look to know it was Conor beside her. She would miss him when he left. She didn't even want to think about it. Yet, the calendar days kept flipping by. Too soon, he would be in Ireland and she would be here. She wouldn't let herself think of him leaving.

That morning she had let him sleep and slipped out of bed. As much as she would have liked to remain with him, she wanted to make a good impression during the week of the Derby. She couldn't afford any mistakes.

Yesterday they had lounged around Conor's

luxury hotel room. They hadn't even gone out for meals. Instead, they had enjoyed room service. They had watched TV, slept and then explored each other's bodies to their hearts' content. She had never felt more desired or satisfied. That day would be treasured in her memories.

"I missed you this morning," he murmured, leaning his head close to hers.

"I had to get moving. I needed to be on time." She leaned into him.

"I know, but that doesn't mean I liked waking up without you."

Unfortunately, that would soon be something she would have to get used to. "I'm afraid it's gonna be like that most of this week."

His voice held melancholy. "I don't even want to think about it. I hate the thought of it."

"We'll just have to take it day by day."

"So what do you have on your agenda? I'm not allowed to see Gold without someone in attendance, and he has to remain in the barn stall unless he's being schooled. I'm pretty much on my own except a few hours of the day."

She looked around at all the police officers within her view. "Security is tight around here. For the horses and the rest of us. I have to admit it's more substantial than I expected."

"I'll just be checking daily with the trainer and grooms to see if there are any issues. I understand that I can't do any care. I can only confer with the track veterinarians. Still, I'll be here when he runs and will run interference if necessary. In case there's any questions about his health and care."

She grinned. "Yes, those track vets can be territorial."

"I hope one feels that way about me." His gaze met hers.

Heat floated over her skin. "This one might."

"Might?"

"Are you looking for some admiration?"

"I'll take what I can get. Mr. Guinness will be here tomorrow. I'll be picking him up from the airport and having lunch with him. Then bringing him by here in the afternoon. He will expect me to be at a meeting with the team tomorrow night."

"Looks like we both are going to be busy this week." Christina couldn't help but be disappointed she wouldn't be seeing him. She needed to get used to it.

"Do you think you will have time to show me around Churchill Downs today? I haven't even been to the stands. I would like to have a look."

"You certainly should do it before Friday or Saturday."

"You mean that all this—" he waved his hand toward the expansive grandstand on the other side of the racetrack "—all of those, will be filled?"

"That and the end fields, and the center of the track. There it's not so much about the races but mostly about the bourbon. Personally, I'd rather see the horses run."

"I would as well."

The sound of horses racing drew her attention. Loud enough that it created an anticipation in her chest. "Here they come."

The thunder of hooves came toward them, then into view as the exercise jockeys rode the horses at full capacity. They went by and into the distance as they ran into the second turn.

"When does Gold run?"

"He'll be coming around in just a few minutes."

"How does he look?" She wanted him to win for Conor.

"I'll let you be the judge."

It didn't take long before sounds of running and heavy breathing filled the air. Soon, two more horses came around the curve and before them. She grabbed Conor's forearm. "Gold looks wonderful."

"He does."

She clearly heard the pride in Conor's voice.

They watched in silence as the horses continued around the track and out of sight.

"I better get to the vets meeting." She turned to go.

He stopped her with a touch to the elbow. "Could you meet me for lunch and then show me around?"

"I'll text you when I know what my schedule will be."

"I hope I get to see you." He gave her a quick kiss on the temple.

"Me, too." She took a couple of steps and stopped again. Headed her direction was the rude man from the party on Saturday night.

"Excuse me."

Conor moved up beside her so he stood between her and the man. She stepped around him but stayed close.

The man cleared his throat. "I want to apologize. I was a jerk the other night. Bourbon loosened my tongue. I shouldn't have said what I said."

Christina didn't move. "I appreciate you coming to tell me. I hope we can work together without any problems."

"That's my intent."

She gave him a tight smile. "Mine as well."

The man looked sincere. "I heard about the colt delivery. Impressive."

"Thank you."

"Then I will see you around." His look flickered to Conor, who hadn't moved a muscle.

"I'm sure you will," Conor said in a tight voice.

The man gave them both a curt nod and left.

Christina looked at Conor. "That was nice of him."

"It would have been nicer if it hadn't happened." Conor released his fisted hands.

Her hand circled his arm. "I would like for it to be forgotten."

Conor spent the rest of his morning in the equine clinic, answering questions about Gold, then attended the track vet evaluation of the horse. Other than that, he was encouraged to leave the backside.

The rest of his week would consist of waiting and trying to catch a glimpse of Christina. Because he was associated with a horse that was racing, he was not allowed for security reasons to do any volunteer veterinary work. Which would leave him with time on his hands. He would have daily discussions with the trainer and the grooms and be at the track for any training, especially when Gold was running the Breeze or being schooled in the padlock. Other than that, he would be restricted by security.

Conor had volunteered to help out. He had seen Dr. Dillard briefly and offered to at least watch along the rail during the Breeze and at the padlock. To be a first responder. Dr. Dillard told him he would keep that in mind. Still, Conor did not anticipate being asked to help unless the man became desperate. Conor's problem was he missed being with Christina. Just the idea of not seeing her hurt.

Why had he let her matter so much? He hadn't planned on that happening. Hadn't thought it could. Despite his fear of being like his father, he had overcome it, and somehow Christina had slipped in and captured his notice. Something no one had managed to do since Louisa. He had never intended to care like this again, then came Christina.

A beep on his phone made him look. His heart jumped. Christina. She was through for the day and would meet him for lunch. She wrote she would wait for him in front of the equine clinic.

Christina greeted him with a huge smile that had him smiling like a fool back at her. It had only been a few hours since he had seen her. The woman had him acting like a love-struck teenage boy.

"I guess your morning went well." He liked seeing her so happy.

She continued to smile. "Very well. I'm going to enjoy this week."

"I'm glad to hear that." He squeezed her hand for a moment. "So where are we going for lunch?"

"There's a restaurant just off the backside. I understand from Callie they have some great burgers."

"Sounds good."

They walked down the gravel drive between the barns then crossed the road to a single-story building.

"I think you'll like this place. It's dark and has a lot of wood. It should remind you of a pub."

Something he hadn't thought of in days. Home. Interesting.

The lighting inside was dim. It took a moment for his eyes to adjust. The older building held wooden tables and chairs that had seen better days. Christina passed them up for a booth in the back. She slid in and stopped in the middle of the seat.

He waved her farther into the booth and took the space beside her. "I want to sit next to you."

"Maybe we shouldn't be so obvious."

He scanned the area. "Who here do you think cares? I certainly don't care if they know I'm attracted to you."

She grinned. "I like the idea that you are."

He took her hand and placed it on his knee.

An older man with a white apron around his waist came to take their order. They decided on hamburgers and fries.

Conor said, "Tell me how it went today."

"Really well. Not that we did anything in particular other than get orders and be reminded of how strict they are about the horses during Derby week security-wise."

"What are you going to be doing?" He rubbed the top of her hand with the pad of his thumb.

"The next two days I'll be helping with taking the daily bloodwork then watching at the padlock during schooling. The next day may be different."

"Then you're going to be everywhere."

The waiter brought their drinks.

"It sounds like it." She took a swallow.

"You'll be having some long days." He saw what little time he would have with her slipping way.

"I will. But I'm looking forward to it."

He squeezed her hand. "I'm glad this worked out for you."

"But I'll miss seeing you. Now, if Gold wins the Derby race we'll both be successful."

Conor was not sure that would make him feel successful about the trip. He already dreaded leaving her.

Their burgers came and they spent their time eating and discussing the horses that would be running.

"Are you off for the rest of the afternoon?" Conor asked.

"Yes, I can be your tour guide." She caught the drip running down her chin with a napkin.

He wished he could have licked it away. "I would like you to stay the night with me, too."

"I wish I could but I have the horses to see about." She ran her hand down his leg.

"I'll miss you."

She met his gaze. "I'll miss you, too. Are you ready to go? We'll go have a look at Churchill Downs."

"When you are."

She took out her phone and sent a text message.

"What's that about?"

"I got us a ride over to the stands. Otherwise, we would have a pretty long walk."

A few minutes later a truck pulled up in front of the restaurant.

"That's Carlos. He's one of the staff here. He said he would give us a lift." She climbed into the front passenger seat and moved over. Conor settled in beside her.

Carlos drove them back along the road they had walked earlier then veered to the left into a tunnel.

"I had no idea this was here." Conor looked around in amazement.

"Most people don't."

They came up into the sunlight on the opposite side of the track. Carlos stopped at the first gate on the grandstand they came to. Conor popped out then helped her down.

"Carlos, thanks for the ride. We'll find our own way back," Christina called over her shoulder.

He nodded and drove on.

They stood in front of the stands for a moment. "I've already told you about the twin spires, which are used as the logo for Churchill Downs. Come on, let's climb a few rows up so you can see."

Conor stood beside her, looking out at the track. "It is something. The big screens and hedges and the Winner's Circle."

"That, it is. As you can tell, we run dirt mostly here. But there is also a grass track. I understand you run mostly grass in Ireland. Both can be a mess on a rainy Derby Day."

"I can imagine. We have practiced Gold on dirt just because of this."

"The track is maintained carefully to make it as safe for the riders and horses as possible." He had seen the track groomers in action. They were a finely tuned and efficient group.

"Down there is where the starting gate is for a number of the races." She pointed to the right near the last turn. "A few races start near the first back turn. But I'm not telling you anything you don't know."

He smiled. "No, you aren't, but I enjoy hearing you talk. I love your enthusiasm."

Conor continued to listen and ask questions.

Christina was in her element and loved the racetrack.

She spread her arms wide. "These stands will be overflowing on Derby Day. All to watch what they call the two greatest minutes in sports."

"I can see why they call it that." Conor couldn't help but be impressed.

"I have more to show you. Doctor Dillard made special arrangements so I can take you up to that balcony where you can see the entire track. Give you a bird's-eye view."

They went under the stands to the elevator. It took them to the sixth floor, where they stepped out into an open area with tables. She pushed through the glass doors that led to a balcony and walked all the way to the rail. "Isn't it gorgeous?"

He watched her. "It is but not as pretty as you."

Christina gave him a lopsided grin. "Thank you but you need to focus on the racetrack."

He put his hand around her waist and pulled her to his side for a little squeeze. "I'd rather concentrate on you." He let her go before she could complain. He looked at the track. "Yes, it is pretty. I still can't get over how large it is."

"It's impressive. Would you like to go see the museum?"

"There's a museum here?" He hadn't heard of it.

"Yes. It not only shows the past winners, but a short movie and history of the event."

"I would like to see it." He also wanted to make the most of the time he could have with Christina.

They returned to the elevator. The doors had hardly closed before Conor took her into his arms. His kiss had her gripping his shoulders to stand.

"I haven't had a chance to do that today and I will miss out tonight, so I'm making the most of this time alone."

The doors slid open. Christina watched him with a dazed look. He grinned. "Weren't you going to show me the museum?"

"What?" She blinked.

He chuckled. Her reaction to his kiss stroked his ego.

They walked the length of the stands and stepped out a side gate to where the museum was located. At the desk they showed their badges and entered the museum. They walked through what looked like a starting gate into the exhibit area.

Strolling along hand in hand, they circled the building, looking at the trophies, jockey outfits and discussing the famous horses that had gone on to win the Triple Crown.

"Remind me what the Triple Crown is?"

"It's when one horse wins the Kentucky Derby, the Belmont and Preakness all in the same year. That's considered the Triple Crown. Only a few horses have managed to do it. And then they go out for stud."

"Which is not a bad job if you can get it." Conor gave her a wolfish grin.

She smiled. "Every man's dream, I guess. To produce many children."

The sadness covered his face.

Her eyes turned concerned. "I'm sorry. I said that without thinking."

"It's okay."

"Would you like to have more children?" she asked softly as if unsure of his reaction.

"I don't think so. It would be too hard to lose one again."

"But you might not."

It hurt to hear her so hopeful, but he had to tell her the truth. "I couldn't take that chance."

"I think children would be worth the chance." She tugged his arm. "Let's watch this movie. That's in the round. You'll like it."

A few minutes later, they were walking out of the museum. They stopped in front of the gift shop. A number of large women's dress hats hung on a stand.

"What are the women's hats about?"

"The women wear hats on Oaks and Derby Day. Some are very extravagant. It's part of the Derby's mystique and fun."

"I'd love to see you in one."

"I'd looked pretty silly wearing one while seeing to a horse." She waved her hand up and down herself. "And one wouldn't go with my outfit."

"You deserve to experience some of the glamours of life." He would like to give that to her.

"Thank you, but I think this week is going to consist of blue jeans and boots."

He took her hand. "I guess you're right."

They returned to the track.

A golf cart approached. She waved it down. "Are you going back to the other side?"

"Yep," the woman said.

"Do you mind if we get a ride?" Christina asked.

"Hop in."

The woman dropped them off in front of the equine clinic. They walked toward her truck.

"I enjoyed my tour."

"I'm glad you did." Christina hesitated. "I guess I should get started for home."

"I wish you were staying with me. I'm sorry I can't go with you. I have to be at the airport early in the morning."

She placed her hand on his chest. "I understand." She opened the truck door.

He leaned toward her. "I want to kiss you, but I don't think this is the place for either one of us to have a public display."

Her gaze met his. "I know."

"Doesn't mean I don't want to."

"Same here." She brushed his hair back.

"Just the same, I'm going to give you a quick one." He took a step closer.

"And I'll gladly take it."

His lips brushed hers for a moment before he straightened. "I'm already missing you. I'll see you tomorrow."

"I'll make sure it happens." She offered him a small lift of her lips.

"You drive safe."

"Bye, Conor."

He watched Christina drive toward the exit. She stopped and waved out her window. She'd known he would be watching.

Christina finished taking what seemed like her hundredth blood test for the day, not to mention the number of daily records of medications that must be reviewed and overseen each day. This had to happen every day for each horse in the stables.

Now all of the competitors were securely on the backside, it had become a busy area. That would continue until Saturday evening after the last race.

She had expected such and loved the excitement of it all. It made her blood hum. Still, she was worn out each evening.

She hadn't seen Conor since she had left him the afternoon before last. She had been busy enough not to obsess over it, but when she did pause for lunch, she scanned the area, hoping for a glimpse of him. She should've anticipated it would be this way. But that didn't mean she liked it.

He was busy with Gold. Had responsibilities of his own. Mr. Guinness would expect him to focus on the race ahead. Understanding the situation didn't mean she didn't miss him. Painfully so.

Maybe it was just as well. She needed to get used to it. Soon, Conor would be gone. The problem was she had become used to him being in her life. There in the morning and again at night. Especially at night. That, she liked the best.

She had known it wouldn't last, but that didn't mean she didn't want to enjoy him while she could. Now their jobs were getting in the way. Not that either one of them could do anything about it.

That evening she drove home exhausted. She took care of the horses before going into the empty house. Where she'd found her home reassuring just weeks earlier, now she found it depressing. Lonely.

She headed for the bathroom too tired to bother with cooking a meal, not that she would have done anything more than microwave something. After a shower to wash off the dirt, sweat and manure of the day, she pulled on a shortie gown and climbed into bed.

She was almost asleep when her phone buzzed, notifying her of a text from Conor.

Come to the back door.

What was going on? She padded along the hall through the kitchen to the door. She flipped on the outside light, pushed back the curtains and found Conor standing on her stoop. She quickly unlocked the door and flung it back. "What are you doing here?"

Conor scooped her into his arms. His mouth covered hers in a deep, wet, hot kiss that shook her to the core.

Her arms went around his neck, welcoming him into her home and her heart. She missed him to the bottom of her soul. She returned his kiss, holding nothing back. Her legs wrapped his hips.

He stepped to the counter and sat her on it, then moved between her legs. His lips traveled down her cheek. He nipped the sweet skin behind her ear. "I've missed you."

"I've missed you, too. What do you mean by coming to my house in the middle of the night and kissing me senseless?" She gave him a defiant look and a teasing grin. "I'm not gonna let you in my bed."

"Honey, I think you're gonna be glad that I came to your bed."

"You have a high opinion of yourself. Do you think you can just bust into a woman's house and make demands on her?"

He studied her face. "You want me to go?"

She wrapped her arms around his neck. "Don't you dare. I've missed you."

He grinned. "Prove it."

Christina kissed him with everything she had in her. She slipped her hand between them and ran it over his tight length.

"Okay, I believe you might have missed me." He picked her up again and started down the hall.

He said between kisses, "I can't believe that I've been in the same half a mile as you for two solid days and didn't even catch a glimpse of you."

"I know what you mean." She nipped his earlobe.

He pressed his manhood against her center. "Can I stay?"

"You can if you make sure the back door is locked. I wouldn't want another man busting in."

Conor growled. "There better not be another man wanting in. I don't share." He carried her to her bed and dropped her. "I'll be right back."

She lay back and sighed. "I'll be right here waiting."

The next morning Christina woke before daylight.

Conor groaned beside her, pulling her to him. "It can't be time to get up."

"I'm afraid it is. The one thing I do hate about running a farm is always having to get up early to see about the horses every morning."

He nuzzled her neck. "You picked the wrong vocation."

"You don't say."

He kissed her cheek and rolled away from her. "You stay here, and I'll see about the horses this morning. Sleep in for a change."

She looked at him in the dim light from her clock. "Don't tease me this early in the morning. I could turn on you."

He gave her a quick kiss. "Hey, I'm not kidding. You sleep and I'll be back in a little while."

"You would do that for me?"

"Sure. Keep the bed warm." She felt the breeze when he lifted the covers.

"That, I can do. I'll owe you one." She had already turned over on her stomach.

"And I plan to collect."

"Mmm."

He kissed her bare shoulder.

Just a few weeks ago she wouldn't have trusted him enough to see to the horses.

Conor returned, crawling into bed. They made love. It was poignant, slow and sweet. None of the rushed excitement of the night before.

"Each time it becomes more difficult to leave you," he said as she climbed out of bed ahead of him.

It hurt her heart to think about him leaving. She had fallen for him hard even in the short amount of time she had known him. She couldn't imagine what the pain would be like in the future. Since she already knew there wouldn't be any tomorrows with him.

The next few days would be impossibly busy. That would be a blessing. There would be less time to think about her future without Conor. She had hoped to spend the weekend with him but instead she would be traveling back and forth from her house to Churchill Downs daily. Unfortunately, he had to remain in town those nights.

She had to break it to him sometime, that she wouldn't be staying with him. Now was as good a time as any. "I'm not gonna be able to stay with you this weekend."

"Why not?" he demanded.

"The person who I had lined up to see about the horses backed out on me. And I don't have time to call around and try to find someone else."

His happy face turned sad with his eyes downcast. "There's no one you can get?"

"Not that I know of right now."

He sat on the side of the bed looking dejected. "I hate for you to travel those extra miles when you could be closer. And with me."

"Our days have already been long and I'm sure they're gonna get longer. We wouldn't see much of each other anyway." She wouldn't be sleeping with him, either.

"That's probably true." He wouldn't look at her.

"I'm tied up all day today. Tomorrow is the Oaks. Then the Derby the next." What she left out was he would be leaving after that. "As much as I hate it, I don't think we need to have any interaction anyway. Us being together might come into question since Gold stayed at my place and we know each other. I don't want there to be any questions about my integrity."

CHAPTER TEN

"INTEGRITY?" HE LOOKED at her as if she had lost her mind. "You have to be kidding."

"There can be no suspicion of impropriety."

He stood. "Then I'll drive out here."

She shook her head. "I don't think that's a good idea."

"What are you scared of?" He jerked his pants on.

"I'm scared of being accused of tampering with a horse or race. My honesty and actions could be questioned. That, I can't take a chance on."

He faced her, his legs spread in a defensive manner. "Nobody's even paying attention and that would mean not seeing me. I'm leaving soon."

"You heard that guy the other night."

"He was an idiot." Conor's voice rose.

"No, he was saying what other people are thinking."

His chin jerked up. "So you plan to go through your life worrying about that."

"I have to get used to it. This is my chance to prove myself."

Conor's brows drew together. "Who are you proving yourself to?"

"My colleagues."

He glared at her with his hands on his hips. "You are a great veterinarian. You did nothing wrong. Why do you think you need to keep telling people that?"

"Because I let them down." She found clean clothes.

"How did you do that?" His disbelief hung in the air.

"Here everyone in the horse-racing world knows everyone else or at least about them. I made them look bad."

His mouth fell open. "You didn't do it. Nelson did. You need to leave that behind and move forward. You. Were. Not. Responsible. You are a good and caring human. You have a business that is admirable. Just because your mother thought you did not measure up that does not mean that's a fact. I think you are wonderful. And enough for anyone. In fact, you are the most amazing woman I know."

"I appreciate that, but that doesn't change the fact that my name has been damaged, and I need to guard it." She headed for the bath.

He followed. "My point is it isn't about what

happened with the drugs. It's about your self-esteem."

"It doesn't do much for my self-esteem to know that you can return to Ireland so easily or that I'm not worth staying here for. You act like you really care but you don't show it."

He looked confused. "What do you mean?"

"What are you going back to? You have family but a lot of people live far away from their family. You could stay here and help run the farm with me. It doesn't seem that you're having any trouble leaving."

He followed her to the bath. "Christina, I can't make that type of commitment. I gave all I had the last time. I couldn't live through a loss like that again."

"What makes you think you would lose me? Louisa killed herself out of despair. The loss of your child was an accident. I'm not going anywhere. This is your chance to start over. To find happiness. Here with me."

He filled the doorway. "Ireland. That's my home."

"You can make your home anywhere. Even here with me."

"I can't, Christina. I can't give you what you want. A husband. Children. I just can't do it again." He glowered at her. Why couldn't he get her to understand?

"I think you could. You're just scared. Maybe it's a good thing we can't see each other for the next few days. We can say goodbye here." She turned her back on him and started the shower.

The idea hurt him more deeply that he would have anticipated. He wanted to shout no, but he just couldn't offer her what she wanted. Now was the time to walk away from her. Even if it was another form of death.

Christina wasn't sure how their conversation had turned into an ugly argument that had gone so bad so fast. Had it been from frustration over not being able to see each other? More likely, it was over the fear they wouldn't see each other again after the race. Whatever it was, she had to learn to accept it was over between her and Conor.

She'd been awake most of the night after their fight when she should've been resting. Instead, she'd spent that time going through different scenarios of how to make their situation better. She couldn't afford to have any hint of impropriety. She had learned that the hard way. Negatives were eagerly believed, while positives were harder to earn.

She worked too hard to get this opportunity to assist during the Derby week. She couldn't fail. She was sorry that Conor couldn't understand that. His reputation had not been called into question.

On Friday morning she drove onto the backside before daylight. Today would be the Oaks Race, all female horses. It would be a full day of racing. The backside was already buzzing with activity.

She had been given her assignment for the day the evening before. There were still a couple of hours before the first race. She and her partner teamed up to help with day-of blood tests. Each horse racing would have to be tested within thirty minutes of their race. This was to look for a number of medicines that could be used to enhance the horse's performance. Those were absolutely not allowed in the racing world. Horses found to have been using were immediately disqualified.

An hour before the first race she returned to the equine clinic. There she caught a golf cart along with three other veterinarians. The driver would drop them at their assigned position at the first turn of the racetrack. If there was an accident, it would only be seconds before she and her colleagues would be there to care for the horse. Other veterinarians would be doing the same along the mile-long track.

She carried medical supplies in her backpack, including different sized splints for the horses' legs, and pain medicines. Breaks and wounds were her largest concern during the actual race.

There was much more to the two days of racing than many people thought. So much took place behind the scenes. It wasn't all about running.

In the distance she could see the stands filling. For once in her life she wished she could dress more feminine, to wear something besides her T-shirt, jeans and boots. She would have liked to look less masculine and more feminine, especially today when so many other women were dressed in their finest, including a hat. Many of them would wear pink in honor of the female horses racing.

Throughout all the activity, she never saw Conor. It wasn't from the lack of trying. She searched for him wherever she went. The chances of her seeing him would be almost nothing from her station on the rail. She was in a restricted area. He would not be allowed there.

Sadness washed over her. She'd known when she stepped out of the shower the day before and Conor was gone, that it was over between them. She had to keep reminding herself of that fact. It was for the best since he would soon be returning to Ireland. At least it wouldn't be a long, drawn-out romantic drama-like parting. That, she couldn't live through.

Friday evening she drove off the backside with a tight chest filled with disappointment. She had been around hundreds of thousands of people all day, yet she felt so alone. This, she should get used to because she would carry the feeling for months and years to come.

Her phone rang. She jerked it up without looking, hoping it would be Conor. "Hello."

"I was just checking in to see how you're doing?"

"Mama. I'm fine. Busy working at Churchill Downs." She put the call in over her truck speakers.

"You got the job?"

Her mother sounded so amazed it grated on Christina's nerves. "I did."

"Even after what happened?"

"Yes, Mother. And I did nothing wrong."

"No, but you should have realized what Nelson was doing."

"We've gone over this before. I'm not up to doing it again tonight. It's been a long day."

"What're you wearing to Churchill Downs? I hope you're wearing something nice."

"The last thing I need to have on while on the ground caring for a horse that is hurt is a dress."

"But it's Churchill Downs. All the women will have dresses and hats on," her mother whined.

"Except for those who have to work like I do."

"I have never understood you and those horses." Her mother's voice carried her usual disapproving tone.

Christina sighed. Here they went again.

"Why couldn't you have done something that didn't require you to get your hands dirty?"

"Mother, I want you to stop there." Christina raised her voice. "You have spent this entire phone call making me feel like I don't measure up. My whole life, in fact. I am a good veterinarian. I have done nothing wrong, and I refuse to act like I have. I'm good enough to take care of any horse at any time, and I love what I do. If you can't talk to me in a positive way then just don't call. I'm tired and I've had a long week. I'm not going to put up with it any longer."

There was a long pause.

"Christina, I think you're overreacting."

"Mother, I'm going to say bye now. Think about what I've said before you call again." Christina hung up. For once, she felt good about herself after talking to her mother. Conor had made her feel strong enough to stand up for herself. She wanted to tell him but that wasn't going to happen.

Because of him, her life would be different. Better.

Conor struggled to act enthusiastic about the Derby Day races. It would be a long day until Gold ran. That left him with a lot of time for his mind to wander. His thoughts were more on Christina than they were on what he should be worrying about—Gold. He and Christina had broken up. Wasn't that what he wanted?

Right now, all he needed was to see her. Just a glimpse. He missed her like he never believed he would. She was so close but so far away. Was she hoping to see him as well?

Over the past few days he had remained busy but not enough so that there was no downtime. That was when thoughts of Christina filled his mind. Was she as miserable as he?

He had not slept since leaving her bed four days ago. Gold's trainer and one of the grooms had even commented on how awful he looked. It did not help that he arrived early in the day, and Mr. Guinness required him for social events in the evening. All he could think about was how much he wanted to join Christina in caring for the horses. He would even help deliver a foal if he could do that with her.

Morning after morning he had stood beside the track, hoping she would join him to watch the horses run. He was disappointed. He had missed the look of expectation that came over her face at the sound of the horses running in her direction. Along with the adrenaline rush it gave him to bring her release.

Around horses and in bed with him she was beautiful. Expressive. In her element. She loved the sights, smells and the trill of horseracing. If he wasn't careful, he would start writing odes to Thoroughbred racing and Christina. There were probably already hundreds of printed poems about the Kentucky Derby. Christina deserved just as many.

What would happen if he decided to stay in America with Christina? His entire life had been built around being true to the one you love. He had seen what it was like when a husband wasn't faithful. It slowly destroys the other person and makes the family rot from the inside out. He had been true to Louisa but now she was gone. Could he be that devoted to Christina? Rebuild his life with her?

Mr. Guinness stepped up beside him at the rail. "You have stood here each morning. At first, I thought you were that absorbed in the horses running. But then I realized you aren't looking at the horses. You're looking everywhere but at them. Who are you searching for?"

Had Conor really been that pathetic?

"Is it the woman who boarded Gold?"

"Yes." Conor continued to search the crowd.

"So what is going on between you two?"

This was not a subject the two of them normally had a conversation over. "Right now, nothing. She told me not to have anything to do with her during the races because she didn't want there to be any appearance of collusion."

"Okay, knowing the security around here I can see that. So why the long face? After Gold's race, find her."

"There's more to it than that."

"And what is that?" When Conor didn't say anything right away, he continued. "You've worked for me for years and because of that we have become friends as well. After your wife died I, along with your other friends and family, have watched you become a shell of yourself. So much so that when your brother and sister came to me and asked me if I would send you over here with Gold I agreed to mess in your life. Not something I make a habit of. We were all worried you would never return to your old self. We all wanted you to have a fresh start. A chance to get away from your memories."

"I had no idea you were in on this."

"You would never have if you hadn't looked so happy when I arrived and now you don't. I would have never said anything. But I knew our plan had worked the second I saw you. This is what we wanted for you. Not necessarily to find someone but to move on past your grief and sadness. To start living again."

"I was that bad?"

Mr. Guinness nodded. "I knew by just talking to you on the phone. Just the difference in your voice said whatever this woman had done, you needed to grab hold of it."

"Being with her would mean leaving everything I've known behind in Ireland."

"You do realize there are airplanes. You can visit. Your family can visit you. Even Gold managed to get over here." Mr. Guinness grinned. "Do I dare to tread on our friendship enough to ask how you feel about this woman?"

"I'm afraid I'm in love with her."

"That's not a bad thing, Conor."

He thought for a moment. "No, it's not. In fact, I've never felt better about myself or life in a long time."

Mr. Guinness gave Conor a slap on the shoulder. "That's what I figured. Maybe you need to give your plans some thought. See what options you can come up with. Even as miserable as you are right now, you look far better than you did before."

"Now, we should concentrate on Gold. We need to go if we're going to walk him over to the starting gate. Maybe you'll catch a glimpse of her as we go."

Conor's chest tightened. Mr. Guinness and Christina were right. There really wasn't anything left for him in Ireland that he couldn't change. His clients had slowly drifted away, and he'd let them. He was down to Gold now. Here with Christina, he could have a fresh start. They could build something together. If she would still have him.

He liked America. He liked living the lifestyle that Christina offered. So why wouldn't he stay? Because he was afraid. Of caring again and losing her, but if he didn't try then he would lose her for sure. He would have no more than he had now. Which was nothing. He knew well what nothing felt like. He didn't like it. Now he understood what it was to have Christina and he wanted that. He had to decide if it was worth stepping beyond his fear to take a hold of happiness.

Christina was worth that and more.

Christina remained in her position at the rail as the groups of owners with their families and those involved with the horses running the Derby race made their traditional walk from the barns to the starting gate.

She tried not to focus on Gold's group, but she couldn't help herself. She got a glimpse of Conor long before he reached her. Her heart fluttered hard enough she worried she might lift off. Was he as happy to see her as she was to see him? Was he still angry with her? Would he leave without telling her goodbye? The idea made her physically sick.

When the group came close enough, Conor's intent gaze locked in on hers. It didn't waver. In that moment it was only them. All the other stuff had fallen away. The thrill of seeing him buzzed through her.

Conor smiled. Concern filled his eyes but a hint of hope as well. She returned a small smile.

He didn't approach her. She appreciated him honoring her request they have no contact. Even though she longed to climb over the railing, run to him and wrap her arms around his neck to give him a kiss. She mouthed "Good luck."

His smile grew a little brighter as he continued past her on the dirt track.

Christina waited with building anticipation as each one of the horses was announced as they were put into the starting gate.

Soon, the track announcer said, "They're in the gate…and they're off!"

The horses came barreling toward her, spread out across the track. By the time they had reached her they had moved into a double line with a group in the middle.

Gold was in the group as they ran past her. She couldn't help but quietly cheer the horse and jockey on. She didn't dare be any louder.

The horses continued to run, picking up speed, and the crowd stood, hollering. From her vantage point she couldn't see even a screen to tell her how Gold was doing. She listened to the announcer as he called names and positions as the horses rounded the back turn. Seconds later the announcer said they're coming around the last curve and into the homestretch.

She heard Gold was in fourth place and the announcer then said Gold was making a move on the outside. He was in third place coming into the homestretch. The crowd was screaming louder. Gold crossed the finish line in second place.

Christina couldn't help but jump up and down. He had done so well. She was proud of the efforts of the horse, Conor and those who worked with Gold.

She wanted to run to the stands, wrap her arms around Conor and congratulate him, but she had to hold her spot. There was one more race before the day would be done.

Would Conor search her out? Or would he be celebrating?

The next forty minutes went by slowly.

She was exhausted and ready to go home by the time the races were over. She slowly made her way to her truck. Still no Conor. The horses were waiting on her. At one time she would've hoped to spend the night with Conor, telling him good-bye. Now she would be going home to an empty house and bed.

She didn't know what she had expected. They were too different. He from Ireland and she from the States. She wanted a husband and family. He a good time while he was there with no attachments. She was messy and he was tidy. He could cook and she couldn't. She wanted to live here and he had his life in Ireland. He was devoted to his dead wife and she wanted him devoted to her. They weren't meant to be.

CHAPTER ELEVEN

THE NEXT MORNING Christina crawled out of bed, fed the horses and returned to bed again. She was exhausted physically, mentally and emotionally after the past week. All she wanted now was to pull the covers over her head and stay that way for a few days, but with animals to feed and care for she couldn't.

She missed Conor with every fiber of her being. He was no doubt packed to return to Ireland. She had hoped, then prayed, he would call. The silence of her phone just added to her agitation and disappointment. She would have to learn to live without him. To be alone.

Working in the barn had been her therapy for so long and now he had ruined that. Memories of them being there hung in the air and settled in her mind. Neither reassuring nor comforting.

Tears stung her eyes. She blinked them away. Last night she had done enough of that.

A good day of rest and she would be her old self. Or at least that was the lie she kept repeating.

She brought this misery on herself. Had become too involved with Conor. Knew it while it was happening. Had told herself that and still, she walked into his arms and invited him into her bed. What had she been thinking? She hadn't been; she'd been feeling.

Rolling over, she clutched the pillow with Conor's smell still attached to her chest and buried her face in it. If she could just sleep today, then get up and start again tomorrow, maybe she could get her life back. With patience and taking care of the horses, the past three weeks would be forgotten. Then she could survive him not being there.

As much as working Derby week had meant to her, having Conor meant more. She had just realized that too late.

In the middle of the afternoon, she hauled herself out of bed. She had to get moving. She had to accept what her life looked like. Those weeks with Conor had only been a dream in the middle of reality. Now it was time to live in the latter once more. After pulling on her work clothes, she headed for the barn.

Cleaning out the stalls despite their not needing the attention would be a good distraction from her worries. She turned the music up and sang along at the top of her voice. The horses gave her a quizzical look but returned to their eating.

What was that noise? Her name? She turned.

There in the half circle of the sun coming through the large barn door stood the most wonderful sight she had ever seen. Conor. Her heartbeat roared in her ears. Her hands were sweaty and they shook. She murmured, "You're here."

"Where else should I be?" He studied her as if her answer was very important to him. "I belong here."

She staggered a moment, then planted the pitchfork into the ground to steady herself. "I thought you were leaving. That you were at least loading Gold to go home."

"No. We are both staying."

"Staying?"

Conor's mouth quirked at the corners. "As in not going."

"I know what *staying* means." She threw her shoulders back.

Conor liked this Christina the best. The one with color in her cheeks and eyes bright with determination. "Would you mind moving away from the pitchfork? It makes me a little nervous. We need to talk. I have a couple of things to ask you."

She placed the tool against one of the stall walls. "So talk."

He had hoped she might fall into his arms and welcome him back. But not his Christina. She would make him work for her. Make him bare his soul. "Gold is being put out to stud. Mr. Guinness wants me to stay here with him. In fact, I gave him the idea and volunteered for the position."

"In America?"

"Yes. In Kentucky. Mr. Guinness asked me to ask you if Gold could be stabled here. He would like me, with your assistance, to oversee the breeding program."

Christina's eyes widened and her mouth dropped, as if he was making it all up. "You would stay here? Stay in my barn?"

Conor chuckled. "Gold would stay here. I was hoping for warmer and softer accommodations."

"I…uh…"

He had never seen her this flustered.

"And where will you stay?" She looked at him.

He gave her a long, lingering look, hoping the desire he was banking did not burst into flames before they finished their discussion. "I was hoping in the house with you." His look bore into hers as he walked closer to her. "Except not in that tiny room off the kitchen."

"Then where?"

"With you."

"Is that what you want, to stay here?"

"I want to be where you are. I thought I left everything in Ireland. What I didn't know was I was coming to everything in America. You are my everything. You brought me back to life. Made me live again."

"You're willing to give up your home, your practice, your family?" She continued to watch him closely.

"I'm willing. I'll do what I must to be here with you. My life was empty and you filled it. I'll gladly do what I have to in order to have you in my life. My home was no longer home after Louisa died. I need to sell it and let somebody else create a life there. My brother and sister are there but I can visit them whenever we want. Which, by the way, I know you will like them and they will like you."

"You shouldn't have to give up everything for me."

"I see it as gaining everything. I can do what I love—caring for horses, helping you build your business and loving you the rest of my life."

She stepped back, shaking her head. "I'm not worth you giving up your entire life for."

He cupped her cheek, stopping her, and looked into her eyes. "Sweetheart, you are important enough and perfect enough just the way you are for me to flip my world. Never doubt that. You are perfect for me. The question is do you want me?"

Her gaze remained locked with his. "Of course, I want you. I've always wanted you."

"Not exactly true. I don't think you wanted me when I first showed up a few weeks ago."

She smiled. "I just wasn't ready for you then."

"And you are now?" He stepped closer.

She nodded. "Yes, because I love you."

He moved into her personal space. She smelled of something floral from her shampoo, hay and a freshness that was all her. He inhaled and savored it. "I love you, too. I never thought I would ever say those words again to a woman. Christina, you took something broken in me and put it together again. You are the glue that makes my life whole. I love you."

His lips found hers. She clung to him as if he were her lifeline.

They broke apart, breathing deeply. He maintained his hold on her. "We are going to find a good farmhand. One we can trust to see after the horses so we can sleep in, have dinner out and visit Ireland without worrying."

She looked at him with love shining in her eyes. "That sounds wonderful. By the way, I spoke to my mother the other day. She started putting me down again and I told her I wouldn't talk to her if she was going to do that. She still doesn't understand the choices I've made."

He chuckled. "I bet she won't understand you falling for an Irishman."

That look of strength filled her eyes again. "She

doesn't have to understand. All she needs to know is I love you. If she starts giving me a hard time, I'll tell her I won't let her talk to me that way. Then I will politely hang up or walk away."

"I'm proud of you. But no matter what your mother says, remember I think you are just perfect the way you are. So much so I want to marry you."

"Marry me?" Her voice squeaked with surprise.

Would she turn him down? "I love you. Why wouldn't I want to marry you?"

"Because you said you wouldn't do that again."

"That was before I knew what it was like to almost lose you. I want you beside me always."

She hesitated a moment, looked away before she said, "What about children? You know I want children."

He swallowed hard. "I cannot say that I won't be terrified of losing you or one of our children, but I can't imagine a better mother. With you at my side I can do anything. I love you and I want what you want."

She threw her arms around him and pressed her face into his chest. "I love you, too. We will have the most beautiful children. I hope they all have your accent."

"If you will take me inside to check out that soft, comfortable bed of ours I'll whisper in your ear in my accent for as long as you like." He nuzzled her neck.

She grinned. "Promise?"

"Sweetheart, I promise to do that for as long as we live. I keep my promises."

EPILOGUE

Eighteen months later

CHRISTINA WALKED ACROSS the yard toward the barn. Conor hurried out, carrying their three-month-old son, Jamie. The baby bounced in his father's arms from the pace Conor set. Wide grins covered both male faces. Jamie obviously enjoyed his father's jostling.

Even at a young age, Jamie strongly favored his father. Christina had no complaints about that. Conor was an amazing and devoted father and husband. She had never seen a man more joyous or grateful than Conor when she had told him she was pregnant. Tears had filled his eyes.

He had to work at keeping his fear at bay during the pregnancy but that had become less evident after Jamie had arrived. Now Conor seemed caught up in the enjoyment of having a child, making the most of every minute.

When her mother and father had visited for the first time, Conor had run interference between her and her mother. He often interrupted her mother when she was about to say something negative and turned the conversation toward something Christina had done recently. Apparently, her mother had gotten the message and thought before she spoke further. Conor's desire to protect her only made Christina love him more.

She looked at her husband and her son. What had she done to deserve such happiness? "What's the hurry?"

"Gold's foal is coming," Conor blurted. "Buzz is with him right now. I was coming to get you. I didn't think you'd want to miss this."

"Of course I don't." Mr. Guinness had allowed them to breed Gold with a mare that had been hurt and rehabilitated on the farm. The mare's owner had no interest in her being returned so they had agreed to keep her. Conor had fallen in love with the horse. He felt she would be a good brood mare.

They all stood outside the mare's stall. Inside, Buzz, a stable hand who had quickly turned into an invaluable employee, softly spoke to the horse. They had hired Buzz so they could have a couple of mornings a week to themselves and soon learned he could handle more responsibility. Enough so they were able to visit Ireland.

Which Christina had loved. She had fallen for it and Conor's family. They had opened their arms to her and couldn't say enough about how glad they were to see Conor happy again. She and Conor were already planning a return trip to show off Jamie at Christmastime.

The horse fidgeted, stomping her feet.

"I better check her." Conor kissed Jamie's head and handed the boy to her then turned to go.

Christina grabbed his arm while holding Jamie secure in the other. "Hey, what about me?"

Conor grinned then pulled her hard against him. His kiss was slow, deep and held promises of later. He released her and her knees wobbled. That grin returned. "I've still got it."

She whispered, "I expect to see more of it tonight."

"You let me get this foal safely into the world and we'll celebrate during Jamie's nap."

Christina giggled and swatted him on the arm. "Go on. Jamie and I'll be right over here if you need help."

Conor entered the stall. She sat in the rocker that had been a gift from Conor's brother. He had made it after Conor had told him how much she enjoyed being in the barn. Conor had positioned it in the hallway so she could be close by while nursing Jamie or for occasions such as this one.

She spent as much time in the barn as possible working around Jamie's needs. The rehabilitation business had grown, and Conor had stepped in to fill her spot there. He had also received his US license to practice. They kept a few regular patients like Mr. Owen but mostly they remained close to home.

Soon, Conor joined her. "How are things progressing?"

"It may not be as soon as I first thought." Excitement filled his voice.

Conor had high hopes for this foal. Not that they had been planning to get into racing, but he wanted to give it a try. Just to see if they could do it.

"It might be a little longer than I thought. If you want to take Jamie inside, I'll come get you." He took a seat on a bale of hay beside her.

"Nope, we are happy right here." Jamie had fallen asleep in her arms.

Conor brushed his finger down her cheek. "You know when I came here I never dreamed I could ever be this happy. I love you."

"I love you, too."

"Conor, you better come," Buzz called from the inside of the stall.

Conor popped up. "Apparently, I was wrong. It's time."

Christina moved to the stall door. She watched as Conor gently guided the gangly foal into the world.

Delight filled his voice. "We have a colt."

She continued to admire her husband as he used handfuls of hay to clean the colt off.

After washing, Conor came to stand beside her, placing an arm around her waist and bringing her next to him with Jamie between them.

Together they watched the colt sway and bob until he found his footing.

"It never gets old watching new life come into the world." Christina sighed.

"No, it doesn't. It looks like a fine colt."

"It does." She shifted Jamie.

"Let me have him." Conor took his son. "Thanks for all these moments. I don't take them for granted."

"Nor do I." She wrapped her arms around him as she watched the mare nuzzle her new baby.

"Life is good." Conor gave her a squeeze.

Christina lay her cheek on his shoulder. "That, it is."

* * * * *

A NOTE TO ALL READERS

From October releases Mills & Boon will be making some changes to the series formats and pricing.

What will be different about the series books?

In response to recent reader feedback, we are increasing the size of our paperbacks to bigger books with better quality paper, making for a better reading experience.

What will be the new price of Mills & Boon?

Over the past four years we have seen significant increases in the cost of producing our books. As a result, in order to continue to provide customers with a quality reading experience, the price of our books will increase to RRP $10.99 for Modern singles and RRP $19.99 for 2-in-1s from Medical, Intrigue, Romantic Suspense, Historical and Western.

For futher information regarding format changes and pricing, please visit our website millsandboon.com.au.

MILLS & BOON

millsandboon.com.au

MEDICAL

Life and love in the world of modern medicine.

Available Next Month

All titles available in Larger Print

Festive Fling With The Surgeon Karin Baine
A Mistletoe Marriage Reunion Louisa Heaton

Forbidden Fiji Nights With Her Rival JC Harroway
The Rebel Doctor's Secret Child Deanne Anders

City Vet, Country Temptaion Alison Roberts
Fake Dating The Vet Juliette Hyland

BRAND NEW RELEASE!

A hot-shot pilot's homecoming takes an unexpected detour into an off-limits romance.

When an Air Force pilot returns to his Texas hometown with the task of passing along a Dear Jane message to his best friends ex, the tables are turned and she asks him for a favour…to be her fake fiancé in order to secure her future. But neither expects the red-hot attraction between them!

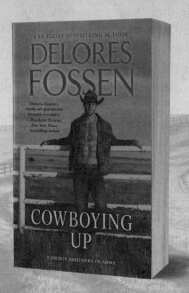

Don't miss this next installment in the Cowboy Brothers in Arms series.

In stores and online October 2024.

MILLS & BOON

millsandboon.com.au